HEART OF IRON

OTHER BOOKS BY THE AUTHOR

The Secret History of Moscow
Paper Cities: An Anthology of Urban Fantasy (editor)
The Alchemy of Stone
Running with the Pack (editor)
The House of Discarded Dreams
Bewere the Night (editor)

HEART OF IRON

Ekaterina Sedia

PRIME BOOKS

HEART OF IRON

Cover design by Telegraphy Harness.

Prime Books
www.prime-books.com

ISBN: 978-1-60701-257-3

To Chris, with all my love.

*Acknowledgements*

I gratefully acknowledge love and support of my family, without whom this book would not be possible. I am forever grateful to Jennifer Jackson, my tireless agent, who provided feedback throughout, and worked diligently on finding this book a home. I thank Paula Guran, my editor, for all her hard work in making this a much more coherent book; and of course I am thankful to Sean Wallace, who continues to believe in my work. Many thanks go to Marcin Jakubowski for his art, and to Stephen Segal for his always expert design ideas.

I am grateful to my first readers—Amy Lau, Beth Bernobich, John Glover, Justin Howe, Leah Bobet, Michael Curry—for their thoughtful feedback, and for helping make it a better book. I am especially grateful to Genevieve Valentine who was there to offer her friendship, advice and encouragement from the very beginning of this project.

Chapter 1

I have been blessed by several good fortunes, and I have no doubt that it is this constellation of luck and circumstance—at least, in part—that allows me to write these words. But foremost among my various and undeserved gifts I count my aunt Eugenia (Countess Menshova to most), for if it were not for her sardonic manner and low tolerance for insincerity, my debut at the St. Petersburg season—and my life thereafter—would have been very different.

Aunt Eugenia had taken care of my mother and me since my Papa had passed on to the mysterious afterlife I had only vague notions of at the tender age of eight. Unfortunately, Papa's passing was not sudden. He had started to succumb to increasingly frequent coughing and fainting spells when I was just an infant. His failing health ensured that I had no memory of his face since he spent most of his time in Switzerland, in successively more expensive and desperate treatments. Time was not the only thing of which the disease robbed our family—the cost of the treatments was such that after my father's passing at some Swiss resort, our fortune was nil, and entered the realm of negative numbers once his body was transported home and interred in the family crypt, just three hundred miles from St. Petersburg in the village of Trubetskoye.

My mother and I were destitute—save for the family manor house, which would have had to be sold at auction, were it not for my mother's trusting love for her sister Eugenia, and Eugenia's clear-eyed practicality. Aunt Eugenia had inherited most of the money on my mother's side of the family. (Their father, an unsentimental man, decided that since my mother was married and Aunt Eugenia was not, that it was Eugenia who would benefit from being named heiress to the title and its monetary accompaniment.) She and my mother decided to pool their resources and save the manor from such indignity. Aunt Eugenia moved to Trubetskoye and set about buying back and administering the estate, hiring help, fixing the manor house, and leasing the land, all the while pouring her own not inconsiderable resources into the enterprise. In a sense, she took over Papa's role in my young heart as well, and provided as admirable a model of masculine virtue as one could hope. The fact she wore a corset and a severe black dress was entirely coincidental.

After Papa's death, my mother had faded both spiritually and physically, acquiring an inspired look one usually imagined in angels or ancient Christians, and while she was never much involved in the daily life of the estate to begin with, she withdrew even further away from mundanity, drifting through the brightly lit spacious rooms of the Trubetskoye Manor, pale fingertips of her left hand trailing along the light-colored paneling of the walls, while her right hand tortured either a lacy handkerchief or a string of rosary beads, a relic from some distant and Polish relative. She only took interest in the news of the St. Petersburg season. This, I think, is what kept her alive—her desire to see me at the Winter Palace, and gossip. She delighted in any news from Emperor Constantine's court, as she delighted in all of his reforms—for he had never forgotten the Decembrists and their families, the ones to whom he owed his throne. He always sent us cards for Christmas and Easter, even after my Papa had passed on.

Ever since I was very young, I had known about reforms—everything changed so fast. Even Aunt Eugenia, interested in the news from the court only if it concerned her directly, used to say that the Emperor's name was ill-fitted to his feverish rush to change change change the ancient injustices that plagued the land.

I was born seven years after the serfs were freed, but ten years later the adults were still talking about the families who had lost their fortunes. The serfs of the Trubetskoye estate were freed with the rest, but quite a few had remained as renters; the rest of the estate was worked by hired labor and, as Aunt Eugenia used to say, the raising of the downtrodden necessitated some sacrifice. Both she and my papa, when he was still alive, had foresight enough to send a few especially bright newly liberated young men to a vocational school. As a result the Trubetskoye now enjoyed its own engineering staff, enough to modify the machinery to do something Aunt Eugenia tried to explain to me on many occasions, but my mind invariably started to drift the moment she mentioned the dreaded word "efficiency."

My education was also Aunt Eugenia's concern—at least she was the one to interview the applicants for the enviable position of my governess, and she dealt with a long procession of French, German, and English noble-but-destitute maidens with her habitual ruthlessness. The winner who emerged from what I imagined as a gladiatorial pit was a long-nosed Englishwoman with closely set eyes who reminded me of a herring. Her name was Miss Chartwell, and from the day I was eight to the day I was eighteen she taught me English, cursive writing, natural history, and calculus.

Perhaps it is worth mentioning that my youth was not just a jumble of family strife and nation-wide reformism—there were also long summers spent playing in the fields, fishing, and befriending the children of the renters, and reading James Fenimore Cooper; there were equally long winters when frost painted the windows with fantastical white flowers while the coal fire blazed in the copper stove, and my mother and her sister sat amiably side by side: one knitting, the other checking over the accounts. They still live like this in my mind's eye, the two aspects of contented domesticity—caring and wisdom, twin guardians of my childhood happiness.

I remember the second winter after Aunt Eugenia took over the household's reins. I played with my mother's cat Murka in front of the roaring fireplace. My mother looked up from her knitting, her dark-hooded eyes smiling at me, the skin around them folding into unfamiliar happy creases. "You're getting so big," she said, wistful. "Soon, I'll be escorting you to the balls in St. Petersburg."

I smiled, happy to see her thinking and talking of me instead of my dead papa. "Am I pretty, Mama?" I asked, coquettish.

She smiled still, but remained silent, and I could see that her eyes were troubled. She stopped rocking in her rocking chair.

Aunt Eugenia interfered with her usual bluntness. "There are better things to be than pretty, Sasha," she told me. "Don't you let anyone tell you otherwise."

"What is better than beauty?" I asked, breathing deeply to stave off the impending heartbreak.

"Not being a fool," Aunt Eugenia said. She was not a great beauty, with her long narrow chin and small beady eyes, her thin hair slicked into a paltry bun. But when she said it, I could see that she would have felt the same way if she were a golden-haired full-lipped nymph. "And if I were you, I would start paying attention to your lessons."

"I am paying attention," I said, indignant as only a ten-year-old child can be in the face of a just accusation.

Aunt Eugenia smiled then, her chin growing even pointier, and turned to my mother. "What do you think, Irina?"

My mother resumed her knitting and rocking; it was difficult to believe that this dark-haired, fragile beauty was related to Eugenia. "I think women in our family are late bloomers," she said. "You watch and see—the girls who are pretty now will be sows in a few years, and my little frogling will become a pretty young lady. Remember the story of the Ugly Duckling?"

Aunt Eugenia and I nodded in unison. Eugenia smiled impishly and said, "Then again, some ugly ducklings grow up to be ugly ducks—not to be helped, that. But having a brain and a heart . . . well, that's the sort of thing a young lady doesn't have to wait for."

Is it any wonder that I took her words more deeply to heart than my mother's?

When I turned eighteen, I was judged to be ready for my debut—even Eugenia nodded and conceded there was nothing to be gained by delaying it further. I was not so much excited about the balls and the season as I was about getting to visit St. Petersburg again—even though we had an apartment there, we spent all of our time in Trubetskoye, and visited only rarely. I missed the leaden Neva and the spire of the Admiralty piercing the fat low winter clouds, and I could not wait to walk those broad and impossibly straight streets, blown through by the cold autumn winds.

Despite my mother's predictions, I had not achieved beauty. Rather, my appearance had become stuck between my aunt's sharp features and my mother's dainty ones—neither an ugly duck nor a swan, I could only claim awkwardness as one feature that belonged to me and no one else.

Then there was the matter of a dress; my mother fully intended to fret about it until Eugenia rolled her eyes and hired a village seamstress. "Here," she told the large, red-handed and rough-knuckled woman as she gave her the money. "Make something not embarrassing." The woman nodded while I secretly doubted the effectiveness of such low-aiming instruction. But to my surprise, the dress turned out to be foam green, simple, and beautiful in a manner of Grecian shifts (if Grecians were to wear corsets and crinolines under theirs.) Thus accoutered, I was ready for anything fine society was prepared to throw at me.

I CONFESS TO SOME ANXIETY AS EUGENIA'S CARRIAGE LEFT THE familiar backwater of Trubetskoye and clanked along the too-wide ruts toward the capital. Squeezed between my mother's warm soft shawl and my aunt's sharp elbow, I had all the time in the world to think and fret, even as Miss Chartwell's fish eyes watched me from the seat opposite ours where she was losing a silent and undignified battle with hat boxes and suitcases that had not fit on the carriage roof.

I felt an impostor, somehow—as if my papa's sacrifice and service had expired the day he had died, and now my mother and I were nothing, just poor relations leeching off of my aunt's kindness; as if my family's past did not entitle me to a place at the emperor's season; as if I did not stand to inherit two titles. All of that was no more than dust to me, and the closer we got to the icy, stony beauty of St. Petersburg, the more perturbed I felt.

Fortunately, my mother and Eugenia's exclamations brought me out of the tar pit of excessive self-reflection.

"It changes every time I come by," Eugenia said. "Every time."

"Indeed," my mother said peering through the window on her side of the carriage. "I guess it is a good thing that the emperor is taking care of the roads." She smiled at me and leaned back into the cushions to allow me a view out of the window.

The road I remembered as being insubstantial and barely passable in the spring floods was being widened—a crew of freedmen labored next to the road, shattering stone with heavy hammers; another crew collected the resulting gravel and loaded it into long, open carts. I surmised the carts would then be sent to pave the road—it was still dirt at our present location, but noises ahead signaled it was paved not too far from there.

Roads and highways and railroads were the emperor's latest obsession. Eugenia had shrewdly observed he had to do something with all the freedmen, now that the fields were modernized and required fewer workers than before. My mother approved of the emperor's actions as she approved of everything he did—he was her connection to my dead papa, his protégé of sorts, even though such an imaginary inversion of power was ridiculous.

To Eugenia, the relentless reformism seemed to signal something beyond imperial magnanimity— I swear she could see farther into the future than any of us with her small beady eyes. "I do insist," she said, and seemed to look past the freedmen on the road's side and past the stone slabs, past the carts and sharp gravel, "that soon enough St. Petersburg will rival the capitals of Europe—London, Paris, all of them—as a beacon of progress and industry."

"You do babble so, Genia," my mother said.

"It's not babbling," Eugenia said. "I want to see this country ascend from the mire of poverty and superstition, for us reach for the light of reason . . . " She caught herself and let her voice trail off.

My aunt was entirely too infatuated with reason, as my mother used to say. She herself viewed rationality as a masculine domain, and occasionally hinted it was not my aunt's lack of beauty but her excess of imagination that doomed her to spinsterhood. My mother seemed to think it should be a lesson to me—at least, the specter of remaining an old maid only surfaced in conversation when I was willful or spent too much time catching frogs and climbing trees with the renters' children. Yet my mother did not seem convinced by her own words—or at least, let them be undermined by the obvious and unrepentant love she had for her sister.

We stopped for the night in the small town of Tosno. At least I remembered it as small from a few summers ago, but soon discovered it had increased considerably in size, not in small measure due to a factory that had sprung up at what had once been its outskirts.

"What does it make?" I asked Eugenia as we watched through the windows of the small hotel at tall smokestacks disgorging clouds of sulfurous steam into the evening sky.

"I am not sure," Eugenia said. "But we can go and find out."

My mother begged off the expedition, citing fatigue, but Eugenia and I walked down the winding dirt street past wooden cabins comprising most of the town's residential buildings. The paint on the dwellings' walls was peeling and discolored, and the acrid air made my eyes water. Even the trees lining the streets were blackened and mostly dead, their branches twisted like pleading fingers reaching for the sky.

The factory was still spitting out smoke and steam when we arrived at its vast doors. I worried that Eugenia, always keenly interested in things that clanged and were made of metal, would drag me inside the horrid building and make me walk across the floors where, surely, rude men swore at each other and operated dangerous-looking machines.

But she never had a chance, because the gates swung open and out came a throng of bearded, half-naked men who shouted excitedly, and pulled on long metallic ropes. There were dozens of them, all straining against thick twisted cables that sang like strings. Eugenia pulled me out of the way and we watched as the factory groaned and opened its doors wider, allowing the men to drag its strange creation forth into the last burnished rays of a setting sun—not quite a ship but a winged golden balloon as large as a three-storied house.

The egg-shaped balloon strained against the containing net. A basket, woven from strips of birch bark, like the lapti on the workers' feet—dangled under it. Tall wings rose from its sides, bracketing both the balloon and a metal cage containing a chugging smoking engine that clung to the basket like a fungal growth.

"It doesn't look like it needs an engine," I whispered to Eugenia.

She shook her head. "Don't be a fool, Sasha, of course everything needs an engine. How will it be propelled, change direction? A balloon is just the wind's toy. An airship has its own mind, though this one could be a tad more balanced."

A few of the men jumped into the dangerously swaying basket, the sweet aroma of birch sap mixing with the noxious smell of sweat and burning peat. The rest let go of some of the ropes, pulling the net off the airship, and the contraption soared. The basket hung lopsided, but this did not deter the men inside it. They operated the iron levers sticking through the bars of the cage that contained the engine, making it chug faster. Other levers lifted and lowered the golden wings allowing the airship to execute slow, swooping turns.

The men on the ground cheered, and Eugenia—quite unlike herself—clapped. The rising wind got hold of the ship and pulled it over the factory, toward the narrow strip of the forest, until its golden glow was hidden from view behind the treetops. The sun had sunk below the horizon, and Eugenia took my arm.

"Let us return to the hotel, Sasha," she told me. "There won't be anything else exciting here today."

The next day, at breakfast, we heard the innkeeper talking about a fire ball crashing in the fields just outside of town and the peat fires that started last night just a few miles to the west. Neither Aunt Eugenia nor I mentioned the airship and its fate to my mother.

IT TOOK US FOUR DAYS OF BEING SHAKEN ALONG THE RUTS AND staying in inns before we arrived at the severe glory of the capital. Eugenia had arranged for the hiring of staff who had uncovered furniture, cleaned, provisioned the place, and laid fires to warm the house in anticipation of our arrival, but it took another day of unpacking and arranging before we were settled in our St. Petersburg quarters. It took even longer before I was allowed to go for a walk along the Neva's embankment.

Oh, but the wait only made it more rewarding—as I strolled across the drizzle-slicked stones of the embankment, a sense of historical *gravitas* washed over me: these were the stones my papa's feet walked over, and the emperor's, and Peter the Great's; every important person who had ever lived in this city, every prominent player in the tragedies of our national life had left invisible footprints here.

I looked at the slick surface of the river and noticed it churn, water frothing white and green as bottle glass until a heavy brass hull, patina-covered, breached the surface. It looked like a monstrous sinking boat that was going the wrong way. A pair of binoculars mounted on a long pole swiveled toward me, and almost immediately the round cover on the convex back of the boat started turning. A few passersby stopped and clustered closer to the water, pointing and gasping. I had to push through the small crowd to get a view of the goings on.

When it opened, a very ordinary-looking freedman, dressed in linen shirt and matching trousers girded with a piece of rope, stepped out of the hatch just as I managed to work my way to the front of the crowd, inches away from the gray stone wall and the black water lapping at it.

"How do you do, miss," the freedman said to me. He then proceeded to walk the length of the monstrous contraption to adjust one of the mismatched knobs studding its tail end like a lace-maker's bobbins. He fiddled with one knob and then another one, as I watched in mute fascination, until he returned to the hatch and climbed inside. The green brass shuddered and several of the bobbins exhaled white clouds of steam. The water hissed and bubbled as it lapped against the knobs, and the boat soon sunk under the water and disappeared from view, leaving only a short-lived white-crested wave in its wake.

Afterwards, I walked along the Nevsky Prospect, the heart of the city laid out so vast, flayed open for the Kazan Cathedral and its square, and I gawped at the rearing horses guarding the Anichkov Bridge. Then I stopped to look at the stately, simple lines of Beloselsky-Belozersky Palace. I tried to guess what silent and luxurious life teemed behind those tall vaulted windows of the second story, who were the shadows sliding past the lacy white curtains like fishes under ice.

I could lose myself in these streets, and even as the rain grew heavier I dawdled, reluctant to go back to our quarters by the Moyka River, not too far from the Yusupov Palace. I had decided to go to St. Isaac's Cathedral and the Senate Square tomorrow; no doubt, both my mother and Aunt Eugenia would be interested in visiting the place of Papa's triumph.

However, upon my return I learned that Eugenia had other plans. Normally my mother and my aunt would arrange for an audience with the emperor, but because of my impending debut and associated emergencies—a tear in one of my silk slippers, a length of soutache coming undone along the front of the dress—they had been unable to arrange for an audience before the ball. The ball at the Winter Palace was two days hence, and preparations had to be made. My aunt was still overseeing getting the apartment and menus in order, and all other business had to wait until after the ball.

The hired maid turned out to be handy with a sewing needle, and thanks to her the clothing emergencies were solved with just a modicum of anxiety, letting us all fret about other matters. I was mostly worried about meeting my peers—even though Miss Chartwell did her best to impart the necessary knowledge of English (no one spoke Russian at the court since Emperor Constantine contracted a profound case of Anglophilia) and manners, I was still more used to the company of peasant and engineer children. I suspected that the young ladies of my own age and social standing would have a much less interest in the life of our estate than I did. Even my treasures, the books by James Fenimore Cooper, were unlikely to interest them.

Meanwhile, my mother seemed to grow even more despondent, the present receding as the deluge of memories of the house and familiar sights of the capital assaulted her. She mopped at her eyes with her handkerchief and drifted from one well-lit room to the next, pausing only in front of the wide bay windows to catch a glimpse of the pavement's rain-slicked stones and the gleaming of St. Isaac's across the river.

Aunt Eugenia was also lost in thought—she had retreated to her room and muttered darkly there, pacing all the while. I suspected that her discontent had to do more with the present state of affairs rather than the memories of the past youth. She seemed to be embroiled in preparations for the ball—her dress of black silk, decorated with charcoal-gray diamonds sewn onto a ribbon that ran all the way down the front was both beautiful and severe—much more elaborate than her usual clothing, and I was flattered that she would go to such length for me.

As it turned out, it wasn't my debut Aunt Eugenia was preparing for.

THE DAY OF THE BALL WAS GLOOMY, BUT IT MATTERED LITTLE as all of society headed for the Winter Palace. The Neva swelled with rain and turned leaden like a corpse, and small white-crested waves lapped at the mottled walls of the embankment. The squares and throughways were choked with the multitude of carriages and horses, and for a while I thought we might never arrive to the palace—I blushed when I realized the thought filled me with relief. I tried hard not to pick at the length of soutache twisting and winding down the front of my dress, and instead played with lace rosettes along my neckline and worried at the buttons of my long gloves.

My mother kept looking at the torrents of rain outside the window, and Aunt Eugenia frowned at her private thoughts. In her black and gray, she was formidable—and a stunning contrast to my mother who wore youthful dark rose and an overabundance of lace and ribbons. Between the three of us, she was dressed most as a debutante.

But, to my disappointment, we somehow managed to arrive at the palace and ascended its grand staircase, chandeliers blazing over the crowd—bright dresses and dark suits, with the occasional royal blue of officers' uniforms and the white of pelisses. There were bare shoulders and enough lace to wrap the Earth three times over. There was an overabundance of glossy marble, too much light and sparkling jewels. My head spun. If not for the strong, dry hand of my aunt steadying me, I would have lost my footing and tumbled gracelessly down the marble staircase. We entered the ballroom arm in arm—or rather with me leaning on her strong, square hand, her surprisingly small birdlike bones belying her evidently supernatural power.

We were announced and joined the overwhelming crowd. There were many young women who smelled of exotic flowers and looked like them too with their bright-colored dresses and pleated lace sewn onto every available surface. Their bodices and bell skirts were stiff with embroidery, and next to them my non-embarrassing dress looked plain, yards of soutache notwithstanding. I even saw a few wearing real orchids pinned to their hair and bodices.

"Goodness," Eugenia whispered. "While we were in our provinces, half of St. Petersburg lost its mind, and now they fancy themselves a greenhouse."

I snickered and immediately felt better. My mother had drifted off to greet some people she recognized, leaving me in Eugenia's uncompromising care. I expected a round of introductions and perhaps some dancing—the orchestra was tuning itself, with low melodic yowls of violins and shy exhalations of trumpets—but instead, Eugenia steered me toward the far end of the ballroom, where a clump of royal blue uniforms betrayed the presence of the emperor and his Polish wife.

He was sitting in a tall chair, not a throne by any means, but imposing enough to suggest it; his wife, a stately woman with watery eyes, sat next to him, with everyone else standing in a semicircle. General Pestel, much older than I remembered him, smiled at Aunt Eugenia.

She nodded, but her eyes and her glare were for the emperor alone. In his blue uniform jacket and white trousers, he looked like an elderly officer; his wig, desperately out of style, gave him an appearance of vulnerability—so light and fine, like the fuzz on a duckling. His pale blue eyes looked past me and at Eugenia, and I could have sworn that for a moment he looked . . . not fearful exactly, but apprehensive.

"Dear Countess Menshova," he said to her. "How good it is to see you! And this"—he nodded at me, smiling beatifically—"must be the Trubetskaya girl . . . I mean, young lady."

I curtsied and blushed.

"Indeed," Aunt Eugenia said, frowning. "A daughter of one of your officers, still waiting for you to wake up and perhaps do something useful with your reforms."

At that moment, I rather resented Aunt Eugenia dragging me into the imperial circle of attention with such a pronouncement. "I . . . " I stammered.

This was clearly not about me, as the emperor did not even glance in my direction. "Countess," he said. "There is no reason for you to be unhappy—your niece will not be hampered by the inheritance laws. You yourself have not been so encumbered."

"I was lucky not to have competition from male heirs," Eugenia parried. "But even then, if it weren't for my father's kindness and forethought, the Menshov lands would be in the hands of some cousins thrice removed."

The emperor shrank deeper into his chair, looked very old, and murmured something conciliatory. By then, those who were queued behind us waiting to pay their respect to the emperor had clustered closely around us, and I found myself quite mortified, the center of a sizeable crowd that surrounded Eugenia, me, and the emperor with his retinue. Even I knew this was not a proper way to make one's debut.

Aunt Eugenia drew closer, her bony finger in his face. "You better fix those laws so that I never see another deserving woman tossed out of her house and sent to live with her relatives," she said.

"But my dear," the empress said. "Most women are not equipped to run an estate. Why, just look at your own sister."

A terrible smile spread across my aunt's features; she no longer looked plain but petrifying, a Fury of old come to avenge the crimes committed against widows and orphans. "Please do not fault my sister for not knowing the things she was never taught," she said, still addressing Constantine, "and I shall never fault your brother for not learning what he was taught."

I could not help but notice that one of the officers, wearing an especially ostentatious pair of epaulettes, turned crimson. I pegged him for Prince Nicholas.

But Eugenia was not yet finished with the emperor. "That reminds me," she said. "You'd best make sure your university starts accepting young ladies, to better prepare them for the rigors of governance. Then you can change the law with no worries."

With that, she turned abruptly, her black skirt swirling, and dragged me along with her. The silence behind us was all the more profound as the orchestra started playing the first bar of a waltz, a waltz, I realized, I would never dance, because now I was the niece of the crazy Countess Menshova who—unorthodox even in her youth—had finally fallen off her rocker in her dotage, and spoke of governing as if it were her birthright. Elizabeth and Catherine the Great notwithstanding, everyone seemed to agree that Eugenia was too bold, and they whispered and stared at us. I could not stop blushing.

My mother, oblivious as always, wandered over to us, and smiled at me. "Look at that," she whispered proudly. "All the eyes are on my little duckling."

Before she had a chance to insist that I should go and dance with some nice young man or another, two officers approached us.

"Countess Menshova," one of them said. "The emperor is concerned that the excitement of the season has reflected poorly on your nerves—he fears you are overwrought. Perhaps you would be more comfortable at home."

The other said nothing, but his posture indicated that if Aunt Eugenia did not leave, he would not hesitate to forcibly exorcise her from the premises. We had no choice but to follow this polite but firm advice.

"Come along, Sasha," Eugenia said. "Apparently, age and wisdom do not always nest together."

Before that day, I had never considered that dying of embarrassment was not just a figure of speech but a distinct possibility.

Chapter 2

THE REST OF THE SEASON WENT SLIGHTLY BETTER—I HAD AN opportunity to meet several young women close to my age, from the families of Golitsyn and Obolonsky, Lermontov and Muraviev—all old families, which shared history with mine. There were balls and there were visits, tea, walks, and carriage excursions. The young women were neither mocking nor particularly kind to me, and I suspected that the rumors of Eugenia's outburst would die if only I could let them. As it was, every time I walked into a room and people stopped talking, I suffered a long spell of blushing and mortification, convinced they were talking about her—about us.

Meeting young men was especially vexing: most of them managed to be simultaneously terrified and scornful of my aunt, and while I suspected that my looks would not detract from the appeal of my future titles and fortune, the mere idea I was related to Eugenia made me, if not a monster in their eyes, then something at the very least deeply unpleasant, like a toad or a water snake.

We stayed in St. Petersburg through most of the winter, and I watched the black Neva waters grow at first a lattice and later a carapace of green ice, turning into a gigantic chrysalis suspended between the gray stone walls, and I wondered if any of the submarine boats were caught under it.

That year, it did not snow until December, and until then the frozen cobbles sung under the thick soles of my winter boots, and I wrapped myself in my coat, while drinking in the sights. I still preferred my solitude, going for walks whenever the wind ceased cutting like a knife, and the damp cold off the Finnish Gulf retreated, allowing the sun to shine.

Anichkov Bridge quickly became a favorite destination thanks to the savage though immobile life of its rearing horses. I could stand and look at them for hours on end; it was a childish conviction, but I believed at times that the moment I would turn away they would spring to life, their muscles knotting and sliding under their stone skin, and thunder away down the embankment, and then I would feel a fool for having turned my back on them. Thus compelled, I stared at them until the cold stung my eyes with bristling tears and my hands grew numb; I stomped my feet to keep warm and stuffed my mittened hands into my sleeves. In retrospect, I recognized this behavior as the first sign of my willingness to search the world for the unusual, a quality foreign to both my mother and my aunt. Yet, it was the latter who furnished me with the opportunity to realize this secret potential.

We returned to Trubetskoye in late January, and as much as I missed Anichkov Bridge, I was relieved to be home. My mother cried a bit because she missed her friends, and Eugenia threw herself into business affairs, since she could not quite believe that the estate had not fallen apart without her. We celebrated Maslenitsa with its usual abundance of blini, and welcomed Great Lent as a relief from such excess. We observed the holy days on my mother's insistence, even though Eugenia was of the mind that such pettiness as keeping track of who ate what when was unbecoming to a deity who had any ambition of looking important.

Before Lent was over, a letter was delivered. The three of us were resting after our supper in the parlor, where the fire burned brightly and my mother's aging cat purred asthmatically in her lap. My mother was knitting, and Eugenia worked on an estimate for the next planting season. When the letter was brought to us, my mother grew agitated at the sight of the imperial seal, convinced that the emperor wanted to honor poor dead Papa in some extravagant fashion; I suspected the emperor had finally recovered from the verbal lashing he had received from Eugenia (the letter was addressed to her), and had come up with a deserving repartee three months later.

I was closer to the truth—the envelope contained two items. The first one was a new *ukaz*, which Eugenia glanced at briefly and then read more closely. She let out a great whoop of joy. "Ha!" she yelled, jumping up and twirling in the most undignified manner. "The old goat listened! Look at this—'St. Petersburg University welcomes young ladies from noble families among its hallowed walls . . . ' Nonsense and circumstance . . . 'to be housed in the newly remodeled dormitories at the Vasilyevsky Island . . . chaperons . . . ' " She looked at me brightly and laughed. "Well, you get the idea."

I did, and felt a little nauseated as I eyed the second piece of paper that Eugenia let drop to the floor in her haste to read the imperial *ukaz*. Presently, Eugenia picked it up and glanced at it, her grin growing even wider. "This is for you," she told me, sly. I took the letter with trembling fingers, and stared at the list of the first ten noble young ladies to occupy the newly renovated dormitory come next August. I recognized most of the names—Golitsyna and Obolonskaya, and Dasha Muravieva was there as well. But my main consternation was directed at the last line—Trubetskaya, Alexandra.

"Why, Sasha, that's you." My mother pointed over my shoulder and beamed; I was not certain if she fully realized what was happening and why I felt simultaneously terrified and elated, but she smiled, Eugenia smiled, and somehow I felt quite certain that the positives would outweigh the sheer terror of having to attend the university—something I frankly had not previously considered but evidently acquiesced to.

I WAS NOT THE ONLY ONE WITH APPREHENSIONS, AS IT TURNED out—five out of ten young ladies named as the occupants of the newly renovated dormitories expressed their gratitude but turned down the appointments, citing various obligations and excuses, from a case of nerves to the impending matrimony. "Same thing, really," Eugenia judged. "Cowards."

I did not allow myself to feel bad about my lack of matrimonial prospects, and spent the summer focusing on my education. Miss Chartwell felt her reputation was at risk, and she spent entirely too many lovely summer days making me conjugate English verbs and calculate derivatives (my hatred for Herr von Leibnitz I could not describe), with an occasional foray into Spinosa or Pushkin.

By the time my departure for the university had arrived, my head felt as if it had swollen three sizes. I suspected, with a hint of wistfulness, that I would probably never be as smart again—and it was all thanks to dear old Miss Chartwell.

The Englishwoman had grown resigned to my leaving, and she came with the rest of the household to bid me goodbye. Her eyes had turned suspiciously red-rimmed and she kept swiping at them with her handkerchief—for her, it was a display of emotion much more extreme than my mother's unabashed keening.

I felt my eyes water as well when I embraced, in turn, my mother and Eugenia. "Worry not about your governess," Eugenia whispered. "I'm not letting her go, and you will see her when you come back home for winter recess."

I hugged Miss Chartwell, tears now running freely down my face, and promised to see her come winter. And with that, there wasn't much to do but to get myself into the coach where my suitcases and a maid—barely older than I and who was leaving home for the first time as well—were already waiting.

The coach took us to the train station. Ever since the railroad had reached Trubetskoye the spring before, the village had rapidly begun losing its backwater status. As much as I feared the railroad's presence would disrupt the village's unhurried, pastoral appeal, I also felt reassured my separation from home would be neither final nor lasting. Returning home would not even be arduous since getting to the capital was now only a matter of a short carriage ride and a day on the train.

From the first time I set a foot onto the throbbing, chugging step of the train, I fell in love with its power and its iron solidity. My maid Anastasia found a free compartment, which she busily filled with our belongings, and I settled on a seat by the window. The great puffs of steam exhaled by the locomotive hid the sight of the train platform and the peasant women with their wicker baskets containing produce and geese. It was like flying through the clouds, with one or another detail of the surroundings momentarily snatched and cast in naked relief before being hidden again in the dense fog. Only the sharp voices and laughter of the women on the platform reached us and convinced me that we were still moored to the earth rather than hurtling through the unending expanse of the summer sky.

Then it was time. The train gave a low whistle, prompting everyone to board in a hurry, and chugged slowly away from the platform. The steam cleared and I watched the yellowing fields run past the windows, faster and faster, and then a forest of tall spruce and ash trees walled the train tracks in on both sides. The train passed lakes and crossed over rivers, it entered villages and towns, piercing through them like a sewing needle, and continued on its way as the scenery opened in front of it and closed behind.

I remained transfixed, my forehead pressed against the window, until it had grown dark.

Only then did I notice that Anastasia and I were not the only passengers in the compartment—we had been joined by a small, dark-skinned and narrow-eyed young man dressed in a silk tunic with a high buttoned collar and matching trousers. A plain white cap covering his long braided hair. He sat next to Anastasia, on the bench opposite me, and smiled when he noticed I was looking at him. He introduced himself as Chiang Tse. "I am a student at St. Petersburg University," he informed me in English. "But I come from the glorious city of Hong Kong, the port of a thousand masts and home of the air dragon ships."

"Sasha Trubetskaya," I said. "I mean, Alexandra. I'm going to the university too."

Chiang Tse proved to be a pleasant companion—now that I could not look outside, I was just as content to talk. Anastasia lit the gas lantern mounted on the wall of our compartment, ran to the restaurant carriage and brought us tea, and the three of us spent a pleasant evening trading stories and carefully skirting around the anxieties of starting a new life as a student.

I learned from Chiang Tse that there were very few Chinese students at the university in St. Petersburg—there were several more at Moscow University, he said, because it was marginally closer to his homeland. He had great hopes for the railroad currently being constructed. The route cut across Siberia and offered an easy passage between Europe and Asia—it had now almost reached Beijing. "I understand there is some apprehension about the Orient moving suddenly close," he said and smiled to show he was only joking.

I smiled back. I could imagine what it was like for him—to be so alone and far away from his compatriots, to be so different from his new classmates, to anticipate their mistrust, their inevitable disapproval. I understood because the same was true for me, and I felt like crying again, even though it was hardly an opportune moment. I could not help but think the girls who declined the imperial invitation were correct to do so—despite being Eugenia's niece, I did not seek to attract attention or to struggle against the current; the only reason I went was because I feared disappointing her more than I feared scandalizing the entirety of polite society.

Chiang Tse was a better sport than I—he changed the topic to his home city, of which I had only a vague notions in connections to the recent war between China and Britain. He told me Hong Kong was now a free port under British control, and I gathered from his reserved manner that he had no love for the British. He also mentioned the unrest that was starting in the Guangxi Province and the dangers it presented to the travelers.

"When one's country is so war-torn and ravaged," he said as he poured another cup of tea, "one cannot help but feel guilt in escaping to a place so peaceful, so . . . " his fingers threaded the air, searching for the right word to pluck, "so *northern*. And yet, I am very grateful for being here. Perhaps, here I could learn to live in peace with the West."

"It's never an easy peace," I said. "Why, our emperor fought in the Napoleonic invasion. And as much as Peter the Great wanted us to become westernized, it is always a struggle; Russians have a deep seated mistrust of the West."

"You do not see yourself as western?"

I thought a little. "My aunt certainly does. My mother and I . . . I'm not so sure. I am less enamored of the reforms, but I certainly find this train convenient."

Chiang Tse nodded, pleased—at least, his sparse mustache bristled in a small smile. "You don't think you're a part of Europe. And yet you speak English."

I shook my head, momentarily despairing to explain the national anxiety about being and yet not being European in a few words, when Anastasia, quiet until then, spoke. "The Countess tells me that you can see Europe from St. Petersburg—across the bay just so, on a clear morning. And how can you see something that you're a part of?"

"Exactly," I said, relieved.

Chiang Tse nodded with some hesitation. "There seems to be much for me to learn."

"You will," Anastasia said generously, and patted his shoulder.

Chiang Tse and I traded a wide-eyed look, and he couldn't suppress a laugh. I suppose he found being patronized by a servant amusing, and I decided not to scold Anastasia for her treprass.

I dozed off for an hour or two, and woke up due to Anastasia's soft snoring. Our companion was sleeping as well—in the uncertain light of the dimmed gas lamp, I could see his head pitched back, exposing his dark throat over the white collar of his jacket, his hands folded in his lap. I would not confess my relief to anyone, least of all Chiang Tse, but I thought it was good to know someone—besides the girls who would be in as much distress and confusion as I—who was not like me and yet understood my discomfort.

Most male students hired rooms in the city. Girls, apparently, could not be trusted to find their own rooms, pay the bills, and protect their own virtue, so they were housed in the dormitories. I was quite pleased with my assigned dormitory—it occupied a low building, with each of the apartments containing two bedrooms, a small room with two cots for the maids, a parlor, and a kitchen. Each apartment was supposed to be shared by two women, but since half of us did not show up, we each had an entire apartment to ourselves. There were three on the second floor and three on the first, with one of the apartments on the first floor given to an elderly woman who was charged with making sure that we were accounted for at all times.

I helped a shocked Anastasia prepare our beds and unpack the suitcases. There was no reason for me to play the lady and not be of use. After all, was I not a modern university woman? Soon enough the kitchen was furnished with shining pots, and a kettle bubbled happily over the stove. Anastasia boiled some water and set an enameled tub in front of the kitchen woodstove so I could wash off the grime and fatigue of the road. Afterwards, Anastasia went to the market to procure supper, and I spent the rest of the afternoon unpacking and hanging my clothes and filling the spacious chest of drawers thoughtfully placed in my bedroom with my underthings. By the time Anastasia had returned and cooked our supper, the apartment felt almost homey.

The chaperon, Natalia Sergeevna, stopped by to make sure we had everything we needed, and stayed for tea. She was a kindly, plain woman, who called me "dearie," and seemed quite pleased to meet Anastasia. I let the two of them babble about the price of wheat that year, and drifted to my bedroom. I had arrived before the rest of the dormitory's occupants, and felt alone in the mostly empty building, its cheerful wallpaper decorated with cornflowers notwithstanding. I wished my mother or Aunt Eugenia had come with me, to at least help me settle in. I chased away my resentments and reminded myself that I was a grown woman now, and honored to be accepted by the university—what else was there to desire? Masha Golitsyna would of course tell me there was marriage, the route she herself had chosen. And yet, even though I was never opposed to the idea itself, I looked at myself in the mirror and knew I would be foolish to have expectations of attracting someone's attention with my appearance. There were better things to be than pretty—the advice I had heeded since I was ten to such good effect that I felt no pangs of regret or self-pity.

The steady rising and falling of the voices in the parlor, coupled with the clinking of teacups, lulled me. I sank into a chair by my bed and closed my eyes for a moment, and then the train was swaying and the steam was covering the windows when we stopped at some station, and the tea was poured and I stared into the dark almond-shaped eyes of Chiang Tse. His voice told me of the tall masts and the awkward flights of the airships. Then his face elongated into the sly muzzle of a dragon wearing a red and gold dressing gown. The dragon winked at me, poured tea, and spoke of his ambitions in calculus, and inquired about Miss Chartwell's availability.

I REMEMBER VIVIDLY MY FIRST DAY AS A STUDENT. I REMEMBER waking up before dawn and looking out of the window at the rows of linden trees, their leaves already turning the color of gold, and maples so red their branches seemed wrapped in living flames.

I got dressed with excruciating care, accompanied by Anastasia's constant nagging. I wore a simple two-piece dress in blue and gray plaid, with a crinoline small enough to not impede sitting in narrow auditorium seats. The weather was cool enough to justify kid gloves and a new muff, of the same soft beige fur that trimmed my cloak.

Classes had been selected for the female students by several deans in consultation with the emperor himself. After I looked at the schedule, I became convinced that Eugenia had a hand in it as well—among expected languages and classics and philosophy, there were swaths of natural sciences, physics, and calculus. In the second year, we were supposed to start taking engineering classes and chemistry. I thanked my lucky stars and Miss Chartwell, and headed for the building indicated on my schedule.

One of the other women students joined me. She was someone I had not previously met, and I was pleased when she introduced herself with none of the languor found in most of the young society ladies I had encountered. Her name was Olga Sokolova, and among the women admitted she was the only one who was not from a noble family; she told me as we walked across the island to the university campus that her father was a mere corporal but he had served the emperor well, and now his service was rewarded by making his daughter an oddity—a strangely hostile gesture disguised as kindness, we both agreed. Despite that, Olga expressed great eagerness for learning, and it made me like her immediately.

Arm in arm now, we found our assigned building; it was newer than most of the university's buildings, and painted bright blue. A copse of poplars surrounded it, and a long flowerbed orange with the last nasturtiums and edged with white stone ran along the path leading to the front door. There were several young men milling outside, and they gave us a few measured and curious looks. Olga blanched and squeezed my arm tighter, and I found myself leaning closer to her. We walked down the path under the veritable assault of the alternately lewd and disapproving gazes directed at us; it felt like running a gauntlet.

"Is it going to be like this every day?" Olga whispered, and her voice shook as if she were about to burst into tears.

"I hope the novelty will wear off after a while," I answered. "But where's that chaperon woman when you need her?"

Olga smiled at that, and we found our assigned auditorium. It was still mostly empty, and the professorial lectern towered at the front. Rows and rows of chairs upholstered in red velvet opened amphitheater-style back from the small stage, like petals of an enormous flower.

"Let's sit in the back," Olga said.

"Nonsense," I replied. "They'll know we are here anyway, but if we sit in the lecturer's sight, no one would dare direct disrespect."

Olga smiled gratefully. "How do you know these things?"

"I don't," I answered honestly. "I'm just thinking of what my virgin aunt would say in this situation."

We rustled our skirts and settled in the first row. Both Olga and I had small notebooks tucked into our muffs—unfortunately, our dresses and cloaks lacked any significant pockets. I considered buying a handbag just to carry pens and notebooks; I hoped we were not expected to transport our textbooks anywhere.

Once we had settled, I watched the door. Several Chinese students filed in, and I recognized Chiang Tse among them. He acknowledged me with a small bow, and I inclined my head. The Chinese students, some of whom were dressed in gray suits while others wore more colorful jackets and long robes, stiff with gold embroidery, and black cloth slippers, settled in a row behind Olga and me. It reassured me—I felt as if I were being shielded from the judging eyes of my male compatriots.

Gradually, the auditorium filled with a shuffling and coughing of young men. Some of them smoked, and strolled through the aisles with a leisurely demeanor that I could easily imagine was a mask concealing cruelty. It was deeply disturbing. Most of these men were not noble, only sons of merchants and engineers. I was their better, and yet defenseless and vulnerable if they decided to vent their unhappiness in my direction.

Three other women soon joined us, and introduced themselves—Larisa, Elena, Dasha —before settling next to us. With the bright jackets of the Chinese students and the girls' dresses standing in such contrast to the prevalent male brown and gray, I felt a part of a small isle of color, and that day my heart chose its allegiance. I turned and smiled at Chiang Tse over my shoulder, and he smiled back—warmly, as a friend would.

The lecturer—a solid, gray-haired and gray-bearded professor—arrived a few minutes late, and he spent a while longer inspecting the front of the auditorium. "Welcome," he finally said, "to our new students. This is a class on human biology, and we will start by examining the differences between races and genders. I expect you—" his gaze locked with mine for a moment before drifting to the next female student—"to take notes. If you feel scandalized by the material, you may excuse yourself." He paused while some tittering laughs flitted about the audience. "I still expect you to know the material."

After the classes were over, I lingered behind, waiting for the auditorium to empty out. Olga and the rest of the girls went ahead, as they chatted in an overly familiar ritual of getting to know one another.

Chiang Tse too split from his companions, and waited for me in the aisle between the empty seats, his profile dark against the golden brilliance of the autumn outside spilling through the open door and tall arched windows.

"That wasn't too bad," I said as soon as I was an arm's length away from him.

He shrugged. "I suppose it could be worse."

Neither of us acknowledged it explicitly, but I was glad he waited for me—at least I assume it was me for whom he awaited. We walked outside together.

The nasturtiums had grown transparent in the sun, each petal like a tongue of living flame rising from the flowerbeds, and without saying a word both of us stopped to look. It was strange to walk with him like that, without speaking, but moving in unison, in some magically silent accord.

The campus had grown quiet in the few minutes between the end of classes and our delayed exit. Only a few figures moved at a distance, with an occasional staccato of hurried footsteps reverberating on the newly laid blocks of pavement. It was all just as well—without knowing why, I was already feeling our walk, innocent as it was, was somehow illicit.

My feelings were confirmed when we turned around the corner of the lecture hall and came across a group of several young men, their clothes betraying means if not breeding—they all wore long sack jackets with upright collars and wide ascots, and formidably tall hats. The five of them crowded the pavement, and I flustered, stepping right and left, trying to find a way between them. They merely watched, dead-eyed and threatening despite their passive demeanor. Finally, I stepped onto the pavement and cringed as my shoe hit a puddle cunningly hid by a narrow strip of the curb; the water splashed all over the hem of my skirt.

Chiang Tse ignored the snickering of the hoodlums, and joined me in the puddle, without regard for the dirty water seeping into his shoes and trousers. I shook the water out of my skirts and thought woefully that this particular arrangement was likely to become a tangible metaphor for my stay at the university.

Chiang Tse was apparently of the same mind. His fingers touched my elbow gingerly as he said, "I enjoy standing in the puddle with you. It is refreshing, don't you think?"

Chapter 3

AND THUS MY EDUCATION HAD BEGUN. I QUICKLY GOT THE impression that even if women students were not admitted solely to prove their inferiority, it was viewed as a desirable outcome.

Professor Ipatiev, the lecturer who had delivered the very first lecture in my student career, proved to be a lasting influence. His class was in turns fascinating and upsetting, and Olga, who had swiftly become my closest friend and something of a confidante, shared my feelings.

"I do not understand," she complained one September evening, as the two of us sat in the parlor of my apartment, drinking strong sweet tea thoughtfully prepared by Anastasia before she left to visit with Natalia Sergeevna. "Professor Ipatiev seems like a kind man. And yet he looks directly at you and me when he talks about women's brains being smaller than men's."

I sighed and remembered the tittering that ran in waves across the auditorium every time Professor Ipatiev spoke about anatomical differences such as that—about how Africans were incapable of any learning, and the Asians could only memorize but not really comprehend complex concepts; about how women's minds were subordinate to their wombs, how their brains lacked the requisite number of folds. One could not help but feel somewhat insulted. "I don't suppose we can argue," I said. "It is true, I guess."

Olga sighed. "Do you get a feeling that we were asked to attend the university just so we can fail?"

"That would be cruel, wouldn't it?" I answered, demurring form the actual question.

Olga was not so easily thwarted. "Cruelty is not exactly uncommon, you know."

"So Anastasia tells me."

Anastasia chose to return at that time, and, eager for a distraction, I made her repeat the gossip she brought home from the market that morning.

Anastasia settled by the table, her elbows on its polished surface and her fists holding up her freckled and ruddy countenance. She enjoyed being a center of attention, and she started with a great sense of foreboding. "I went to the shop just the other day, to get some pickles and raspberry preserves, seeing how we didn't make any this year—I guess they did at the Trubetskoye, but the countess didn't send us any, even though she *could* have, but I'm not complaining. So I went to the shop, and there was this man—really shifty, and he wasn't buying anything, only looking as people went and came, all crooked-like. And then there was one of these Chinamen, all in silk and with a long mustache and a straw basket on his head. He just bought a twist of tobacco and a pound of tea, but that shifty man followed him right out, and I said to Marfa the shop girl, what is he doing? And she says, oh, that's a Nikolashka. Goodness me, what is that, I say. And you know what she says?"

Olga and I shook heads in unison.

Anastasia sighed with happiness. "Marfa tells me that ever since all the foreign people started coming to St. Petersburg, Prince Nicholas took charge of keeping an eye on them. And he now has policemen—only they're not in uniform and they are all secret-like—and people call them Nikolashki, after the prince. And they follow the Chinamen around, for our protection." She nodded to herself, satisfied, and fell silent.

"That is so strange," Olga said. "Are the Chinese really up to something?"

I shrugged. "The ones I talked to certainly aren't."

Olga smiled at that. "That's right," she said. "There is that young man you talk to, and his friends. They always sit behind you."

"Behind us," I said. "And if you want to meet them, come with me this Saturday—they are having a social at their club."

"Club?" Olga asked, apprehensive.

"Just off Fontanka, "I said. "A few blocks from Anichkov Bridge. The Chinese students always go there—I think they feel unwelcome everywhere else."

"This could be fun," Olga decided. "It's not dangerous, is it?"

I shook my head. "Of course not. We'll take Anastasia with us for propriety's sake, and they are harmless, really. Besides, I'm sure Prince Nicholas and his secret protectors will be chivalrous enough to come to our rescue if the necessity arises."

Olga smiled a bit and shook her head. "I know you're just joking, Sasha. But doesn't it worry you, even a little?"

I shrugged. "Let the government worry about such notions. I'm much more concerned about my human biology exam."

"Me too." Olga rose to her feet. "I suppose I better go study."

She departed to her apartment located just down the hall from mine, leaving me with my uneasy thoughts. I looked through my notes and thumbed a thick volume written by Ipatiev himself, where he illustrated some especially savage and sloping foreheads as indicators of intellectual inadequacy. He had a chapter on Chinamen as well, and I tried reading it before flinging the book across the room—the faces illustrated there, all toothy and barely human, bore no resemblance to the gentle features of Chiang Tse and his countrymen, who were all polite and soft-spoken, and who were kind to me. Yet, I suspected that the majority of my classmates would rather believe the book than their own eyes. This is why, I decided, I could not possibly fail this exam—as unfair as it was, all five women were closely scrutinized, and any shortcoming on our part would reflect on future generations. A sense of historical responsibility weighed on me until I had a cry and went to bed early.

SATURDAY WAS UPON US BEFORE I WAS READY FOR IT—DROWNING in readings and incomprehensible problems, I was entirely too preoccupied. It was a blessing, since it allowed me to barely notice the habitual mockery of my classmates. That in turn seemed to enrage them further, and I rarely had a chance to walk to class without hearing a snide remark. The day before our scheduled visit to the Crane Club, as I was leaving the auditorium, I heard a man's voice say, "Look at her. Takes after her aunt Menshova." This was not a surprising statement—my aunt was well known and almost universally disliked. I turned around to see a clump of several younger men, some of whom I recognized from last season. There was no indication as to which one of them spoke, and all smiled, almost predatorily.

I gave them a long measured look and continued on my way.

The same voice spoke again. "I hear this one is going to be an old maid too."

I did not dignify it with a reaction, until someone else added, "I hear she'll marry a Chinaman."

I spun around, feeling my face burn. "Instead of marrying a brainless cowardly lout like any of you? Why, it's a capital idea!"

A few laughed, the rest appeared outraged. I continued on my way. By then, we had left the building and early dusk was descending over the campus. It occurred to me then that I was alone and rather helpless. Six or seven of the men followed behind me, never closing the distance between us. I almost regretted my insolence when Dasha Muravieva and Larisa Kulich caught up to me, and the pursuers dispersed.

"What happened?" Dasha asked me.

I caught my breath and let my heart calm down before I answered. "I don't know, but I think it would be a good idea for us to walk in pairs, and never alone."

Dasha and Larisa nodded and grew serious. I thought bitterly that I did not need to explain to them what I meant when I said "us." They knew we were separate from everyone on campus, and that even our families could not protect us from the subtle menace of our fellow students.

So I was relieved when Saturday had arrived, and looked forward to visiting the very mysterious Crane Club. I had only heard rumors of the place, and wondered if there would be any opium smoking, or any of the other indulgences ascribed to the foreigners. Chiang Tse did not seem capable of anything unwholesome—and neither did his friends. I had heard, however, rumors of strange devices housed in the Chinamen's club.

The rumors turned out to be true. The outside of the building was an unassuming storefront, painted pale green. Inside, Olga, Anastasia, and I encountered a foyer filled with lacquered display cases, where a number of interesting contraptions sat on the shelves protected by thick glass.

Chiang Tse met us in the foyer, and smiled at my obvious befuddlement. "These are the projects of the Chinese engineering students who went to this university," he said. He pointed out a cigar-shaped object with a basket under it. "This is a model of an airship used in the Opium War," he said. "And next to it is a device that transcribes sounds."

We politely examined a brass contraption that consisted of a huge funnel-shaped horn on top and a large gutta-percha membrane on the bottom, connected by wires to a series of slender quills. When Chiang Tse spoke, the quills twitched nervously, but remained stationary.

"There are quite a few interesting things," Chiang Tse said. "But for now, let's go and meet the rest of my friends."

Inside the club proper we found it was fashioned after a large parlor. There were chairs and cushioned sofas, as well as a large central area covered in rugs woven in simple green patterns and surrounded by wide, low couches. All of the furniture was upholstered in sea-green and golden silk, and the paintings on the walls depicted bug-eyed black fish and peculiar, long-bodied dragons that reminded me of eels more than the stocky lizards one saw on St. George icons. There were also long scrolls hanging between the paintings, with plum flowers and mountainous landscapes drawn in spare brushstrokes of black and red ink. I had to stop and stare. I marveled at the economy of these drawings and how they still managed to evoke such expansive beauty.

Olga pulled at my sleeve to draw my attention to three young men reclining on the couches in a state of extreme languor. Long-stemmed pipes held by their weak hands exhaled wisps of sweet-smelling smoke.

Chiang Tse frowned. "Opium," he said. "A terrible affliction of my countrymen, for which they cannot be faulted. Please come with me, and do not let the weaknesses of a few color your perception of the many."

We followed him through the parlor and into a room dominated by a single long table, covered with crisp linen cloth of European fashion. The servers, dressed in less elaborate versions of Chiang Tse's black and red silk robes, hurried along, pouring fragrant pale tea into small cups. The men sitting around the table were engaged in animated conversation, which politely halted once we walked in. Chiang Tse introduced Olga and me to the rest of the gathering, while Anastasia blushed and remained standing until one of our hosts brought her a chair at Chiang Tse's urging, and she settled in the corner of the room, by a spacious window, where she could keep an eye on me, and the street.

"You're trying to stick her as far away from you as possible," I whispered to Chiang Tse. "You're afraid that she might be condescend you again."

He smiled at my teasing, and even blushed a little.

Olga and I took seats at the table. She looked a little apprehensive, I thought, in her striped black-and-white two-piece dress and hat with a thick veil. But soon enough the friendliness of our hosts dispelled lingering doubts, and she chatted with one of Chiang Tse's friends, Lee Bo, who was in our physics class. By mutual consent, Ipatiev's name was never mentioned, and instead we laughed about some of the unsuccessful static electricity demonstrations we had all witnessed.

I waited for a lull in the conversation and turned to Chiang Tse. "You're very quiet," I said. "Do you miss home?"

Chiang Tse sighed wistfully, and for a moment I was entranced by the way his thick eyelashes cast a shadow over the steep curve of his cheekbone. When he looked up, his eyes reminded me of blackberries, dark and shiny in the eyelash thicket. "Sasha," he said, "I wish you had been there, I wish you'd seen it. It is so difficult to explain when you have nothing to compare it to. When my family lived in Canton for several years, there were boats and ships sailing from the sea to the delta of the Pearl River. I cannot forget the way the golden ships—the color of the sun—would push softly through the emerald reeds. Ships, winged dragon boats, war junks . . . There were so many ships in the harbor you could not see the water under them. There were boats that sold books and actors on boats that put on plays—floating theaters! There were boats selling moon cakes and sweet rice, dumplings and slices of mango, sweet bean paste and wood-smoked chicken."

"From the boats?" I asked. "Where did they all go?"

He shrugged. "They kept floating along the shore and into the mouth of the river, and up the river and then back down. When I first saw it, it was like heaven—green reeds and the river, and the beautiful stately buildings . . . I thought of taking my examinations there, in that city, when I was old enough, and I thought of what happiness it would be, to live in that place of floating palaces and theaters and bookshops. In Hong Kong, there are ships, but nothing like I saw in Canton. And back then, there were no foreigners allowed in Hong Kong, although there were smugglers. But in Canton, the foreigners had a whole sector to themselves. We would go outside of the city walls to watch those solemn men in their strange clothes." He looked up from his teacup, smiling at the fading sunlight in the streets outside of the Crane Club. "And now I cannot help but feel there were little hints then of things to come, as if my life prepared me for being here."

I smiled back, content that his life—and the lives of his friends—turned out the way it had. I was certainly happy he was here now, and that I was fortunate enough to have met him.

Wong Jun, another student at the university—distinguished by his luxurious golden robes—sat across the table from us without joining in our conversation. "He's Manchu," Chiang Tse whispered into my ear. Noticing Olga's uncomprehending look, he explained, "Qing, the ruling dynasty of China, is Manchu, while most of the people—including quite a few students here—are Han. So if you notice any tension . . . "

"There's no need to whisper," Wong Jun said with a wave of his hand and a grimace of mild irritation. "Then again, there's no need to bring up petty disputes either."

"I'm interested," Olga said.

Wong Jun shrugged and grinned. "See how most of the students here wear black or dark blue robes with red ones underneath? That's *xuanduan*, Han formal dress. My robes are Manchu."

Olga and I nodded politely. "It can't be just about clothing," she whispered to me.

I shook my head and gestured that I would explain later—thankfully, my friendship with Chiang Tse prepared me for at least a vague discussion of Ming and Qing differences, and the commonly professed Han hostility toward the Manchu.

Wong Jun and Chiang Tse expressed no outward enmity toward each other, but instead joined forces in explaining the Opium War to Olga; apparently, dislike of the British brought the Manchu and the Han together. We drank the tea that smelled faintly of flowers—a taste both familiar and strange, and watched the sky change color from almost white to blue to streaked with pink. Just as the sun was touching the roof of St. Isaac's Cathedral, Anastasia squawked from her perch by the window. "You have to see this, Miss Alexandra," she called. "That's the man I told you about."

Olga and I both bolted for the window, arriving just in time to see a stocky man cross the street toward the club. He was dressed in a non-descript blue coat and trousers splattered with mud at the hem. His top hat was pushed low over his brow obscuring his face, but Anastasia insisted he was the man she had seen at the shop.

Chiang Tse joined us at the window, and watched our discussion with a somewhat puzzled expression. I hurried to explain the rumors of the secret informers to him.

"We're not doing anything untoward," he said. "We have nothing to be afraid of."

"Except the opium smokers in the parlor," I said. "You might discourage their public consumption. It is not illegal, but . . . "

Wong Jun left the dining room, and his whispered words spread a mild agitation among the students. Some hurried to the parlor to make sure that there were no non-presentable activities, and opened windows to chase away the sweet, lingering smell of the opium smoke.

Olga and I traded looks, unsure if we were in any danger. If we were to leave right away, would the Nikolashka outside start questioning us? I suddenly realized what my aunt had meant with her attack on Prince Nicholas. The idea of the Nikolashki was somewhat sinister; the appearance of one outside the Chinese club betrayed the prince's proclivity for unsavory business.

"Do you think the Chinese are truly are spies?" Olga whispered into my ear.

I have to confess the question had not previously entered my mind, but I now weighed the possibility. "No," I finally said. "They are just students, just as we are."

"They could still be spies."

I sighed and pulled Olga away from the window, and made her sit down by the table. "Listen. They are our friends. Shouldn't we trust them?"

Olga's eyes filled with doubt but she said nothing.

"Come on," I said. "What did they ever do to you?"

Olga stood, and would not meet my gaze. "I better go."

"You can't go by yourself." I turned to Anastasia. "Please take Miss Olga to the dormitories."

Anastasia scowled. "And leave you here alone? No, miss, I cannot."

"Consider it an order," I said. "Please don't argue, or I'll send you back to Trubetskoye and you know what words my Aunt Eugenia would have for you."

Anastasia paled, impressed by the thought of Countess Eugenia's wrath to such an extent that even her freckles disappeared. "How will you get home, Miss Alexandra?" she dared to ask.

"I'll walk," I answered. "Don't worry, I know the way, and I'll be along as soon as we know what these men want."

"You don't have to stay," Olga said, still not looking me in the face.

"I won't be long," I answered. "I just want to make sure that Mr. Chiang Tse and his friends are not harmed. I cannot do much other than offer my word as to their character, but my family might mean something to these people."

I walked Anastasia and Olga to the door and promised to join them soon. When I returned to the dining room, the servers had cleared the table. The Chinese students had congregated in small groups, some speaking English, others conversing in what I assumed was Cantonese.

"What is going on?" I asked Chiang Tse, who was speaking to Lee Bo and Wong Jun.

All three turned toward me with tense smiles.

"We must thank you for warning us," Lee Bo said. He was the most soft-spoken of the three, and I was surprised to hear him speak for the rest. "Several of our countrymen disappeared recently. Initially, we believed they were compelled to return home on urgent business. But my own brother, Lee Jin, disappeared yesterday. Suspecting foul play, we went to the authorities. But if what you say is true, I now worry we will find no assistance from government officials for my brother and our friends."

I sought for words with which to reply, shocked by the realization of the severity of the situation. Its grievous nature was reinforced by the fear written so clearly on copper-dark faces surrounding me. "This makes no sense," I said. "Surely, the emperor . . . "

I could not finish the thought—of course the emperor would trust his brother over foreign students. As for the students' war-torn native country, even if made aware of the harassment and abuse of its children abroad, little attention could be spared from more profound national problems. I remembered the group of menacing male students following me, and—once I recognized with crystal clarity how defenseless all of us were, how vulnerable—my head began to swim.

"I will go out, I will try to reason with the scoundrel," I said.

"What will you say?" Lee Bo said.

"This is ridiculous," Chiang Tse interrupted. "It is only one man in the street, and we have no reason to think he's looking to arrest someone. We've allowed fear to overwhelm us."

"It is understandable if you consider my brother's disappearance," Lee Bo interjected.

"At the very least, I can ask," I said, and resolutely pulled my gloves on.

When I stepped outside, I realized Lee Bo's fear was not exaggerated. The Nikolashka Anastasia claimed to have recognized stood under a small arch next to the club's doorway. Moreover, there were another six men in street clothing milling about and trying to look inconspicuous. When they saw me, most of them turned away, as if looking at something fascinating down the street. The sun had almost set by then, and long shadows twisted around them, hiding their faces and pooling under their eyes.

"Excuse me, gentlemen," I said. "I could not help but notice you've been here for some time. Are you waiting for anyone in particular?"

Anastasia's Nikolashka frowned in my general direction. "Pass along, miss. Official business."

"Really?" I stepped closer, even though my heart was fluttering high in my throat. I was close enough to smell onions on his wheezing breath. "Is anyone in this club of interest to you then?"

He did not answer but turned away with a sigh and a show of irritation.

"My family," I said with as much weight as I could muster, "is close to the emperor. I will gladly offer my word of the good character of those inside."

Nikolashka jerked his shoulder. "Good for your family then, miss. Now, let me do my job, and I won't spoil your friendship with the emperor, how's that sound?"

I stepped back, unsure of what to do next.

"And you better not go back into that club," he said. "You don't want to be caught consorting with that element, believe you me. Just walk home and get yourself some sleep." He never addressed my by name, but I got a distinct feeling he knew who I was.

For a moment, I was tempted to follow his advice. I think what stopped me was a slowly rising anger at being dismissed for not presenting a real threat; in any case, I headed back to the club's entrance.

There were a few men leaving the club, none of whom I recognized. Still, I stood and waited for them to pass through the doors and by the arch. I hoped the Nikolashki would not dare anything while I watched. Perhaps my mere presence would be enough to avert a disaster.

The next to emerge were Wong Jun, Lee Bo, and Chiang Tse. I pressed my lips together and inclined my head in the direction of the arch. They seemed to understand, and hurried into the gathering darkness.

"Halt!" called the Nikolashka who smelled like onions. At his command, a few of his comrades stepped forth, surrounding the three men.

I am not exactly sure what was I hoping to accomplish, but I stepped between Chiang Tse and the Nikolashki. A part of me hoped that the latter would be dissuaded from their pursuits if there were a witness; it had never occurred to me that any real harm might befall me.

The one who smelled of onions moved to shove me aside, and his arm caught me across the chest, pushing me into the waiting arms of others, while three more stepped forth to apprehend the Chinese students. I struggled out of the men's hands, appalled by the unclean touch of their corrupt fingers, all the while demanding that my friends be left alone.

The gas streetlamps were coming on, but the passersby were few, and clearly uninterested in getting involved. All four of us were held by the arms now; only I continued to struggle, still willfully oblivious to whose side the power was on.

I was lifted bodily off the ground, and used this opportunity to try and kick at my capturers, but they were apparently used to such attempts and the onion-breath avoided injury with surprising deftness. Before they could carry me off to the carriage now waiting at the corner, a part of the night sky suddenly grew darker—both starlight and lamplight disappeared, and before I had a chance to wonder at this phenomenon, the dark patch resolved itself into a wide cloak.

I could not see the face of the man who fell like a stone from the sky—a suicide, I thought at first, even though there were no tall buildings in our proximity. Our capturers saw him too; I felt the grip on my elbows relax, and used the opportunity to wrench free. I was not the only one: I saw Chiang Tse and Lee Bo wrestle out of constraining hands as well. Noting their hesitation, I screamed, "Run!"—furious that they might waste this opportunity with unneeded chivalry. They wisely obeyed.

The man who fell out of the sky backhanded one of the Nikolashki, and the rest of them stepped back, understandably stunned by his appearance as well as his rude behavior. I could not see the face half-hidden under his wide-brimmed hat—only a long, clean-shaven chin was visible.

He grabbed my elbow. "Come on," he said, and pulled me along. I ran after him, into darker streets with only a scarce smattering of streetlamps. He ran quickly, changing directions as to confuse any pursuit, and I did my best to keep up. My skirts tried to twist around my legs, and my chest felt as if it would explode against the confines of my corset. "Wait," I gasped.

The stranger paused and let me lean against an anonymous brick wall where I stood gulping air.

"Wong Jun," I finally managed. "They still have one of my friends."

The stranger gave a soft chuckle. "I am awfully sorry to hear that, miss," he said in perfect English, "only I'm not going back. Look at the bright side though—two of them got free. Maybe for long enough to leave the city and avoid further trouble altogether." He had an easy, pleasant manner of speech. By then I had decided he had not fallen out of the sky, but had a good enough heart to interfere with injustice when he stumbled upon it. It was his sudden appearance that had confused me.

"I appreciate your assistance, sir," I said. "You came seemingly out of nowhere."

"Just happened by." A flash of teeth under the brim of the hat, and another soft laugh. "Name's Jack Bartram. I do believe I've seen you in my philosophy class."

I shook a proffered hand, very long, with square-tipped fingers. "If you say so."

"Forgive my lack of manners, miss." He took off his hat, and I saw an entirely unremarkable, pale visage—even if he was in my class, he had one of these faces that was easily forgettable. But he was quite tall and gangly under his cloak, and that made him memorable enough.

"I am Alexandra Trubetskaya," I said. "It is a pleasure to meet you, and I thank you for a timely and dramatic rescue."

He was laughing still. "I hope your friends will get a chance to say the same to you."

I smiled then. "I hope so too."

He put his hat back on, and stood a moment listening for the sounds of the pursuit. Satisfied that there was none, he offered me his arm. "It would be my pleasure to escort you back to your dormitory, Miss Trubetskaya," he said.

I nodded and took his arm. "Thank you. Anastasia must be worried sick."

Chapter 4

I did not get a chance to tell Olga about my miraculous rescue and the terrible behavior of the Nikolashki —by the time Mr. Bartram and I arrived at the dormitories, all windows but mine were dark. I listened to Anastasia's relieved exclamations and then went to bed, but not before peeking out of the window, and observing that, to my disappointment, my rescuer was gone.

I saw him on Monday in my philosophy class. It took place in the afternoon, when most of those present, full and contented after lunch, dozed to the monotone of Professor Zhmurkin, who informed us of the Prime Mover and other such fanciful notions. I, however, was alert, and looked past Olga and Dasha's nodding heads (it was like watching a seesaw) to the back of the auditorium. When I looked behind me, my heart fluttered painfully in my chest. The colorful robes and long braids were gone now, replaced by a row of empty seats. There were three Chinese students left in attendance, and all of them had their hair cut in the current style and wore Western dress.

My sorrow was quickly replaced by blushing, fluttering joy as my eyes met the steely-gray gaze of the Englishman from last night, who smiled and nodded to me as if I were an old friend. I quickly turned away, and listened to the lecture, flustered by my embarrassing joy. I should not be feeling elated with Chiang Tse and Lee Bo missing and Wong Jun no doubt languishing in some prison. But what could I do help them?

As always, I imagined what Aunt Eugenia would say. Her stern voice crystallized in my mind with perfect clarity. "Foolish girl," she would've said if she were here. "You have plenty of connections in this city—don't tell me your poor mother and I wasted our time introducing you. If you want to find something out, nothing's stopping you."

That was true enough, I thought. Yet Eugenia had never been subtle, and I suspected that the matter of arrested foreign friends required at least a modicum of subtlety. Unfortunately, I was too much of Eugenia's niece to think of anything artful. My first inclination was to march to the Winter Palace and shout at the emperor; my second was to spit in his brother's smug face. Either course of action was unlikely to yield the desired results.

I barely heard the end of the lecture, and nudged Olga when we were dismissed. She woke with a start, rubbed her eyes, and shot me a look of mild irritation. "What did you do that for?"

"Time to go," I said timidly. I still hadn't apologized for Saturday; I wasn't planning to even though I knew she expected it.

Olga rose and followed Dasha Muravieva out, and I lagged behind, angry at myself for feeling guilt even though I had done nothing wrong. I was almost ready to apologize anyway, so as not to feel so shut out.

"Miss Trubetskaya?" I heard a soft male voice behind me. I knew who it was before I turned around.

There was a sly quality to Jack Bartram's smile, and it made me think that he was always hiding something wonderful, that he held some magical secret in the hands he clasped behind his back.

I couldn't help but smile in return. "Mr. Bartram. It is a pleasure to see that you are well."

"As well as your friends." He followed me out of the auditorium and offered me his arm, which I took with a sense of developing habit.

"What do you know about them?"

He leaned closer, his warm breath tickling the tip of my ear. "A friend of mine was at the train station yesterday, early in the morning. He saw two young men of Chinese origin board the train, and I'd wager they were those fine gentlemen I never got a chance to properly meet. I thought you might like to know that."

"Thank you, Mr. Bartram," I said, an enormous weight left my shoulders with such alacrity that I stumbled. Only Jack's arm allowed me to maintain my upright posture. "That is wonderful news. Now, if I could only find out about Wong Jun and where they are keeping him . . . "

Jack only shook his head. "I cannot help you there, Miss Trubetskaya."

"You've already accomplished a great deal," I said. "I am quite grateful. I will now look into the matter using my own resources."

"I wish you good luck," he said. Once outside, he put on his hat—not a top hat like most men wore that season, but the wide-brimmed, soft contraption he'd worn the night before. It hid most of his face from view—although not from me, because I walked closely enough to peek under it.

I had forgotten about Olga and Dasha who had gone ahead, quite content to walk along with Jack Bartram in whatever direction he cared to point the tips of his black scuffed boots. Even though his legs were ridiculously long, he took care to match his loping stride to mine, and seemed as pleased to walk along the paths covered in yellow leaves as I was. We breathed the bitter autumn smells and the scent of coal from the river, and I found myself in front of my dormitory quite a bit sooner than I expected.

As much as I found Jack's attention flattering—especially because, rightly or wrongly, I assumed he was less aware of my impending titles and fortune than my compatriots, and therefore I could ascribe unselfish motives to him. As soon as I was alone in my apartment, I turned my mind to finding out about Wong Jun. It really would be more convenient, I mused, if one had an ability to not worry about people one had just met and seen arrested by the secret police. For better or worse, however, such ability was as beyond my grasp as the clouds now gathering outside of my windows.

Anastasia busied herself in the kitchen, and I sat by the window, resting my chin on folded arms, various possibilities bumping against each other in my mind. I had deferred worry over Lee Bo and Chiang Tse, having decided to trust Jack's word of their safety. Wong Jun still seemed a natural target for my concern.

I took out my notebook and leafed through the notes, past diagrams of Newtonian and Da Vincian machines, to the meager still-empty section. I settled my lap-desk and snatched up my pen. Uncapping the well, I inhaled the rich smell of ink. I tore a page from my notebook, each page bearing the insignia of St. Petersburg's University. Of course I had my own stationery, with the Trubetskoy crest, but the use of a page torn from a student's notebook seemed a better choice. I was not above trying to project an image of artless and studious youth and innocence if it could help Wong Jun.

I addressed my query to Prince Nicholas himself and sealed the letter with the Trubetskoy seal, to ensure that it would be read. With nothing else to pursue as far as Won Jun's predicament, I turned to studying for my impending exams.

I looked forward to the end of term and the short respite before the next one began—and I fervently hoped I would be able to see Eugenia and my mother during the recess.

Exams had filled me with enough sense of impending doom to chase almost every other thought from my mind. The increasing gulf between Olga and me seemed almost natural considering recent events, and the new friendship with Dasha Muravieva filled what little need for companionship I felt. But Jack Bartram occupied what thoughts I had other than study—quite disproportionately to our short walks between the philosophy class and the dormitory. During these strolls we spoke little, and I wondered about the role these ritual walks were starting to play in my life.

Jack rarely spoke about himself—I only gleaned that philosophy was his main focus and that he hoped to attempt a course of study in Germany, perhaps next year. I asked him about London, but he grew recalcitrant and spoke only in generalities. He complained about the smell from the Thames, and mentioned its gas-lit streets as something he was trying to leave behind, not dwell upon. I was left to imagine the infamous fog and Buckingham Palace by myself.

With October came rains and mists. Jack grew more wistful during our walks. He said a few times that the river and the severe stone city on its banks reminded him of home, but mostly we shared our anxiety about the impending exams. We never mentioned Wong Jun or the fact that there were now no Chinese students left at all. If he ever visited the Crane Club since the night of our first meeting, he never told me about it. I had almost forgotten about the letter I sent to Prince Nicholas—or rather, I assumed it was glanced at and discarded, and I would have to wait for December when my aunt arrived in St. Petersburg and perhaps felt inclined to exercising her influence on my behalf. There was nothing else to do until then.

The exam week started on October 17th, and I was so terrified that I could spare no thought for anyone but myself. Olga and Dasha, Larisa and Elena were also quite agitated. On the morning of the exam in human biology we all could be mistaken for ghosts—we had grown pale, and even though we didn't moan or clang spectral chains as we walked toward the auditorium, I thought our inner anguish more than made up for lack of outward effects.

We gathered in our usual auditorium; the exam was administered by Professor Ipatiev himself and two of his colleagues, neither of whom I had encountered prior to the day of exam. Their anonymity made them all the more desirable as examiners in my eyes. I said my little prayers and approached the dais covered in green felt, where the examination questions, each written on a long paper strip, were laid out, text facing down. I drew a question and dared a glance at it as I walked to my seat. A mix of relief and gratitude washed over me when I realized that I had to do nothing more complicated than describe the human circulatory system.

The second stroke of luck occurred when it was my turn to present my question—Ipatiev was deeply engaged in interrogating poor Larisa Kulich, and another examiner, a young man with a soft flaxen beard and gentle eyes motioned for me to sit in front of him.

I settled, not quite believing my luck. My heart beat so loudly, I feared the examiner would hear it rather than my voice, but I calmed and began explaining—appropriately, considering my physical reaction—the circulatory system starting with heart and lungs. The examiner smiled encouragingly and nodded along, and I could not quite believe what was happening: it appeared as if I would pass this—the most difficult—exam. The rest of them did not warrant a slightest worry in my mind.

I was almost finished—only the capillaries left to expound upon—and the professor had smiled and reached for my examination booklet, when the doors of the auditorium squealed open, and rough boots pounded the floors. Several uniformed men squinted in the murky air of auditorium. Their attire was not that of the civil police, but indicated they were from the Ministry of Internal Affairs.

Professor Ipatiev looked up, irritation spreading from him in almost palpable waves along with the smell of sweet pipe tobacco. "What do you want?" he called. "Just tell me who you're looking for, and let us get on with our examinations, if the emperor does not mind."

One of the men cleared his throat and looked at the sheet of paper crumpled in his large fist overgrown with sparse red hairs. "Alexandra Trubetskaya," he announced loudly.

All eyes were on me, and I felt as exposed and tiny as I did during my debut, only this time I was the sole cause of everyone in the auditorium turning toward me, and there was no aunt to shield me from their hostility. I stood, gathered my muff and parasol, and walked toward the policemen.

The one who had called my name reached out as if to grab my arm, but I had quite enough humiliation for one day, and being manhandled by his ilk was still fresh in my memory. I whipped my parasol across his knuckles, and he withdrew his hand with a hiss.

"Now," I said with as much dignity as I could muster, "there seems to be some mistake, for there is absolutely no reason for you to interfere with my schooling. I have done nothing illegal. I will gladly come with you to clear up any misunderstanding, but please do not lay your hands on me. I have heard of a number of unfortunate maiming accidents involving parasols. You would not wish such to befall you."

He grumbled under his breath but did not attempt further contact. As I exited, surrounded by a cluster of uniformed men and my heart in my stomach—not because I feared them but because I worried that leaving an examination room would count as failure—I noticed Olga looking straight at me, with a brave and encouraging smile on her face. I smiled back, even though my own circulatory system felt as if it was filled with ash instead of blood.

As we headed away from the building, my thoughts took a dark turn; I suspected that Professor Ipatiev would be more than pleased to fail me for not completing the examination. Further, the news of my undignified arrest would soon spread to the palace and the emperor would be glad for an excuse to disassociate himself from our family—what my aunt's outbursts could not accomplish, my consorting with a dangerous foreign element would. I could already think of all the things they would say about me and the Chinese students, about the hazards of admitting women and Chinamen into hallowed halls . . . my ears burned just thinking about such indignity.

We approached the Palace Bridge when a familiar swirl of a gray cloak caught my attention. There was no reason for me to expect Jack's appearance; yet the moment I saw him, I realized I had been holding my breath, hoping he would to come to my aid. When he did, I thought he had an extraordinarily sharp nose for police—secret or uniformed—and could not help but smile.

He approached us in an easy step, his eyes curious and bright. I thought he couldn't very well attack any of my capturers, since they were in uniform and it was broad daylight. Still, I waited for miracles. Jack did not hesitate to produce one—or rather, he pulled a sheet of paper from the inner pocket of his jacket, and handed it to the apparent officer in charge. After a few whispered words he joined our party. I kept quiet and he did not say a word to me.

We passed the Palace Square and the Decembrists Square, close to the embankment, away from the streets dedicated to the tenements of the mercantile classes and the offices of clerks and minor governmental officials. They took me to Gorokhovaya Street, to a large nice-looking building. All five stories teemed with intense activity—everywhere I could see clerks coming and going, most of them dressed in uniforms of the Ministry of the Internal Affairs. There were other policemen, too. The clerks' uniforms differed from the officers who surrounded me, and lacked swords, but it was apparent my captors belonged to the ministry—and the ministry was overseen by Prince Nicholas. Evidently Nikolashki could lurk about in civilian clothing or wear uniforms in public: both a secret police and the uniformed gendarmes.

I was led into a roomy office, the parquet floors and tall windows looking out on the silvery gray autumn daylight. Only one of the gendarme officers, his epaulettes golden and red, followed me inside. Jack Bartram remained with us as well, although I still had no idea on whose sufferance he was there.

The officer in the bright epaulettes offered me a seat on a stiff little sofa that rested against white-and-gold striped wallpaper by the door. He himself took a seat behind a massive oak desk, and Jack stood by the door, which he had carefully closed behind him. I got the distinct feeling the two men were keeping some secret from me, and I was about to be scolded. That made me feel slightly better, because a scolding was much preferable to accusations of sedition and treason and a tribunal of some sort, or any of the other such things I had imagined on my way here. I rested my parasol across my lap, took off my gloves, and prepared to listen.

The officer and Jack traded a look, as if each expected the other to speak first. After a short awkward pause, the officer cleared his throat.

"You know why you are here," he told me.

I gave a one-shouldered shrug, unwilling to commit. I then stared at Jack.

"Mr. Bartram here claims to have some information," the officer said. "And since Her Majesty's interests and ours happen to coincide, Mr. Bartram and his colleagues have been quite helpful in our recent investigations of the Asiatic menace with which, I hear, you are involved."

"Not at all," I protested.

He shuffled a few papers on his desk, and pulled out a single sheet. I recognized the page from my notebook; I think I blanched, because the gendarme gave me a humorless smile. "We have a report," he said, "that one Wong Jun was arrested, while in company of two compatriots and a lady, reportedly of European appearance. With your letter, I am forced to conclude you were that lady—a lady who resisted arrest, interfered with the performance of police duties, and escaped lawful custody."

"Wong Jun is a classmate of mine," I protested. "And I am not blind—I know how many Chinese students have disappeared."

"And yet, you've inquired only after the one in our custody." The man seemed to enjoy the effect of his words. "Not anyone else. You know why you are dealing with this special branch of the police and not others, correct?"

"Military crimes," I said, sullen. "Which I did not commit."

"And yet, you've consorted with spies."

"They are not spies," I said, starting to lose patience. "You have no proof that any of them is involved in anything untoward, just as you have no proof that I was in any way connected with illegal activities."

"Do you have proof that you weren't?" he asked. "Where were you on Saturday September twenty-fourth?"

I sought feverishly for an answer—Olga? Anastasia? Both would swear they were with me the entire day; unfortunately, there were likely others who saw the two of them return to the dormitories without me.

Jack spoke. "The lady was with me," he said. "After she separated from her maid and a friend, she went for a walk with me. Not entirely proper, perhaps, but quite legal."

The officer's eyes lit with understanding and a sly smile curled the corners of his mouth under his mouth under his mustache. "I see," he said.

I nodded, speechless. I wasn't sure whether to feel grateful Jack would lie for me, suspicious because he was probably more eager to conceal his role in the event than mine, or furious because he never told me that he represented the interests of the British crown in addition to being a student. It did explain his taciturn demeanor when he was asked about his homeland though. I finally settled on seething resentment, softened a little by regret.

I declined Jack Bartram's offer of walking me home, and asked for someone to be sent to fetch Anastasia. She arrived soon after the paperwork was finished and I was let go with no greater punishment than admonition to be careful about writing letters to the emperor's brother, and about who I chose as friends. I had decided to take the latter to heart, and frowned all the way home. Anastasia prattled about how worried she had been ever since Larisa and Olga told her about my sudden detainment, and how she was "this close" to sending a messenger to Trubetskoye.

I brooded all the way home and long after Anastasia made tea and supper and retired to bed. I thought it silly to be angry with Jack—if he was indeed in St. Petersburg to somehow work with Prince Nicholas and help him spy on the Chinese, then his help with Lee Bo's and Chiang Tse's escape made no sense. Nor did it make sense for him to help me, to lie for me in direct violation of what the policeman claimed was his mission. On the other hand, if the gendarme was deceived, then Jack was carrying forged papers, and his interests diverged quite greatly from those of both empires. *That* sounded even more dangerous than having Chinese friends and resisting arrest.

I finally slept, only because my philosophy exam was the next day and I had already lost an entire afternoon of studying; I did not need to add a sleepless night to the list of my disadvantages.

THE NEXT MORNING, OLGA BURST INTO MY ROOM TO INFORM ME of the events following my extraction from the examination room. It was a pandemonium, she said. There had been laughter and speculation, and Professor Ipatiev said rather loudly to the professor who had been examining me—his name turned out to be Parshin—that since I had not finished my exam, I should be required to retake it.

I gasped at this point in the story, since I could think of nothing worse than being re-examined by Ipatiev who would surely not let me pass. It was just unfair, I thought—of course the professors knew more than the students, of course Ipatiev could fail me quite easily.

Olga, however, wagged her finger in my direction, and continued. "Only as soon as he said it, Professor Parshin jumped up and said that yours was one of the best examinations he had ever had an honor of witnessing—I swear, he did say 'honor.' And then he took your examination booklet and wrote 'Excellent' in it, so Ipatiev and everyone else could see. I offered to take it to you." Olga extracted my booklet from her muff and handed it to me, smiling. "I didn't think Ipatiev could be taken aback, but there he was. Here, don't leave that behind again."

"Not unless they decide to drag me to jail or something," I muttered as I stared on the first page of the booklet, my first grade. Professor Parshin had beautiful penmanship.

Olga's voice intruded. "What was that about then?" she asked. "I don't even know what happened to you at the club . . . and afterwards. And who is that Englishman who follows you around."

I did not want to place blame, but saw no way around it. "I thought you did not want to know."

Olga's gaze met mine. "Surely you can understand my position.

My father is a nobody, our family cannot shrug off political scandals."

"Neither can mine," I said. After I gave it some thought, I touched Olga's hand. "But I see your point, and it would be more dangerous to you."

Olga beamed. "Now that they let you go, everything is well again, right? Well, come on! We have to be on campus in an hour or so, and you can tell me of your exploits on the way."

I let her drag me cheerfully along, but my thoughts remained troubled. For one, I did not share Olga's happy certainty that everything was well again, or even if such a possibility existed. My idea of things going well was not compatible with disappearances of my friends, or with being arrested and questioned for inquiring about their whereabouts.

It was unseasonably warm that day, and we still had time, so we decided to sit down on a park bench—not far from the Palace Bridge, with the view of the river, yellow and red with floating leaves, and Nevsky Prospect and the Palace Square on the other side. St. Isaac's dome blazed like fire, and Alexander's Column shone in the sun. It was easy to imagine it as molten gold touched by sunbeams reaching down from heaven. I looked toward Gorokhovaya, and even though I could not see it, I imagined the five-storied building with police and seemingly innocuous clerks and functionaries inside. Really, a city this beautiful had no right to have such a loathsome, shriveled heart. I tasted the bitterness in the air, the metallic under taste of the approaching rain, and felt pensive.

"Well?" Olga said. "Who is he?"

It made no sense to make as if I did not know of whom she spoke. I told her about Jack. I told her about the night at the Crane Club and the horrible Nikolashki, of Wong Jun's arrest. I downplayed the drama of Jack's appearance and mentioned only that he helped me escape, never explaining his propensity to fall out of the sky and commit violence against the secret police, who then for some reason treated him as if he were royalty. Really, even without the exams my mind was filled to bursting, and I thought it would be best to not further contemplate these things for a while, not if I hoped to avoid crying in a public place.

"He seems nice," Olga said. "He does follow you all the time—I think he fancies you. Dasha and Larisa, they both were saying there are a lot of Englishmen in St. Petersburg this year."

"Indeed," I whispered. My thoughts tumbled, directionless, unable to reconcile the contradictory elements. The British had just made truce with the Chinese, and the emperor thought the Chinese were spies. And His Imperial Highness was greatly infatuated with all things British, and Jack was greatly infatuated . . .

"Sasha!" Olga gave me a troubled look. "Are you all right, Sasha? You are . . . drifting. Are you all right?"

"No," I said. "I'm not exactly all right. I just feel there is something happening all around us, as if there are heavy stones waiting for us . . . imagine what a grain of wheat feels like—it sits there, listens to some distant rumbling, and before it knows it, it is ground into flour by some millstones it never knew existed."

Olga's eyes had grown as large as those on Byzantine icons. "Such strange things you say," she whispered, clearly concerned.

I managed a smile and got to my feet. "I'm not trying to frighten you, Olga. I'm warning you—to not be ground up."

The sky above us changed color—from cornflower blue, it silvered like the side of a fish, and slowly darkened into leaden. We hurried toward the university buildings, looking apprehensively at the sky swelling with imminent rain. "Nothing will be well again," I whispered to myself; I wasn't sure if Olga heard.

Chapter 5

THE REST OF THE EXAM WEEK WAS UNEVENTFUL. ALL THE GIRLS, undoubtedly spurred by the same sense of necessity as myself, passed. I did better than I expected but not as well as Eugenia would've liked—human biology was the only class in which I rated "excellent"; most of the rest were "good," with "satisfactory" in philosophy. Jack Bartram teased me about it, but gently.

I decided not to go home for the break. It was only a week long, and my fervor to see my aunt and mother had abated due to a part of me—a brand new part that had not existed until recently—that felt the time would be best spent getting to know Jack Bartram and figuring out exactly what his position was, as well as why the British crown was interested in Chinese students in St. Petersburg. Luckily, Jack, deprived of our daily walks from the university to the dormitory, showed keen interest in standing outside my domicile in plain view from my windows. On the first day of break, I slept late, greatly aided by an interminable drizzle. When I eventually looked out the window, I saw all of Vasilyevsky Island was weeping—the buildings and the trees dripped water the same ashen color as the sky. There was a man standing outside, and even though his collar was raised, I recognized Jack Bartram by his gaunt physique and soft-brimmed hat. He huddled under his black umbrella and smoked a long thin cigar, thick clouds of smoke drifting and twining with the fog.

"Your suitor's here, miss," Anastasia informed me helpfully as she peered over my shoulder.

"He's not my suitor," I said. "At least I don't think he is . . . "

"He sure ain't here to enjoy the weather," Anastasia pointed out. "Maybe you should invite him in then—he seems to get wetter and sadder by the minute."

Natalia Sergeevna was in a kind mood that morning, and allowed a visitor, so Anastasia ran outside to extend the invitation while I put the kettle on. When Anastasia returned, she was disappointingly alone.

"He's too shy," she explained. "He just asked me to give you this."

I unfolded the piece of paper Anastasia handed me. It was an invitation to a concert of chamber music to be held in a club called Northern Star. I could not help but think of the Crane Club, and miss Chiang Tse acutely. Chamber music seemed a pleasant enough way to spend the evening, but no one could argue that at the same time it was quite unadventurous and dull.

I sighed and rolled my eyes at Anastasia. "Prepare an evening dress," I said. "I'm going out tomorrow night."

The Northern Star Club was surreptitiously tucked away among the tenement buildings not too far from Moyka and the Yusupovs' palace—that reminded me painfully of my first season. It was hard to believe it had been less than a year since my debut. I certainly felt more adult and more sympathetic to my aunt after just a couple of months on my own. I could now understand the deep irritation those who ran this city caused her.

Jack had collected me by the dormitories—he still refused to come inside, and waited stubbornly by the main entrance as I made sure that my dress had not developed any rips or stains while I was not watching. Jack had the good sense to hire a coach, and as soon as my crinoline and I settled inside the carriage, I began asking him questions. And I had quite a few of them.

"Why did that gendarme listen to you?" I asked, not bothering to waste time on how-do-you-dos and other polite nonsense.

"He told you," Jack said. "I have diplomatic papers."

"Even though you claim to be a student."

"I claim to be both." He smiled. "Is that not allowed?"

"And since when do the English have jurisdiction over the police, which are, if I recall correctly, a part of Russian Internal Affairs?"

Jack swallowed and looked out of the carriage window, no doubt longing to be outside or at the very least away from me—even though just an hour before he wanted nothing better but my company. "Collaboration in the cases of Chinese espionage," he finally said. "You understand."

I shook my head vehemently enough to displace my bonnet. "I most certainly do not. If you indeed think they are spies, why did you let them go?"

"But you . . . "

"It was not about me," I interrupted, with Eugenia's stern tone cutting into my voice. "You did not know who I was . . . " A sudden thought struck me and I peered into his face, undeterred by darkness and flopping brim of his hat. "Or did you?"

"I did," he said. "But that is not why I was there."

"You were there to help with the arrests?"

He shook his head. "My . . . my own business, I swear to you. And I just happened by and could not bear to see your distress."

He seemed sincerely anguished, and I decided to scale back my interrogation. There's only so far you can push a horse before it collapses, Eugenia used to say. I suspected the maxim applied to bipeds as well as the equine species. We traveled the rest of the way in silence, me smiling as beatifically as I could manage, and Jack hiding under his hat, his nervous fingers worrying an unlit cigar.

The club could rival any of the imperial palaces in the number of chandeliers, candelabras, and score of other contrivances blazing light. It seemed that the Northern Star had one mission—to banish every scrap of darkness and shadow—and it succeeded admirably. Even Jack's long, narrow countenance, usually hidden by his hat, was cast in stark relief. I could admire the austere hollow of his cheek, like that of an ancient saint. I thought my mother would approve as we entered the club, arm in arm.

In the main hall, as large as any ballroom I had ever seen and probably quite capable of serving as one, the light was dazzling. Men and women spoke and mingled in the excessive illumination, some sitting at the small round tables, others in armchairs and on sofas positioned invitingly in the alcoves of the ornately decorated walls. Soft music was playing, and I had to squint to discern four musicians and their instruments on a small stage at the far end of the hall. Two violins, a cello, and a flute complained about something beautiful and sad, and the music served as a fine counterpoint to the low hum of human voices, tinkling of Champagne glasses, and occasional burst of soft laughter.

"How do you like it?" Jack whispered.

"It's very bright," I said.

He took my words as a cue, and led me toward one of the niches in the wall, to an unoccupied table framed by two chairs. I sat down and waited for my eyes to adjust to the somewhat lessened light. A waiter stopped by our table to deposit a bottle of Champagne in a silver ice bucket, a pair of flutes, and a plate of hors d'œuvre, which I found quite welcome. I had forgotten to eat dinner.

Jack leaned back in his chair and drank. His gray eyes searched the crowd and seemed troubled, and I hoped my questioning had not upset him. It is with a small amount of shame that I confess my concern was not indicative of the goodness of my heart but rather worry that if I upset him, he would be less forthcoming with answers.

He nodded at a few men who walked past our table and they nodded back, but showed no inclination to stop and chat. I thought it rather strange that people did not seem to speak to anyone but their immediate companions, and precious little mingling was occurring.

"How peculiar," I said. "I don't think I've yet seen people change tables or move to talk to someone else."

"It is by design," Jack said. "People come here to enjoy a social setting where one is not compelled to interact with one's fellow men. I find it refreshing."

I shook my head and laughed. "If one wants to be quiet, then why leave one's house?"

"As you can see, most come here with their friends. It's a good way to be alone in a crowd."

I wanted to say that being alone in a crowd seemed to miss the point of both crowds and solitude, but bit my words back. After all, how would I make Jack like me enough to tell me his secrets if I argued with his every word? I was certain my mother would be proud of my feminine deductive abilities if she only knew.

My self-congratulations were cut short due to the sudden cessation of music which distracted me. I watched as several men wheeled around a piano, and moved it to occupy the stage the four musicians had just left. The mahogany piano gleamed, and its white keys were so bright in the blinding light they seemed to fuse together into a single strip of pearly radiance. They seemed pure light, with an occasional dark gap of the black keys. The smell of burning wax added an almost religious atmosphere to the proceedings.

The men also brought around a chair in which the pianist was already sitting—I thought that it was someone crushed with age or disease, and assumed the upcoming performance would likely be more about honoring the unfortunate than actual entertainment.

Imagine my surprise when the figure in the chair raised its stick arms and rained its fingers onto the keyboard in an avalanche of sound, cascades of loud clear notes filled with both passion and precision.

"Bravura" was the only way to describe the performance. All conversation and laughter ceased, and even the waiters dawdled with their trays, reluctant to move for anything as mundane as delivery of drink and food. Even I was enraptured.

My own relationship with music had always been uneven and fraught with doomed romance, much like any good novel. Despite a string of teachers and a variety of instruments from clavichords to flutes, I showed no proclivity toward musical performance whatsoever. My fingers got entangled in themselves and my breath came out ragged and wrong. I could not hit a proper note if my life depended on it. All this was, of course, a cause of bitter disappointment to my mother, who herself was quite an accomplished, albeit infrequent, piano player, and who remembered too acutely it was her skill at the piano that had initially enchanted my father. It took both Eugenia and Miss Chartwell reminding her rather cynically that what I lacked in musical education I more than made up in titles and impending wealth to console my dear mother.

Despite all that, I quite enjoyed music as a listener, and I could not have been happier sipping my Champagne and discreetly tapping my foot under the cover of my bell skirt in tempo with the music.

Jack smiled at me. "You seem to enjoy the music."

I nodded. "I do."

He looked sly, almost impish. "Notice anything unusual about the player?"

"Not as such," I replied. "Unless you consider being carried around in a chair unusual."

"That's because he does not have legs." Jack seemed to enjoy his grisly words.

"I'm sorry to hear that."

"And no head," he added, laughing openly. "Look."

The music stopped and while the applause still hung in the air, the stagehands approached the pianist's chair and swung it around. There was laughter from those in the know and a drawn-out "ooooh" from the rest of the audience. The pianist was nothing but a stout metal can, the size and shape of a small water barrel, with two long jointed metal arms attached to it. Each arm ended with a set of ten unnaturally long and flexible fingers.

"That's cheating," I said.

Jack laughed. "Still quite a marvel of ingenuity, isn't it?" he said. "It is quite impressive how much mechanical and engineering talent is gathered in this city and what things they can achieve."

I inclined my head, agreeing. He was right. There was a sense of vibrancy and invention, of novelty: the submarines that popped up in the middle of Neva had been growing larger and sleeker lately; newspapers reported on new railways and the creeping expansion of St. Petersburg's many newly constructed factories. There were rumors of increasingly successful airship flights. Maybe it was enough, I thought, enough to make up for the plain-clothed policemen and silent disappearances.

Jack looked at the crowd, as if searching for someone. I drank my Champagne and waited politely, half listening to the human musicians who resumed playing on the stage. A tall, regal woman caught my eye as she walked past our alcove, her hand resting in that of a slender man who seemed to be her senior by a few years.

The woman turned to regard Jack with a long and apparently disapproving look. "Mr. Bartram," she said. "What are you doing here?"

Jack stood and introduced me to the woman, a Dame Florence Nightingale. Her taciturn companion was Mr. Sidney Herbert—an

Englishman, but he quickly informed me his mother was Russian, from the Vorontsov family. He even greeted me in Russian, and I responded in kind, noticing he was only slightly rustier with the language than I was after months spent in St. Petersburg.

While Mr. Herbert and I exchanged pleasantries, Jack and Dame Nightingale entered a fierce whispered argument. She leaned over the table, hovering above his chair like some sort of vengeful angel dressed in a gray two-piece silk dress.

I would've eavesdropped, but Mr. Herbert distracted me quite effectively, occupying my attention by asking me about the subtler points of declension of female nouns ending in "ch" and "sh," and I got so flustered as to completely forget I was supposed to be listening for Jack's secrets.

My linguistic embarrassment was thankfully cut short when Dame Nightingale pointed her very straight nose at me and smiled, her dark eyes boring into me as if I were some curious thing she happened to come across during a nature excursion—she looked like one of those overly healthy individuals who called their walks "constitutionals" and had an extreme interest in the out-of-doors, vegetarianism, and other ways of artificially extending one's life, not really caring whether it was God's intent or not.

"Hello," I said, trying to keep the hostility I felt out of my voice. "Are you in St. Petersburg for the upcoming season?"

She laughed and shook her head slightly, offering no further response. Instead, she launched an offensive of her own. "Mr. Bartram tells me you are one of those curiosities, a woman they are attempting to educate."

"Quite successfully," I said.

She waved her hand, dismissing my words as if they were mere child's babblings. "Of course. I myself once had interest an in medicine—nursing, to be honest. Thankfully, I had parents who cared about my wellbeing and friends who dissuaded me from such foolishness. It is not a woman's place."

"Your queen would beg to differ, I am sure," I said.

Dame Nightingale snorted rather loudly. "What nonsense. Her Majesty is most concerned with the recent trend of women abandoning home and hearth, as well as their duty to their fathers and husbands. I'm sure she would not at all approve of your little . . . excursion into the male realm."

I glared. "Surely a woman who is capably ruling two countries . . ."

" . . . is especially sensitive to the demands a male sphere of activity puts on the female constitution." Dame Nightingale smiled unpleasantly. "Besides, Her Majesty has a husband. And you . . . ?"

"I do not," I said, feeling as if it was Aunt Genia's will that animated my lips. "And I would prefer to not have one. If I were audacious enough to dare compared myself to an English monarch, Queen Elizabeth would be my example."

"A spinster."

"No man's chattel."

Dame Nightingale grew bored with me, and turned to eye Jack. "Is that what you like then?" she inquired. "A complete lack of femininity?"

"I've never felt particularly attached to abstract attributes," Jack said earnestly, and I managed not to laugh. Suddenly, I couldn't wait for the season to start so Eugenia would be here and could meet Jack. I thought the two of them would enjoy one another's company.

"I see," Dame Nightingale said icily, and again leaned over the table, planting both hands firmly next to our nearly empty hors d'œuvre plate, in a pose that struck me as almost comically at odds with her expressed views about propriety and femininity. I had to stifle another giggle as Mr. Herbert kissed my hand and murmured he was charmed, truly, and was looking forward to meeting my aunt in December, for he had heard so much of her keen political mind. I responded in kind, assuring him she would most certainly be delighted to speak to one who served another great empire, all the while straining to hear Dame Nightingale's whisper. I was especially curious because, out of the corner of my eye, I saw Jack draw away from her, his back against the wall. I only caught the end of her words, but that was enough to seal my dislike of her forever.

"Just remember, Mr. Bartram," she hissed, "who your true friends are and where your loyalties lie, and any trouble could be avoided."

I felt sick to my stomach when Jack whispered back, "Yes, madam. I always remember."

THE NEXT DAY, THE SKY DRIZZLED AND GRAYED. THE RIVER, VISIBLE now through the bare branches, black—as if drawn by the same hand that had executed the Crane Club's ink paintings—against the pale enamel of the weeping sky. I idled in bed until Anastasia exiled me from my bedroom because she needed to sweep, and cleaning waited for no one.

As much as I enjoyed the music the night before, the events had left an unpleasant deposit deep in my soul, like the dregs that settle in a glass of seemingly acceptable wine, spoiling forever one's appetite for it. Dame Nightingale was surely the cause of the dirty murkiness that clouded my spirit that morning.

I peered out the window, and was somewhat consoled to see the rising cigar smoke and the wide-brimmed hat, the black umbrella and a black glove holding it aloft, a wide cloak flapping in the wind like wings. At least, Jack did not hate me; I found the thought comforting.

He looked up just then, and, well aware it was too late to conceal

I wasn't looking, I smiled and waved. He waved back, turned, and walked away abruptly. I wasn't sure then whether to feel pleased or insulted. I settled on calling Anastasia and asking for tea and breakfast—thick slices of bread, loaves so rich and golden, their crust as fragile as March ice on the river, butter, slabs of cheese.

I drank my tea, sweet and strong and hot, and read the newspaper as a diversion—it had been weeks since I read anything other than a textbook, and soon enough the next quarter would start, plunging me into more human anatomy and Newtonian fancies. But by God, I was going to read the newspaper that Sunday.

I skipped over the news from abroad, unwilling to relive yesterday's irritation with the English, and let my eyes travel over the black newsprint describing the construction of Trans-Siberian railroad. The article was accompanied by several daguerreotypes of smiling freedmen standing next to gigantic piles of dirt, with horses and mules dragging rails in the background.

It was only when I got to the last page that my tranquility was subsumed by indignation and anger: in a single paragraph, the newspaper reported a break-in and subsequent fire at the Crane Club. No one was hurt, however the cases containing all the engineering marvels of which Chiang Tse was so touchingly proud had disappeared. It was especially puzzling since the cases were heavy and made of glass and metal. Additionally, they had been bolted to the floor and the article mentioned that when the police examined the burned out ruins, they came to the conclusion the bolts had been ripped out, damaging the floor previous to the fire. There were no suspects, and no one—neither the newspaper nor the police—seemed especially concerned with this convergence of vandalism, arson, and theft.

My first thought was to blame the Nikolashki—only they could've seized whatever property they desired without attracting attention, without the newspapers even knowing what was taken, and without having to engineer a fire. Since there were no suspects mentioned, they were not trying to frame anyone either. I decided the crime was genuine—that is, no official governmental bodies were involved.

Of course, my mind could not help but worry at Jack's sudden appearance on the night that I first met him—he was there, by the club, soon after sunset. That was nothing, I told myself—plenty of people happened to visit the club, and plenty of others had made appearances in places that later became scenes of crimes—why, it was practically impossible to avoid.

I folded the newspaper, finished my bread and butter with grim determination, and decided to go for a walk along the embankment, to clear my head.

Thankfully, the rain had lifted, and the pale sun lit the sky, coloring it pearl gray at first and then pale blue. The tree branches, still studded with water droplets, shone in the sunlight, and as I left the dormitories, I thought of the winter, of how soon enough it would change everything—it would enclose the tree branches with a carapace of ice, as glorious as it was alien and terrifying; I imagined snow crunching underfoot, its virgin expanse quickly tracked and split with many footpaths, like veins on pale skin. I thought of all the birds—yellow, red-breasted—flocking from woods to the cities, to be cooed at and to feed shyly on breadcrumbs and grains of rye thrown to them. I walked alone, tracing the outline of Vasilyevsky Island with my slow footsteps, and thinking about school and Jack.

I tried not to think of my friends, especially of Chiang Tse—I tried not to guess if he had ever encountered snow, or if he would delight in learning to skate on the frozen surface of ponds and lakes. It felt so terribly unfair, that he, perhaps one of the gentlest people I knew, was chased away and denied the opportunity to enjoy the winter in St. Petersburg—not its shallow season and vapid self-aggrandizement, but its true and natural beauty offset by a frame of snow and ice into which it would be placed like a gray precious stone.

I realized then how much I missed Chiang Tse and his friends, how this final violation of their beloved club was a blow struck to a heart already wounded. How I missed them then, and how guilty I felt about the Manchu Wong Jun, locked up in a jail somewhere, not knowing that there were people who still cared about him. I couldn't imagine whether it would be a comfort if he knew or not.

On Monday, my tormented unease was assuaged by Olga's return—she did not say it outright, but I suspected her family preferred her here, safely away, where she was fed and looked after and taken care of. I greeted her with open arms, and felt only a small pang of guilt at the selfishness of my joy.

As soon as she had settled—which did not take at all long, seeing how she was gone only a couple of days—I told her about the Northern Star and Crane Club. She seemed, however, less interested in mechanical piano players and robberies than she was in Jack. She made me repeat everything Jack had said to me, and what I said back, and describe the way he was looking at me.

"Clear enough," she said after our third cup of tea, and sat back in her chair. Anastasia took the gesture as a permission to retire, and was gone in the direction of Natalia Sergeevna's apartment before I had a chance to dissuade her.

"What's clear?" I asked, looking after Anastasia longingly. I was hoping for more bread and butter, since worry usually had an effect on my appetite—somehow, the state of the world seemed more tolerable to me when there was fresh and crusty bread and the sensation of butter melting on my tongue.

"He loves you," Olga explained, exasperated with my stupidity. "How can you not see it?"

I shrugged. "It's not that I don't—he clearly wants to spend time with me. It's just that I am not sure why."

"It is obvious," Olga said and poured herself another cup of tea. There was so much steam in my little living room that the windows had completely fogged over. "Men want to spend time with the girls they like. And he is clearly an important man—I hear that Mr. Herbert is a brilliant politician, and knowing him is quite an honor for anyone. So that Mr. Bartram of yours is obviously a great catch—and he is certainly interested in you. The only question is, are you interested? Do you think you love him?"

"I cannot say that the question had occurred to me," I mumbled, and bit into a lump of sugar like a peasant, chasing it with a sip of very strong tea. "How do you know if you love someone? How do you even know what love is—I mean, if you never felt it, how do you know what it's supposed to feel like, and if you're feeling it right, and if what you're feeling even has a name?"

Olga stared at me in dismay. "You speak such nonsense, Sasha. What is it with you?"

I only shrugged. I never knew what it was with me, how things that apparently looked like simple questions and basic emotions to others grew enormously complicated for me—I felt as if I was tripping over my own feet, trying to disentangle meanings of words such as "love" and "interest" and "like" and "friendship." They seemed simple on the surface, but the moment I attempted to use these words as measuring sticks against which to hold my emotions, they wriggled and slipped away, leaving only confusion and frustration behind.

Olga attempted to help—at least I think that is what she meant when she said, "All right then. Think about how you feel when you see him. If he were standing outside of this window right now—what would you feel?"

I smudged the condensation on the windowpane, clearing a sickle-shaped sliver of clear glass. There was fog outside, its tendrils rising from the ground and curling into the mist that already concealed everything from view, except the gas streetlamps and their reflections in the Neva. There were lights on the opposite bank but only vague and blurred, distorted by the fog like ghost lanterns. Jack was not there but I could picture him clearly as I said, "I would be glad, I suppose. A little embarrassed that he's out there for all to see, so obvious. Maybe a bit angry because he is so conspicuous, as if trying to make me feel guilty for not returning his affection quickly enough. I would be curious too, and impatient to ask him about his friends, his work, what they want with the Chinese—or with the Russians, for that matter."

Olga heaved a sigh and shook her head. "You are making it so very complicated, Sasha, and it doesn't need to be. Life is really very simple."

I nodded as if I agreed to avoid further argument, but my mind raced. It was nowhere as simple as Olga claimed. To her, life was people falling in love and marrying. But I did not understand love, as I did not understand its connection to marriage. Eugenia's words from my childhood, forgotten until now—until I actually needed them—floated to the surface. "Marrying is not difficult," she said. "Who isn't smart enough to make babies? Only this is the thing, Sasha—love is nothing, it is empty. If you must marry, don't marry someone you love—you're too much of a fool for that; we all are. Instead marry a man who is kind to you and who would be your friend ten, twenty years later. Love passes by all too quickly, and if you must be stuck with someone, at least make sure you can stand him."

"I don't love anyone," I told Olga. "I am much too preoccupied with other things. If I drop out of the university to get married, my aunt would never forgive me." Olga moved to say something, but I held up my hand. "I mean it. I'll be dead before I let anything interfere with my schooling—even if that something is the most wonderful man in the world."

Olga took a long sip of her piping hot tea. "You'll change your mind," she said. "You just wait."

I did not argue, but thought bitterly to myself that everyone seemed to think they knew more about me than I did, from Dame Nightingale to my best friend. Oh, how I hoped they were wrong.

Chapter 6

I SPENT MORE TIME WITH JACK, SINCE EVERY CONVERSATION I attempted to have with Olga ended up with her asking about him anyway. Jack was a pleasant companion in his own right, even if one were to ignore the fact I attempted to use our new closeness to find answers to the questions that plagued me. He, however, was very good at avoiding sly hints and the subtle verbal traps I set for him. When the break came to an end, I knew no more about his purpose, Dame Nightingale, or the burglary at the Crane Club than I did when it started.

The last Sunday before the classes were set to resume, Jack and I went for a walk along the Nevsky Prospect. It was late October, and the snowfall and the cutting winter winds were not far away. I was eager to enjoy the last of the tolerable weather, even if it meant contending with light rain and occasional wind gusts forceful enough to almost rip the hat off my head despite many pins specifically embedded to keep it in place.

Jack too had to keep vigilant hold of his hat. He did not look particularly pleased about the walk, but I described the horses at the Anichkov Bridge and the impression they made on me last year, and he agreed to pay them a visit. As we both stood transfixed—I was caught up anew in the violent yet still life of the sculpture—my thoughts churned. It was as if the horses gave me the presence of mind and courage to enunciate the question to which I so desired—and perhaps dreaded—an answer.

"Mr. Bartram," I said then, "Do you know what happened with the Crane Club? Did you have anything to do with it?"

He kept looking at the horses, his head tilted back, one gloved hand holding the brim of his hat. His eyes, squinting against the wind, did not change their expression and the Adam's apple on his long pale throat did not bob. Yet, like the sculpture he was studying, his still frame filled with silent tension, and just like that, without him uttering a word or making a gesture, I knew.

"No," he said after a very long pause. "Why would you think that?"

"That night, you were at the club."

"I was just passing by."

"And at the Northern Star . . . that awful lady told you to remember your loyalties. The Crane Club was vandalized, soon after."

He finally looked away from the bridge, his eyes meeting mine. His coat flapped, and something twinged in the depths of my memory. "And why would one thing have anything to do with another?"

"Your country was at war with China."

He smiled, as if I were a child he had decided to indulge a bit longer. "We have signed a peace treaty. But even if we had not . . . do you think ransacking a Chinese club is the same as declaring military hostilities? It was more likely some drunks or thieves who were hoping to find alcohol in that place—it was all but abandoned recently. So they took some trinkets to sell. Really, Sasha, you're too smart for your own good—you're making things so complicated."

I did feel very young and very foolish then. "We can go," I whispered.

He offered me his elbow and I hooked my hand over the crook of his arm. "Don't feel bad," he said. "I know you are upset about your friends. Only I wish you wouldn't cast me as an enemy."

Those words made me blush. "I remember that you saved us," I said. "You saved me twice, and I told you I was grateful. But there are things happening now that I do not understand, all I know is that I do not trust Prince Nicholas and his secret police, and I do not trust your Dame Nightingale."

He seemed amused by my words, as we turned toward the Palace Square. "She may be a bit brash," he said.

"And a bit rude," I added. "I really don't appreciate being insulted, but this is not why I do not trust her. I think she may be a spy."

His face retained the same smiling expression but mirth left it momentarily, only to return with an exaggerated chuckle. "Nonsense," he said.

I thought he was an awful liar but did not challenge him, content to see my guess hit near its target. "And you are here to help Nicholas," I said. "The gendarmes listened to you. What do you want with the Chinese? Is this why Nightingale and Herbert are here?"

He shrugged, uncomfortable. "I cannot tell you much, but be assured that it has little to do with your friends. However, I can say Prince Nicholas once sought an alliance with Britain to help protect Russia from the Chinese threat."

I snorted. "This is nonsense. There is no threat."

Jack only shrugged. "If you say so. If there's no threat then the Chinese have nothing to fear."

"This is not true and you know it," I said. "There has been enough damage done already, and I still don't know what happened to Wong Jun."

"I cannot help you."

"I do not need you to." I freed my arm from his. "I wrote to my aunt about this injustice, although in vague terms and naming no names." I had learned from my encounter with the police. "I expect she will set things straight when she arrives in December."

A gust of wind grabbed my shawl and flapped it in my face while simultaneously tearing off Jack's hat—he had foolishly forgotten to maintain a grip. He lunged after it, just as the wind picked up force and hurled the hat down the street with the speed of a locomotive.

"You can always get another," I said, but discovered Jack was no longer in my immediate proximity—somehow, he was a few hundred feet ahead, picking up his hat from the pavement and shaking it free of puddle water. I was still rubbing my eyes when he returned to my side. "How—" I started to ask.

"I was a sprint runner when I was younger," he said with an apologetic smile.

But that was no sprint. That night at the Crane Club I had been willing to let myself believe panic and darkness had deceived my eyes, but now, in somewhat weak but sufficient light of the afternoon, I had no excuse. He had not run, he had hurled himself . . . flew . . . jumped . . . he moved faster than was possible, faster than my eyes could follow him. I realized he had, indeed, fallen out of the sky that night.

I looked around. Nevsky was not crowded, thanks to rain and chill in the air, but there were a few passersby and couples walking arm in arm, some clerks hurrying along on business, their long gray overcoats heavy with rain. No one seemed to have noticed Jack's unusual behavior. There was no one I could appeal to for confirmation.

"I see," I said slowly. "Do you expect me to believe that?"

He smiled wider, but humor was gone from his eyes. "You should," he said, "if you know what is good for you."

I glared. "Are you threatening me now, Mr. Bartram?"

He shook his head, rueful now. "Not at all. A warning, perhaps. A worry." His gloved hand took mine and squeezed it, almost desperately. "Please believe me, Sasha. I would never do anything to let any misfortune befall you, but sometimes you really must look away."

He walked me to my dormitory in silence, and I spent a sleepless night, angry and elated and generally uncertain how to feel.

CONSIDERING MY RESTLESS NIGHT, IT CAME AS NO SURPRISE TO find myself dozing through most of my classes the next morning, revived only by Dasha's sharp jab to my side at the end of each lesson. I was ready to take my confidences to Dasha instead of Olga, in hopes she was slightly less obsessed with matrimony, but the fates interfered: when I came back to the dormitory that night, I found Anastasia in a nearly hysterical state, precipitated, as I discovered, by my aunt who was currently sitting in the living room, drinking tea, and scolding Anastasia for dust under the lampshade.

"Aunt Genia!" I exclaimed and ran across the room to embrace her. "What a pleasant surprise!"

She let me kiss her dry, papery cheek. "Good to see you too, Sasha. What is it you're telling me—Nikolashka went and lost what little mind God blessed him with?"

It was shocking to hear my aunt to refer to the prince by his nickname, like a gossiping peasant. Refreshing, too. Before I even took my hat and gloves off, I told her about Wong Jun, my own almost-arrest, and Jack's interference. Oh, it was such a relief to pour my heart out to a sympathetic soul. She listened, not moving, until her tea went cold and Anastasia recovered enough of her wits to bring in supper and to inquire whether Eugenia was planning to stay with us or to go back to her St. Petersburg apartment.

"I'll stay there," Eugenia said. "No need for me to crowd you here."

"It's no trouble," I said quickly. "There is a spare bedroom, it is not much, but it is tidy and I'm sure it will suffice until your apartment is ready."

"Thank you, niece," Eugenia said. "I won't be in the city for long—just a few days, to have some business taken care of. I'll make sure to look into your friend's whereabouts." She wrote down Wong Jun's name in her notepad with her small, exacting letters.

Over supper, we talked about things at home. Eugenia complained the horses were getting expensive to feed since oats had grown poorly this year and prices were now sky-high. She spoke about buying some mechanical plows, since coal and peat seemed in less demand than oats. "And the machines are certainly better tempered. The horses are such fiends—give them one finger, they'll take your whole arm. I kept them for your riding, but now that you're gone . . . "

"I'll be back," I said quickly.

"You don't say." Eugenia waited for Anastasia to clean the table and then excuse herself and go gossip with Natalia Sergeevna before asking more. "You think you'll come back to Trubetskoye, with your Englishman and all?"

"It's not like that." And before I had a chance to worry that Eugenia would think me insane and talk myself out of telling her, I told her how Jack dropped out of the sky and then chased his hat by leaping a hundred yards in one step. "There's something about him, only I don't know what and how it is even possible."

"Stranger things have been known to happen," Eugenia said. "We better turn in—you have classes tomorrow, and I will be going to the ministry offices first thing. They always make you wait forever, so I need my rest."

When I was in my bed, drifting to sleep, there was a creak of the floorboards and weight on the edge of my bed. My aunt's hand rested on my brow, just as when I was small and ill. A sense of deep calm and belief that everything would turn all right filled me. "You came because of my letter, didn't you?" I murmured, comforted like a child.

"Of course," she answered. "Not that I don't have business of my own, but know one thing, Sasha: all you have to do is ask, and I will be there."

I sighed, happy, and fell asleep before her dry cool hand left my forehead. I had not slept that well since arriving in St. Petersburg.

I WOKE UP MORE HOPEFUL THAN I HAD FELT IN WEEKS. EUGENIA'S mere presence seemed enough to instill a sense of rightness in the world, as if nothing bad was possible when she was nearby. She ate breakfast with me and then departed toward the Palace Bridge the same time as Olga and I left for our classes. I almost skipped on my way; I had not realized how heavily the latest events weighed on my mind until the burden had lifted. Even Professor Ipatiev could not affect me with his explanation of the female reproductive system and rather excessive insistence that ovaries were nothing more than defective and listless testes. I caught Dasha's attention, and we rolled our eyes at each other as our only recourse. I did hope, however, I would not have to draw the reproductive system at the next exam.

In philosophy, I took my usual seat. To my surprise, Jack came in earlier than was his habit, and took a seat next to me, the one usually occupied by Dasha. When Dasha came in, she smiled and moved down the aisle, leaving me in unasked-for tête-à-tête with Jack Bartram.

"Listen," he said. "I've been thinking."

"So have I," I whispered back. "Shh, class is starting."

"Promise you'll stay after class and talk to me."

"Very well."

He didn't move away when the lecture started, and I found I had trouble concentrating on chained men in the cave and the shadows that they somehow mistook for real people when Jack was sitting next to me.

The lecture was finally over, and I could've cursed my friends—Dasha and Olga, and Elena and Larisa all ran ahead, leaving me facing Jack with no excuse to escape the situation. Even our classmates who could be counted on to follow us around and make rude jokes when they were least welcome left the auditorium. I sighed and faced Jack, even though it was the last thing I was interested in doing at the time. He smiled and motioned that we should step outside.

"I know I was harsh the last time we spoke," he said, and matched his long stride to mine. "I just . . . I wish I knew the right thing to do."

"Sometimes it is hard to decide," I said. "But you can start by not lying to me."

"I'm fond of you," he said. "Really, quite so." His voice was steady, and his hat concealed his expression as well as ever. "I don't want to lie to you, but I see no choice sometimes."

"I appreciate the sentiment," I said, blushing rather hopelessly. "But if you want me to return your interest, your sincerity would be most effective."

As much as I resented such manipulation, I had to sternly remind myself that it seemed to be the only way to find out what was going on. I had tried straightforward sincerity before, so I felt I was morally in the clear.

Jack nodded a few times, thoughtful. "You were right about me," he said. "I am here on orders of my government, and I am gathering information of . . . sensitive nature."

I held my breath not quite believing he was finally supplying some answers. "And the Crane Club?"

He hung his head. "I cannot talk about that. Please believe me, if it were not for necessity . . . I had no choice."

"There's always a choice," I responded. "You could've refused."

"I face severe punishment should I disobey my orders," he said. "More severe than most others."

"What have you got against the Chinese?"

"Nothing," he said. "There was some interest in the models they were building, but it is secondary, and served mostly as a diversion. That is why I, a criminal, was trusted with it—it is not important in itself, but only as a symbolic gesture."

Although I did not wish to, I had to lean on his hand. My head spun. I had assumed Chiang Tse and the rest were victims of continuing British hostility. The emperor's preference for all things and causes English coupled with his brother's fear of foreigners had made matters worse. I assumed they were arrested and pursued to please the British, and that Jack and his compatriots were here to direct and to supervise. It had not occurred to me that all this was a deliberate setup, a distraction engineered by the English. The unavoidable conclusion stared me in the face, and it had the mean pinprick gaze of Dame Nightingale.

"You're telling me," I whispered with numb lips, "that you are not here to spy on the Chinese."

He shook his head. "No. But please, please, be careful. Don't tell anyone. I can protect you if need arises, but no more than that."

I was overcome with the onslaught of information and Jack solicitously led me to a bench by the path. It was still a bit wet from the recent rain, and he laid down his cloak so I could sit comfortably. I stared for a while at the yellow leaves covering the paths and the lawns, at the students walking and laughing, their voices carrying far in the still air. I realized there was knowledge in the universe that had the ability to decisively separate one from the rest of the world—some things you could not know and continue to live like everyone else. Blood roared in my ears, and I helplessly shook my head at Jack and his moving lips—I could not hear a word he was saying. I could only acutely experience the bitter smell of fallen leaves and distant peat smoke.

"If you're a spy," I finally managed, my tongue slow and woolen, "and if you're found out, you'll be in more trouble than you can imagine."

He smiled then. "If I ever do anything to jeopardize my task or to expose those who give me my orders, I'll be in more trouble than you can imagine."

"Can't you quit? Promise to keep what you know a secret and just stop?"

He laughed, a slow mirthless sound. "As I said, it is not my choice."

"Because you're a criminal." The last word was difficult for me to get out—it was something I did not want to believe.

There was one more thing I needed to know, but I could barely bring myself to ask. It seemed too much for one day, too much disappointment and heartbreak. Still, I thought it would be better to confront it all at once. "What are your crimes?"

He stood facing me, took his hat off and tapped it against his knee, absent-minded, and yet aware enough to answer my question with his face unobscured, his eyes on mine. "Armed robbery," he said. "Theft. I never killed anyone though, if it makes it any better."

Strangely enough, it did allow me to feel a measure of relief. I feared that the man I had spent so much time with, a man I had started to trust and liked enough to consider a friend was a murderer. I didn't know what I would've done if that had been the case; as it was, I managed a smile. "This is not so bad."

His face flushed pale pink. "I'm glad you think so," he said. "However, you now see my predicament. My attempt to shake off the thrall I find myself under will surely lead to me being taken back and imprisoned."

I nodded and stood. "I understand why you would want to avoid that. Still, I would imagine there are other possibilities. Hiding, for example."

He smiled and shook his head. "It is not so easy, Sasha. Dame Nightingale . . . they say, you couldn't hide from her on the bottom of the sea if she wants you, and she certainly wants me."

"Why?" I asked, even though I already knew the answer. If he was a thief, he was good at spying—he could take things without others noticing, and moreover do so without the moral reservations most people would have in his place. But even a thief might have a sense of duty and patriotism—or at least, so I imagined.

"Because of the things I can do," he said.

Falling out of the sky, leaping a hundred feet in a single bound. I felt slightly dizzy again, my step faltered, but his arm remained a steady support and I quickly recovered. It seemed that once he had found the strength to talk to me, confession became easier.

"The display cases—they were too heavy for a single man, and how would you drag them out of a building? Surely several men carrying glass cases would be noticed."

He laughed. "It took only me . . . and my gifts. We carried those cases to the roof, and leapt."

He spoke without hesitation now, his voice full of passion, as if he had to empty his overburdened heart, before it burst or gave out.

The visions of his superhuman and terrifying abilities were almost too much for me. I imagined him as a wild, possessed thing, leaping like a demon from roof to roof, glass and metal cases rattling on his shoulders—like a *vurdalak*, a terrifying grave-robber from the old peasant tales, with two coffins on his shoulders.

"Why the Chinese?" I finally mustered. "If you said they were not important, then why wreck their club?"

"Opium," he said simply. "The East India Trading Company will not stop selling it, and the Chinese government won't cease trying to stop its importation. There was one war, there will be others. And they know that as well. Chinese airships are second to none, and those display cases contained some of the best examples of their ingenuity: traditional Oriental engineering combined with the modern discoveries of the West. Such equipment and devices would be invaluable in any war. Even if they are just models, our engineers may gain ideas." He gave me a meaningful look, just as we stopped in front of my dormitory. "Remember that, Sasha. China is subdued for now, but there are other wars the empire could be fighting."

I wanted to ask him more questions, even though my knees wobbled and threatened to yield at any moment. But he swung around and walked away, never looking back, leaning into the wind with the desperate determination of a man with no secrets left, his chest flayed open and heart torn out for all to see. For a moment, I feared I would never see him again, but a new thought made me rush through the door, in wild hope that Eugenia would be there. A sudden realization descended like a piercing and merciless beam of light which cast the unpleasant reality in stark relief: the English played Prince Nicholas' hatred not just to gather his help against the Chinese, but also to distract him—everyone—from the fact that English spies were looking for weaknesses in Russia. They watched the submarines, they had access to the engineering students at the university and to the offices of the Ministries.

I rushed into my apartment, to see Anastasia setting the table for supper and Aunt Eugenia reading the newspaper by the table.

"Aunt Genia," I exhaled. "Aunt Genia! There's going to be a war soon."

I AM FIRMLY CONVINCED THAT IF MY AUNT COULD BE PERSUADED to take on the problems of the world, we would be living in utopia. However, she preferred to concentrate on the domestic, and instead busied herself with making me raspberry tea and a slew of other old-fashioned remedies meant to lift my spirits and strengthen my obviously shaken constitution. Anastasia was sent out for valerian tincture and chamomile, and Eugenia made sure to loosen the laces of my corset to let me breathe better.

"I am all right," I assured her. "I swear."

"Just drink your tea," she said. Her presence made my small living room more inviting somehow, more like home—she had adjusted the wick of the lamp so light fell only on the table and chairs around it; the rest of the room remained swathed in pleasant velvety shadows. She wrapped a plaid throw around me and made me comfortable in the best chair, situated on the border of light and dark. She brought my tea and pulled up a straight-backed chair to sit next to me. "Oh, Sasha. I forget how strenuous it is for you—you've never even been away from home before, and now you're on your own, and your studies are difficult."

"It's not that," I protested weakly, even though I did enjoy her attention. "The British are worried, their spies are everywhere. They are using the Chinese as a diversion."

Eugenia stopped mopping at my brow with a cold towel and gave me a long, critical look. "I would think that you speak nonsense, Sasha," she answered after a while, "but today I'm not willing to dismiss anything as nonsense. Something very strange is afoot, and I am a bit dismayed the emperor has decided to abandon those who have been loyal to him."

I sat up straighter. "I told you they dragged me to Gorokhovaya as if I were a common criminal. I needed an Englishman to intervene."

Eugenia nodded. "I spent all day sitting in waiting rooms, and no one would receive me. The entire government is either away or in meetings, the emperor has stopped giving audiences, and all the clerks are snooty upstarts who act as if they have never heard of our family."

"That might be my fault," I said, timidly. "I'm sorry."

"You've done nothing wrong. If you didn't stand up for your friends, I would have been disappointed. And if Constantine wishes to forget who *his* friends are . . . well then!" She huffed and rose to pace across the living room in her habitually large, unfeminine steps—two steps forward, two back. "I'm afraid you are right though—things are about to get much worse."

"What can we do to make them better?" I asked.

Eugenia shrugged. "What can anyone do? I would tell the emperor he is not looking at the real danger, but will he listen?"

"To you, maybe," I said. "I also think China would be a good ally against the British."

Eugenia paused. "Perhaps. Only how would that be achieved?"

"Perhaps I can help," I said. "The man who is, I think, in prison—Wong Jun—is of the ruling dynasty. And the others . . . they are from families of wealth and influence or they would not have been studying here."

"You'll have to speak to your imprisoned friend," Eugenia said. "And as God is my witness, I won't leave this city until I help you with that. Then we will see what we can do to convince the emperor that China is his friend, not the British Empire."

It would be a lie to say I didn't feel intimidated by the enormousness of these events. Two women, sitting in a tiny apartment disentangling a complicated standoff between three empires—four, if you counted the Ottomans, and Eugenia assured me that if Russia were to show any weakness, the Turks would surely make a grab for Crimea and the Russian shores of the Black Sea. They may already have made an alliance with the British, making it even more urgent that Russia and China stand shoulder to shoulder—no one would dare to defy such a show of power.

I tried to force my mind to think on such a scale and it recoiled. My thoughts were like lumbering boulders, impossible to shift by mere human will, and I felt defeated by the very act of contemplation.

I would have gone mad if not for Eugenia's presence. She spoke of politics until Anastasia, who had returned from the shops, walked smack into the middle of our plotting. She fell asleep at the kitchen table, a cheek resting on round freckled arms still folded around the bag of fragrant roots and potions she'd fetched.

Eugenia filled in more of my lacking understanding of foreign politics and made more tea, raspberry and chamomile. She made me drink the valerian root seeped in hot water. It made me warm and drowsy.

It was almost morning when I had been calmed enough—with Eugenia's talk and no small amount of valerian tea—to go to bed. My aunt did the same.

I did not ask for this, I whispered to myself as I fell asleep. I did not need this, not on top of my classes and the constantly smirking Professor Ipatiev, not with friends in jail or missing, or a suitor who robbed people and leapt from one building to the next. It all seemed excessive for one person, and I would never have dreamed of taking on additional burdens if my aunt had not been with me. But since she was, efficient and severe as always in her black dress, sleeping in the bedroom next to mine, it didn't seem all that impossible.

Really, it was mostly because of my aunt that I rose in the morning, determined and ready. As Anastasia snored peacefully in her little room and I made tea, I made the decision that was to alter the course of my life forever: I had decided that if there was a war brewing, it was my job to stop it. My first step was to convince Jack Bartram to come to my side.

Chapter 7

THWARTING THE IMPENDING WAR TURNED OUT TO BE MORE complicated than I imagined. While Eugenia was getting nowhere with her petitions and being irritably sent from one waiting room to another and then back again, I suffered under the uncompromising instruction of Professors Ipatiev, Zhmurkin, and several of their assorted colleagues. Physics caught up with me rather unexpectedly, and I realized that to pass the exams I would have to study more than previously. And of course I was not going to abandon my studies, so the entirety of my campaign would have to be confined to my winter recess. Or so I thought.

Jack presented another problem—after his passionate confession, he seemed to consider the matter closed, and we returned to our amiable walks after philosophy class, with an occasional outing to a concert of chamber music, of which Jack was inordinately fond, or an engineering exhibit. I felt uneasy about those, even when they featured something as innocuous as the piano-playing automaton. I could never forget he was there to observe closely and report.

He too seemed to be aware of the awkwardness—at least, he never made any further incursions into romantic territory, to both my small relief and greater disappointment. A man in love was easier to manipulate, and I was prepared to feel only a modicum of guilt about it.

Because of him, I had also gained access to the Northern Star—the English favored it, and I discovered that even though the smoking room adjacent to the main hall was off limits to everyone female, the library on the second floor was available for my use. Jack spent much of his time there, and I started to occasionally join him, while procrastinating or simply looking for a quiet place to study.

My natural curiosity had driven me to explore the heavy oak shelves and bookcases in the library. The selection of novels was decent but not breathtaking, featuring some old books and some newer ones, such as George Henry Borrow (I flipped through one that looked like a gypsy romance, and decided to save it for later). What interested me most however were thick sheaves of newspapers—*The Times of London,* going decades back, all stitched together and bound into massive tomes.

I was able to read them only when there was no one else in the library—I did not want to attract attention to the fact that I selected newspapers between last year and five years previous, and combed through them looking for reports of arrests. Jack might have shown me himself if asked, only it did not seem right to inquire. Besides, I rather enjoyed the sense of secrecy, the feeling it was I who spied on him. It somehow fulfilled my sense of justice.

Because of this situation, I only learned of Jack's past in brief snatches, in short but illuminating glimpses between the creaking of floorboards and consequent slamming shut of heavy volumes. Garnered in this constant atmosphere of vertiginous trespass, his tale seemed all the more marvelous. I tried to reconstruct the chronology, from the first brief report of a robbery and two drunk eyewitnesses swearing they saw the robber leap onto a nearby roof of a three-storied townhouse and sprint away, jumping from rooftop to rooftop, to much more detailed accounts, dozens of witnesses—a growing and calamitous impossibility of denial.

One of the more recent stories struck me as especially telling: it spoke of a hansom cab hired to transport a jeweler and two men he employed to protect his person and the diamonds and gold he had with him. The valuables were in a heavy chest held together by three iron strips that ran the circumference of the chest. The chest was locked, and the key was hidden under the jeweler's jacket, cravat, and shirt, hanging from a plain velvet cord. The newspaper was especially insistent in listing all these details.

Eyewitnesses reported that a man fell out of the sky, landing on both feet with such force that his knee had to touch the ground to absorb the impact, and that the cobblestones on which he had landed splintered with the shock of his arrival (I did a quick calculation in my mind, trying to figure out the force of a falling human body, and decided that—by itself—it was not enough to split stone, but the newspaper was quite adamant about the fact. The image of Jack splintering stone consequently haunted my dreams.) The horses spooked and reared, upsetting the cab and rendering the jeweler and his bodyguards ineffectual. As they struggled to free themselves from the cab and avoid the horses, the man who fell out of the sky grabbed the chest and heaved it over his head—which was a feat in itself, as the chest was quite heavy. He then brought it down with such force the strips of metal holding it together broke as easily as violin strings, and the wood burst into a shower of long splinters. Gold and jewels showered the street, and the man shoved a few handfuls of the treasure into the pockets of his long overcoat, leaving the rest for gawking onlookers and the street urchins, who fell on the bounty like scavenging magpies. No one saw what happened to the robber, although most felt that he probably jumped onto a nearby roof and was gone in his usual manner, taking one roof after another with his gigantic, inhuman strides.

I felt exhilarated just reading the story, but did not understand why. I supposed that it was the sheer fact of Jack's existence, the very impossibility of there being a man such as he—impossible, I whispered, impossible. A man who could jump atop buildings now studied philosophy in the same class as I.

The London newspaper dubbed him "Spring Heeled Jack," and the nickname made me laugh at its levity and simultaneous accuracy.

I heard footsteps, and quickly slammed the volume shut. I shoved it into its nest on the shelf, while grabbing for something else to read. By the time Dame Nightingale peered over my shoulder, I appeared to be quite absorbed in my reading and gave a little start when she said, "Ah, *Pride and Prejudice*—a fine work indeed, and offers much for a young lady such as yourself to learn."

"Quite," I agreed. I expected Dame Nightingale to point out how everyone in the book married, as if it somehow bore relevance to my life, but instead she sighed and rested her long, well-shaped hand on the crease of my white sleeve.

"You see, Alexandra," she said in a tone of soulful intimacy, as if we were best friends sharing secrets, "it is good for a girl your age to understand that not all people are suitable for your friendship. There are rough beasts masquerading as gentlemen; I wish I could tell you that the reverse is also true. However, those who seem as beasts are bestial, and so are some of those who seem as gentlemen. Do you understand?"

"Yes," I said. I did understand her words, although the reason behind her saying them escaped me—unless she meant to intimate that Jack Bartram (which was not his real name, as I had surmised) was a beast; but then again, I already knew as much.

"Very good," Dame Nightingale said, and nodded at me as if dismissing a class. I reacted as if it were exactly that, and left the library, book still clutched in my hands, even though nothing could be further from my intentions than reading.

I found Jack in the hallway—an open corridor that ran along

the front wall of the building, its wide windows offering a view of the Nevsky Prospect and the moody dark river. I stood for a bit, as I always did, captivated by the wide expanse of water. More than ever-present, the River Neva did not merely run through the city, the city arranged itself along it—every palace, every cathedral had a connection to it, or to one of the smaller rivers such as the Moyka and Fontanka.

Jack finished his conversation with Mr. Herbert and some other gentleman I had not previously met, and smiled at me, his hat in his hand, ready to depart. Always willing to walk me home or to the club or to the embankment, wherever I wanted to go, he was right there next to me, my gangly criminal shadow.

"Such a nice view," I said to him.

He nodded. "I almost feel bad," he said. "I mean, that we English have taken this club over. We really do not deserve that view."

And there it was, that elusive quality in him I could never understand—on one hand, he was considerate of others to an enormous degree; yet, if newspapers and his own words could be believed, he had no trouble robbing people and scaring the daylights out of them. I avoided thinking of the darker tales, where the victims claimed Spring Heeled Jack beat them or committed some other violence. Perhaps I was foolish, but I was not afraid of him.

"Mr. Bartram," I said as he escorted me across the bridge, back to Vasilyevsky Island, "I have a favor to ask of you."

He looked down at me, quizzical. "What is it?"

"You have informed me of your . . . special capabilities," I said. "You think that I would not be believed if I were to tell anyone. But it is still quite a risk, no matter whether I am believed or not. What if I were to tell Dame Nightingale?"

"You wouldn't."

"No, I would not." I would not give the dreadful woman the time of day if it could be avoided. "But there are those who know of them. I have read about you."

He smiled. "In the newspapers?"

"Indeed. It was very thoughtful of you to show me where they were."

He laughed. "You seem to enjoy sneaking behind my back."

I blushed a little. "I could not be sure if you wished me to discover more about you, so I had to finish my readings before I told you. And now you are laughing about it."

He grew serious then. "Not at all," he said. "Although you are right. I did want you to know about me. But to tell you straight out did not seem right."

We stopped in the middle of the bridge. The wind was especially cutting there, and the black water churned below, occasionally silvering and growing choppy with the silent passing of submarines underneath its surface. I watched Jack observe their movement, and a quiet certainty grew within me. All this time I had agonized about ways of swaying him to my side, but he wanted nothing more. This is why he told me about the Crane Club. He could not help but tell me, yet he could not tell me all. Nor could he ask of me what he wished to ask.

"What is it that you want from me?" I asked.

He smiled, started saying something jocular, but then his eyes met mine and he stopped.

"You want me to free you," I said. "Correct?" It was starting to feel like a parlor game, where a summoned spirit could answer only yes or no; all that was missing was a medium and table rapping.

He nodded, turning back to stare at the river. A submarine surfaced, and a freedman wrapped in an overcoat of sheepskin and shod in felt boots climbed out of the hatch awkwardly, and tinkered with something on the tail end of the contraption.

"These submersible craft are rather complicated," Jack said. "Very interesting, really."

"Of course you have plans of their inner workings," I guessed. "You stole them, just as you stole the Chinese airship models."

"And some other war machines," he said. "When all of those documents travel to London, the British Empire will be impossible to oppose."

"Especially if you have the Ottomans on your side," I said. At that point it was a mere supposition, even though I had seen a Turk or two in the Northern Star, their red fezzes as visible in the crowd as blood on the snow.

"Yes," Jack said. "I'm afraid there is nothing to be done about all that."

"And you hate being a spy."

"I was compelled. One cannot help but resent any sort of indentured servitude, be it slavery or something a little more genteel."

"So if I were to offer you something else?"

"I would consider it," he said. "Only what can you offer that Nightingale won't take away?"

"Who is she, really?"

"The head of Her Majesty's Secret Service," Jack said. "She supervises all the spies."

"So she has access to everything any of you bring along."

Jack nodded. "Mr. Herbert, her . . . friend, is hoping to head the War Office, and she will do anything to help him get there. She calls herself his 'helpmeet,' if I recall correctly."

"That is from your King James's version of the Bible, I think."

"Probably." He sighed, still looking at the freedman and his bushy beard, at his thick clumsy fingers adjusting the membranous fins of the submarine's tail and the lattice of bronze rods and gears that held them in place. "Everything she says is from somewhere."

I pondered. It made sense that Nightingale would keep all the intelligence—copies or originals—gathered by her spies. Knowledge is power and she intended to gain such for her Mr. Herbert. "Do you know where she keeps her documents?"

He nodded. "A safe."

Neither of us said it aloud, but Jack had experience with safes. The man who stole display cases from the Chinese students' club could just as easily obtain all the secret materials from the British spymistress. The question remained what to do with them.

"She will not be leaving St. Petersburg before Christmas, will she?"

He stared at me. "I don't think so. Why?"

I sighed, feeling petty and selfish. "I have exams to take. When I'm done, I think you should take those documents from her."

"She'll get them back. She has many men under her command, and your family can't help you."

"No."

The freedman had finished his tinkering, leaving one of the fins hanging aslant, clearly broken. Cursing under his breath, he crawled through the hatch and the submarine sank from view, leaving only a small trail of silver bubbles in its wake, like a drowning man.

I continued along the bridge and Jack followed. "My family," I said, thinking aloud more than addressing him, "may not protect me, but if anyone can make the emperor listen, it's my aunt. It may take her a while, but she will find a way."

"I hear she's in disfavor."

I shrugged. "She is, but in his heart the emperor knows she always speaks the truth. He may try and ignore her, but he won't succeed. We must make sure she has proof the British . . . that you are spying and planning an alliance with the Ottomans. Can you obtain such proof? Something even a delusional man can not argue with?"

"A delusional man can argue with anything," Jack answered, catching up to me with no effort and walking so close his arm brushed mine. "However, I can provide your aunt with enough that the emperor will have to admit he is delusional to ignore it."

"That would do," I said. "And I will help you avoid Nightingale."

He made an amused face, but I could not miss the savage hope that flashed in his pale gray eyes. "And how would you do that?"

"You will come with me to China," I said. The plan had just formed in my head—rather, all the sleepless nights and musings and political conversations with my aunt had crystallized into this solution, as perfect as it was simple, or idiotic, depending on one's viewpoint. All I knew was that I liked it.

"China," Jack repeated, not bothering to affect amusement any longer. "To do what, exactly?"

"To avoid Nightingale," I said cheerfully. "We can find those men you freed that night, remember? I need to see Wong Jun first, to ask him where we can find them and who else would help us. My aunt will work on the emperor here, while we convince the Chinese that they need to ally with Russia against Britain. We can bring the documents, the diagrams of the airships. We will take submarine plans to them as well, as a bargaining chip."

"Seems risky," Jack said. "Although I do not suppose Russia would have much to fear from the Chinese—the British East India Company would surely be their main concern."

"And submarines would help against China's ships," I concluded. "Really, it is disgraceful what Britain is doing with the opium trade."

"I wish I could argue," Jack said, "but you are correct—and you are correct about traveling to China."

I couldn't help but smile at his docile readiness to follow me across an entire continent the same way he followed me to my dormitories, protective and yet defenseless. I, of course, had to admit that fear of Dame Nightingale probably provided a stronger motivation than whatever attraction he felt toward my humble person, but enjoyed the realization nonetheless. Besides, I had read enough James Fenimore Cooper and Alexander Dumas in my youth in Trubetskoye to appreciate the challenges of our lonesome heroics. We were two noble friends standing against the cruelty and small-mindedness of the world, and we had no choice but to do what we believed in, circumstance be damned. I almost felt guilty about still worrying about my exams, and my secret hope that it will take us long enough to gain access to Wong Jun for me to finish the exams. One thing I did not worry about was my aunt's compliance—I knew that she would have nothing but agreement with my proposition.

One day in mid-November Eugenia arrived at my apartment with an expression of triumph on her red, chapped face.

"Don't ask me how I did it," she said as she pulled off her gloves and gestured to Anastasia to get the kettle on, "But I got you an appointment with your Chinaman friend."

I ignored the explicit prohibition—more of a dare or an invitation, really. "Who did you bribe?"

She took off her hat and bustled into the kitchen, rubbing her cracked, rough hands and pulling her shawl tighter around her shoulders. "Never you worry about small indignities—you have an aunt for that."

I had to smile, sure this is what she told my mother—my mother who was comfortable and content in the family home, with a tabby cat purring in her lap and her knitting in her hands. "Thank you, Aunt Genia. Where is he?"

"They stuck him in the Petropavlosk Fortress," she replied. "On Zayachiy Island. Apparently, he's important enough."

"Of course he is," I replied. "He is a Manchu." It was silly to feel such a sense of pride, but I felt flattered that someone I knew warranted an imprisonment at the place that housed only the most notorious and highly regarded among political prisoners. Then again, the fact that no one had ever escaped from it filled me with gloom. I sighed.

"He's in Alexeevsky Ravelin." Eugenia shook her head, troubled. "So many good people have perished there—I only thank God there weren't more. Every time I think of your father and his friends' rebellion, my heart almost stops when I consider what could have happened. Can you imagine what would become of them if they had failed?"

"Ravelin," I guessed. "How am I getting there?"

"I'll hire you a coach—unless, of course, you would like me to come with you. Or do you have another escort?"

"I think I should go by myself," I said. Anastasia had finished her preparations for tea, and Eugenia and I drank with great enjoyment, trying to chase away the bitter, wet cold that settled deep into our bones.

Eugenia drank in large gulps. By all rights the scalding hot tea should have peeled the epithelium right off her esophagus, but she had apparently trained it to withstand temperatures hot enough to melt lead. "Is that so? Still enjoying solitude?"

I blew on my tea and waited for it to cool down. "I think that a young woman alone tends to invoke the instinct of protectiveness in men—and I am assuming that I will be dealing with the guardsmen and the commandant of the fortress. I do not want them to wonder about my purpose, I just want them to be concerned and to want to help me."

Eugenia gave a short incredulous laugh. "Oh dear niece. Not even three months you're away from home, and already you're plotting and calculating like a government official. This city has bureaucracy in the bones, and black ink for blood."

"When is my appointment?" I asked.

"Tomorrow," Eugenia replied. Before I could object, she held up her hand, commanding. "I know, I know, you haven't missed a day of classes yet. I'll send Anastasia to your professors so they know we had an urgent family affair only my heiress could deal with. And I'll make sure those friends of yours come for tea after and tell you everything they learned. Which probably won't be much, what with the way they've been filling their heads with dresses and men and nonsense, but enough to get you by. You're so much smarter than any of them, I swear."

I knew my aunt well enough to recognize this praise as disguised question—she wanted to know whether I was filling my head with nonsense. I suspected that dresses she wouldn't have minded so much, but Jack must have been a concern to her. I still had not told her about her expected role in my designs, reasoning that the less time she had to contemplate my request, the less likely she would be to decline it. Despite her many eccentricities, Aunt Eugenia was not insane. Rather she possessed the courage and iron will to stand up to the emperor or anyone in his court. But she lacked the ability to ignore the facts and barrel through—her hope hitched to that least reliable of movers, expectation of luck and simple refusal to think through one's actions and their unavoidable outcome—against all odds.

If I were to think everything through as thoroughly as Eugenia, I would not go to the Petropavlovsk Fortress, or made plans to travel to China. My ignorance and optimism sustain me when sober reason fails; I am not convinced that I like this conclusion, but I cannot deny it. Whatever the case, I had decided to conceal my intentions from Eugenia for as long as my conscience would allow me—and it was proving to be surprisingly robust.

Eugenia touched my hand. "What are you thinking about?"

I realized I hadn't answered her question, so I laughed. "Rest assured, Aunt Genia, I am not interested in dresses or men. Or rather, I am interested in the man in Alexeevsky Ravelin, but my interest in him in strictly political."

Eugenia smiled with visible relief.

I shrugged. "I have my education to worry about."

Eugenia had never been stupid, and she sat up, looking at me closely with her piercing eyes. "And pray tell, why are you so interested in it all of a sudden?"

I could never lie to her about these things, and yet I had trouble articulating why I had undergone such a change of heart. She knew, of course, that I had first gone to the university out of obedience rather than enthusiasm. And now, as much as I would hate to disappoint her if I quit, the drive to stay and to excel was entirely mine. "I am not sure," I said after some soul-searching. "I suppose this is one thing that is entirely mine."

She raised an eyebrow at me, but finished her tea and stood. "The coach will be here tomorrow at eight in the morning. Be ready."

I slept surprisingly well that night. I suppose I should have fretted and been concerned for Wong Jun's well-being and for my own impending and perilous trip. If there were to be a trip, if Jack managed to steal the necessary papers and we escaped the unpleasant attention of Dame Nightingale. Instead, I stretched like my mother's tabby cat and went to sleep, not a worry in my mind . . .

. . . and it was morning with Anastasia whispering fiercely for me to wake up, wake up, miss, please wake up.

She got me dressed—I chose a sophisticated two-piece tweed ensemble trimmed with lace that simultaneously signaled refinement and naiveté—and made me breakfast. Eugenia had already gone for the day, and I wished I could talk to her a bit before leaving. Instead I had to content myself with admonishing Anastasia to not forget to take the message to all my professors, and not to spend too much time gabbing with Natalia Sergeevna.

The coach took me along the University Embankment, all the way around the eastern tip of Vasilyevsky Island, and turned north toward the Tuchkov Bridge to Petrovsky Island. I briefly considered the folly of building a city on several islands, and the dangers spring floods always presented. I had heard a few stories of the Neva and other rivers overflowing their banks despite the tall containment walls; hundreds of people drowned. I supposed the trick of living so close to water was to never contemplate the damage it could cause longer than strictly necessary. I stared out the window instead.

The coach traveled east and north, along Bolshoy Prospect, a crowded, noisy avenue that was not nearly as pleasant as Nevsky, and much dirtier. The northern wind brought clouds of acrid smoke and exhaust from the factories by the Malaya Nevka River, and I covered my nose and mouth with my handkerchief. The scent of lilac sachet was comforting and far less objectionable than the air. We turned east and traveled over a small wooden bridge to Zayachiy Island. The carriage stopped at the gatehouse of the fortress—a place of grim aspect—and the coachman assisted me out.

"I'll wait for you here, miss," the freedman driver said. "Here, on the outside."

I could not blame him for not wanting to go into the fortress. I hesitated myself, suspicious this was all a ploy to lure me here. I soon realized that was rather irrational. Surely, a simple arrest would get me into jail just as securely and more efficiently than laying an elaborate trap. I knocked on the small side door by the gate.

A guardsman in full uniform the epaulettes as large as his face let me inside, and I admired the trees and the carpet of orange and red leaves lining what in the summer was likely to be a very soft lawn. The guardsman escorted me to the commandant's house.

Commandant Mishkin, a stout, mustachioed man in shining black boots and very thoroughly pressed uniform, checked my papers and asked me a few perfunctory questions. As he walked me along one of the many twining paths toward the Ravelin itself, he smiled. "You know," he said, "this fortress is quite prestigious, far as jails go. Some of the brightest minds have stayed with us at one time or another."

I found the idea that the caliber of a prison was measured by the talents of those unjustly contained within terrifying and funny at the same time, a comical nightmare. I managed not to betray my thoughts but only nodded thoughtfully.

Commandant Mishkin smiled. "We have been undergoing some wonderful renovations. The emperor is very concerned about the humane treatment of prisoners. We just finished expanding the cells and introducing all possible amenities. I think you will be pleasantly surprised."

My suspicions revived again. "How do you mean? Surely, you do not expect me to evaluate these amenities by myself?"

He laughed, a great belly laugh suitable to a man much bigger and more rounded. "I should've known," he said between guffaws. "You take after your aunt. She always makes me laugh."

"You know her?"

"We are old friends," he said, as if it was an obvious fact that should've been known to me. "I owe my position here to her—not in a direct way, of course, but still. It took her long enough to call on our acquaintance."

"Why is that?"

"She always tries to do things the right way, no bribes, no calling in favors—unless there's no other way, of course." Mishkin stopped mid-stride to cross his eyes and give his mustache a critical look. He wetted his thick thumb and forefinger with his tongue and twisted the mustache tips into points. Satisfied with the results, he continued. "She is old fashioned, your aunt, no matter how much she loves progress. She still expects things to be as they used to—as they ought to. Only you and I, we both know that progress has its price, and this price includes the cost of doing business." He winked. "And here we are."

If there ever existed such a thing as a cozy jail, Alexeevsky Ravelin was it. Gone were the stone walls weeping cold and moisture from cracks in crumbling mortar, and the hallway between the doors—all padded with cheerfully colored cloth—was straight, well-lit and dry. Mishkin was not lying about Constantine's humanitarian inclinations.

I followed him along several corridors, almost losing my footing when he turned the corner abruptly and entered another one. It was like traversing a labyrinth, and my suspicions intensified once more. The smell inside was also starting to bother me—not the clean cold smells of the river that surrounded the fortress like mother's embrace, but a tepid, faintly rotted miasma that was bound to breed consumption and fevers.

Mishkin stopped outside of a door no different from any other. There was an observation slit in the door at eye level, and another one just above the ground, no doubt for passing through meals or other objects. I peered through the observation slot, steeling myself for the worst.

Wong Jun looked quite comfortable, sitting on his bed with a book in his hands. There was a wooden door separating his room from a small stall in the back—a garderobe, I assumed. Overall, it was rather more civilized than I expected.

Wong Jun was wearing a long silk robe in green and yellow, a bit frayed at the collar. His face was paler and gaunter than I remembered, and his mustache, still long, looked as frayed as his collar. In addition, his beard had been growing without much care or grooming, which gave him a slightly mad and hermitlike appearance. To be expected out of a political prisoner, I supposed.

I nodded to Mishkin and he let me in. He locked the door behind me, and I briefly wondered if he would be right outside, eavesdropping. "Wong Jun," I said.

He looked up then—I supposed the clanging of the door was not unusual or promising enough to attract his attention.

Wong Jun startled at the sound of my voice, and his book fell to the floor. He jumped up and grabbed my hands as if I were a dear friend, not someone he met only a few times and spoke to once. But I found myself overcome too. After a moment when we both were at a loss for words, tears forced their way out of my eyes. Wong Jun embraced me and cried too.

"I am so sorry I couldn't come and see you before," I said. "When I made inquiries, they arrested me . . . "

"And yet you are not in prison," he interrupted, then grinned. "I apologize. It was not my intention to imply anything but my sincere joy that you remain free."

"I had assistance," I said.

He nodded. "I must say I am surprised to see you. I did not expect any visitors at all, except perhaps for a wayward Chinese diplomat who might remember I was in this godforsaken city. But tell me, what of Chiang Tse and Lee Bo?"

"I have not seen them," I said. "I heard they escaped unharmed—I only pray they have reached their . . . your homeland by now. The man who saved them and me is my friend; he's English. I don't understand all of it, but the English are more influential in St. Petersburg than Russian aristocracy."

He shook his head, mournful. "There are only two ways in which the English relate to the world—they either take what they want or they destroy what they don't."

"Not Mr. Bartram," I said, rather defensively. "You see, he agrees the Opium War was a disgrace for his countrymen. In fact, he is helping me, and we are going to go to China, and . . . "

"You must speak more slowly," Wong Jun said. "And keep your voice down."

I hesitated, realizing that if Wong Jun had a chance to buy his freedom in exchange for information, everything I told him could be just as well printed in the newspapers. Still, there didn't seem to be anything to gain by not asking questions he had answers to. I sighed and related the plan Jack and I had devised with, omitting the details and keeping the general thrust—that is, our need to go to China and to reach someone in the position to gain the emperor's attention.

Wong Jun listened thoughtfully, his eyebrows doming occasionally as if he were troubled. He made a sound only once—a small, disappointed moan when the fate of Crane Club slipped through my lips.

"I'm so sorry," I said then. "But you do see why it is important. The English have your airship models."

He looked at me as if my words made no sense. "Those were not secrets, they were there for display. No one had to steal them, they could go in and see."

"But if they want to make something that works, they would need the models," I said. I remembered my visit with Eugenia to the factory in Tosno, the ill-fated airship. I wondered what happened to it, if there were any more.

Wong Jun nodded. "I see. If something isn't a secret, it doesn't mean it cannot be stolen and used. I do have to say I think your idea to ally our countries against the British is a good one—China would certainly benefit from not having Russia as an enemy. And I will be able to help you. Do you have any paper? I used up my monthly allowance on poetry." He gave a dry smile. I wasn't sure if he was joking or not.

I rifled through my handbag, and found the programme from a chamber music concert Jack and I had attended recently. Fortunately, the reverse side of it was blank, and I handed it to Wong Jun. Under his bed, he kept an inkwell filled with black ink and a brush—just a piece of bamboo splintered into fibers on one end. With these simple implements, Wong Jun started drawing symbols similar to those I'd seen at the Crane Club, but of course could not read. When he was finished, he handed me the paper and I folded it, feeling rather like either Rosencrantz or Guildenstern.

"What does it say?" I asked.

"Just show it to any official you see," he said. "Or rather any who wear Manchu robes—Ming loyalists and most other Han are idiots, and they may decide this letter has better uses than helping two Europeans, one of whom is . . . English." He said "English" as if it was the most distasteful word in the world. "But you need to get to a real official with that, understand? They will take you to the Xian Feng Emperor—I wrote that it is the matter of our country's very survival. I wrote that you would help us stop the East India Company. Don't make me into a liar."

His smile, hidden by his beard so that only the corners of his eyes creased and his mustache lifted a bit, was unexpected but welcome. I had not realized how tense my back was, how tightly my hands clenched on my jacket sleeves until I smiled back and heaved a sigh of relief. "It's a tall order, but we will do our best. Meanwhile, my aunt will keep asking for your release."

"Please convey my deepest thanks to your aunt." Wong Jun smiled still. It struck me, how stoic he was, how accepting and yet how brave. If I were imprisoned, I would be throwing myself at the door and screaming, I would be hitting my head against the walls that enclosed me . . . the violence of my reaction surprised me, as if the very thought of being imprisoned was enough to drive my imagination wild and make me panic with the possibility.

"I will," I promised. "The commandant is a friend of hers, and I think he is a good man. Let me know if there is anything you need—"

"To be set free." He gave a mournful smile. "But I suppose this is rather asking too much."

"My aunt is trying."

"Other than that, I am being treated well," he said. "What is interesting to me is that no one is interrogating me. I was arrested and delivered here, and then left alone. If they really believed I was a spy, they would have at least asked me some questions, don't you think? Instead, it's just this." He spread his fingers and raised his hands palms up.

"At least it is . . . agreeable," I said.

"It's a prison."

"I know. I'm trying to be comforting."

"You're trying to absolve yourself from guilt of leaving me while you and your friends ran away."

It was true, I realized, even though it was something I tried not to think about for a long time now. "I couldn't have done anything to help you," I said. "You know that."

He kept quiet, smiling.

"Is there anything you can do to help us?"

The look he gave me was a hair short of annoyed. "I am doing what I can, but as you can see, I am rather limited by current circumstance. I will however offer you this advice: you Europeans have an unfortunate tendency to assume the rest of the world exists to assist you and to help you. But please remember as you travel that the Chinese people you will encounter have excellent reasons to neither trust nor help you. And the emperor—you must have compelling reasons for him to approve of your proposed alliance, he has his own problems, what with the East India Company and the Taipings. He is quite busy; but if you will, please let him know that I am well and my rescue is not an urgent matter, although I do hope he could get to it eventually—if your aunt's attempts do not succeed, of course."

I blushed—I could feel my cheeks heat up and glow crimson. "I did not mean to imply that I consider myself in any way more important than you."

"Your Englishman certainly does," Wong Jun said.

Just then there was a knock on the door, and Mishkin's round, smiling face that reminded me of an especially ripe and red apple looked in. "I'm afraid I must interfere," he said. "This visit had gone on longer than I agreed to, and the lady must be going."

I took Wong Jun's pale hand in mine and gave it as strong a squeeze as I could. "I promise I'll do anything I can."

"I believe you," he said, gripping my hand firmly in return.

As Mishkin escorted me through the winding corridors in reverse order, I felt lightheaded and barely answered his prattle. Wong Jun's letter nestled safely in the pocket of my jacket, and I could not help but brush my fingertips against every now and again, just to make sure the feel and rustling of the paper and the smell of ink remained real. I was still foggy on Wong Jun's relationship to Qing dynasty, but the fact that he expected the emperor to know him made me feel optimistic. I had decided even before I left the Ravelin that the letter was a cause for celebration, and promised to take Eugenia to the opera as soon as it was practical, and before of course I had leave the country and start peace negotiations with China.

Chapter 8

THE EXCURSION TO THE OPERA OCCURRED SOONER THAN I HAD expected. My bare mention of the possibility to Eugenia provoked a terrifying outbreak of enthusiasm and emotion. She was tired and disheartened, desperate for a distraction as the first snow, angry and biting, sifted from the clouds. Her fruitless daily visits to various offices and failure to make any progress were humiliating by themselves, but she was also not used to being rejected. She had always had access to the emperor, and now that it had suddenly taken away angered her. Her usual stubbornness left her no recourse but to continue knocking on locked doors. What she hoped to achieve, she never told me. I wasn't the only one with secrets then.

So the opera seemed like a salvation, but preparations were needed. Usually indifferent to clothes, Genia insisted that we have new dresses sewn for the occasion. We found a seamstress she felt suitable, but the woman charged twice as much as others. Eugenia, contrary to her usual level-headedness, decided she would be the one. Her name was Maria Verbova, and she commanded an entire army of girls, all dressed in plain but well-made checkered dresses and white caps. Her atelier had appearance of efficiency and expensive simplicity.

Eugenia was usually thrifty, but the prospects of attending the opera excited her into ordering two very expensive dresses (although she did note they would serve as ball gowns as well). She kept to her usual widow's black, and I wondered if she wore it on my mother's behalf. I do not remember my mother wearing anything but pastels; she grieved for my father deeply when he passed away, but did not seem to think that changing the color of one's clothing made a difference.

For me, we decided to go with a silver-gray taffeta, with just a hint of pearly sheen. I never understood how people could become so enchanted by fabric until that day—looking at that taffeta was like looking into the autumn sky over St. Petersburg, at clouds so low they tore on the cathedral crosses and the Admiralty spire; it was like gray river reflecting that sky. I asked for white lace, to remind me of the frothy water whipped by the rising submarine hulls. They made my skirts wide and flounced, and the bodice clung to my shoulders, while mercifully covering most of my chest with lace and ruffles.

"It's very nice," Eugenia said. "A good color for you—it reminds me of a sword blade."

That week, I went to my usual classes and for fittings afterwards. By Saturday Eugenia and I had new dresses, and tickets had been procured. Despite Eugenia's humiliation and disgust with everything, she made sure our tickets were for the balcony, to the right of the emperor's private box.

Getting dressed took longer than usual—the dress required an unreasonable number of starched petticoats, and Anastasia had to spend a few minutes making sure that the lace of the hem lay evenly. I ruffled the lace at the neckline, making it looked even more like foam.

We arrived to a full house, and I was simultaneously dismayed and thrilled to see that Dame Nightingale, Mr. Herbert, and Jack were present as well. They were seated in a balcony across from ours, and I smiled and nodded to them. It was a perfect opportunity to point Jack out to Eugenia and I did so.

She squinted at the trio through her lorgnette, and whispered to me, "Is this the Englishman who always walks you home?"

"Yes," I said. "What do you think?"

"A bit stringy," Eugenia said. "Then again, I don't suppose you're intent on cooking him, so it shouldn't matter all that much."

I laughed and covered my face with my fan—I didn't want Jack to think I was laughing at him, even though I was. "And that lady in pearls and a blue dress is Dame Nightingale," I said to Eugenia. "She's with their Secret Service."

"She is one of the spies then," Eugenia said and gave a slow, bitter laugh.

"She is," I said. "I got the impression that the man next to her is the reason. She is doing it to help him."

"Surely there are other ways to help loved ones," Eugenia said, frowning. "Besides, a little selfishness in certain people would be a blessing to the world."

"I'm sure some are saying the same about you," I said.

She laughed. "Indeed, I'm sure some people would be quite happy if I left the public sphere. But I am getting better—I have decided to only concern myself with matters that affect my blood relatives."

"Funny you should mention it," I said. "But I was going to ask you to interfere on behalf of Wong Jun."

"I've been trying."

"You haven't been giving bribes or pulling favors."

Eugenia looked shocked, and her lorgnette trembled. "Sasha! How can you even suggest that!"

I shrugged, feeing my shoulder slip out of the taffeta and then dip back again. "It doesn't matter, Aunt Genia. No one is playing by the rules anymore, not the emperor, not the English. You're the only one who perseveres."

"Sometimes one's integrity is the only thing one has left." She turned away, sighing, and pointed her lorgnette at the orchestra tuning their violins in the orchestra pit. I thought the time was right to talk to her about my expectations for her help.

"Yes," I persisted, "but let's try to save more than our integrity alone. Jack may be able to obtain proof the English are planning a war—but you will have to do everything you can to get it in front of Constantine."

"He would do that?" She laughed softly. "Just be careful you don't put your trust in those who are not worthy of it."

I was about to reply, but the first bars of the overture sent a hush over the theater. I knew from experience that Eugenia took her music seriously, and it would be wise not to annoy her by talking during the performance. Besides, I thought, it would be good for her to consider my request.

I sat back in my chair and watched the velvet-draped figures bumping against each other and singing in Italian. Someone jumped off a papier-mâché wall, and then they sang some more. I could never follow an opera (probably because I never bothered to read the programme that helpfully explained the plot), so I just tried to enjoy the music, while watching Jack out of the corner of my eye. Between studying and dress preparation I had not had time to talk to him of late. He also seemed preoccupied with concerns of his own. Exams were drawing closer, and I surmised he was working on getting the documents from Nightingale. I couldn't wait to show him Wong Jun's letter.

During the intermission, Eugenia and I went to the foyer, where unobtrusive waiters dressed in white weaved in and out of the crowd with trays of Champagne glasses. Eugenia and I nodded to a few acquaintances but kept to ourselves—primarily, to spare the Obolensky and Orlov families the embarrassment of finding excuses to avoid us. I had been so engrossed in the life of the university that

I had not noticed how the position of my family had deteriorated; it wasn't any specific misdeed or overt scandal, but a cumulative effect of Eugenia's unorthodoxy and my own small and unwomanly trespasses, coupled with the withdrawal of the emperor's support. We were now considered somewhat less than desirable company.

"So what," I whispered to Eugenia. "We don't need those people."

"Those people used to be my friends," she said, and drained her Champagne flute in one long swallow.

"Mishkin still is," I said. "Look, Aunt Genia. You told me yourself that you get to know who your friends are when things are not going well."

She shook her head, sadly. "This is how one learns that one has very few friends."

THE END OF SECOND QUARTER AND EXAM WEEK CAME QUICKLY AND unavoidably. Beyond them yawned the abyss of the unknown—China. I'd soon embark on an important mission, more dangerous but only slightly less terrifying than the season with its social visits and occasional ball. Still, I thought myself lucky to be given this opportunity. I did not concern myself with idle thoughts of from whence it came—God, or destiny, or some other unknowable entity.

By the time classes ended, I was feverish with excitement, and Olga and Dasha both insisted that I looked consumptive. I was less worried about the exams, although I did study, than about the approaching journey.

To my surprise, Eugenia had agreed to assist us, and did not argue with me going to China. I wished she had; I wish she had some of my mother's irrational protectiveness that would make her cling to me and beg me not to go. But Eugenia only sighed, and wrote letters for me to carry to bureaucrats in Moscow and every major city east of it. She cried at night, when she thought I could not hear her.

Jack and I were supposed to take a train to Moscow and then proceed east. Anastasia insisted on coming along, but really, there was no point in dragging silly Anastasia with us. She was a good, hardworking maid, but I decided she would be better off keeping the place fit for my return a few months hence.

"You cannot go dressed as yourself," Eugenia told me two days before my exams.

She did have a point: a young woman traveling alone with a man would surely attract attention. Moreover, if Jack was to succeed in his thievery, both the English Secret Service and the homegrown Nikolashki would surely be looking for us. Traveling as a married couple on a honeymoon was briefly considered but discarded because, rings or not, the police would not be fooled. However, Eugenia very sensibly suggested no one would not be looking for two men.

"But men's clothes are so drab!" Anastasia exclaimed. "No offense, miss, but you have to glitter."

Leaving aside that mysterious pronouncement, I considered the gist of her words. "I need a military uniform," I said, finally. "A grenadier, perhaps."

Eugenia shook her head. "Don't be a fool, Sasha, you're not built for infantry. You will pass as a young hussar, or a Guardsman officer."

"Why not a dragoon?"

She sighed. "In our apartment, there's a chest of old clothes. Your father's guardsman uniform is in it still, as well as your uncle's—he was a hussar. You can try them on, and see what fits best."

"Uncle?" I asked, confused.

"My older brother," Eugenia said. "Pavel Menshov. He was

killed during the Napoleonic invasion, but he was a small man. His uniform is old-fashioned, but surely we can use his sword and insignia."

Eugenia told me a little about my dead Uncle Pavel—he was young when he died, she said, barely more than a boy. His uniform, had it been wearable, would have fit me. It was strange for her, an old woman now, to think of him as her older brother. She told me how hard she cried on the day she realized she had forgotten his face.

Maria Verbova, my aunt determined, could sew me a uniform quite similar to my dead uncle's; moreover, Eugenia predicted, since the woman charged so much she must be used to keeping secrets. My aunt was proven correct. When I stopped by the atelier and requested Madame Verbova make me a hussar uniform, the seamstress only nodded and asked me if I would need to have my hair cut too.

"Yes," I said. "In a week."

She smiled then, dark lids hooding eyes that seemed too old for her well-kept face. "If you let me cut off a lock now, I will have a mustache ready for you as well," she said.

I laughed at the idea but conceded it was a good one, and with a swift clip of scissors she sheared a lock of hair near my temple. "You've done this before, haven't you?" I asked.

She inclined her head. "As you can imagine, there are many reasons for women to disguise themselves as men and men as women. If you wish, I will make you a corset to flatten your chest and thicken your waist."

"That would be helpful," I said.

"Don't worry," Maria assured me. "You are paying me enough to take care of it personally—my girls are quite reliable, but sometimes it is better to be safe than sorry."

The fittings at Maria Verbova's atelier evoked an almost sinister but giddy mood. The hussar uniform was still wide in the shoulders, but the corset (a disturbing-looking contraption of satin, whalebone, and cork with metal grommets) was designed to widen my shoulders, and its weight, aided by a set of particularly strong hooks and laces, pressed my bosom until it was as flat as a boy's. The cork-and-whalebone bodice surrounded my waist, thickening it. It had joints that allowed me to bend, and generous padding made the device surprisingly comfortable.

The breeches, white and tight fitting, took a bit of getting used to—I felt naked without my petticoats and skirts, but soon enough I discovered the trousers were quite comfortable as were the tall boots that squeaked with every step. The blue jacket, its chest stiff with gold braid, and a fur-trimmed pelisse completed my attire; a tall bearskin hat gave me much-needed height. My uncle's saber hung off my belt, its sheathed tip knocking reassuringly against my left boot, and Eugenia and Maria both agreed that I made a youthful but convincing hussar: short, squat, and broad shouldered.

Maria kept her word and made a mustache out of my hair. I was secretly hoping for an elaborate concoction, like the one decorating Commandant Mishkin's face. Instead, Maria produced several thin strips of sheer fabric covered in sparse hairs and a small bottle of glue. When she glued it to my face and held up the mirror, I laughed. As a woman, I was plain, but as a boy hussar with a nascent mustache, I looked . . . handsome. Maria nodded, pleased. "You look like you are about seventeen," she said. "Don't tell anyone you are older or no one will believe you. If your mustache gets dirty, replace it promptly; the glue dries fast. Now we need to work on your walk."

I just had to think of the way Eugenia moved around the manor in Trubetskoye—with long, hasty steps, her footfalls loud and haphazard, and tried to do the same. Maria nodded, smiling. "You're good at it," she said. "Have you practiced before?"

"No," I said.

I did not ask the questions on my mind, foremost among them my conviction that Maria herself had helped many women appear to be men, and perhaps had done so herself. I could see the advantage, of course, but I had no idea that such behavior was in any measure common. As it seemed impolite to ask, I practiced walking like a man late at night, after all the seamstresses were sent home, in Maria's vast and empty atelier. I weaved among the gypsum dummies, most wearing half finished dresses and frocks, sack jackets and evening coats, several drowning in a sea of handmade lace. I walked among them, practicing bowing and shaking their imaginary hands. I practiced talking.

"Don't try to make your voice too low," Maria advised. "It will sound artificial. Just lower it comfortably, and the rest will be attributed to your youth."

I waited to have her cut my hair until the last day of the exams.

I think my lack of nervousness helped with the examinations, for my grades were better than the previous quarter. I was pleased and Eugenia ecstatic; nonetheless, my thoughts were with Jack.

We had it all planned out. On the night of the last exam, Jack was to obtain the papers and then I was to meet him at the Moscow Train Station. Eugenia took me to Maria's to have my hair cut, and helped me pack when we returned to the dormitory—I had some civilian clothes as well as spare britches, six shirts of good cotton, and my underclothes. It all fit into a single satchel. Anastasia cried a little, worried I would need all the dresses and lace and pretty things I was leaving behind. In truth, I too felt like crying, even though I kept reassuring the silly girl I would be back soon.

Eugenia, always preoccupied with practical matters, gave me some last minute instructions. "You're Alexander Menshov now," she told me. "No need for fancy aliases, and it was easy enough to get you papers in this name. I'll tell your mother you are visiting classmates in Crimea—it is warmer there, she'll understand. You know how to handle yourself, so I won't nag you without need. But tell that Englishman that if he dare lays a hand upon you or shows any disrespect, I shall have his hand and his heart brought to me."

"Aunt Genia," I said, sighing. "You do love melodrama too much."

She stared at me. "Fancy that," she said after a few silent minutes. "Now I'm starting to think this is exactly what Pavel looked like."

She dabbed at her eyes as I searched for something to say. "Don't worry," I finally managed. "I am not he. I will not die, I promise."

She sobbed outright at that, and hugged my padded body to her chest. "You have no idea, Sasha, how frightened I am. The situation here now, the possible threat of war looming . . . you are too young to remember the Bonaparte, but I do. The terrifying thing is, if there is a new war, young people will be fighting it, and we, the old ones, we'll mourn and watch and relive our past losses and then lose even more. So you make sure it doesn't happen."

I pulled away. "I'll do what I can, Aunt Genia."

She dried her eyes and smiled then. "Time for you to go, young hussar. You'll miss your train."

"I'll try to avoid wars," I said, and picked up my satchel.

Everyone was asleep when Eugenia and I snuck out of the dark and quiet house, and walked to the Palace Bridge where we hailed a coachman. She kissed me goodbye once more, and I was on my way to the station.

At night, the building of dark granite and light gray marble towered against the sky pale with moonlight and impending snow. The station seemed deserted, but once inside, I discovered there were quite a few people, some stretched out on the wooden benches asleep, others sitting on their sacks and parcels. A few urchins played marbles by the far wall, away from the ticket windows and the gates leading to the tracks. I drew my pelisse around my shoulders, moved my satchel from one white-gloved hand to the other, and went to buy my ticket.

At this dead hour of the night, only one train left the station—a train to Moscow that ran primarily for the convenience of business travelers. It departed St. Petersburg at one in the morning and arrived in Moscow at one in the afternoon, early enough to conduct necessary business and possibly head back the same day. In my childhood when we visited relatives in Moscow, the journey from St. Petersburg took more than a week, and I felt nostalgic. One had to be determined to travel in those days. Nowadays, it seemed almost too easy, too casual.

That was Eugenia again, speaking in my mind, and I shook my head, dislodging her. With all her love of progress, she did miss those days, and Mishkin was correct about her essential old-fashionedness. I, of course, was happy with the speed of modern travel—it meant we would arrive to China in two weeks' time. If everything went well, we would be back before February when the next quarter started. Oh, how I hoped we would avoid complications! I let my hand slide over the front of my jacket. Under all the gold braid and over the whalebone, I could sense the faintest rustling of paper, the theater programme with Wong Jun's message. The message he promised would make our task possible.

I paid for the ticket and looked for a place to sit. A gangly young man, a student by all appearances, slept stretched out on one of the benches. I remembered I was currently a man in military service. I cannot describe the satisfaction I felt when I dislodged the young man's scuffed shoes with a swift kick of my polished boot.

He woke up and glowered, but when his gaze fell upon my uniform his grumbling turned into a loud yawn and he sat up, surrendering half a bench with an almost apologetic expression. I settled down and smiled to myself.

The clock above the ticket window showed half past midnight, and I hoped Jack would be on time. As the minute hand crawled closer and closer to twelve, I prayed the train would be delayed. But a man in a tall red hat announced the train, and passengers woke up and stretched and shuffled wearily toward the gaping mouth of the gates, beyond which I could see only the glow of a gaslight and the white sifting of another snowstorm. Jack was still not here.

We had decided long in advance that if one of us was to be delayed, the other was to go to Moscow anyway and wait in an appointed place. We had selected a tavern Jack knew of not too far from the Kremlin. I had memorized the simple directions to it. Waiting in St. Petersburg would have been too dangerous, especially if the missing one was caught or found out. After waiting three days in Moscow with no sign of the other, the one who was still free was to continue on to China alone. I did not like that idea—even with Wong Jun's letter, I lacked any proof of my words. Worse yet, I had nothing to bargain with—and it would not be unreasonable to expect bargaining, for one's life or freedom at the very least.

I settled in an unoccupied compartment of the last carriage, and watched the platform through the thickening snow as it fluttered about, whipped by the wind into elaborate whirlwinds and eddies; occasionally it even looked as if it was falling upward. Every time I saw a human figure, I clung closer to the window, but was rewarded with nothing but disappointment—it was never Jack.

I could picture him so clearly, with his gangly frame that concealed his superhuman strength and agility so well, one hand on his hat, a satchel in his other hand . . . possibly a briefcase, for all the papers. Oh, how I feared Dame Nightingale then, how certain were the moments when I thought Jack captured by her and imprisoned. I hoped if that were the case he would be important enough for Alexeevsky Ravelin.

The locomotive chugged and its whistle sounded one piercing note that became quickly muffled by the snow and the night. Clouds of steam fogged the windows and obscured the view, my heart jumped to my throat when I had to seriously consider that even if I waited three days, I might never see Jack again. The thought constricted my throat—I had lost too many friends lately, and to be completely honest I would've liked some company on such a perilous journey.

The locomotive was gaining speed and I felt restless. Unsatisfied by the view from my window, I went to stand by the door—I was in the last carriage, and the back of it was occupied by a door with a large square glass window. In the snow that seemed to fall faster as the train sped ahead, I could discern nothing but the endlessly receding rails behind us, glinting in the starlight. It was quiet, save for the train whistle and an occasional crow cawing. I glimpsed an intermittent palimpsest of one building or another—black against speeding dark—but had no hope of identifying them. Beyond the overwhelming feeling it was the second time in less than a year I had left behind everything I knew, I was so overcome by nostalgia and self-pity that at first I did not notice a quick shadow moving behind on the rails behind the train.

Curiously, the shape did not disappear from view but remained—as if it were impossibly following the train and matching its speed. Then it began to grow larger, and I realized it was gaining. It resolved from a dark speck into a figure of a man. I gasped, and clasped my hands to my throat. There was no one in the world who could run like that—except Jack.

He was close enough now for me to see his breath pouring out of his mouth in one continuous ribbon, the mad pumping of his arms. He had lost his hat, it seemed. As his feet struck the crossties, the frozen wood groaned and splintered, geysers of pebbles flew into the air.

He had almost caught up, and I struggled to open the door for him. Of course he could not see me—the train was dark inside, and he was too preoccupied to notice me struggling with the lock. He jumped, and I barely had enough time to get out of the way.

I threw myself into the empty compartment on my left, just as the glass shattered with the impact and Jack . . . There is no way to describe it. He did not fly or break through or do anything else comprehensible. For a moment, it felt as if time had stopped: jagged fragments of thick glass hung in the air, frozen, shining like Christmas tree ornaments. Jack was suspended amongst them, a sleepwalker with one foot in front of the rest of his body and the other behind, both of his arms folded in front of his face to protect it.

Then I heard the tinkling of broken glass as it rained to the floor. Time resumed its flow and Jack landed on his feet, crouching, not a yard away from me.

His gaze lingered on my prostrate form, confused and apprehensive, and I remembered he had not yet seen me in my hussar disguise.

"Jack, it's me," I said, and sat up on the floor.

He laughed, delighted. "Sasha?"

"Of course." I stood up and waited for him to unwind from his crouch—he had remained in it since landing. "Now, let's go—I have a compartment claimed, and the conductor has not yet come by."

He looked behind him, at the shattered window. The look in his eyes struck me—he seemed confused and a bit apprehensive, disoriented. He was like a man who woke from a dream and found himself on the roof of his house in a nightgown with no idea how he got there. "What will I say about that?" He pointed at the jagged hole in the door, like a guilty child.

"If you come with me right now," I said, "we can act as if you were in the compartment the whole time. There is no one else awake in this carriage, and the train is too loud for people to have heard the glass breaking."

He followed me, his satchel clasped so tightly in his hand that—when I finally managed to pry his fingers open—I saw his nails had cut semicircles into his palm.

Jack seemed in a state of shock, and I wondered if that was common in cases of extreme exertion. I had not noticed it before, but then again, I never witnessed him chasing a train for miles. His first instinct seemed to be to retreat into himself, and I let him. I even went as far as to ask the conductor, when he finally came by, for two glasses of hot tea.

"Yes sir," he said, and adjusted his billed cap, the red stripe going around it the only color on his entire person. He was dressed in a gray overcoat and even his hollow face looked gray in this light. "It is very cold in here, sir. Perhaps you would like to change cars? Some hoodlums seem to have broken the door."

I nodded. "Yes, we felt a draft. Perhaps we will move later. My companion is feeling somewhat ill, so for now, my good man, just the tea."

"I'll see about some blankets then," he said.

The conductor brought us tea and two woolen blankets. Jack drank his tea and soon resumed his customary demeanor, although he kept looking at me and my uniform.

"Unbelievable," he said. "Who would've thought that the best disguise would be so . . . colorful?"

I shrugged my new masculine shoulders. "As long as it's a change, it doesn't matter what one changes into."

We occupied a couchette carriage. Jack and I each claimed a seat, opposite of each other, and attempted to sleep the rest of the night. At first, I thought I would never fall asleep with the chugging of the train, its whistling, and the desperate cries of crows overhead. But before I knew it, I was in another train, in my proper clothes, and talking to Chiang Tse who drank his tea in a seat next to me. I dreamt of his knee accidentally brushing against mine, and woke with a start.

The sun was well up and the locomotive sped along the gleaming tracks, a black line singing through the expanse of white snow walled in by naked black trees. It was vertiginous, to think of my gigantic, flat, frozen country, crisscrossed with the black lines that connected Moscow to St. Petersburg to Sochi to Minsk, every single city in the empire. I imagined a multitude of metallic spiders weaving this web, ensnaring smaller and smaller towns, until no white snow was left.

"Sasha?" I looked up to see Jack, stretching and yawning on his bench. He sat up—or rather unrolled his long spine into a sitting position. "Did you sleep well?"

"Yes," I said. "And you . . . you are better?"

He nodded, still eyeing me cautiously. It seemed that with my disguise I had become a new person to him, and we had to get reacquainted. "I obtained everything we need last night," he said. "Do you wish to see?"

Of course I did. He handed me a sheaf of papers from his satchel, and I leafed through copies of submarine diagrams and long letters detailing boring but apparently important diplomatic details. Much of it revolved around Nightingale's instruction to her spies, and Herbert's hopeful letters to Her Majesty back in England.

Some of the letters were private correspondence—these were tied together with an ice-blue satin ribbon that reminded me strongly of Dame Nightingale. Without even looking at the signature, I recognized the meticulous, precise handwriting as hers. Interspersed with her letters were offers written with loopy, generous, words running off the page—surely Mr. Herbert's. As revolted as I felt about reading private correspondence, I peeked with one eye, and blushed. The letters were passionate—an emotion I could see in her, boiling and bubbling like a tar pit deep beneath the icy surface. They made me jealous, too—I wondered if I were capable of such love, not to mention detailing it so fearlessly on paper. Among the fiery confessions, the muffled cries of longing and desire, were references to the post of Secretary at War, to the Ottoman negotiations, and to war with Russia.

It felt almost obscene at times, the way she toyed with the fate of nations in letters interspersed with proclamations of passion, where longings of lovers forced to be apart lashed out at the entire countries, a forbidden love that raged against the world and promised to destroy it. The seas that separated them were to be conquered by the navies and submarine fleets, the impossible expanse of land was to be crossed in airships of stolen designs, to be marched across by armies in red and gold of Britain and Ottomans. Dame Nightingale was denied, and it was the world that would have to pay for it.

"We'll have to send these to Eugenia." I gathered a sheaf of letters and a few other papers that made it clear that Nightingale and quite a few frequent visitors to the Northern Star had been using their positions to gather information and to use it for military planning. "I'll hire a reliable courier in Moscow."

Jack nodded.

"My God," I said, blushing even more, and handed the letters back to Jack. "They love each other so much. And yet they are so proper when they are together."

"Mr. Herbert is married," Jack said.

"I guessed as much." I looked out of the window. "And yet, she would turn the world inside out to please him."

"This is what love does," Jack said. He leafed through the letters, absent-minded. "I wish I could have had a chance to drop them off with your aunt last night," he said. "But . . . "

I remembered his mad run, something from a nightmare, not a waking memory. Something my mind tried to forget it even saw. "Does she know? Dame Nightingale, I mean."

He nodded. "They chased me."

"So they know where you went?"

Jack yawned and stretched, smiling. "I don't think so; I jumped over the roofs and doubled back a few times, so I am fairly certain I've lost whatever pursuit was sent my way. "

"We still have to be careful."

"Yes."

We spent the rest of the morning in private ruminations. Jack's thoughts were of course a mystery to me, but my own contemplation ran toward the possibility of pursuit. They would figure out he had left the city, and they would look for him in Moscow sooner rather than later. Our only hope was to continue moving, not attracting notice. Keep running, I thought, in rhythm with the wheels; keep changing trains and cities. It occurred to me there was a seductive danger about such life, the temptation to keep moving and never look back, and to never arrive at the final destination.

Chapter 9

Moscow greeted us with fresh snow and blazing golden cathedral domes. We had to cover our eyes to protect them from the brilliance from above and below.

A hired coach took us to Balchug Street in the Zamoskvorechye District by the river. Tsar's Tavern dated back to the sixteenth century, but its old-fashioned name was now a misnomer. After recent renovations the establishment was a small hotel, with a portion of the first floor still occupied by a kitchen and a dining hall that served food and liquor.

We took rooms on the second floor. We did not plan to stay longer than was necessary, but we needed papers to travel abroad. Thankfully, my aunt's letters were enough to hasten the process.

After lunching, we went to see the Minister of Oriental Affairs. The ministry was instituted in Moscow after Siberian exploration started—as the sad result of Prince Nicholas' eagerness to exile his enemies as far north as possible. The landlocked and eastern location suited it and a few other agencies better than the imperial capital of St. Petersburg.

The ministry was not far from Balchug Street. We had only to cross the bridge over the Moscow River, already seized with black and green brittle casing of ice, pass the Kremlin, and enter a labyrinth of small twisting streets. Snow slushed underfoot, dirty and weeping, kneaded by a multitude of feet.

I kept looking at the street signs. Moscow's warrens depressed and confused me, and it seemed that no two streets met at the right angle. I was used to the orderly grid of St. Petersburg, streets razor-straight, wide. We got turned around a few times, but finally found the three-storied building of white sandstone decorated with a carved dragon painted red. I assumed the dragon was intended to be symbolic of the Orient.

Inside we found a roomy foyer with a marble fountain that was not working, and a dusty waiting room adjacent to the main office. It appeared to have been converted from what might previously have been an apartment for a struggling merchant family. A guard in full uniform nodded to us.

"What can I do for you, poruchik . . . ?"

"Menshov," I said and presented the papers with a confident flourish. "Poruchik means lieutenant," I explained to Jack's puzzled look. "This is a friend of mine, Mr. Bartram from England. We are traveling to China, and need travel papers. This is a letter from my aunt."

"Wait here," the guard said. He took my papers and disappeared into the office. We sat on the narrow sofa in the waiting room.

"I do not understand Russian bureaucracy," Jack whispered.

"No one does," I whispered back. "Just go along with it."

I was grateful to Eugenia for laying out the places for us to go to, and writing letters to present so we did not need to do or say much. It made me feel as if I wasn't really on my own, alone in the strange city.

An hour or so passed. The dusty clock on the wall ticked loudly at first, but when three in the afternoon arrived, it rang out the hours while a counterweight traveled downwards until it touched the floor and the clock stopped. There was no longer any way for me to keep track of time. Jack had a pocket watch, but it seemed improper somehow to ask him to look at it—as if the empty waiting room would be offended by my rudeness.

Finally, the guard reappeared, carrying our papers. They had been properly stamped and signed, and the guard handed them to me. "The minister asks after your aunt's health," he said.

"She is well," I assured him.

"He says he did not know the countess had a nephew."

"A distant one, on her father's side. Thrice removed." I had that small story memorized and was ready to diagram a Menshov family tree if necessary, claiming to be one of the provincial Menshovs descended from my great-grandfather's bastard brother.

The guard only nodded. "Good family. And the old countess takes care of her relatives."

It was already dark when we left the building and walked back to the tavern—the sun set early here; it wasn't even six and already the lampposts had grown hazy round halos of light, like ethereal giant dandelions. Shadows pooled by the walls of the townhouses and engulfed the river, an insatiable black mouth swallowing everything.

The tavern keeper, a man as stout as his bow-legged oak furniture, sent a kitchen boy to fetch us a courier, and Jack and I took our supper in our room while preparing the package for Eugenia. The room was furnished with two beds, a stand with a basin jug of cold water, and a couple of chamber pots. Modest but sufficient, and it allowed me an opportunity to practice washing my face while carefully avoiding my mustache.

Jack sat on his bed, his elbows on his knees, his hands dangling. The tray with his supper stood by his feet, and he didn't pay it much attention. "Are you not uncomfortable sharing a room with me?" he said.

I shook my head, still marveling at the sensation of breeze on my bare neck. "It's better than being alone in a strange place. If Nightingale and her underlings catch up with us, I'd much rather you be here than behind a wall."

"Safety in numbers," he agreed.

I finished wrapping the letters into a silk scarf I had purchased on our way to the tavern earlier that day, and wrapped the scarf in butcher's paper. This way, a casual inspection would present the package to be a modest gift. I even enclosed a note saying, "Dear Auntie, I hope you like this scarf. All is well. Love, Sasha."

We ate some cold bread soup, fortified with no small amount of sour cream, and started on the potatoes and fried fish.

"There has been a great deal lot of paper sent back and forth," I said somewhat unintelligibly, since the food in my mouth interfered with the clarity of my enunciation.

"This is what politics is all about, I think," Jack answered. "Paper. It's a good thing you have a letter from Wong Jun—it should help us."

I thought of how sad Wong Jun looked in his cell. "Yes, it should. But we also need to remember his advice: while we are in China, we will be judged by their laws."

"Ignoring that is what brought on the Opium War," Jack said, "although the Chinese call it the Unfair War—and it was. The English are . . . uninterested in behaving in any manner contrary to their own immediate benefit. It's a national shortcoming."

"Chiang Tse mentioned an official in Canton," I said. "Lin, I think—Commissioner Lin. Lin Tse-Hsu. He wrote letters to your queen, and he said again and again it was wrong to smuggle opium, that profit was a poor excuse for spreading such misery. He thought that if only she knew about it, she would stop the trade on moral grounds. I thought it fascinating that someone expected others to forego self-interest for the sake of doing the right thing."

Jack shifted uncomfortably on his bed, the plate on his bony knees tilting perilously before he steadied it. "I was not proud to be

English when the war started. However, Lin and the rest of the Qing are not so innocent—just ask your Manchu friend."

"I know about the Han people not liking the Manchu," I said. "I know they conquered East Turkestan. But you studied philosophy, you know that this is a poor rhetorical maneuver: whatever the Chinese had done does not justify what the British did."

Jack looked suitably chastised and continued picking at his supper in silence. I finished mine, addressed the package, and headed down the stairs to hand it to the courier.

The tavern was full for dinner, mostly with merchants and an occasional freedman. The owner and his contingent of waiters—all greasy young men in long aprons that once were white at some point in their tragic existence—hurried to and fro with dishes of borscht and heaping plates of pickled herring and boiled potatoes, sauerkraut and thick slices of bread.

"Hey, poruchik!" a loud voice came from behind me and I turned, feeling my stomach turn to ice, afraid to see the Nikolashki or Nightingale's spies. Instead, there were three hussars sharing a table in the corner, and they all gestured at me happily.

I held up one hand indicating I had some urgent business but I would join them as soon as I could, and went to look for the courier. He—a tall thin man whose face expressed great doubt that there was anything in the world at all worthwhile—took my package.

"Request a response," I said. "When will you return?"

"I take a train tonight," he said. "Return tomorrow, early afternoon." So he would be taking the same train we did; it seemed reassuring. "Any instructions in case you have to unexpectedly leave?"

I pressed a few silver coins in his palm. "Yes. Forward as fast as you can in care of the stationmaster at Nizhniy Novgorod." The courier nodded and even managed a wan smile once he counted the coins. With that, he disappeared, leaving me with nothing else to do but talk to the hussars.

Judging by the color of their faces and the empty vodka bottle in front of them, they were sufficiently inebriated. While Eugenia enjoyed an occasional nightcap of brandy with lemon, I had never picked up the habit of distilled spirits. It occurred to me however that in my male guise I could attempt it with minimum of judgment.

"Which regiment?" the tallest and burliest of them greeted me. He also had the most impressive mustache, and I almost felt dejected over my sparse stubble. I was sure a youthful lieutenant would have felt that way.

"Semyonovskiy," I told them. A well-rehearsed lie.

They all nodded, and the burly one offered me his hand. "Rotmistr Ivankov," he said. "And these here dolts are Cornets Petrovsky and Volzhenko."

I shook hands as firmly as I could, but doubted I inflicted any damage.

"Sit and have a drink with us," the Rotmistr said.

I nodded my agreement. The rotmistr looked like one of those people it was easier to say "yes" to than explain why you didn't want to have a drink with him.

The rotmistr ordered a round, and as we waited, the conversation took on a familiar form—we compared places of birth and length of service (I decided not to lie too much and pegged mine at six months, which provoked gales of laughter). The rotmistr in his thirties and the cornets in their twenties were clearly not old enough to had participated in the Patriotic War of 1812 —they had not even been born—and regretted it. Yes, they had traveled abroad—mostly to pacify whatever natives protested the construction of the railroads or somehow found themselves unhappy the empire's influence had reached them. And wherever it was, there were these friendly, loud, drunk men on horseback, ready to burn houses and do unspeakable things. By the time four glasses filled with vodka arrived, I felt that I needed a drink.

I had seen people drink before, and I tossed my shot back rather confidently and took a quick bite of one of the thoughtfully supplied pickles to keep from coughing.

They asked me about my life and I answered truthfully that I traveled with a friend—an Englishman, I hinted, of considerable importance. I was his local guide but said I could not tell them more.

They nodded that they understood, and I could almost see the ideas forming in their skulls, the slow, laborious movement of minds used to only the simplest of operations—they saw my uniform and heard the word "Englishman," and assumed I was on a secret mission of a great military and governmental importance. In fact, I was. In any case, I was grateful to be spared any additional lying. They started talking about their squadron—Rotmistr Ivankov was their leader—and I, relaxed by alcohol and warmth and fatigue, let my mind drift.

I thought of my conversation with Jack and wondered if I had been too harsh with him. If, really, one could not help but take the side of one's country. And then I thought of the letters to the queen written by Commissioner Lin, and I felt so angry—one of the passages Chiang Tse quoted to me from memory spoke of sameness, of how essentially alike the Chinese and the English were. It was the English and the Russians who kept denying the similarity, and instead they found Professor Ipatiev and others like him who wrote stupid books about beastliness of everyone who was not them.

The word "Turkestan" caught my attention and brought me back to the table. My new friends spoke of their impending departure to that distant province, and lamented the fact it would take the cavalry so much longer to get there than the train.

"We've been there before," the rotmistr told me, his voice made soft and intimate by alcohol. "You won't believe what it's like there, lad—steppe, yes, but also a desert. Not a single tree as far as the eye can see, just golden dry grass and red clay ringing under the hooves and the blue mountains on the horizon."

One of the cornets (I had forgotten which was which) leaned on the table with both elbows and whispered to me, "I wonder sometimes, what right we have . . . The Turks who live there, they live on horseback and always move around. They take their yurts with them, and they just go—Turkestan, Mongolia, China-land . . . all the same to them. And there's such beauty all around, I wonder why we have to take it and call it ours."

"That's empire building," the other cornet said, without any noticeable trace of irony. "If the tsar-emperor wants it to lay a railroad through, then he can take it. Not like those people are doing anything with that land anyway."

"Commissioner Lin was sent to Turkestan," I slurred, both my memory and my tongue getting away from me. I felt his hurt, his puzzlement: If you know it is poison, why are you bringing it to us? If you know that opium destroys lives, if you know enough to make it illegal in your country, why do you keep selling it to our people? I felt like crying—I recognized that puzzlement of a noble man in the face of betrayal, I recognized it from Chiang Tse's look back in the Crane Club. The inability to recognize such callous, cynical disregard for truth and justice because he was as unable to harbor such feelings as I was unable to fly.

"Cheer up, lad," the rotmistr told me. "There's hope for the empire yet. Now, how about a toast to the emperor's health?"

Jack came down the stairs, concern written clearly on his long face, to find me in the company of three fairly drunk hussars—truth be told, I was getting a bit tipsy myself, because they kept calling me a bare-faced youth and buying me drinks. I consumed tremendous quantities of gherkins and pickled herring attempting to stave off intoxication, but by the time I saw Jack, my vision was blurred, I laughed quite readily, and the hussars had persuaded me to join them in a song.

"This . . . this is my charge," I explained to my new friends, while poking Jack in the chest repeatedly. Then I swept my arm in the air, indicating the rotmistr and both cornets, and informed Jack, "And these are my friends. We were just singing 'God Save the Tsar'."

"How nice," Jack said. "We do have to turn in—we have a long day tomorrow."

"Just one more drink," the rotmistr said in passable English. "Please, join us for one drink, and then we'll return your boy."

"Very well." Jack pulled up the chair and shook hands.

I felt misty-eyed, so happy everyone was getting along so well, and that Jack did not seem inclined to snub anyone. I also missed my mother with a sudden intensity, and wished we had taken a long route to Moscow, stopping by Trubetskoye. I decided to write her a letter instead, as soon as I could hold a pen. Meanwhile, Jack and the rotmistr started a discussion about Asia.

"The thing is," the rotmistr was saying, swaying a bit with liquor, a fire of righteous conviction bright in his eyes, "Russia needs to embrace its Asian nature. Scythians, yes? Our ancestors, and yet Asiatic. We need to embrace that."

"Is that so?" Jack said, smiling. "It seems to me that Emperor Constantine along with Peter the Great and a few others tsars are quite intent on being embracing Europe."

I rolled my eyes: this was a discussion I had heard many times, and even participated in myself. It did not seem to have a resolution or even any purpose beyond providing a thin excuse for discussing Russia's destiny as a nation and its delicate position perched as it was between the East and the West, like a Georgian circus rider between two horses. Their voices buzzed in my ears as my mind drifted to the train ride with Chiang Tse, who seemed so curious then of the entire notion of westernization. I was half asleep by the time Jack tapped me on the shoulder and dragged me upstairs, to the accompaniment of the hussars' laughter.

THE NEXT MORNING I WOKE UP WITH A HEADACHE AND A SENSE OF calamity; there was an uncomfortable sensation burning in the pit of my stomach as if I had done something inappropriate the night before but couldn't quite remember it. I had slept in my clothes, and my shoulder hurt where my reverse corset had rubbed it raw. I sat up and stretched, trying to readjust everything that had shifted during sleep. My mouth tasted especially foul.

The other bed was empty, and I worried until the door opened and Jack appeared with two plates of fried eggs, cheese, and bread and butter. "Eat this," he said and set one next to me. "Believe me, there's nothing better for a hangover than a full stomach. I'll get tea."

He disappeared again and I ate, my mind clearing as eggs and bread and butter smothered the queasy feeling in my belly. I was glad to have Jack on my side.

"What are we doing today?" I asked when he returned with two glasses of very strong and sweet tea.

"I would suggest staying where we are," he answered, and started on his breakfast. "I went out this morning, picked up newspapers and a few penny dreadfuls—some French ones, and *The String of Pearls*."

"I like those," I said. A day spent indoors reading appealed to me; I also saw an opportunity to talk to Jack about some of the conversation from last night.

We read most of the morning; both of us felt anxious to keep on our journey and yet eager to hear from Eugenia. We scanned the newspapers, but apart from a brief mention of the robbery of the St. Petersburg house of a visiting British dignitary, it contained nothing pertaining to us. Finally, I had got a grasp on the elusive memory that had been nibbling on my mind on and off all morning. "Jack," I said. (It was easier for us to be on first name basis when we both were men; I suspected we would revert to the polite form of address once I was back in proper clothing.) "I heard what you said last night to the rotmistr."

He put down the magazine he was flipping through. "What exactly are you referring to? If memory serves, the rotmistr and I had quite a prolonged talk."

"You said that you've been to China. And you mentioned something about East Turkestan."

"They all served in West Turkestan," Jack said. "They said they were going there again."

"And Commissioner Lin was exiled in East Turkestan. And you went to China. And there was no mention of you in those newspapers before 1841. About ten years ago."

"What are you asking me?" He had such a direct, steady gaze, it was difficult to suspect him of anything unsavory.

"Have you ever worked for the East India Trading Company? Did you return to London in 1841 after the hostilities started?"

"You are astute," Jack said. "I was never involved with the smuggling; I was a mere youth, a member of the crew on a merchant ship. We were caught in Canton Harbor in March 1839 when the Chinese demanded the surrender of all opium and detained all foreign ships so that the smugglers could not escape the country. We were only allowed to leave after all opium was destroyed."

"Why didn't you tell me this before?"

He shrugged. "I have told you more about myself than I ever told anyone, except under duress. I worried that your . . . idealism would not allow you to judge me kindly. And, to be quite honest, you already had quite a lot to contend with: my criminal past and my neglect of the natural sciences."

I had to smile at that. I could also understand his omission—he did want me to like him, of that I had no doubt. "I understand," I said. "I was simply curious, and never had intention of judging you."

He laughed, visibly relieved. "Oh, thank you," he said. "I should've known that your infatuation with Commissioner Lin would lead you to the truth of the matter. I've never been to East Turkestan myself, but I do have an acquaintance who has—who went there to see Commissioner Lin."

"Who was it?" I awaited the answer with a superstitious dread that I had already guessed it.

"Dame Nightingale," Jack said. "She does not miss a chance to see an old enemy of the British Empire humiliated."

I put my book away. "But you told me she's not really interested in China."

"That's what she told me."

I searched through my satchel to get my pen. "Fine, but now I need to write a letter to my mother."

"Make sure you do not mention where we are in case it gets intercepted."

"You need not tell me things I already know," I said. I tried not to be uncivil—he did bring me breakfast, after all; I just disliked being treated as a child. Somehow it was more acceptable from the hussars: at least, they thought I was sixteen and fresh out of a military academy. But even so, they spoke to me in a way men had seldom spoken to me before—as if I were their equal, to be teased a little due to my youth, but otherwise as one of them. I worried I might get used to it.

Jack went back to his reading as I contemplated my letter. I was supposed to uphold the lie of staying with friends, and I could betray neither my whereabouts nor my concerns. Instead I poured my anxiety into the only form available to me, which, by happy coincidence, was something she would most likely understand. I did not think my mother a dull woman, but her interests lay firmly in the sphere of the domestic and the courtly.

"Dear Mother," I wrote, "I miss you every day, and I cannot wait for the summer when we will be able to spend our days together in the happy embrace of our home. I hope your cats and servants are well, and your days are filled with serenity and contentment. Is the river frozen yet? I hope it is, and that the village children skate and amuse you with their merriment.

"I have to confess I write to you not only because I am feeling deprived of your company or because it is my duty as you daughter, but I also hope to receive advice from you on matters of the heart. Even though Eugenia visited with me before my departure, you know well she is not the one to advise on courtship matters.

"I confess also that despite my great interest in my studies and my hopes to continue them until I accumulate enough courses to be called a Baccalaureate, two young men came recently to my attention. Both are of foreign origin and both possess pleasant qualities; although neither had proposed, I feel reasonably confident that at least one of them might be compelled in that direction with a most subtle demonstration of my benevolent interest."

"Sasha," Jack called from his bed, where he sprawled, reading. Apparently, the change of costume on my part allowed him to dispense with any semblance of courtly behavior—which was an asset, I supposed, since traveling together and being elaborately polite seemed unnecessarily taxing.

"What?" I answered, also unceremoniously.

"Did you know that the Masked Temerain could peel his face off?"

"He was burned to the crisp, as I recall, and disfigured. What of it?"

Jack smiled at me fondly. "I just wondered if you knew. He is quite an extraordinary creature, that Temerain."

"So are you," I said, still a bit uneasy about Jack's leaping prowess. "Maybe I should write a penny dreadful about you."

His grin grew wider and he folded his long arms behind his head, staring dreamily into the ceiling. "Someone ought to. As long as I don't die in it."

"You can't die in a serial," I told him. "Maybe if someone wrote about you they would explain how you were able to do the things that you do." It started to snow outside, and I felt grateful to be inside, where it was warm and cozy. I pulled the woolen blanket around my shoulders, making a nest of sorts for myself, my ink bottle, and my unfinished letter. "Well? Are you going to tell me?"

"You're busy," Jack said.

"I'm not. I can finish this letter later."

He sighed then. "No, I wasn't always capable of leaping over buildings. I was born poor, and quite undistinguished in any way. My parents managed to make ends meet, and I helped as I could—sometimes I worked in a textile factory, sweeping the floors and cleaning up; sometimes I stole. When I was fifteen, I left home and got hired as a sailor on a ship named *The Oxford*, and we left for China. I had a propensity for languages, and I learned a smattering of Cantonese from a Chinaman traveling with us by the time we landed in Canton. This was in 1839, when things were deteriorating so badly. My ship stayed anchored at Canton, unable to take cargo or unload, because no one was not even thinking about anything that wasn't opium."

"I get the picture," I said. "Chiang Tse told me about it."

"There were Chinese merchants who helped with the smuggling. The streets adjacent to the English factories were choked with opium dens and supply shops. I was a boy, with nothing to do. It was in these shops that I found something unusual."

"A wise Chinese mystic," I suggested, being familiar with the conventions of the penny dreadfuls.

"No," he said. "A Portuguese man, from Macao—he had come to Canton to patronize the opium dens there, and he . . . I don't really know much of his story, but he said he would teach me to do things that no one else could do."

"And the fact that he spent his days in the opium den did not seem suspicious?"

He laughed. "As I said, I was bored. But he did keep his word."

Jack smoothed his hair, remembering. "This Portuguese man, Paolo was his name, he spoke of strange things—of how opium unlocked something within him, enabled him to fly. He said he would teach me to fly."

I made a face. "Please tell me that you didn't become one of . . . those."

"You mean opium smokers?" Jack smiled. "No, although hashish eating was something I picked up later in India. But no, Paolo spoke of unlocking my mind's hidden abilities . . . I suspect that he was intoxicated, insane, and extremely dull, but there wasn't much else to do. His teachings seemed to be based on imperfectly understood Confucian philosophy and local superstitions, as well as whatever foolishness he had learned in his homeland."

"And? He told you some magic words, made you a potion?"

Jack grinned and picked up his booklet. "I shall not tell you anything more if you keep interrupting me."

"Sorry."

"Oh no, it is too late. You'll have to wait for the next time I feel like talking."

I sulked. "You are just trying to be like one of those serials you love so much."

"Maybe. Go read about your Sweeney Todd."

"The stories are all the same," I complained. "I read *The String of Pearls* a million times, and all the other Sweeney Todd stories are the same. Tell me how you became Spring Heeled Jack."

"I will," he said. "Just not now: I have to maintain my mystery, after all, or you won't ever want to talk to me."

I sighed and went back to my letter. There was at least two weeks on the train ahead of us and I decided he would tell me during the journey. At least it would keep the boredom at bay.

"I feel conflicted," I wrote to my mother, "for even though I have no immediate plans of marriage, I feel I should be moved by the attentions of at least one of these young men. One of them especially has proven himself a loyal friend who has risked much to help me, and who was always considerate and kind. I feel I should be returning his interest, and I wonder whether I should compel myself to develop affection for this fine gentleman.

"Now, the other gentleman is a more complicated case—he is also a good friend and a kind companion, but I fear I have not have many opportunities to talk to him of late. Moreover, I fear that if I were to start a courtship with him, society would not approve. He is a foreigner, and recent political tensions may prevent any possibility of marital happiness. And yet . . . "

A knock on the door interrupted my epistolary exercises. I

rushed to the door before Jack, and found myself face to face with Rotmistr Ivankov.

"Looking good, lad," he said and slapped my shoulder with enough force to make my teeth chatter. "Wild night last night, yeah?"

"I've seen wilder," I lied. "What can I do for you, rotmistr?"

"There are some Englishmen downstairs, interviewing the staff," he said. "They are looking for a very tall Englishman and someone who's traveling with him. I don't suppose you'd know anything about it, but I figured better safe than sorry and that I should drop you a word. In case it's someone you know, even though I've never seen those folks they're looking for, and neither have my cornets." He gave me an exaggerated wink and was gone before I could muster a thank you.

Chapter 10

Jack and I tried not to panic as we threw everything we had unpacked the day before back into our satchels—at least, I tried not to panic. Jack seemed composed, but I felt certain it was playacting. Who could stay calm considering the terror of facing Dame Nightingale? I was afraid of her even before her letters had shown me a true depth of her passion—and I now knew of how much love and, conversely, hatred she was capable. Now I was mad with fear.

"Sasha," Jack called me. "You must control your emotion. You are as pale as a ghost and look guiltier than sin. Appear casual, walk easy. They are looking for a girl, not a hussar."

It felt like a bad dream, listening for footsteps and voices. Finally, the sense of fear and helplessness solidified into a piercing realization the people who were looking for us would not stop, and they would unlikely have any reservations about killing us. I forced these thoughts out of my mind and pulled the straps on the satchel closed. Jack stood by the window, eyeing the snow outside.

"We could jump out of the window," he said. "I mean, I could jump. You won't be recognized."

"You think so?" I said, uncomfortable with the idea of going near the spies all by myself.

"Unless you want me to carry you as I jump," he said. "I have never tried it before, with a person."

I did a quick calculation in my mind. "If you jump out of this window carrying me, the impact will either kill me or break some bones at the least."

"There's the answer then." He smiled, encouraging. "You can do it. Besides, someone has to pay the bill."

I picked up my satchel and sighed. "I'll meet you at the bridge. Then we can go to the station, meet the train from St. Petersburg, and see if Eugenia sent any messages."

Jack nodded and opened the window. Cold wind lifted the thin white curtains and a few snowflakes danced into the room, melting the instant warm air touched them. Jack stood a moment with his foot on the windowsill, looking at the street below. The next second, he leaned out of the window as if estimating the distance, and then he was gone in a swirl and a flap of his long coat.

I fought the temptation to rush to the window and see but there were voices outside. I shut the window with nary a look and swiftly exited our room. In the hallway I saw three men in tweed jackets that were much too light for the weather, and it took great effort to not speed my steps or otherwise betray my distress. I nodded to them as I passed with my newly developed swagger, and they nodded back, showing no signs of recognition.

I thundered down the stairs, forgetting decorum, and felt like I drew a breath for the first time in years when I entered the downstairs dining room. Warm smells of cabbage and fish washed over me. I found the owner, let him know we were leaving earlier than anticipated, and paid for our lodging.

The rotmistr and his two cornets sat at the same table as before—in fact, in my panic and confusion I thought for a moment that they were always there, not real people but mere decorations. The rotmistr raised his gigantic hand and waved at me; I had the presence of mind to wave back. The cornets saluted without getting up, and I returned the salute. Just as I turned to leave the tavern, there was a commotion outside, a ringing of hooves and terrified whinnying of horses, and a woman's scream.

The usual din in the tavern died down; but only my friends the hussars and myself were foolish enough to bolt outside. The picture we discovered made my heart feel like it was frozen to my ribs by a sudden gust of especially cold wind.

Dame Nightingale herself, dressed in furs, screamed and pointed, as several men in civilian clothes—but with military bearing—circumvented an upset carriage, under the wreckage of which two heavily dressed figures struggled weakly. I assumed Jack had spooked the horses with his leaping, and it was he Dame Nightingale directed her pursuit after.

Passersby gathered around the wreckage and helped the passengers out; one of the horses thrashed on the ground with a broken leg. Discussion started among a merchant and two bureaucrats about whether it should be put down and by who. Freedmen, factory workers, waiters from the tavern as well as a few diners with their napkins still around their necks appeared, and a sizeable knot of people assembled, clogging Balchug Street. The English had to wrestle through the crowd, and their progress was slow and reluctant.

Dame Nightingale turned and saw me; her eyes tore through my disguise as if it were mere smoke, flimsy enough to be dispelled with a single breath, and gave a slow smile. “Sasha,” she said. “How good to see you.” With a flick of her wrist she directed the attention of the men in civilian clothing to me. The immediately moved toward me.

“Now now,” the rotmistr said. (I was so terrified of Nightingale I’d forgotten he was there.) “Leave the young man alone.”

The cornets drew closer to me, their hands on the hilts of their sabers, and I remembered that I wore one as well.

My dead Uncle Pavel had a larger, broader hand than I—the hilt of his saber felt too wide and too heavy, but its curve fitted into my palm snugly enough.

The English, all moving at once, as if their movements were mutually articulated by invisible strings, put their hands in the pockets of their coats. I assumed their attire concealed weapons, pistols or knives.

The rotmistr moved to my left, his shoulder almost brushing mine, and advanced half a step in front of me, as if to shield me from the English. Thankfully, his broad back obscured the sight of Dame Nightingale's snakelike stare, freeing me from her hypnotic influence.

"Stand down, rotmistr," I whispered in Russian. "They won't dare do anything here, in the middle of the street, with all these people around them."

"Right you are, little hussar," the rotmistr said. He turned to glance at me, his grin flashing a full foot over my head. "They'll wait till you're all by your lonesome somewhere secluded. You better run along and find your friend. We'll keep them entertained here, if that is acceptable?"

"Thank you," I whispered, and stepped back until his large frame concealed me from the English view entirely. I had left the sidewalk, and struggled through the bushes fringing the side of the tavern. I turned and ran, Nightingale's voice echoing faintly behind me, my boots sloshing through the snow.

I dashed across the street and ducked between two buildings. The yards behind them connected and I ran through them until I was well clear of the crowded scene on Balchug Street. The yards, surrounded by tall townhouses with dark windows, had accumulated veritable mountains of snow. The din of the street was extinguished by its softness, and—stumbling through knee-deep drifts—it felt as if I were miles away.

The rotmistr and the cornets had done a wonderful thing for us, even though they had met us only the night before. I was lucky,

I supposed, that the rotmistr was so kind, and didn't take my behavior as an affront—he seemed rather amused by it, truth be told. I smiled when I remembered the way he grinned and winked, like a conspiratorial child.

I found an exit back onto the street, and stumbled out of the snow, stomping my feet on the pavement. The crowd thronged far behind me, and I could just make out the rotmistr's head above the crush. I could discern some shuffling and pushing where he and the cornets were, and could hear a shrill rising female voice, but could not understand what she was saying, or even who it was with any certainty. However, there didn't seem to be any Englishmen emerging from the crowd, so I sheathed my saber, changed the satchel from my left hand to my right, and ran toward the bridge. As I crossed it, the icy air pricked my chest from the inside with a million stinging needles.

I stopped to rest only when I reached the embankment on the opposite side. It seemed quieter there in the deep blue shadow of the Kremlin, and I walked slowly, looking for Jack. He wouldn't have gone far.

I found him sitting on the frozen, snow-covered steps leading from the foot of the bridge down to the water, black and sluicing over the fringe of ice that was forming on the embankment's stone walls. "Are you well?" he called to me.

"Yes," I said. "But they are after us—they'll get here soon if the rotmistr fails to hold them off."

"The rotmistr?"

"Come on—we have to hurry."

Jack leapt up the steps and I had trouble keeping up with his pace. We decided to walk to the next bridge and cross back into Zamoskvorechye, and head for the train station. We would meet the St. Petersburg train and intercept the courier returning with a message from my aunt. We planned to then hire a coach to take us north, to the Eastern Station where we could catch the train heading to Nizhniy Novgorod and further east, all the way to Turkestan and China. I hoped we would confound our pursuers enough to lose them—there were five train stations in Moscow, and they had no way of knowing which one we would head to, even if they guessed that we were leaving the city.

There was a thundering of hooves behind us, and a small group of hussars rounded the Kremlin wall and headed toward the embankment. They wore the same colors as the rotmistr—blue and red with white pelisses. I waved at them and called out, "Are you with the Muscovy Regiment?"

"Yes, lad," one of them replied. "Semionovsky?"

"Indeed," I answered. "Listen, if you're heading down Balchug, there are some Englishmen who started fisticuffs with three hussars just a little while back. Rotmistr Ivankov was there."

"The rotmistr?" the man sat straighter in his saddle. His breath clouded the air and left a thin patina on the silver tack of his bay gelding. The horse snorted, breathing out great plumes of dense white vapor, and I could see hairs on its muzzle rimed with hoarfrost. "We better go see if he needs help. Thanks for telling us, lad."

"What was that about?" Jack asked as the hussars departed.

"You don't understand any Russian?" We had always spoken in English, but I was taken aback to realize he never understood a word I said in Russian, as infrequently as that happened.

He shook his head. "I know, very lacking on my part. Maybe you can teach me on the train . . . after you explain about the rotmistr and the hussars."

"Only if you finish telling me about your life," I said.

"It's a deal," he answered. "We better hurry, though, to avoid Nightingale's men catching up with us."

"No need," I said happily. "Those hussars will detain them and perhaps incapacitate them altogether."

IT WAS SO COLD THAT THE INSIDE OF MY NOSE FELT FROZEN SOLID, and my lips split and chapped with every breath I took. Jack loped ahead of me, intent on arriving at the train station before the St. Petersburg train, his boots moving through blackened slush with aggravating ease as I struggled after, wondering if I would ever restore the shine to my boots.

We made it to the station just in time. As Jack forged fearlessly ahead, I looked around, dreading I might catch a glimpse of the Englishmen or Nightingale. It did not matter that, rationally, there was no possibility of finding us so quickly, especially waylaid by the hussars—Dame Nightingale had become a creature of a nightmare to me, omnipotent, omniscient, and unstoppable in her malice.

Jack turned around and waved to me. I hurried after him, pushing through the dense crowd with my shoulder. Say what you will, but I took a certain relish and satisfaction in behaving in such an unladylike way. I now understood why Eugenia walked as she did, why her strides were always so long and unrestrained and mannish.

The courier had returned, and he had a letter. A wave of relief washed over me—I did not allow myself to think about everything that could go wrong up until this moment. I tore into the envelope as Jack paid the courier—who looked tired with his stubbly cheeks and red-rimmed eyes.

"Dearest Sasha," Eugenia wrote.

"Thank you for your thoughtful gift—it was received as well as the notes from your friends. Give them my thanks for housing you for the time of your vacation, even though you do have to miss the season. Your mother was quite distraught about that, but she came to share my view that the warm climes are beneficial for a young lady of your fragile constitution. I hope Sochi is nice, and you are having a good time with your friends.

"Regarding your question—I should be able to take care of your request soon. Unfortunately, the parties involved are both stubborn and inaccessible, but I am certain a small payment will ease my attempts to gain their company. As for our mutual friend who is in the care of Captain Mishkin, he is well and sends his regards. I have started a correspondence with him via the captain, who has been quite kind about it. Your friend expressed his hope for your success, and I join my wishes to his."

"What does she say?" Jack interrupted my reading. I looked up only to see that the crowd had dispersed considerably, and was probably boarding the outbound train. Jack and I stood nearly alone in the middle of the waiting hall.

"Let's sit down," I said.

We found an available bench where I hunkered down and derived a small measure of comfort from being somewhat hidden. "Everything is well," I said. "She received the documents, and started correspondence with Wong Jun. If we need to find something out from him, we can write to her."

Jack kicked out his long legs and stuffed his hands into his pockets, sighing impatiently. "Everything takes forever."

"You're welcome to leap all the way to St. Petersburg if you want."

"I can't."

"Of course not. So now you have to obey the same limitations as the rest of us mere mortals. Come on, we need to get to Nizhniy Novgorod."

We walked out into the cold, and hailed a coach cab.

"Eugenia will get those documents before Constantine, I'm sure," I said as we settled snugly into the dark interior smelling of leather and horse sweat. "I just hope that Wong Jun's letter will be sufficient when we reach China."

"It's better than nothing," Jack responded. "But the Chinese do not trust foreigners and they know very little about them . . . us, I mean."

"And?"

"Sometimes, they think you're the devil and want you away from them. I can't tell you how many times I was shot at for no reason."

"Well, you are English."

"Is that a good enough reason?"

I thought for a moment. "If there is a war? Of course. You can't expect people to extend the courtesy you're not willing to give. I bet the English did not stop to see whether they were shooting at peaceful Chinese civilians or soldiers."

"How do you know?"

"That is how wars are." I wiggled my fingers, trying to find a suitable way of explaining this phenomenon. "They are fought in a very general way. Chinese shoot at English, English shoot at Chinese, and no one stops to verify credentials. I just hope that with the war over they at least look at your papers before shooting."

"Of course," Jack said. "At least, for the Europeans. I hear that the Manchus and the Taipings happily shoot each other on sight these days. Some of the Taipings have defied the Manchus by wearing their hair long and loose rather than in a braided pigtail as the law requires."

"I am not surprised if you consider how the Manchus enforced their hairstyles."

Jack gave me a long look and laughed. "You know quite a bit about Chinese politics, don't you?"

"No, just what Chiang Tse told me." I peered out of the window of the cab, to avoid meeting Jack's gaze. "I hope he is well."

WE CAUGHT THE TRAIN TO NIZHNIY NOVGOROD WITH NO TROUBLE, and as soon as we settled in our couchette compartment, I stretched on one of the seats and slept, exhausted. Even the whistles of the train could not rouse me.

They could not rouse me, but they colored my dreams—I dreamt about being on the train, swaying, clanging, sparks flying from the chugging iron wheels. I stood by the glass door at the tail end of the last carriage, watching the tracks recede in a dazzling flash—shining metal, hoar-frosted ties. And I saw a dark figure cutting through the brilliance. My heart jumped to my throat as nameless unreasoned dread enveloped me and the figure approached, fast, faster than the train could travel.

It was Dame Nightingale, running in a strange, simian gait, her impossibly long thick arms with giant hands dragging on the ground aiding her. She ran almost on all fours although remained upright. Nightingale thrust her massive arms forward, grabbing onto the crossties, and pulling the rest of her behind; her neck had elongated and her eyes, unblinking, fixed me with their hypnotic stare.

I sat upright before I even realized I was awake, and came to awareness gasping for air, my arms outstretched, reaching or pleading. My eyes snapped open a split second later.

Jack who was reading on the seat opposite of mine carefully considered me, his eyes especially pale and gray that day. "Bad dream?"

"Not just a dream," I said, and rubbed my eyes. "The waking reality is altogether lacking in cheer as well."

He laughed. "We're safe here, at least for now. Rest, sleep, read."

I stared out of the window instead. Dazzling white all around us, with black dots of crows and the blue smudge of forest on the horizon. We passed an occasional small station, where the locomotive did not deign to stop, and the village women, wrapped in woolen shawls, holding chickens and geese plump and ready for Christmas, watched the train as it sped by, momentarily locking eyes with me and losing this contact as our carriage flew by. It seemed fitting, such great speed so contradictory to making more than fleeting human connection. I thought of it for a while, as villages and their wooden cottages half-buried in white appeared outside of the train and melted back into brilliantine mist of snow and cold; the faster we went the less time there was to simply look. Then again, I couldn't really complain—because of this speed, we would be in Nizhny Novgorod in a few hours, and then the train would take us all the way to Kazan, Perm, Yekaterinburg, Omsk, Novonikolaevsk, Irkutsk, Ulan Ude, and finally . . . Beijing.

"Have you ever been to Siberia?" I asked. "I wonder what Irkutsk is like."

"It's a trading town," Jack answered. "Trading with China—there's gold and silk and tea. Lots of mosquitoes in the summer, but now everything is frozen solid. Even Yenisey is frozen, I reckon, and it is such a grand river."

"What else?"

He shrugged. "As I understand it, the town not that large, really. There're traders, a lot of Chinese, and the railroad business. Some furriers go through every now and again. There are some local tribes, herding caribou or whatever it is they herd, but I've been told that ever since the Russian Empire took a foothold there, they've declined. A price of progress, I suppose."

"What about Ulan Ude?" I asked. In my anxiety, I was eager for any information about new places, however vague or incomplete. I wished I had a book of some sort—only there were no travel guides for Siberia, because who would go there voluntarily, on their leisure?

Jack scratched his head. "In Ulan Ude, there are Buryats who look Asiatic . . . I only know what Nightingale told me."

"Nightingale? How did she know that you were going to Siberia?"

Jack made a face, shook his head. "Sasha, what do I have to do for you to stop suspecting me at every turn? We talked about Siberia while discussing the possibility of land war with China, after Russia is taken care of. She thought if the south of China is already overrun by the Taipings, a strike from north would finish it. But these are idle speculations."

I nodded. "Sorry, I did not mean to accuse you."

"It is of no matter." He still frowned, and unrolled the booklet detailing some adventure or another of one Dick Turpin. It didn't seem a good time to ask him more questions, and I decided to let him be.

I remembered about my letter to my mother, and settled to write some more. I could mail it from Nizhniy Novgorod, I told myself, or any other city on our way—the stops were supposed to last anywhere from half an hour to two hours, sufficient time to mail it whenever the letter was finished. In truth, I think I just enjoyed the opportunity to write down my thoughts. The act of writing was as important as my intent to mail it to mother.

"It is difficult for me to think about that," I continued, "and my thoughts, unless they are pinned to the paper with my pen, get away from me. I know that you fear deep in your heart I will end up like Eugenia, and you think it would be a tragedy. While I have not made up my mind, I can see many benefits to such an arrangement, at least until the emperor turns his attention to the inheritance laws. Unless I am legally allowed to possess property while being married, I will surely feel much less conflicted on this matter.

"As it is now, I would have to surrender everything that is

mine by birth to the dubious care of whatever man that becomes my husband, and how am I to know that he would be wise in its dispensation? Moreover, why does the law seems to think I would not be capable of making decisions about what belongs to me? In our classes, we always hear that a woman's or an Asian's brain is inferior to that of a European man. Yet the Chinese and the girls get grades as good or better than any Caucasoid male, even in classes which are designed and taught by European men—as are the texts we study. It surely seems to me that women would be capable of administering an estate—Aunt Eugenia certainly is—and the Chinese are capable of taking care of their own country.

"And this brings me to another concern, dear mother. I know how indifferent to politics you are (I am not talking of the palace gossip here), but please do bear with me this one time. I fear our contempt for our own Asiatic origin has blinded us to who our allies truly are. I wonder how the world would be reshaped if Russia allied itself not with the degeneracy and false superiority of European empires, but with the might of the Orient?"

Just as I wrote these words, the train slowed down and soon stopped entirely. I looked up to peer through the window, and discovered it had completely frosted over. I scratched at the frost with my fingernails, and saw an iced over wooden platform which could not—I hoped it was not—be Nizhniy Novgorod, for its apparent lack of any interesting architecture or cathedrals.

"Why are we stopping here?" I asked Jack.

He shrugged, without looking up from his penny dreadful. "Probably picking up some passengers. Some chose to board in remote regions to avoid the crowded stations for personal reasons. More discreet that way."

There was a small hut on the platform, as I could discern after pressing my cheek to the frozen windowpane to melt the frost. A pavilion with a flat roof on which the snow mounded like sugar in a sugar bowl, and three wooden walls. Inside it were two figures, bundled up against the cold in what looked like fur cloaks made of the skins of the entire contents of Noah's ark—no two pelts were alike. The whole gave an impression of a moving cat-and-dog fight as they started to shamble slowly toward the train, dragging behind them two fairly large sea chests.

They came through the doors of our carriage a moment later, and even though the carriage was almost empty, took a compartment across the aisle from us. I studied their chests, covered in intricate carvings of whales and fishes and dragons, and secured by wide leather straps. The two chests occupied most of the floor of the compartment, and the passengers had to carefully arrange their feet shod in heavy boots with fur spats. I couldn't help but feel they were overdressed for the weather, even if it was frigid outside.

It took the new arrivals a while to unburden themselves from their fur hats, fur gloves, fur everything. Their cloaks were lined with gold-colored silk, an unexpected flash of refinement.

I noticed Jack was watching them too: his pose, while seemingly nonchalant, was wound with hidden tension—his right hand dangled between his knees, still holding the booklet, but his left was thrust into the pocket of his coat. His feet rested flatly on the floor, his leg muscles tightening under the fabric of his trousers.

The strangers were not English, as I had feared, but Chinese—there was no mistaking their facial features and soft voices that spoke in what I recognized as Cantonese. Yet, their hair was not braided into a long pigtail, but hung loosely around their faces, looking as if it had not been cut in some years. The clothing they wore under their furs was made of silk, but tattered and dirty, and I could not decide if they were Han robes. I was certain they were not Manchu.

One of them realized that I was staring. "Kuan Yu," he introduced himself and bowed, withdrawing his hands into sleeves sporting an unintentional fringe.

"Poruchik Menshov," I said brightly in English. "Any relation to Admiral Kuan Tien Pei?"

The man laughed then, showing small white teeth. "Not that I know of, but I do suspect the admiral honors Kuan Ti, the god of war, as do I."

Jack listened to this exchange, visibly relaxing. It occurred to me that he did not lower his guard when he realized our new neighbors were Chinese, but only at the mention of some pagan deity I was sure Chiang Tse mentioned to me at some point. "You're not a Christian then?" Jack interjected.

Our interlocutor and his companion traded a quick look. "No, of course not," the one who had remained quiet so far said in fairly good English.

"You have long hair instead of shaved temples and queue," Jack said.

"My father died," said Kuan Yu.

"Mine too," added his companion. "We are not Christian. You're Christian, you're an Englishman."

Jack nodded.

"Funny," said the second man. "There were other English at the station with us, and now I don't know where they went."

"There were?" Jack and I said in one voice.

"Yes," the man said. "My name is Liu Zhi."

"Nice to meet you," Jack said, but already his gaze drifted toward the doors of the carriage.

We did not have to wait long—the door opened, and eight men, dressed in civilian clothing, tweed and fur collared-cloaks, filed in. In the narrow corridor of the couchette carriage, their numbers would be of no advantage, I thought, even if they noticed us. To prevent such recognition, I wrapped my shoulders in my pelisse and acted as if I were asleep sitting up, my head resting against the windowpane. Jack's gray eyes flicked toward me, and he shot me a quick smile as he unrolled his Dick Turpin booklet.

The Englishmen looked at all the passengers as they passed; I could not see through the walls of the compartments, of course, but I could see their slow progress down the corridor, their heads swinging to the right and then left. I peeked out of the compartment, and wished we had chosen the sleeping carriage with closing doors; it was Jack who objected to those, on account of avoiding potential traps.

The first of the Englishmen reached us. I saw the back of his head as it swiveled to look at the Chinese. He had tiny black hairs on the back of his neck, fine as cat fur, bristling over the white scarf he wore over the ruddy pelt of his fur collar. When he turned toward us, my gaze drifted toward the letter in my lap. Out of the corner of my eye I noticed Jack sink lower in his seat, slouching forward and hunching over.

The man did not move on; he remained where he was, staring at us. When the silence became uncomfortable and I looked up, reluctantly meeting the stare of his pale watery eyes. "May I help you, sir?" I said in my most masculine voice.

He smiled slowly and gave a half-turn half-nod to his accomplices. While his back was turned, Jack sprung. He lacked grace, but he made up this shortcoming in raw power. He barreled into the man and sent him stumbling backward, into the arms of his colleagues.

Someone in the front end of the carriage screamed, and there was a shuffling of steps as passengers fled the carriage. Soon, it would be just the two of us, eight Englishmen, and nowhere to run. Jack, however, was undeterred by the circumstance. He strained like a man trying to single-handedly move a heavy piano, pushing the knot of Englishmen back the way they had come in.

A shot rang out. I smelled smoke, and the acrid scent of burning sulfur and paper. I unsheathed my dead uncle's saber and made my way into the narrow corridor.

I wanted to help Jack, but there was no getting around him to reach the struggling Englishmen. I was so intent on finding a way to circumvent him that I did not immediately notice both of the Chinese gentlemen had arisen as well, their fur cloaks donned anew.

"Stand aside," one of them shouted. I obeyed on instinct, falling into one of the empty couchette compartments as they pushed past me. I expected them to be stopped by the obstacle of Jack as I had, but instead—I do not quite know how to describe it, since my eyes refused to believe the sight—they leapt into the air and sailed with the slow grace of birds riding air currents, over Jack and the Englishmen he was struggling with, and landed softly on the far side of Nightingale's agents.

Confused shouting and thrashing of limbs filled the end of the corridor, and the fur of the Chinamen's cloaks became quite animated—I saw it rise above the commotion flapping like mangy wings.

I glimpsed a sudden flail of an arm and the piercing shine of something metallic and sharp. Even Jack stopped pushing and his Englishmen scrambled to turn around. All I could see was a blur of motion and shadow. One of the Chinese gentlemen (I think it was Kuan Yu) jumped nearly to the rail car's ceiling, and his foot, shod in a surprisingly refined-looking satin slipper, connected with the back of the head of one of the Englishmen, sending him spinning and tumbling into the clump of his countrymen, already exceedingly cramped by Jack's effort at our end.

Even though it was difficult to make out who was hitting whom and with what, the Chinese gentlemen and their disturbing fur cloaks seemed to be gaining an upper hand. The English were defending themselves only half-heartedly, squeezed as they were between the Chinese and Jack who, by then, had stopped pushing and only administered an occasional and judicious slap or poke, keeping the agents tightly contained. He would make a good shepherd dog, I thought, as I managed to wedge in next to him and poke and prod the men with my now-sheathed saber. It wasn't strictly necessary, but I wanted a closer look at the strange balletic species of fisticuffs our new friends were employing, and I enjoyed feeling useful.

The Chinese had beaten the agents bloody, all of them slumped or staggering in the narrow corridor, blinded by their bruises and disoriented, a few split lips bleeding and a few eyes punched bruised and shut. Jack and I herded the Englishmen toward the carriage door. Kuan Yu pushed the door open; Jack smiled and nodded to him. "Jump," he said to the English.

The ground sloped down from the tracks, coated with a crystalline blanket of snow, and yet my heart was uneasy as the English jumped, one by one by one, and rolled down the slope, raising brief, low flurries in their wake. I hoped they would find their way to safety.

"How close is the nearest town?" I asked Jack.

He smiled, shook his head. "They'll be fine. Unfortunately."

Kuan Yu laughed. "Indeed. Why not kill them?"

"Diplomatic nightmare," I said.

We returned to our compartments, but after a quick unvoiced exchange, I went across the corridor to speak to the Chinese. Kuan Yu seemed a bit more talkative, and I sat down next to him, making sure my posture was both casual and masculine: I rested my elbows on my knees, letting my hands dangle.

"So," I said. "What do you gentlemen do?"

Kuan Yu grinned. "How do you mean, poruchik?"

"Just in general. What brings you to Russia, business or pleasure?"

The men laughed, their bright teeth twinkling in their dark beards with great mirth. "We are traders," Kuan Yu said.

Liu Zhi laughed again, throwing back his head, and gasped for breath, overcome by too much merriment. "Yes, traders," he confirmed once he regained his ability to speak. "Business is bad in Siberia, had to go west to sell all the silk and tea we had. Now going back home, to Beijing. Will be selling fur." He pointed at their cloaks that were now hanging placidly on the wall of the compartment, and I determined the unnatural mix was composed of mink, fox, ermine, and otter furs.

"Us too," I said.

"Trading fur?"

"Going to Beijing," I said.

They nodded, expressing no further curiosity. "Long trip," Kuan Yu said. "Rest up, young man—who knows when you will be able to sleep in such security and comfort as now. We always rest while we travel by train. We know when there's an opportunity for danger to arrive, and when it is safe. Sleep while the wheels rattle on and wake up when they stop."

"Thank you," I said and rose, realizing I was being politely encouraged to leave. "And thank you for your help."

Liu Zhi nodded, smiling. "Our pleasure," he said.

I did not doubt his veracity.

Chapter 11

I WOKE UP WHEN THE SUN WAS HIGH IN THE SKY. EVEN WITH MY eyes closed I could feel the air outside had a mature, late-morning quality rather than the slanted, insistent early morning light that prodded at one's eyelids, forcing them open. I stretched before my eyes opened, and felt a warm breeze on my cheek—a barest whisper of air sliding against skin, tugging gently at the fine hairs of my carefully trimmed temples. I glanced between my eyelids, opening them just wide enough to sneak a peek. In a halo of distorted light, I saw Jack's face, leaning so close to mine and peering so intently, it was as if he was trying to read his fortune in the veins of my eyelids, in the creases of my lips.

He sighed again, his breath like a slow caress at the ridge of my jawline; I opened my eyes, slowly, to give him time to move away.

He did not. "Good morning," he whispered, his soft, gravelly voice rumbling with recent sleep and great fatigue.

"Morning," I said. I had to pull myself back with my elbows, so that I could sit up without my forehead smashing his high arched nose. "You seem troubled with thought."

"That I am." He sat on the edge of my seat, leaning on both his arms, his palms planted on either side of my legs. He was too close, and his proximity was constraining enough that I had to fight a mild panic. If he were to try and kiss me, there would be little I could do to avoid it, save for a hearty slap in the face. "Can you talk?"

"Sure." I pulled up my knees to my chest, circumventing the arch of his arms, and felt immediately better as soon as my feet touched the floor. "What do you want to talk about?"

"My past," he said. "Remember what I was telling you about Canton?"

JACK STAYED WITH THE REST OF THE ENGLISHMEN IN THE ENGLISH factory—or, as the Chinese called it, *hong*. From what he described, it seemed more a vast complex of apartments, stores and secondary buildings than a place where anything was manufactured; every western nation represented in Canton was in control of one such sprawling building, surrounded by shallow gardens and allocated to the outside of the city walls. They were not allowed to house women, and the merchants who made homes there kept their families at Macao, where the Portuguese opium addict Jack had befriended came from. The two of them often took long walks by the port and around the city perimeter, all the while arguing about religion.

Jack was bored, and he used his time to learn the local Chinese dialect in addition to the pidgin they all used to communicate with half-naked coolies at the docks and the shopkeepers who hung signs in Chinese and English, undeterred from trade by neither imperial edicts and threats of death nor apparently latent patriotism. They always had good advice on bribing the officials.

Jack's knowledge of Chinese made him useful, and his Portuguese friend and mentor told him he was interested in leaving Canton and traveling up the Pearl River, to distribute some of the religious tract he had cobbled together and printed in Chinese courtesy of some Englishman working at the *Canton Herald*. The book was the usual mix of misunderstood mysticism, catechism, and drugged fancies, such as his assurance of human ability to fly.

Missionary work was nothing new. However, in light of the recent souring of the relations due to the opium impasse and the mulish stubbornness of Captain Charles Elliot, the man who tried to negotiate the conditions of trade on the English side, it had become even more thankless and dangerous than before. Paolo's plan was to have Jack dress in Chinese garb and send him up the river to distribute the religious pamphlets. His Chinese would be passable enough to keep him out of trouble—at least they both hoped this would be the case.

Jack told me he did not know who the men who captured him were—they spoke a dialect of Chinese strange to his ears, and they had no knowledge of pidgin whatsoever. They were not Chinese officials. They took his books and his clothes and beat him with great vigor, but did not put him into jail. Instead, they lowered him into what seemed to be a dried up well and tied large stones onto his back, around his neck, and to his arms and feet, so that he could not move.

"This is where it gets interesting," he said and smiled when I leaned closer, enthralled. "I started trying to move, so as not to be squashed by that weight, and I sang those little nonsense mantras Paolo had taught me. The more I moved, the easier it got. Soon, I stood up with the millstone still on my back.

"Then, I tried climbing the walls of the well. It was slow at first, but soon enough I could ascend twenty feet before having to climb back down. Not long after I began jumping in my well. It was a full year before I was strong enough to get out of the well, millstones and all."

I held my breath. "And then . . . "

He nodded. "Yes. I could run and jump and climb with these stones, easy as any man without them. But when I reached safety and had them taken off me . . . that first moment, I took one step and I thought I could fly! The barest movement made the world fall away from under me. It was like a dream, only for weeks I couldn't take a step without soaring to the clouds. The war had started by then, and no one was paying much attention. As soon as I could walk, I went to Macao—I jumped from boat to boat, to tell you the truth, and when I couldn't, I just jumped bouncing off water."

"Nonsense."

He put his long-fingered hand over his chest. "I swear to you, it is all true. I sailed for home on the first boat taking English families back."

"This . . . " I gulped one breath after another, my heart pounding. "But you make it sound as if it was natural. However, I am certain that no other person would succeed the way you did—they would've died in that well."

He inclined his head, agreeing. "It allowed me to discover that I had such an ability—a confluence of an inborn talent and circumstance had brought it forth, do you understand? And either of them is nothing without the other—this is what is so extraordinary about it. Don't you agree?"

"I do," I said, and only then noticed a small burnt hole in his jacket, just below his right shoulder. The hole was almost invisible as it was obscured by a crust of dried blood. "My God, you're injured."

He followed my gaze, and probed the hole with his fingers, thoughtful and flinching. "Must have been that shot we heard. Who would be mad enough to shoot in such narrow confines? A ricochet is almost a certainty."

"They did get you," I pointed out. "Let me get my scissors and some thread—I can at least try to dig out the bullet and close the wound."

"There's no need."

I stared at his visage, just a shade paler than usual. "Of course there is. You're still mortal. Aren't you?"

He grinned. "I assume so. Very well, you've made your case."

I suspected he enjoyed being ministered to, as he took off his jacket and undid the collar of his shirt. His skin looked sallow, smeared with thick dry blood. The bullet entry stared at me like a solitary black eye, and I wished I had a more suitable tool than a pair of scissors. I probed the wound carefully, and felt a subtle scratch of metal under metal almost immediately. Some bone must've stopped it. I sighed with relief.

Jack closed his eyes and looked paler, but made no sound as I dipped the scissor tips into the wound, pushing them next to the bullet. I pivoted the scissors—easy as turning a key—and a stained black metal cylinder slipped out into my hand. One end was flattened where it had encountered Jack's bone.

"That's it," I said. "You want stitches?"

He shook his head as he touched the wound and the single drop of blood that had squeezed out of it. "It seems pretty well cauterized, and I do heal well on my own. Thank you, and I promise to ask for the stitches if they are at any point necessary."

"You're welcome," I said. I did not feel particularly useful, or helpful; I suddenly worried about Jack. The more I thought about how close he had come to being seriously wounded, the more I panicked. What if he were to be killed or gravely injured? As selfish as I felt when I thought that way, a part of me keened in a high, childlike voice, *What would happen to me then?*

Jack seemed pensive all day, quiet, and I did not think it was due to his injury. Rather it seemed as if he regretted opening up to me so much. I worked on my never-ending letter, which had acquired a worrisome similarity to a diary, especially once I realized I was unlikely to mail it from anywhere, be it Nizhniy Novgorod or Omsk or Beijing.

Jack read his booklets, only looking up at me when he thought I was not watching him. The fur traders played a game of cards, happy and angry exclamations alternated in an almost constant stream from their compartment. Ever since we had dispatched the English, in what I hoped would be a summarization of any future untoward encounters, the carriage belonged to us, as if the other passengers somehow got a wind of the events and worried of being thrown off the train as well. Even the conductor appeared infrequently, usually after dark, and only to offer woolen blankets or clean linens.

I folded my letter that had grown to seven pages in length, and went to refresh myself. The reverse corset was comfortable enough, but its weight and mere proximity to my skin induced almost fearful fits of sweating. The washroom in the end of the carriage was small, and boasted only a washbasin and a bucket of cold water the conductor refilled at every stop.

I wet a towel and loosened the collar of my jacket. Even though I shivered at the touch of cold water, I sighed with relief as it removed a layer of grime from my face and neck and chest. I was looking forward to the day when I would be able to take a proper bath. I hoped it would come before we reached Beijing. This cleaning myself with a rag soaked in cold water was starting to feel lacking.

After I felt sufficiently refreshed—or, at the very least, cold and shivering—I took the opportunity to affix a fresh mustache to my lip. I returned to my seat, to find Jack asleep with his head propped against the window. The fur traders, on the other hand, were wide awake—they had finished their card game and drank tea, talking loudly in their language. That made me sigh and think back to the social at the Crane Club. Poor, defiled Crane Club. I couldn't help but glare at Jack a little, even though it wasn't really his fault.

"Join us for tea, young hussar," Kuan Yu called to me from across the aisle. "You sleep so soundly, you missed the last night's stop. We bought fresh tea and local bread. It surely is better than stale sandwiches and cheese you get from the restaurant carriage."

"Thank you," I said, and crossed the aisle.

The compartment across from ours was thoroughly inhabited by the traders—it even smelled different from ours, of tea and sandalwood and some unfamiliar spices, of tanned leather and slightly wet dog. Ours smelled mostly of Jack's cigars and pulpy reading material with a whiff of my ink and stationery. I relished the difference.

The three of us crowded on one bench, while the opposite one served as a sideboard: there was hot tea and round bread specked with poppy seeds, butter and raspberry preserves. Kuan Yu and Liu Zhi did not seem discouraged by the unfamiliar food—or, I supposed, they had traveled back and forth enough that food made no difference whatsoever. I hoped I wouldn't look too provincial in the foreign land, where I would probably have to eat things that would be slightly confusing.

We drank our tea and ate in silence. "Do you live in Beijing?" I finally asked after my hunger had subsided and I did not have to converse with my mouth full.

Kuan Yu shrugged. "Sometimes. Here and there we go. I am originally from Hua County, in Guangdon Province."

"He's a Hakka," Liu Zhi explained. "It is close to Canton."

"I have heard of Canton and Hong Kong," I said. "And Macao."

"Hua is like that but different," Kuan Yu said.

The word sounded familiar, and after turning it in my mind a little, I remembered I first heard it from Lee Bo, when he explained Heavenly Kingdom of Great Peace to me. "Isn't Hong Xiuquan also from there?" I asked. "The man who started the Heavenly Kingdom?"

The men traded a quick look. "Indeed," Liu Zhi said. "How did you know?"

"I have friends who were in the university with me," I said, momentarily forgetting my disguise and my story. In any case, there was no reason why a man couldn't be a student before becoming a hussar. "A few of them talked about what was happening in China . . . before they left. St. Petersburg was not safe for them anymore."

"So we heard," said Kuan Yu. "Well, you'll be happy to know the Heavenly Kingdom is doing quite well. If your friend is a Hakka, he might even be in great power." He lowered his voice, looking furtively at the compartment Jack and I shared. "Hong Xiuquan, the Son of God, has taken Nanjing, and it is only a matter of time before Beijing and the devil Qing fall."

I decided not to draw Kuan Yu's attention to the fact that he had lied to us before when he assured us he was not Christian but worshipped old gods. Not that, from what I'd heard, Hong's Christianity was the one I was familiar with. "You sympathize with the Taiping then."

Kuan Yu shrugged. "I am just a fur trader," he said. "All the ins and outs and great men and children of gods—all that escapes me, or doesn't concern me. I do want the Manchu gone, and I want the Chinese to be in charge of China."

"I want my daughter to grow up with her feet unbound," Liu Zhi said. "Hakkas don't bind their women's feet—this is why Hakka women cannot find non-Hakka husbands, their feet are too big. But if no woman walked with lotus gait . . . " He shrugged, without finishing the thought.

I nodded mutely. At first, I wanted to argue against such terrible mutilation as foot binding—I had seen depictions of folded over, disfigured feet that did not look human—and yet I did not want to sound like Ipatiev, who always tried to make everyone think that he was the final arbiter and judge of what was barbarous. So I drank some more tea and changed the subject. "I hear that in Taiping Tianguo they let women take examinations to become state officials. I wonder if women would ever be allowed to hold administrative posts in China."

Kuan Yu shrugged. "Either way, I do not care. As long as the Manchu are gone."

Liu Zhi nodded. "I could not agree more. Let us hope the English will not get involved."

I held my breath, my mind racing with what I knew and what was advisable to mention. Ever since I met Jack, most conversations felt like trying to navigate an unfamiliar carriage drawn by wild horses through a strange city in a moonless night. Sometimes it seemed best to let the reins drop, and to count only on luck rather than trying to guess the intentions and motives and political alliances of every person I spoke to. "If the English got involved," I said slowly, "wouldn't they support the Taipings? You know, Taipings being Christian and all."

Both men laughed heartily, and I felt very young and very foolish.

"Of course not. They won the war with the Manchu, they signed treaties with the Qing emperor letting them trade opium. The Taipings punish opium smoking and selling by death."

"So they would put profit before religion?"

They nodded in unison. "And besides, what foreigner would ever admit that their God Yasoo might have a Chinese brother?"

I considered the question. "It seems only right," I said. "The Bible recounts these people being chosen or that. Priests and kings and emperors always act as if they have God on their side. I heard that during war with Napoleon, everyone thought it was God's will that the French took Moscow, and then it was God's will it burned and then it was God's will the French lost. He always seems to be taking different sides. I think He only cares that we put an entertaining spectacle, not who's right or who's wrong."

"Gods like spectacles," Kuan Yu agreed. "And sacrifices, although they tell me that Yasoo does not like sacrifices?"

"His Father used to," I said. "I think in the days of the Old Testament you were supposed to burn cows for Him."

"Terrible," Liu Zhi said without much conviction. "In any case, we honor our ancestors and old gods, and hope that Manchu are gone."

I finished my tea. My thoughts were racing with the possibilities I had not previously considered, and as soon as it was polite to do so, I fled back to my compartment. I kicked Jack's shin until he woke up.

"What is it?" he mumbled.

"Shhh," I hissed. "I was thinking . . . the letter from Wong Jun is addressed to the Manchu officials, and to the Qing emperor himself."

"Yes." Jack stretched and yawned. "Is this why you woke me?"

"Yes. No. I mean, I woke you because maybe we shouldn't be talking to the Manchu. Maybe instead we need to make alliance with the Taipings—looks like they just might win this. They've taken Nanjing, and looks like it's only a matter of time before they advance further north."

"They are barbarians," Jack said. "At least, the Manchu are civilized."

"They are a hated foreign government. I am just not sure that Emperor Constantine should make an alliance with such a tenuous power."

Jack laughed. "The Qing have been in control for centuries. My dear, empires are all about hated foreign governments."

I laughed too, stretched, and looked at the fir forest whizzing by the window, so close to the train tracks that I could've touched the branches if I had opened to window. "I do see your point."

"Make no mistake about it," he said softly. "When we visit Turkestan, you'll see. Emperor Constantine, of whom you seem so fond of for some reason, is as hated there as the Manchus are in Canton."

"Emperor Constantine is a good man," I said. "He is being misled by his brother and his advisors, but I think—"

Jack threw his hands into the air. "What is it with you people! Even you, Sasha, and I thought you were smarter than most. The entire country seems to believe in some imaginary good tsar, as if nothing is ever his fault. From the sixteenth century to today, you all mumble about how your ruler doesn't mean to do anything bad, he or she is just being lied to by corrupt boyars. Do you realize how silly it sounds?"

I did, but was not yet ready to admit to it, so I just turned beet red and stared out of the window, seething, and imagining suitable insults for Queen Victoria, even though I suspected that they would never wound Jack as deeply as his words had wounded me.

IT WAS THREE DAYS BEFORE WE REACHED YEKATERINBURG, AND BY then I had moved beyond vague dissatisfaction and into a ravenous lust for a hot bath and a meal that was not bought on a platform from portly peasant women bundled up in shawls and kerchiefs all the way up to her eyes. They sold sauerkraut and boiled eggs and hand-sized minced meat pies of dubious freshness but nevertheless a welcome relief from the monotonous bread, butter, and two-days-old soup from the restaurant carriage. But even those treats were starting to grate, and I would kill for a pancake or a plate of pelmeni.

The conductor informed us we were to stop for a few hours in Yekaterinburg, and recommended a tavern where we could take a room and, I fervently hoped, find some hot water. And pelmeni.

"Perhaps it would be better to stay on board," Jack said when I expressed my plans excitedly. "It may be wise to avoid being seen."

"We are much more obvious on this train," I pointed out. "Besides, this train is the fastest thing in the country—how can they catch up to us?"

Jack shrugged. "There are ways. What does the train need to stop for anyway?"

"Pick up more coal and tea and water and food," I said. "I was bored this morning and stopped by the engine compartment—it is rather horrifying. All those half-naked freedmen, covered in coal dust, black as devils, shoveling coal into the maw of the furnace . . . scary to think one furnace is what's driving the entire train, isn't it?"

"Fire and steam," Jack mumbled under his breath. "It is staggering to think how much the two of them reshape the face of the land."

"I suppose." I stared out of the window, impatient for the sight of the city or any human habitation, but so far nothing but a spruce forest and a bridge over Chusovaya River broke the monotony of snow and sky. "Quite a bit of reshaping going on lately. I still wonder if we should take our offer to the Taipings."

"You have no connection to them. Wong Jun's letter would be a liability to their eyes."

I sighed and continued staring. It felt like we were doomed to variations of this argument until we arrived in China and took one course of action or another; until then, it felt rather futile.

We entered the outskirts of Yekaterinburg—wooden single-storied cottages, fenced in yards with an occasional barn, but mostly poor but neat houses. It reminded me of home so much—I imagined the insides of these cozy tiny houses, their floors covered with straw and a few chickens milling about in the kitchen, a single living room half-occupied by a brick whitewashed stove that gave warmth to people and livestock alike, and was also good for cooking and heating water. Simple but comfortable accommodations—most peasants and freedmen in Trubetskoye lived like that, and my heart was squeezed tightly by the cold, steely hand of nostalgia.

By the time the train pulled into the station, I felt misty-eyed and sentimental, missing my mother and Eugenia and even the freedmen and engineers so terribly. Only the thought of the tavern cheered me up a little.

We said temporary goodbyes to the Chinese gentlemen who expressed no desire to explore taverns, and stayed in their little compartment crowded by their trunks and playing cards, speaking in soft voices. I promised to see them again soon but took my satchel with me. It was conceivable we would miss the train and would have to wait for the next one.

The tavern our conductor had recommended was a small one, curiously empty—although I supposed few traveled so far east in winter. Indeed, the cold had been strong and biting, and in a few minutes that it took us to walk from the station to the tavern, my fingers had grown white and my pelisse (woefully inadequate as a protection against the cold) developed a thick coating of frost that hid the gold braiding entirely from view. Jack seemed as uncomfortable—he kept blowing on his fingers, his breath thick and milky in the clear air, and tossing his satchel from one hand to the other.

"Maybe we should take separate rooms," I said.

"Not safe," he said in a voice strained by cold.

"It's just for a few hours," I argued. "And I would enjoy little time to myself."

I could not tell whether my words upset him or not, but I did not care. I was relieved to finally arrive at the tavern and let the warmth and the thick smell of sour cream and baking potatoes engulf me in its welcoming embrace.

In my own room, I almost wept as I stripped away my uniform and my shirt, gray with sweat and dirt, and the reverse corset—I'd been wearing it for so long I worried my body would forever retain its shape. Two buckets of hot water were generously prepared for me, and I sunk gratefully into a tin tub by the stove with the full intention of not leaving it until impending departure absolutely demanded it.

I closed my eyes, savoring the water hot enough to fill the tiny, whitewashed room with thick fluffy clumps of steam. I sighed, feeling my body gradually reacquire its God-given shape, almost weeping with gratitude for small mercies. Truly, if I could spend the rest of my days in this tub, I would be content.

I must've slept a little, because the water was suddenly no longer hot and I found myself shivering. I climbed out, dried myself, and put on a clean cotton shirt. Before restoring the monstrosity of the reverse corset to its rightful place over my shoulders and chest, I decided to clean it. The cork and the cloth could definitely use a bath as well—there was a distinct smell of sweat lingering about them, and I decided to eliminate it, even at the cost of appearing less masculine.

I kneeled before my tub and lathered the contraption until it smelled of nothing but soap. I rinsed it in cold water and hung it by the brick stove to dry.

The steam had dissipated, and only a few forlorn drops of condensation slid down the windowpanes. I took a look around me. The room was almost shockingly clean, with an uneven but freshly swept wooden floor that was now decorated with half-moons of my wet footprints. Whitewashed walls, adorned only with two cheap woodcuts depicting some peasant celebration embarrassing in its earnestness, still smelled a little of chalk, as did the recently whitewashed stove. The tiny windows, decorated by an elaborate tracery of hoarfrost vines and flowers, still let in the pale afternoon light, but soon it would be time for me to go back to the train. I sighed and stretched on my bed, covered by a coverlet decorated with poppies and cornflowers, telling myself that if I were to fall asleep, Jack would surely wake me up.

When I opened my eyes again, I felt rested and refreshed, and the quality of light streaming in had barely changed. I put on my corset and stretched, and then I smelled something burning. At first, I rubbed my eyes leisurely and thought of a giant kitchen downstairs, with a woodstove of gargantuan proportions exhaling fire and smoke like the mouth of Gehenna: hypothetical but nevertheless terrifying. The smoke persisted, and it was only when I tasted ash in back of my throat that it occurred to me the fire was not related to the kitchen, and promised not a meal but a disaster.

I put on my uniform, grabbed my satchel, and pushed the door. It remained closed. I jiggled the handle, my mind still fuzzy after sleep but growing sharp once I realized the door was not stuck but deliberately locked from the outside, and saw tendrils of smoke seeping under the door. I threw myself against the door; my cork shoulder did not hurt, but the door did not budge either. After several attempts, I gave up primarily because the thick veil of smoke made my eyes sting and my throat constrict with irrepressible cough.

My room was on the second floor and I rushed to the window, coughing and calling for help—not too loudly, because even though my life was in danger, I feared that outright panic would be unbecoming for a hussar. I yanked at the window, but it was frozen solid.

Irrational fear flared up then—the realization I was trapped, alone—for the first time in days, I was alone—and that I had no one but my own self to help me. Terrible visions crowded by mind—charred remains, red blisters opening like flowers in a twisted coal form no one would ever recognize as human, would never recognize as me . . . I had to slap my own cheek to regain a semblance of sense.

With my face burning from the slap as well as heat, I put my shoulder to good use again, managing to shake loose the frozen frame. As the heat in the room and my own exertions made my face bead with sweat, I pushed the window open with what felt like an effort almost too colossal for my arms. The window swung open, and I looked into a small back street, empty save for a bundled up old woman on the corner, who was screaming (very unhussar-like) for help, gesturing at the thick pillars of smoke pouring out of the windows of the first and the second floors. I panicked at first but soon realized the inhabitants and other visitors must've escaped through the front door. I hoped that I was the only one locked in.

Thankfully, tall snowdrifts had built up by the back wall of the tavern—the snow seemed to have been shoveled against the wall, all the way up to the first floor windows. I crossed myself, tossed my satchel out of the window, and jumped. My breath caught at the sudden hard impact—the snow was packed tight, and felt little softer than the pavement below it. My right ankle shifted inside my boot with a sickening grinding sound and a wrenching sensation, and I staggered away from the building. My right foot throbbed with pain and refused to support even an ounce of my weight. I cursed through my teeth, picked up my satchel, and hopped on one foot down the street, along the two long tracks worn by the wheels of carts and carriages. I headed for the corner, where I hoped to find a way into the front street, to make sure that Jack was there, alive and unharmed. Worry gnawed at me as I hopped, painfully, laboriously—this was the first time since we had met that I needed Jack and he failed to come to my aid. One hand resting against the solid, packed snow, helping to maintain my balance, I rounded the corner, to the sound of shouts and the sight of orange flames reaching from the windows of the first floor like questing fingers. The commotion overwhelmed me and I was jostled back and forth by people rushing about; I almost lost my balance a few times. Still, despite all, my eyes searched the crowd; the absence of Jack's tall figure was more obvious than I dared to admit to myself.

Chapter 12

It took a few minutes for the fire wagon, drawn by four stout, small horses with shaggy fetlocks, to arrive at the tavern. The long yellow tongues of flame wagged from every window and licked the blistering walls. The paint burned and peeled, and the stone underneath charred. I bit my lips, seized by the ancestral memory of Moscow burning at the time of Napoleon—even though I did not experience it myself, I heard stories from my aunt and my mother often enough to be able to taste ash and crumbling brick every time Napoleon was mentioned. Now I tasted it regardless.

I waited with everyone else, my teeth chattering, as the firemen unrolled the hose and brought out a pump. The water in the wagon's barrel was frozen, and one of the firemen had to crack the ice with the blunt end of an axe.

They pumped a thin, uncertain stream that occasionally rose as high as the second story windows but quickly abated, and then reared up again. The flames guttered and went out when the water hit them, then quickly grew to their former size. It was becoming obvious the fire and water could chase each other like this forever, neither gaining an upper hand, as the tavern gradually charred and grew disfiguring tumors of ice. The water froze the moment it touched any portion of wall not in flames. As I watched the icy gray lumps grow, I realized how cold it was—how cold I felt. My twisted ankle, so swollen by then it filled my boot as tightly as rising dough fills a too-small bowl, was thankfully numb; so was the rest of me. At least, this is the only explanation I could find for the sense of curious calm that enveloped me. I thought of Jack, who was not among the throng outside; surely, he wouldn't be trapped inside and burned to death—he would be strong enough to break the door if it was locked from the outside, he could jump from any window and do so without hurting himself . . . he must have gone to the train, I said to myself. I should hurry there too.

There was no chance of finding a carriage near the sluggish inferno, so I hobbled away, my injured foot numb enough to put a modicum of weight on it. I wondered as I hobbled who had started the fire. I assumed, it was the English, but it seemed possible that Nightingale would not be above having the Nikolashki or some other unsavory branch of secret police doing as she bid.

It occurred to me I had seen neither foreigners nor plain clothed policemen at the tavern—the arsonists either escaped before I got there, or found their way out the back of the building. Would they chase me? I could not run, and felt too tired and distraught to hide. It wasn't quite despair that hung over me like a thick veil; it was the sense of resignation. If I were captured I would probably feel only relief. I stumbled along, smelling the pungent scent of smoke permanently trapped in my clothes and hair, hoping for either a carriage or a policeman to come along and take me somewhere I could sit down and finally stop running.

I had not thought about the university in days, and now I yearned to be there. It was becoming increasingly plain I might never make it back at all let alone in time for the third quarter. If I survived this adventure and returned home, I only hoped the rector would be merciful and allow me to resume my studies next year. Otherwise, I would be expelled, tossed out. If that were to happen, death by the hand of Dame Nightingale would be certainly preferable.

I managed to hail a carriage; a sullen freedman and his large, bay horse studied me with suspicion and a remarkably similar shine of dark, bulging eyes, but agreed to take me to the station. My breath clouded the air inside, as the driver sang to himself and clapped his mittened hands. His horse, evidently encouraged by this, snuffled and neighed.

The train was still there. I found the compartment empty of Jack but also empty of policemen or spies or any other foes; only the two Chinese gentlemen, Kuan Yu and Liu Zhi nodded and smiled at me. I settled in my seat and immediately pressed my forehead to the frozen window, to thaw out a clear patch large enough to observe the goings-on on the platform.

I worried about Jack, although I could not imagine him dead—such a little fire, such an obvious and feeble arson were designed not to kill but to scare him, to drive him away—I imagined him running, leaping tall buildings, leading the pursuit away from me . . . something he would do. Sweet old Jack.

Every passing second resonated in my mind like a heavy stroke of Grandfather's clock that used to decorate my father's study when I was an infant—I still remembered the heavy, weighty sound. I felt the ghostly clock hand move, slow and inexplicable, its blade shredding my heart with worry, each little step another opportunity lost.

I attempted to distract myself by checking on my ankle, but the boot would not come off because of the swelling, and I gave up soon enough.

I wished I hadn't insisted on taking my own room—I would have known where Jack was, if he was still alive, and whether I should stay in Yekaterinburg and wait for him or continue on my way. The remorse tore at me, and yet there was no fixing it. It was the same truth I had realized only gradually after my papa had passed away, so long ago: the truth that some things could not be fixed no matter how much you turned them in your head and wished they would be otherwise. The realization often descended early in the morning, in that fuzzy domain between sleep and wakefulness, where—despite what your dreams still whispered in your head—those who were dead would remain dead. Grief was always freshest in the mornings, but I now allowed the memory of it to distract me from my current misery.

"Where is your friend?" Kuan Yu asked.

"I don't know," I answered. In my distress, I could not even start making up a plausible lie, and so instead I told them we had been separated while in town, and now I couldn't decide whether to continue or not.

"Of course not," Liu Zhi said. "You don't leave a friend behind—there will be another train tomorrow."

"But we are in a hurry," I said. "Besides, I worry those people you helped us push off the train will come back."

"All the more reason to not abandon your friend," Kuan Yu said, the confusion written on his honest, broad face that reminded me of Anastasia at that moment. "What sort of a soldier are you?"

"Not a very good one," I said, simultaneously afraid and giddy with the thought that between them Liu Zhi and Kuan Yu were generating enough guilt to chase me off the train, and wondered how far would my shame push me. The role of embarrassment in human history was vastly underestimated. As I picked up my satchel and hobbled on my distended ankle toward the doors of the carriage, it occurred to me that many instances of heroism, acknowledged in books and history records and Jack's beloved penny dreadfuls, were likely to have been inspired purely by embarrassment, by fear of looking foolish or cowardly in front of total strangers. So I smiled and waved at Kuan Yu and Liu Zhi. "It was nice meeting you. Have a safe and pleasant journey."

They waved back and whispered to each other fiercely, their

words obscured by their language as well as hissing of the steam—the train was getting ready to leave, and its breath, a cloud of milk in the clear water of the winter air, curdled and billowed all around me as soon as I stepped onto the platform. I thought I heard voices calling after me, but I was too fatigued and frightened and hurt to turn back and ask what they wanted.

There will be another train tomorrow, I consoled myself. If I cannot find Jack, I can go by myself—stay on the train, make friends, remain in a full carriage so there are always eyes and ears around me. There were advantages in going by myself, too: no one to argue with over giving the letter to the Taipings and insisting on Qing legitimacy. It also occurred to me that whether Dame Nightingale had Jack or whether he was simply lost in Yekaterinburg, now that we were apart we would not be as easy to find as before—a tall Englishman and a girl dressed as a hussar were slightly less obvious apart than together. In fact, I thought, I wouldn't have needed Jack at all if only I wasn't so frightened. If only Jack did not have the documents and submarine schematics.

The train whistled and the passengers hurried aboard. I hoped with every fiber of my soul Jack would manifest somehow, that his tall figure would appear cleaving the crowd like the prow of a steamship—almost as much as I hoped he wouldn't. It was so difficult to decide whether Jack was an asset or a liability, especially with my fear muddying my feelings further.

The train chugged, faster and faster, and I had to step away from the platform's edge lest I be burned by the steam that poured from the stack of the locomotive and curled along the length of the train like a cloud dragon.

I was still undecided regarding how I felt or what I was going to do next—should I search for Jack or simply wait for him here?—when the locomotive gave a last mournful whistle, spooking the crows sitting on the roof of the station, like so many monks waiting for Easter service to start. The train shuddered and moved, faster, faster. It was leaving now and it was me receding behind it. I could feel myself getting smaller in the eyes of the passengers, until the train curved behind the horizon, and I disappeared from its view, as if I had never existed.

Cold and pain, resurrected from the overwhelming numbness like a particularly cantankerous phoenix, jolted me from my reverie and reassured me—rather rudely—of the existence of my mortal body. Considering the advantages of being an incorporeal spirit, I hopped on one foot toward the station building. There, I found a bench free of village women and their baskets with chickens, eggs, and minced meat pies as well as fur traders and their bundles of freshly hunted and badly smelling furs, and sat down. Rather, I let my leg give under me, and tumbled onto the bench in utter exhaustion and misery, not even caring how ungraceful I looked. It seemed like a good time to decide what to do next.

I did not want to go back to the burned tavern, not with the risk of encountering the arsonists, which happily coincided with the most sensible course of action: waiting for Jack to find me. The train station would be the most obvious place in the absence of other contingency plans. It was just common sense, I told myself, since lacking other information I had to assume he was looking for me, and thus starting to look for him would almost certainly guarantee we would never find each other.

I considered another meal of meat or cabbage pies and shuddered with disgust. Instead, I opened my satchel to work a bit on the confessional (and increasingly sentimental) letter (diary) addressed to my mother (or my aunt) in her sane (female) world. Truly, it was getting too complicated and parenthetical for its own good. Except as soon as I opened my satchel, I realized it was not there.

I cursed under my breath, using words my mother would never believe I suspected the existence of, and dug through several times. It was of no use, and I sunk back into my bench, clutching my cropped head as if I were hoping to crush it between my hands. I wouldn't have minded so much if the letter contained only troubles of my heart; but as I written quite a bit about Wong Jun and Chiang Tse, and even though I avoided committing to paper the exact details of our task, I suspected I had referenced too many people, including Aunt Eugenia. My only consolation was the hope the letter had either burned in the tavern or was lost somewhere, kneaded by a multitude of feet into the dirty slush, at one with the city's frozen refuse now.

The throbbing in my ankle had subsided enough to allow me a brief venture toward the back of the station, where a small sectioned area smelled of food, and two harried women with lined, drawn faces worked the woodstove and cast iron skillets, serving pancakes with butter and sour cream to the few passengers who lingered by the small wooden counter, carved with a heart and someone's initials. There was nowhere to sit, except the usual benches of the train station, so I leaned against the wall, inhaling the smells of sizzling dough and sour milk, and feeling my mouth fill with saliva. Pancakes were sure to make everything better—their smell alone made the pain in my twisted foot almost tolerable.

I waited patiently for my turn, my hunger growing with every passing minute, so that by the time I received a scalding-hot plate with a stack of golden pancakes and a small dab of sour cream dwarfed by a spreading lake of melted butter, all thoughts other than those related to my meal became but a distant whisper deep in the recesses of my mind.

I burned my mouth with my first bite, but did not care—it was as if today's fear in the fire, concern over Jack, and worry about the lost letter had all combined to push me toward focusing on the very basics of survival, one of which was eating. As it turned out, another instinct—and one I had been neglecting—was paying attention to my surroundings.

I REGRETTED, AT TIMES, LEAVING BEHIND THE FEMALE WORLD inhabited by my mother; I even missed the gray, ambiguous area where my Aunt Eugenia dwelled—the world of influence and responsibility, where she still wore female clothes and relied on men to exercise her influence. Now I was truly on my own, alone, and dressed as a man, ready to cut my swath through the world as men did. I gritted my teeth and felt determined, and only because of that was I able to not weep with relief when a familiar voice called out, "Poruchik!" One needed friends, I had discovered, even in the male world—especially in the male world.

Rotmistr Ivankov grinned at me, and both cornets nodded politely.

It was all that I could do not to rush over and embrace him. "Rotmistr! I wished I had had a chance to thank you for your timely intervention in Moscow. Please, join me."

The rotmistr sat next to me, the bench creaking under his bulk, and sent the cornets to procure pancakes with a flick of his wrist. "No need, lad. You did well enough by sending those reinforcements our way."

I nodded, grateful for his willingness to play along with my disguise, even though I suspected he could see through it as easily as Dame Nightingale. If he addressed me as "miss," it would've been awkward. "I am sorry we could not stay to help."

He waved his hand in the air dismissively. "Worry not. We can certainly understand the need to get away in a hurry. Speaking of which, where's your friend?"

When the cornets came back with food, I told them about the fire and the missing Jack, and they nodded along, suitably concerned-looking. It was good to have friends—and the rotmistr and his cornets certainly felt like very old ones. "But how did you get here so quickly?" I asked.

The rotmistr smirked. "Remember when I complained about horses not being quick enough? Wouldn't you know, there are now trains that carry cargo, and they take horses too." He laughed happily and opened his arms and eyes simultaneously wide, surprised and delighted by such development. However, he stopped smiling when he saw my face. "What's the matter, lad? Don't you think horses might enjoy being passengers every now and again?"

I shook my head. "Nothing against your horses or your hussars, rotmistr, but I wonder why they suddenly decided to start transporting soldiers east? I thought you were on garrison duty?"

He confirmed with a nod and frowned. "I suppose freight trains would be useful for trading. It is just incidental that they used them for troops."

"Your orders said nothing about any urgency of your journey to Turkestan then? Nothing about heightened preparedness for military action?"

He scowled. "Tell you what, son. If you're so smart and well-connected, why don't you join us—we are leaving tomorrow, and we can keep you company at least to Turkestan. If your friend shows up, that will be all for the good. If not, we can offer some protection. We can talk if you feel like it, too."

"Why are you doing this for me?" I whispered, my eyes filming over and threatening to spill sudden, warm tears.

"Hussars stick together," he said, smiling. "That's why."

The rotmistr (who I was by then suspecting of being my guardian angel in a hussar uniform) led me to the other side of the station, to another set of tracks. There was no platform, and the only train there was merely a few carriages long, the rest of it composed out of open carts covered with sailcloth, housing the impatient, snorting horses covered with felt and blankets to keep them warm against the Siberian winter. Through the walls made of thick wooden slats, light and resinous, I could see the horses' breath and the small mincing steps they took in their narrow prisons, I could hear the muffled strikes of their shod hooves, iron against frozen straw, brittle as glass.

"Poor beasts," one of the cornets (I think it was Volzhenko, younger and sadder than his doppelganger Petrovsky) said, tracing my gaze. "They want to be out of those tiny stables on wheels so bad. They want to run and to feel the dry grass against their flanks, not this cursed cold . . . " He noticed the curious stare of the other cornet and let his voice trail off, to my chagrin.

I, of course, wanted to hear more—I was always intrigued by how many of my compatriots had such poetic and earnest souls below their jaded exteriors, an almost embarrassing sincerity and blazing conviction one found in certain kinds of drunks.

The rotmistr slapped my shoulder to gain my attention and almost sent me tumbling down on my hands and knees; instead, I managed an awkward hop, stepped too heavily on my injured foot, gave a loud hiss between my teeth but recovered. We stood before one of the carriages of the hussars' train, and the rotmistr helped me climb its wrought iron ladder-steps, covered with festoons of transparent ice.

Inside, the carriage did not have compartments but merely rows of wooden benches, sparsely populated by soldiers who smoked, played cards, talked loudly, dissected pickled herrings on greasy newspapers, and washed their foot wraps in buckets of murky water. It smelled of stale sweat and mold, and I feared I would not last a day in this place—I would probably shout at someone or hit them with a wet wrap in the face or choke them by shoving a deck of card down their throat. I laughed then, and the rotmistr gave me a concerned look. "You don't look well, poruchik," he said. "Let's show you to the doctor right away."

The doctor was found in the end of the carriage, where he drank and played cards with a few soldiers. He was a small, balding man with a sharp goatee who seemed genuinely sorry to leave the game in favor of taking a look at some stranger his rotmistr had dragged in.

I sat on an empty bench and the doctor leaned in, as the rotmistr and his cornets watched on. Of course, I refused a too-close examination, and reassured him that taking a look at my ankle would be sufficient. My ankle and leg were so swollen he had to cut open the upper portion of my boot in order to remove it. I peeked at my ankle and felt immediately nauseated—it was red and black and purple, certainly not the color flesh was supposed to be.

"It's a bad sprain," the doctor reassured me after he contented himself with what felt like many interminable hours of poking, prodding, and twisting of the tender flesh. "It'll heal—just stay off it, keep some ice on it, keep your boot off and your leg elevated—you don't want blood pooling in there. You do seem to have a fever, but I suspect that it is unrelated."

The moment the word "fever" touched my tympanic membranes, the carriage around me tilted and swam, as if the doctor's words allowed something I had kept away from my consciousness with a sheer act of will to coalesce and take shape, to fill my ears with sticky cotton so that the din of the carriage became subdued and remote as the tide of my own blood pounded at my ears like waves of the Pacific, toward which I had been moving so slowly, so unavoidably. I leaned into the back of the bench, and felt cold sweat slithering under my uniform. The sensation of these chill, somehow greasy drops, made me want to cry about everything I had lost that day—Jack, the documents he carried, my letter, Kuan Yu and Liu Zhi, my ankle . . . that would be regained, of course, but still. Instead of crying, I eased into the hard wooden bench and hugged my satchel to my chest, terrified of losing anything else. I heard the rotmistr's soft voice ordering the cornets around, and after a short pause there was a scratchy woolen blanket over me and a pillow that smelled like wet feathers thrust under my head. Large calloused hands eased me into the corner so my head rested against the pillow wedged between my cheek and the wall of the train, by the window. I felt the light diminish outside, and then it was night. The darkness brought an intensified fever and wild imaginings—there were stars exploding across my closed eyelids and I heard voices—not the hussars in the carriage but menacing voices that whispered on the very edge of my hearing in a language I could not understand but sounded unmistakably hostile. It felt as if I strained just a bit more I would understand their vague threats, but I avoided it. I dreamt and hallucinated and was buoyed by the waves of fever, until the morning came and there was weakness and drenching sweat, and a slow rumble of the moving wheels.

I SLEPT AND DREAMT, AND WOKE UP TO A STEAMING GLASS OF TEA, my fingers slipping on its sides. I drank my tea and slept again. Then I woke again and had someone help me walk to the end of the carriage, where the tiny privy (much smellier and considerably less comfortable than the one in the couchette carriage of the Trans-

Siberian train) offered necessary relief. Three days had passed, and we arrived at Novonikolaevsk before I was ever cognizant enough to realize that without thinking of it much, I had left Jack behind and it was too late now to go back.

In my defense, the fever I contracted in Yekaterinburg had bound me in a delirious dream from the moment I snuggled into the blanket provided by the very thoughtful rotmistr. The rattling of wheels had separated from its meaning, from signaling movement east, and only resonated in my ears as mindless percussion, as metronome beats.

The sleep was constant and yet uneven—I was often startled from it by laughter and voices, but even those remained meaningless, inconsequential, as if mere music and not the indication of a train full of hussars. Even the neighing of the caged horses in their wooden prison right behind my carriage did not jolt me to reality. One night I thought I heard thunder but then heard the rotmistr and others talking about horses' hooves shattering a slatted wall and two of them jumping off, breaking their legs as the train kept speeding along. I did not know whether the story was just a dream or a real memory.

In the end, I woke up three days later, when the train had stopped by a snow-covered platform, everything around us pristine and white, and for a moment I thought I was still dreaming, of some quintessentially Russian heaven. My face pressed against the window felt cold and numb—I must have been sitting like that for a while, but did not realize it until just now. The cessation of movement and sound must've jolted me to awareness.

Silence was too profound not to notice and I lingered in the same position, fearful of shattering it with a careless movement, with a clinking of an empty tea glass resting on the bench by my hand, ready to be sent tumbling onto the floor and splintering into shards

. . . the image of the breaking glass was so clear in my mind, I jerked my hand away from it, to prevent it from coming true.

"Menshov," someone said behind me. "You're awake?"

"Yes." Silence ruined, I sat up and rubbed my eyes with my fists. The carriage was empty, save for Cornet Volzhenko stretched on the bench behind mine, reading a volume of Pushkin's newest poems (I disliked his newer ones, finding that the poet was growing sentimental in his advancing years.) "Where is everyone?"

"Novonikolaevsk," the cornet replied. "Heart of Siberia. Everyone's probably buying vodka and food off the local Buryats. The rotmistr told me to stay here, keep an eye on you."

"Thank you," I said. Then, "Sorry."

"What are you sorry for? It's no bother. I'd rather stay here, in the warmth and quiet. They'll bring us something to eat tonight, after they're done painting the town." He thought a bit, looking at me as if wanting to ask something.

"I have been ill," I said. "When the rotmistr gets back, will you ask him to speak to me? I need to find out what happened in Yekaterinburg . . . where my friend Mr. Bartram went."

He nodded. "Don't you remember, Menshov? You sprained your ankle and decided to come along with us to Krasnoyarsk. You collapsed as soon as you sat down, and there was no waking you or talking to you."

I shrugged. "I don't mind. It is going to sound strange, but with the fever I am not sure I made the decision myself."

"God has a way of guiding us sometimes," he said with a serious, deep conviction.

I felt disinclined to speculate about God's designs, so I changed the subject. "Is there somewhere to send a letter from?"

Cornet Volzhenko shrugged. "I reckon there is a post office nearby. Novonikolaevsk is a new city still, but it has everything a city needs, although God help me if I know why the emperor decided to build it here. Then again, he named it after his brother, suitably enough."

I couldn't help but snicker. "You don't care for Prince Nicholas?"

The cornet shook his head. "My father was at the Senate Square in 1825," he said. "And he always told me it wasn't so much that they were keen on Constantine, but rather that they were terrified of Nicholas becoming tsar-emperor. Can you even imagine such a thing?" His dark eyes opened wide and rounded in exaggerated fear. "At least now, all he has is this city named after him, frozen in winter and a stinking, mosquito-filled swamp in the summer."

"And the Nikolashki," I added. "His secret police—he has those too."

"And they are not too keen on the Chinamen. Is that why you're going to China? Spying for the emperor?"

I shook my head, relieved I did not have to lie in this instant. "Nothing like that, I assure you."

"But you have a reason to go there, and a reason why you're upset the Englishman is not here, with you. And why all the other English are chasing you, as they were in Moscow. And now your friend is nowhere to be found."

"There are reasons for everything," I said. "But we are neither spies nor traitors."

He pinched his upper lip, the vegetation decorating it as wispy and scarce as mine, pulled on it as if testing its resilience. "I believe you, Menshov. The rotmistr seems to have taken a shine to you, and that's good enough for me. He's like a father to Petrovsky and myself, yeah? So he likes you—I like you, I even play nanny to you if he tells me to. But understand this: if you betray his trust, you're dead. Boom!" His fist smashed against the wooden bench. "Nothing left but a wet spot, like a bug."

"I see what you mean," I said, and eyed his young but knobby fist respectfully. "Don't worry, I hold the rotmistr in high esteem and am indebted to him for his kindnesses."

"Damn right." Volzhenko nodded and grinned, visibly relieved to get his worries off his chest. "Now that you're awake, want to test that foot of yours?"

My right ankle was indeed much better; it only produced a dull ache when I put my weight on it. I was able to sew the upper of my boot back together with some string and an awl Aunt Eugenia had thoughtfully packed in my satchel—which I still held against my bosom. I wondered if the hussars had noticed how desperately I had continued to clutch it, and whether they thought there was something exceedingly valuable in it other than a couple of clean shirts and a letter written in Chinese on the back of a theatrical bill.

Chapter 13

If there were anything I could wish for besides finding Jack or returning home, it would be some clothing designed for the Siberian winter. The moment I stepped foot outside, I realized that even though I had been cold before in my life, I had never been cold like this. Twiggy icy fingers grabbed my very heart and froze even the insides of my bones; my teeth chattered and I shook as if in St. Vitus' dance.

"You need something more than your uniform," Volzhenko, who stood on the platform next to me, draped in a thick shearling coat, said. "Pelisses are suitable for winter most places, but here . . . "

"Where . . . can I get a coat?" I stammered between my teeth that did a little tap-dance of their own.

"There's a furrier near the station," Volzhenko said. "Come, you'll feel better once we're walking."

He was right to an extent—walking indeed sent blood coursing through my legs but only to remind me bitterly that I had toes, albeit numb, which would be ripe for frostbite. Not to mention the low fever that made my forehead burn, and the disparity made the rest of me even colder, if that was at all possible.

I did not ask where the rotmistr and the rest of their regiment went. I assumed they had better things to do than pass an entire day on the train, and I did not blame them.

It was indeed a new city, although the appellation of *city* was rather generous, considering its wide, empty streets lined with a few sparse, single-storied cottages. The dwellings themselves seemed aware of their own insufficient number and volume to create a proper street. The trees around the houses were cleared in fits and starts. While some blocks had a white and deserted appearance, others looked as if they were about to be swallowed by a dark-green wall of spruces and furs, sneaking up from behind. There were a few stores that appeared to be closed, and we passed a tavern that exhaled clouds of smoke from its chimney, and clouds of steam from its open door along with gusts of great laughter.

"We can stop by there if you want," I said to Volzhenko as I noticed his long, forlorn look toward the tavern's door.

"As soon as we get you dressed," he agreed. "Or the rotmistr will kill me—he thinks you've fallen ill because of the cold and the wind."

"And stop by the post office," I reminded. I had already written a worried letter for Jack, and copied it several times to send to every city between Novonikolaevsk and Yekaterinburg.

"Of course. It's by the furrier's store." Volzhenko pointed toward an especially dense stand of trees, before which the street stopped rather abruptly, like a small child who had run against a glass door and now stood disoriented and puzzled, ready to cry. "Both right over here."

The furrier's shop pressed against the tall skinny trunks of three black spruces, as if too shy to step away from their protective skirts. TRUBKOZUB AND SON announced the hand-painted sign. I studied it, momentarily forgetting the cold, puzzling at such an exotic name in such harsh environs—mysterious, like its namesake creature. It was rather strange to find a shop in Siberia owned by a man named after an African mammal; I tried to remember its name in English, so I could tell Jack later. *Aardvark*. A furrier shop named *Aardvark and Son*. I snorted and entered, followed closely by puzzled-looking Volzhenko.

What the shop lacked in stature and location, it made up in selection. There were skins, furs, and pelts from every animal that ever had the misfortune of meeting man, some already arranged into coats and hats, others were flattened caricatures of their former owners.

The man sitting on the counter, his thick legs folded under him, didn't look up from his sewing—a curved needle in his fingers moved with the fluid grace of a boat as he made small careful stitches, joining forever two thick Arctic fox pelts, so smoky-gray they seemed blue in this light. I almost had to slap my own face to remind myself that I was Poruchik Menshov, a military young man from a military family, and it would not suit him to walk around in a coat clearly meant for a woman.

"He needs a coat," Volzhenko said by the way of greeting. "Shearling coat and a hat—muskrat, or rabbit, or whatever you have."

The man on the counter—whom I guessed to be Trubkozub the elder—looked up with his small beady eyes, which clearly longed to be together, but were prevented from achieving unity only by Trubkozub's large bulbous nose of strangely beautiful lilac hue. "Can help you with that," he said. And yelled, addressing someone hidden behind the curtain of tails, paws, and snouts with glass eyes, "Hey, Petro! Take your thumbs out of your ass, and come help the customer." He gave me an apologetic, yet tender smile. "Kids. You know how they are."

I nodded, hoping that his supposition regarding Trubkozub Junior's thumbs' whereabouts was nothing more than speculation, and feeling otherwise ignorant of ways of furriers' children.

Thankfully, Petro appeared—a small, square boy of maybe fourteen, and seemingly Trubkozub to the bone: he did not waste words but indicated with a brief toss of his flaxen curls that I was to follow him to the back of the shop, where, behind the curtain of various pelts and half-finished hats, there hung a few shearling coats, short and long, as well as some especially warm looking boots, mittens, and hats—all tailored with the fur in, and all originating from sheep rather some more exotic and adorable creatures. Then again, those were probably reserved for women, and I sighed, appalled at my loss of femininity anew.

Petro chose a coat that appeared quite bulky but fit beautifully over my uniform. He then found me a pair of very furry large boots that not only fit over my existing ones, but also went all the way up my legs, secured with belts and buckles, keeping my lower limbs warmer than any woolen trousers or stockings in the world could. Mittens and a hat seemed an unnecessary luxury, a bonus I was grateful for but could have done without. A few moments in Petro's care transformed Siberia from a place of abject terror to something tolerable.

I paid Trubkozub Senior and thanked both Aardvarks profusely; I considered asking about the origin of their name but decided it would be an imposition. Instead, I said, "You wouldn't happen to know when the post office is open, would you?"

Trubkozub the elder nodded. "It's open when I open it," he said solemnly. "We used to have a postmaster, but the winters here proved to be too much for him, so he left. Brave man, he put up with the mosquitoes and the drought, but the winter got to him. Feel like howling, he kept saying. Left after the second winter, took the first train west, and never heard from him again. I'm the postmaster now." He put on his hat, made of the fur of a wolverine or some other menacing beast, and tossed aside the tangle of furs he had been sewing. "Petro," he said. "Mind the store. If the Chinamen come again, you tell them that it's five per pelt and not a penny less. I'll take a few bolts of silk in barter, but very few."

My heart fluttered and then settled, expecting unavoidable disappointment. "Chinamen fur traders?" I asked. "Do they come by often?"

"Not in winter," Trubkozub the elder answered as he wrestled his thick arms into the sleeves of his voluminous coat. "These two showed up yesterday, on a train going back to China. What they were doing so far west, who knows. The strange thing is, they still have a lot of their silk and tea with them. Why didn't they trade it all for pelts, I ask you? And why did they have to go west then back here, hmm?"

"Who knows other people's business?" I answered with as indifferent a shrug as I could manage. "Only I think I met those two before, on the train—I should probably say hello to them."

"That won't be difficult," said Trubkozub as he headed out the door, the keys on a heavy iron ring clinking like icicles. "They'll either be here, haggling over nothing, or at the tavern, where the rest of you hussars are drinking now. The cook there is a Chinaman too, a good cook. Makes those Chinese pelmeni, calls them pot stickers—very much recommend them, young men. Try them when you join the rest of your army or regiment or whatever they call it nowadays."

He chatted amiably and we followed. The three of us crossed the windswept street, dodging handfuls of snow lobbed at us by fir branches roused by particularly frisky gusts. I only smiled into my new collar that smelled faintly of milk and barn warmth, immune to such shenanigans.

The post office was a log building, single-storied, with shuttered windows, like everything else in this street. Trubkozub unlocked the door and let us inside with significant sighing. He took his place behind the counter and took off his hat. "What can I help you with?" he said in a much more official voice than the one we had been subjected to so far. It was almost as if he truly believed he became a different person, a postmaster instead of a furrier, the moment he stood behind the official counter.

"I need to mail these." I handed over six envelopes and paid, as he laboriously calculated the exact price of delivery and tax for each of the letters. He did not seem surprised they were all addressed to the same person—all except one, that was heading back to St. Petersburg and addressed to Eugenia, a letter in which I said very little but did my best to convey the emotional drain this journey had been subjecting me to.

Trubkozub collected money and promised my letters would go out that night, with the first train heading west. It perplexed me still, this single line of travel and communication, this rut of steel and creosote-soaked wood along which we traveled, constrained by the rocking trains on their iron tracks. How could one not long for the three dimensional freedom of airships and submarines in a world such as this? I wished I had the plans Jack had spirited away. I also felt guilty at the thought that I should be missing Jack more than I actually did.

True, I was concerned about his well-being—as I would be concerned for any friend whose whereabouts were unknown and surrounded by danger; but I did not miss him in a way Olga and my other friends would expect, in a way that Jack himself might have liked. It occurred to me that by traveling with him I took a significant social risk; it would be a pity to ruin one's reputation for a man one was not romantically interested in.

"Well," Volzhenko intruded upon my reverie, "maybe now we can go and have a drink."

"And get something to eat," I agreed. "I haven't eaten in three days."

"Come on then!" Volzhenko bounded for the door like a very

large and a very enthusiastic puppy, and I followed in a more sedate manner.

At the door, I waved goodbye to Trubkozub. "Thank you."

He smiled, and lit a kerosene lamp—I hadn't realized it was getting dark despite it still being afternoon. "You be well now," Trubkozub the elder said. "And if you ever need any furs or pelts, you know where to come."

I promised I would, and ran after Volzhenko, my new fur boots squeaking on the smooth snow, colored lavender by the long slow shadows.

THE TAVERN WAS NOISY, SMELLY, WARM, AND WELCOMING. THE rotmistr presided, as one would expect, over several tables pushed together. It was a Roman bacchanal in spirit if not in exact letter, and there was shouting and singing and spilled wine and awkward dancing cut tragically short by gravity, the cruel mistress of drunks and children.

Right away, I realized that as much as the rotmistr was always kind and welcoming, I would be better off trying to find some food by myself rather than joining the party already in progress. A young man, his dirty apron betraying his occupation as a scullery helper, loitered by the kitchen door but did not dare to venture into the tavern hussars had taken over so completely. I smiled at him. "Say, fellow," I asked. "Is the kitchen still open?"

He scratched his freckled button nose thoughtfully. "The cook is there, only he has some friends with him since no one here seems to care and winters are generally slow. But go right in, see if he will make you something."

I pushed the door and entered a cloud of steam smelling of sesame oil, and plowed through the dense artificial fog toward the sound of voices speaking Chinese.

I found the cook and Kuan Yu and Liu Zhi sitting around a thick wooden slab all the way in the back of the kitchen, next to a vast sink filled with boiling, steaming water, and a busy day's worth of dishes. A woodstove blazed with red flames, and crackled with the resinous sap of the pine and fir branches.

"Hussar Menshov!" Kuan Yu cried out in English. "We wondered if you would be along with your fellow hussars. Have you found Mr. Bartram?"

I shook my head. "I worry the English have him, but I found no trace of him."

Liu Zhi gave me a penetrating look. "You got here fast enough; you didn't look for long."

"I fell ill," I said, and felt my cheeks blaze with shame.

Kuan Yu whispered to his friend and smiled at me. "Do not worry," he said, reassuring. "Do not pay attention to Zhi—he's a busybody. Here, meet our friend Woo Pei, the cook here."

I shook hands with a very tall and very thin Chinese gentleman, who wore his hair braided in a long queue. His lips pressed tightly together, lest a word or a smile escaped from them.

"I hear you make great pot stickers," I said.

He nodded. "My fame precedes me. Or rather, it escapes my kitchen and wanders about looking for new customers. Sit with us then, as I was about to make food for my friends. You are welcome to join us, but you mustn't get angry if we speak our own language."

I shrugged. "Why would I be? Surely if it is something that concerns me you would tell me. Correct?"

Woo Pei said something in Cantonese, and the three of them laughed. I busied myself taking off my new furs and watching Woo Pei boil water in a copper kettle, and pour it over flour. He mixed the dough and kneaded it with his long, thin fingers, then cut it into small pieces and flattened them. With minute, precise motions that seemed more suited to a watchmaker than a cook, he chopped onions and mixed them with ground meat and sesame oil, dusted the mixture with potato flour, and stuffed all the tiny dough circles with meat.

Before I knew it, he was heating a large iron skillet. As it hissed and sputtered oil, he dropped perhaps three dozen of the tiny meat dumplings into the skillet. He then poured water over them, covered the skillet, and sat down with the rest of us.

"Five minutes," he told me in Russian, and then went back to talking with Kuan Yu and Liu Zhi. By then, the aroma of onion and meat had grown strong enough to distract me from any other thoughts but how hungry I was. Jack was an afterthought now, as I concentrated on not looking too impatient.

The pot stickers were delicious—fried golden on one side and steamed perfectly otherwise, served with brown salty and spicy dipping sauce , they seemed to me a most delicious meal I had ever tasted. I always got such an impression when eating after a long hike or a protracted riding lesson, something about the combination of physical exertion and fresh air made even the simplest food taste divine, a joy meant to be savored only infrequently, distinct in my memory from all the other mundane, everyday meals.

After the four of us had finished eating, I sat back in my chair, enjoying the pleasant sensation of fullness and warmth, accompanied by the first twinges of fatigue. I listened to the three Chinese men, and imagined myself back in the comfortable confines of the Crane Club, its vast windows gilded by the setting sun, its mysterious tiny machines and airship models humming and whirring, the tiny jointed wings folding and unfolding like paper fans . . .

Two words pulled me abruptly back into the tavern kitchen in a brand-new Siberian town. The words *Taiping Tianguo* stood out clearly in the otherwise incomprehensible speech.

I sat bolt upright and leaned over the table, as if sheer effort of my will would be enough to decipher the indecipherable syllables, and I wished I had learned Cantonese back in St. Petersburg when there was still someone to teach me. As Eugenia had warned me when I was just a child, no one grew up with no regrets; the best one could do was to make sure one's regrets were not stupid.

Woo Pei noticed me straining to understand, laughed softly, and spoke to Kuan Yu, his gaze still lingering on mine. I felt rather like a dog, trying so hard to understand what the men around me were talking about, and vaguely hoping for something good, trying to discern their mood from their intonation—but their language was so alien, everything sounded the same.

Kuan Yu finally turned to me, and if I had a tail, I would've wagged it in relief and jubilation. "Apologies," he said. "Woo Pei is away from home, so we tell him what we know about the Heavenly Kingdom of Great Peace. We also tell him about your Englishman, because everyone who travels through this town, they come here to eat and talk. At least, when there are no hussars around—they make it too noisy."

"Well?" I sucked in my breath and leaned back, my hands fisted in the pockets of my britches, trying to feign impatience I did not feel. "Will he tell me if he's seen my friend or not?"

Kuan Yu smiled, his anthracite eyes narrowing like those of a sated cat. "He hasn't," he answered. "But we have something we found in your compartment, after you left in Yekaterinburg. A letter."

"Give it to me!" I cried, forgetting all proper decorum and reaching out with both hands, like a child. "Why haven't you told me?" Relief and fear alternately lapped at my heart, making it soar with hope that this was my lost letter, my confession that did not belong in anyone's hands but mine, and then plummet with grief when I thought that it was nothing, a useless scrap discarded by the previous passengers, a train schedule, a nothing.

Kuan Yu smiled still. "If I give that letter to you, will you do something for me?"

I heaved a sigh. Everyone wanted the same thing—information. Who spied on whom, why the British were forming alliance with the Turks, why there had to be a war . . . if only I could answer such questions to anyone's satisfaction. It was intimidating, really, to realize how little I knew, and how little business I had meddling with forces and powers too great for anyone, least of all me. "What do you want?"

"Nothing much. Just your word that you do not mean to harm us, to harm the Taiping."

I smiled, relieved. "I . . . we mean no harm, I swear to you. We want an alliance between China and Russia, because both are in danger of aggression from the West."

Kuan Yu nodded, solemn. "That is true. There's fear that the British will start another war, if the Qing do not get the Taiping under control fast enough."

"So you do not think the Qing would be interested in allying themselves with Russia."

"No." Kuan Yu's smile was frozen, a sliver of white ice in his dark beard. "Qing . . . you know they are foreigners, you know how Han hate them. But there's also this: they have chosen their demon. They know it is a demon, a demon that torments and kills and mutilates them every day, and yet it is familiar and they tell themselves that it will protect them from other demons."

"You think all westerners are demons?"

Woo Pei shook his head, impatient. "It is not that. Your god is taking over our gods, and maybe it is all right, maybe they can all live together or they will battle and the weak ones will perish. What it is, however, is this: we do not yet believe we must ally with any demon. Maybe we are naïve and foolish, but we do think like this: maybe we don't have to honor demons, maybe there are angels, or maybe we, ourselves, are enough. Qing, they believe in nothing but the demons and are eager to strike a bargain without ever thinking that maybe they don't have to."

Despite his faltering words and circuitous manner of speaking, his explanation made sense to me. Moreover, I recognized myself, Eugenia, Jack: we all were too fearful to expect anything but disappointment. I thought maybe this was why all of us were constantly rewarded with it. I nodded, wordless, and sat back in my chair, no longer tense and reaching. "Maybe we are not demons," I said.

"Maybe so." Kuan Yu put a folded envelope in front of me. I opened it to find a sheet of paper covered in Jack's careful hand. My heart fluttered, and I forgot to even feel disappointed once I realized it wasn't my letter.

"My dearest Sasha," the letter opened, rather dramatically, "I hope this finds you well. I must beg your forgiveness for not telling you earlier, but I fear that our pursuers (and I am ashamed to recognize them as my countrymen) may have too easy a time following us. Yet, I worry that if one of us were to be captured, the fate of the other would be as good as sealed. So I have made a decision to travel separately—and I hope you will forgive me for not betraying my means, for to tell you would be to put you in a greater danger." I stopped there and thought peevishly that he knew the way I was traveling and therefore was in a position to betray me while not extending me the same courtesy. Or was he so certain that he liked me more than I liked him? I continued reading.

"I will wait for you in Krasnoyarsk, and only hope you will do the same for me if you get there first. If we do not meet in one week's time, proceed without me. If it is at all in my powers, I will make sure the documents you need to achieve your purpose will be available to you."

Strange—how could he make sure of something like that, unless he had a trusted courier? Moreover, there was no place of meeting indicated anywhere. I turned the page over, and found a faint, spidery scrawl that I would have missed if I had not searched so intently any sign at all.

"Follow your heart," it read. "Believe your heroes."

This advice seemed both too general and too hackneyed for Jack, so I decided it was a secret way of telling me where to meet him. The trouble was, I had no idea what was in Krasnoyarsk, and who I could possibly follow there, let alone which ones of my heroes he was talking about.

I folded the letter and stuffed it carefully into the inner pocket of my uniform, as Kuan Yu and Liu Zhi watched. I wondered if they had read the letter.

"Are you going to Krasnoyarsk?" I asked them.

"Eventually," Liu Zhi answered and twisted his mustache thoughtfully. "Who knows when the next train comes? In winter, there's snow, there's cold and breakage. Trains unreliable. Unless the hussars let us join them."

"This could be arranged, I'm sure," I said, and rose. "Come along, it is high time the two of you met some of my colleagues."

Liu Zhi and Kuan Yu nodded to Woo Pei and followed me; their docility and easy manner kept surprising me. After all, I had barely made their acquaintance before witnessing them kick in several English heads. I puzzled whether traveling with me would be of some benefit to them—if it were, it would be easier for me to accept their willingness to come along.

We found the party in the tavern had grown subdued, as most

of the participants had either left for the train and its warmth and benches, or fell asleep where they sat. The rotmistr and still sober Volzhenko were the only two who seemed in possession of their faculties. A few hussars were leaving, and Volzhenko barked orders at them, telling them to all stay together, to take a head count when they left and when they arrived, and to report the irregularities to Cornet Petrovsky who was already on the train. When Volzhenko saw me, he grinned. "Has to be done," he shouted by the way of explanation. "These sorry bastards get drunk, wander through the snow, fall over and pass out, and then we find them dead, like logs frozen solid. We make sure that if anyone falls behind, there's someone there to go back and dig him out of a snowdrift. Necessary, that."

"I see," I said, and smiled.

The rotmistr winked and laughed, and gave an exaggerated head tilt in the direction of Kuan Yu and Liu Zhi. Woo Pei remained invisible in the kitchen, but his presence was still palpable in the sweaty, musty din of the room. "Your friends?"

"Fur traders from China," I said. And added in a burst of inspiration, "I am paying them to escort me around Beijing. May they travel with me?"

The rotmistr scratched the back of his head, and then opened in his arms in a gesture of wide wonderment. "Oh, young Poruchik Menshov. How I envy your gift of making friends, of finding what you need to find. Of course they may travel with you—we have space."

"Thank you, rotmistr." I leaned over the table to shake his wide, calloused hand that reminded me of a piece of leather tack more than human flesh. "I cannot thank you enough for your kindness."

He waved his hands in the air, as if suddenly shy of gratitude and praise. "The pleasure is all mine, poruchik," he said.

I had to admire how quickly his speech changed from educated and businesslike to lilting and folksy, as if he was so used to playing one of his hussars, all peasants in their past lives, that it took him effort to remember how to speak as an educated man, while the reverse transition came as easy as breathing. "The pleasure's all mine. You see, it's winter, the nights are long, the days have all but disappeared, and the road is long and snowy and difficult. There are rumors of roaming wolves and rails busted open from the freeze, but—and call me a superstitious man if you must—but I look at you and I wonder. I wonder at how you manage to slip away from those who are looking for you and how you continue—as unstoppable as an arrow—and the world turns to spread itself under your feet so that you may get to wherever it is you're going. With you on board, I am sure our journey will go well, little hussar, so you bring whoever you need to bring with you, and may God be with you all."

I wasn't sure if he was serious or joking, but I could not doubt that his sharp eyes saw Kuan Yu cross himself when God was mentioned.

Chapter 14

I WONDERED OCCASIONALLY WHETHER I HAD FALLEN ASLEEP and dreamed this entire journey, if I would wake up back in St. Petersburg—or even in Trubetskoye, and discover that the last year of my life was just a dream brought on by a too late and too filling meal. I could hope, couldn't I?

Not that I was unhappy, but I felt so detached from everything I had ever known. I drifted among the strange people and occurrences, missed my mother and my aunt, and still moved inexorably east, along the narrow steel tracks that pierced the heart of my country like a shining needle piercing the thorax of a butterfly.

Kuan Yu and Liu Zhi made fast friends with the hussars. Here, without the compartments, we all shared the same living space, and it felt like a gypsy encampment where people moved from bench to bench, forming temporary alliances and knots of conversations and laughter and card games. We consumed ridiculous amounts of pickled herring and pot stickers and wine; the rotmistr made sure that we were well stocked with food and drink, since the military trains did not bother with a restaurant carriage—or many other amenities. Besides the engineer and the freedmen feeding coal to the insatiable maw of the locomotive, coal that powered its terrible blazing heart, it was just the hussars, two Chinese fur traders, and I.

Kuan Yu and Liu Zhi had fulfilled the requirements of their professed occupation, and bought a goodly portion of Trubkozub's inventory, as well as bartered several bolts of white and blue silk. I had made a mental note not to leave China before acquiring several miles worth of this smooth, shimmering material in pale blue for my mother, and a few bolts of black for Eugenia. Both would surely enjoy it.

Krasnoyarsk used to be a frontier town, Cornet Volzhenko who seemed to consider himself my friend now, told me. It was built to guard the eastern reaches of the empire back in the seventeenth century, and now it had retained some of its old forts. "All wood," Volzhenko said as he sipped wine from his tin mug, his legs stretched across the aisle between our benches, and his large boots propped comfortably next to me. "Nothing really modern there. There's a garrison though, all Cossacks, I think."

"That's good," I said. "What are they doing there?"

Volzhenko shrugged. "Guarding the border, I suppose."

"They are not near the border."

"Somewhat near."

"Not near enough to guard it."

Volzhenko smiled. I noticed he looked particularly young when he grinned like that—lopsided, showing a chipped canine tooth on the left side of his mouth, his faintly freckled nose wrinkling. I frowned, thinking that if there was to be a war, Volzhenko would certainly be sent to fight and likely to die. Eugenia's words floated back in my memory—her lamentations for her brother who was killed in the previous war, the helpless cry of those who were left alive and had to carry the burden of remembering the dead. "I'm sure if there's a war with China, the Krasnoyarsk garrison will be there in spades. When we get there, I'll take you to one of the Buryat teahouses—I swear, their tea is the strangest thing I had ever seen. They make it with lard."

"That doesn't sound like something I would want to try."

Volzhenko laughed, slapped his knee for emphasis. "You have to. For the experience, see? It's not as awful as it sounds."

"Right."

"Well, it is pretty awful," Volzhenko admitted. "But you have to have experiences like this, you know." He removed his feet from my bench and leaned forward, elbows in his knees. "This is one thing I believe. You know how Father in church, how he always tells you about your soul, and how he's always yapping about soul this and soul that?"

I nodded. "I know, although I haven't been to church in a while."

"No matter, you remember. And how they always make it sound like your soul is something you always have, how you get it when you're still in your mother's belly and have it till you die, and how it is always the same and unchanged?"

"That's the long and the short of it, yes."

"But I think they are wrong, and I don't care if they say it's heretical and such. I think that we are born only with a capacity for the soul, and the things we experience and learn and think about, this is what makes the soul up—the layers of everything. I heard there was that Father, a priest in Moscow who wanted to take a picture of God, so he bought this contraption for taking daguerreotypes, and took pictures of everything—his room, trees, streets, birds, just everything around him. And he took them all on the same plate, because he hoped that all these images one on top of each other, all of them translucent, would make a portrait of God."

"Did it work?"

He laughed and ruffled his hair, his hand traveling a familiar path from the back of his neck to his forehead. "I don't know; I doubt it. But I think it works with us—we, people, we are just cameras, and every image, everything we see and experience becomes us, becomes our soul, all of them layered and translucent . . . " His voice trailed off as his gaze grew remote, directed at something far away, beyond the walls of the train carriage.

"That's beautiful," I whispered, entranced by the delicate elegance of his heresy. "I didn't realize you were a philosopher."

"I took a course at the seminary in Moscow," he said. "The rotmistr, bless him, persuaded me when I was still young enough to listen that one didn't have to serve God by repeating the most trivial babblings of his most unimaginative servants." Like the rotmistr, Volzhenko possessed the valuable gift of changing his diction to suit circumstance. I was starting to feel I was in a den of shape-shifters of a most peculiar kind—those who changed from simple and uneducated bumpkins to sophisticated gentlemen in a wink of an eye.

"It's hard to imagine you a priest," I said.

He nodded. "I was going to join the black clergy too—to become a monk. White, the parish priests, are too well fed and too content with their wives and children and being pillars of the community. The monks at least have a greater purpose than keeping their belly full. Monks . . . one could become an archimandrite. But yes, higher purpose is what I wanted."

"None higher that the cavalry," I said.

"You said a mouthful there, Menshov. Maybe you're not as dumb as you look."

"Look who's talking."

He laughed. "Fair enough. What I learned in the seminary—that was all nothing. I really started to develop true understanding when I started listening to the rotmistr."

"I know. He is your teacher, prophet, and God."

Volzhenko did not laugh but grew serious instead. "You need to talk to him more, maybe you'll understand what a great man he is."

The rotmistr towered two benches over, so we took our wine and migrated to sit next to him, disrupting his whispered and, by all appearances, emotional discussion with Petrovsky. If the rotmistr was indeed a messiah, he couldn't have wished for more dedicated disciples than his cornets.

"Sit with us, you two," he addressed us when we approached. "I was just telling the dolt here why I joined the military."

"The Napoleonic war?" I guessed. "Lost your father in it?"

"This, my young poruchik, is all coincidental although not wrong," he replied. "But the real reason is that unless you die with a weapon in your hand—and what is a better way to ensure such manner of death than joining the military?—you cannot reach Valhalla."

"Valhalla," I repeated. The rotmistr appeared to be one of those rare individuals who managed to combine a perfectly traditional upbringing with unexpected paganism of the school that greatly exaggerated the nobility and acumen of our Scandinavian neighbors, but I was at least willing to give the rotmistr a chance to talk about his unorthodoxies, since we had a few hours until arrival to Krasnoyarsk.

"Valhalla," the rotmistr said and sobered up visibly. "Not because of what you think, Menshov—not just weapons or the flying wenches . . . whatever they are called."

"Valkyrie," Petrovsky offered in a reverential tone, his eyes glistening. I guessed that he harbored some ideas of his own as well.

"Right," the Rotmistr said, nodding. He pulled a wine bottle from under the bench where it fit for easy storage, and topped off the mugs of both cornets. He handed the bottle with the leftovers to me, and I guessed that I was to drink directly from it. "But flying wenches or no, this is not why. You know that in the great hall, in

Odin's hall—and Odin is the one who takes the warriors fallen in battle—they drink and then they fight, and whoever falls in that battle wakes up whole again, so he can drink and fight and die again. In Valhalla, it's not like heaven, where you get to stay alive forever and play some lute or harp . . . there, the world is destroyed every day, and then rebuilt anew, so nothing is ever old, ever stale."

I took a cautious sip of the wine. "But everyone gets resurrected and they're still the same."

The rotmistr wagged his thick, calloused finger at me, dirt around his fingernail black as gunpowder, and I suspected that it had become incorporated into his skin and could never be washed out. "No one is the same after resurrection. Read the classics, Menshov. Cannot step twice in the same river, and everything changes even if you go away from home for a week. What do you think happens to everything, to the world, if you daily destroy and rebuild it? It changes, because nothing can ever be recreated perfectly."

"So what do you want with it?" I asked, wine making me bolder. "You want to be killed and resurrected too?"

He shook his head, sly. "No no. I'd sit in the corner and watch and take notes, on how everything becomes different from day to day to day. I would keep track of all the small alterations, of all the tiny fault lines and cracks that appear from one resurrection to the next. And I will be there when everything finally crumbles to dust."

"What will happen then?"

"Ragnarok," he said. "When the new world will be made from scratch instead of rebuilding an old one again and again, from a broken mold that wasn't that great to begin with."

"You want an apocalypse?"

He shook his head vigorously. "Aren't you even listening to me, lad? Apocalypse means that the world ends and we all go live in the clouds with harps, or in the eternal flames with pitchforks as the case may be. No, what I want is a new, better world, and the only way to make it happen is to go to Valhalla, and to go there I need to die with a weapon in my hand. Believe me, I've given it a lot of thought, and Ragnarok seems like the only way to a new world rather than a mere destruction of the old one."

I suppose I could think the rotmistr was simply insane, raving mad, and yet charismatic enough to attract two youthful and foolish cornets as followers. But talking to Kuan Yu had prepared me for such things. When he talked about Hong Xiuquan, it seemed rather immaterial whether he was insane or not, and whether Hong was indeed Jesus' younger brother. In some situations—and most of those seemed to deal with religion, I had noticed—sanity seemed a meaningless concept, and one had to ask whether such convictions would harm the world or make it better. It was difficult to decide that about either the rotmistr or Hong Xiuquan; although I had no doubt both meant well, and this was more than I could say about almost everyone else.

By the time we had reached Krasnoyarsk, I had developed a feeling that I was still at the university, so many lectures about philosophy and religion I was subjected to. I rather enjoyed the experience, and between the rotmistr and his disciples and Kuan Yu, who was also quite given to theological speculation, my mind swelled with ideas. Kuan Yu too seemed enthralled by the rotmistr's stories of Odin and the entire choosing of the slain process. Kuan Yu managed to tie it in with his thoughts on Kuan Ti and a variety of goddesses he claimed to honor—deities I was hearing about for the first time. I liked the goddess of the sea best, because she was the one in charge of all waters and oceans, and in my own oblique way, without betraying much of my thoughts to myself, I decided she would be the one looking over Hong Kong and other port cities, and—by extension—after Chiang Tse.

The rotmistr and the cornets in turns argued with and listened to Kuan Yu, and I could sense their minds turning and absorbing new gods, turning them this way and that, fitting them into their view of the world.

"And what about you, poruchik?" the rotmistr asked me when we were about two hours away from Krasnoyarsk. "What do you think of this whole God balderdash?"

I shrugged, my attention riveted to the black tunnel of fir forest we sped through, to the glistening of the diamond dust in the still air—I could tell, with some mysterious sixth sense, that it was very cold outside, colder than Novonikolaevsk, cold enough for birds to freeze in their flight and fall out of the sky like small feathered stones. "I don't know," I said. "I'm Orthodox, as I was brought up, and I do wish I had more opportunities to go to mass and to light a candle for my father's soul."

The rotmistr grinned from his seat across from mine. "You were brought up one way, and you never questioned it?"

"No," I said. "Why would I? There was never any reason—I guess I do not find myself trapped in a carriage full of amateur theologians often enough."

That made him laugh. "So you believe in the clouds and the souls and all that."

"I suppose." I looked away from the black-and-white landscape streaming past the window, regretful to be dragged into yet another argument I had no particular desire for. "I do not believe that questioning everything is necessarily a virtue."

"So you prefer obedience."

"No, but sometimes it is easier to follow a simple path rather than guessing everything about it. You question so much, it is a miracle you manage to get yourself dressed in the morning."

"I have a batman for that," the Rotmistr answered but grinned.

"However, I see your point. Only God ought to be more important than getting dressed."

"To you maybe," I answered icily. "I take my attire quite seriously, and when I'm not in uniform, I assure you I'm quite a stylish dresser."

The cornets laughed and the rotmistr smiled into his mustache and dropped the subject. The train whistled and steamed and whined, and pulled into the station an hour later.

We found the garrison in a state of disarray and alarm. It was a small one, protected by a palisade of pointed thick logs aimed at the sky like spears. Behind the palisade, there were a few wooden barracks, a training ground, stables and a kitchen, and officers' quarters. All of the buildings and the snow-covered training ground, its snowy surface broken by chaotic chains of footprints, indicative of panic rather than proper military maneuvers, were surrounded by bearded soldiers, many only half dressed, some armed. All looked startled and kept calling to each other trying to see what had happened.

A few horses bounded across the training ground, almost up to their bellies in powdery snow, kicking up white fountains as they strained against the resistant substance. The horses whinnied and thrashed, silly animals that they were, firmly convinced the stuff holding their legs meant them harm and that they had to fight for their very lives. A tall bay gelding lost its footing and skidded, landing hard on its flank. I hoped it was not injured.

The rotmistr, the cornets and I, all of us bundled in our yards of furs, stood just inside the gates, surveying the mass confusion. "What's going on?" I said, succumbing to the apparent need of repeated demands for information that ruled the garrison.

"Let's find out." The rotmistr moved ahead with the confident but lopsided strides of his slightly bowed legs; the cornets and I followed like oversized, fur-clad ducklings.

The rotmistr approached a man dressed in a pelisse and dragoon uniform jacket decorated with a few medals and officer's epaulettes; he would had cut a lot more impressive figure of he wore his britches rather than the bottoms of his under flannels tucked in his shining, spurred boots. "Excuse me," the rotmistr said. "What's the trouble? I have a trainload of hussars here, and we will be more than happy to assist you if you only tell me what's going on and what's to be done."

The man's eyes cast about wildly, as if he had just woke from a terrifying dream. "The English," he rasped. "We were attacked by the English, leaping over the fence, stealing horses . . . one of my men tried to apprehend the trespassers, and he had his musket torn out of his hands, and its barrel tied into a knot. He says, the man who did it did it with his bare hands. Tied solid iron into a knot."

"How many were there?" I asked, my heart fluttering with excitement and relief. One thing about Jack, he could rarely be confused with anyone else.

The man shrugged, distraught. "There was the one who ambushed the man guarding the stables . . . and then there was shouting, and they grabbed horses . . . no one expected an attack, not here, not in the middle of the winter."

"I understand," the rotmistr said, his voice even, soothing.

By the time the terrified horses were caught and put back into their stables (adjacent to the barracks for warmth) and the soldiers had regained their composure and disentangled themselves from the horses' tack and each other's muskets, the sun had almost set, and we were led to the officers' quarters—a grand name for a log cabin divided into three apartments, each with a small bedroom and a sitting room, plus a common kitchen and a dining room with a long rough pine table. The table looked as if it was waiting for an opportunity to stuff someone's unsuspecting palm full of splinters. Paisley drapes struggled valiantly to disguise the room's rough-hewn severity, but failed miserably.

We waited for two batmen, both Cossacks, to prepare the table for dinner. It was barely afternoon, and yet the sky had grown dark and star studded— fat yellow stars, spreading like wiggly-legged spiders over the royal blue of the sky, not the pale, cold white pinpricks one saw in St. Petersburg.

The moon was also out—large and peach-colored, with a few spots that looked like decay. It hung outside of the officers' dining room window as if eager to eavesdrop on our conversation. It was quiet now, with an occasional sharp bark of an Arctic fox or some other small predator, cold and hungry and ecstatic to be alive, to feel the steam of its blood coalescing against the solid cold of the night.

The garrison's commander, Captain Kurashov, told us the story again over dinner. He had calmed down, and for a while I wondered why a real soldier would be so distraught about the theft of a horse or two, even if it was accompanied by the appearance of Spring Heeled Jack. Surprise must have had something to do with it; but it also seemed the source of his unhappiness was internal—brought about by his disappointment at his own inability to deal with a sudden unpredictable situation. It was the sadness of a man who had been tested and found himself lacking.

I wished I could offer words of comfort, but at the time my mind was preoccupied with Jack's whereabouts as well as those of Dame Nightingale and her contingent of agents. Anything that did not get me closer to the answer grated on my nerves .

"You have to know where they might have gone," I blurted out half way through the dinner, interrupting the soothing speech

Rotmistr Ivankov had been delivering. "I mean, there are not that many places here, are there?"

Captain Kurashov gave me a mournful, lingering look. "It is a small town," he said. "There's a Buryat village nearby, but in this cold the horses won't get far, even if they are well cared for. I do not know if the man who took them, or the rest of the English, would know how to handle such fragile animals in the Siberian winter. They are not locals."

I supposed I should've felt bad for the horses, but my focus allowed no distractions. "So they couldn't have gotten far. When can your men go after them?"

The captain's face folded into an accordion of surprise and concern. "Should we go after them?"

"Of course," I said. "If you don't, rumors will spread. You don't want to become known as a cowardly garrison, do you? Word does get around."

He scowled at me. "Don't talk nonsense, young man. I am forty-two, and your stupid challenges are not going to work. If you want to go and look and bring our horses back, then please be my guest; we will appreciate it. We, however, need to assess the damage and investigate how that man got over the fence."

"You said he jumped."

He scratched his chin, thoughtful. "A few of my soldiers swear that this is exactly what happened. And yet, he must have used some device—a trampoline, or a spring of some sort, or spring-loaded stilts . . . " His forehead furrowed, and I could see the brain of the poor captain working as hard as his jaws, grinding down a piece of rye bread. "He would've used something like that, wouldn't he?"

"I don't know." I wasn't sure he was quite ready for the Spring Heeled Jack exposition. "But I thank you—tomorrow morning we'll look for your horses . . . I hope it doesn't snow tonight."

There was a loud pounding on the door, and the Cossack batman let in a small, shivering boy of perhaps fourteen, in a uniform that was criminally large for him. He was black-haired and his eyes had a curious almond shape, as if he had more than a small portion of Chinese or Buryat blood in him. Whatever the mix of his blood, it was not keeping him warm enough as he stood in the middle of the dining room, squinting and blinking at the light of the kerosene lamps, apparently oblivious to our presence.

"Well?" Kurashov nudged.

The boy startled, then fell back into a military stance and saluted his captain. "Sir," he said. "You better come and look. They found something in the stables."

THE SOMETHING THE YOUNG MAN WAS REFERRING TO TURNED OUT to be a piece of paper, folded over so many times it was ready to fall apart at the seams. The paper was also soaked with melted slush, and bore a distinct hoof print. Still, I recognized Jack's handwriting.

"It's addressed to Sasha Menshov," the young man said.

Kurashov yielded the missive without argument, and he and the rotmistr watched me intently as I read, as if they expected the contents to appear, by some literary osmosis, on my forehead.

"My dearest friend," Jack wrote.

"I hope this letter reaches you. I hope my appearance has created enough of a stir to circulate rumors and to attract your perspicacious attention. I also hope that the commander here will be good enough to pass this letter along, and that my pursuers will not intercept it: it is quite a bit of hope.

"For the fear that it might never reach you, I will be brief and remind you of the night we first met. I certainly hope you would keep the same company, and, moreover, appreciate their inventive spirit. The rest, I leave with the Providence, and hope it will be enough."

I folded the cryptic letter, and looked around the table.

"Well?" the rotmistr said.

"This may seem odd to ask," I said, "but is there a place nearby where Chinese engineers gather?"

Captain Kurashov did not seem surprised. "There's a Chinese settlement near the Buryat village," he said. "Furriers, but there may be engineers too. If you want to get there, you may want to hire a caribou or a dog sled, but caribou would be easier if you're used to horses. I assume you will be looking for our horses or them men who took them?"

I SLEPT IN THE BARRACKS—SIMPLE ROOMS SMELLING OF PINE, with narrow wooden benches which were about as comfortable as the ones in the train. I was so used to sleeping on wooden benches that beds seemed a half-remembered and puzzling extravagance, a nice conceit but something that had little to do with me. When I stretched out on my bench and closed my eyes, the barracks thudded and swayed with the steady rocking movement of the train; I imagined a lonesome whistle, and fell asleep right away.

Volzhenko shook me awake what seemed like moments later. The dark barrack was filled with dozens of soldiers' bodies, their sour smell and uneven snoring. "Wake up," Volzhenko said. "It's six in the morning, and we'd better get moving if we want to get to the Buryat village."

"Are Kuan Yu and Liu Zhi coming with us?" I asked and sat up, rubbing my eyes with both fists, the grit of sleep grinding into my swollen eyelids that wanted only to close and get some more sleep.

"Yes," Volzhenko said. "Kurashov found us a sleigh and three horses, and it shouldn't take us more than an hour to get there. Are you sure that this is where we should be going?"

"Somewhat," I said. "In any case, I guess I'll have a chance to try that Buryat tea you were so eager to share."

Volzhenko's teeth flashed in the dusk. "I told you that it was an interesting experience, not necessarily a pleasant one."

"You're just mad that you fell for it and now you want everyone else to do the same." I rolled out of the bed, and cringed when my bare feet hit the frozen floor with an uncalled for thud. "It's cold here."

"The sort of thing you would expect in the middle of winter in Siberia," Volzhenko said amiably. "Put your furs on, you'll feel better."

I collected my jacket and the coat from the foot of the bed where they were folded for safekeeping as well as providing additional warmth for my feet, and put them on. I could've used a clean shirt, but Volzhenko standing next to me deterred me from putting one on. The reverse corset felt unpleasantly mushy, as if it was welding itself to my skin, becoming some porous and smelly flesh. I only sighed and hoped that I would be able to detach it when time came for me to become a girl again.

The sleigh and horses, covered with felt blankets, waited by the stable adjacent to our barracks. Kuan Yu and Liu Zhi, barely visible in the gray morning light, outlined against the long blue snowdrifts hopped from one foot to the other, their hands stuffed in their sleeves. By mute consent, Volzhenko took the reins, and the rest of us piled in the back of the sleigh. There were blankets and felt spreads, and Kuan Yu offered me a flask filled with hot and sweet tea. Thus equipped, I felt prepared for the trip to the Buryat village, and only hoped my interpretation of Jack's note was correct. Finally, I had time to sit and think about the meaning of it as well as the tremendous leap of faith he had taken leaving his note—a mere trifle, so easily lost—in the wake of his destructive appearance. Of him staging the distraction—so much like his old self in that—to attract my attention. Such dramatics, however, also seemed excessive.

Volzhenko steered the horses along the narrow road, packed snow hard as a pavement. A sliver of the sun curved over the black treetops on the horizon and the three horses neighed in unison, as if greeting the new day with jubilation it did not, in my opinion, warrant. I sat back and waited for the trees to open up, showing us the village.

Chapter 15

The Buryat village loomed between the trees, a small cluster of low octagonal wooden houses, a strange russified species of nomadic yurts. The tall spruces, their palmate branches weighed down by the snow, shielded the pointed roofs covered with more snow. The nearest roof showed traces of dried grass—I suspected that in the summer this grass was alive and green, a sure sign the yurt hadn't been moved in many years. The rest of the village similarly retained the illusion of nomadic mobility but with walls that had sunk into the ground and grown roots.

At first, I thought the yellow glow came from some sort of lanterns left outside, but as we pulled closer, I saw that the doors stood open and light emitted from the inside of these yurt-houses. Smoke rose from the tops of most, and the air smelled like wood smoke. My hair and furs and the Trubkozub hat I wore low on my forehead became saturated with the smell instantly. I noted with irritation that I would likely smell like a campfire for weeks to come.

Volzhenko rubbed the horses dry, as the Chinese furriers and I danced from one foot to the other and clapped our mittens together. Only when he was satisfied with the horses' condition and content they were unlikely to catch some insidious form of consumption, did he let us move to the nearest yurt, which was bigger than the rest, and boasted an especially thick and straight pillar of smoke coming from the hole in its roof. I guessed it was inhabited by . . . I realized then that I had no idea what Buryats had for authority, but assumed it wouldn't be a superior officer or an emperor, two authorities I was familiar with.

Volzhenko knocked on the wooden wall, close to the doorway opening. Inside, I could see the central room covered with a bright carpet. A hole in the carpet allowed a view of a fire pit dug in what seemed to be bare dirt. Over the fire in the hole there was an iron rack, where a copper kettle bubbled away.

Volzhenko grinned and winked at me. "That would be tea," he said.

"Who lives here?" I whispered.

"The shaman," he said. "When we cross over the Baikal, you'll see more Buddhist Buryats closer to Mongolia, but here they were christened but reverted to their pagan ways." He shrugged. "What can you do?"

"Accumulate experiences," I answered with more acidity than I felt.

The man who came to the door looked short in stature but wide in girth, and his tanned placid face seemed a mere background for his very bright and very black eyes that looked at us with great curiosity. He looked past Volzhenko and myself to Kuan Yu and Liu Zhi, grinned, and said something in the language I didn't understand. Judging by the enthusiastic response from Kuan Yu, it was some form of Chinese, although it sounded different from his usual speech.

Volzhenko tired of waiting, and pushed past the small round man into the yurt. I hesitated, not wanting to be impolite, but the small shaman caught himself and ushered us all inside. My eyes watered from the smoke—most of it managed to escape through the hole in the roof, but enough of it lingered inside to cause some discomfort.

"Sit down," he said to me in good Russian. "Have some tea with me."

I sat down and looked around to distract myself from the unpleasant thought of larded tea. The walls of the yurt rose and cupped above us, in a surprisingly smooth and elegant curve that reminded me of the sweep of the St. Isaac's Cathedral dome.

The yurt was clean and spacious; one corner of it was separated from the rest of the central area by a partition made of green bamboo, pounded flat and woven into a curtain. Along the walls, there were sable pelts tied together in multi-pawed bunches, and small statues interspersed with tall lacquered baskets. There were dried herbs and mushrooms hanging along the walls, and, most mysteriously, despite the wide open door, the interior of the yurt was warm and cozy enough for its owner to wear nothing but a thick quilted robe. All his warmer clothes were piled up on what seemed to be a bed by the wall opposite of the entrance.

Kuan Yu and Liu Zhi, still immersed in a discussion as lively as it was incomprehensible, settled next to me, by the fire and the bubbling kettle. The pine and spruce branches glowed a menacing red in the fire pit, and our host tossed in a few more, needles still green and attached, to liven up the flames. The spruce needles hissed and caught fire, crackling, exhaling great clouds of resinous smoke that smelled like Christmas. It occurred to me that I had missed Christmas, probably asleep on the train somewhere. It was so hard to keep track of days in a place so vast and so distant.

The host, apparently in no hurry to inquire about our business, poured tea into tin mugs, covered in an elaborate filigree of smudged soot. The tea was boiling hot, and devoid of flavor other than butter that left an unpleasant film on my lips. But the liquid made my head swim and gave my nerves a bit of a jolt.

"Drink carefully," Volzhenko whispered. "It'll keep you up all night—this brew is strong; they boil it for hours, you know."

"I didn't," I hissed back. "You could've told me earlier."

"Then you wouldn't have drunk it." Volzhenko laughed softly.

"Probably not."

"You see my point."

I was about to suggest a glaring flaw in his argument, when the small shaman held up his hand. "What do you want?" he spoke to me directly, and under his piercing black eyes I stammered and burned my lips on the edge of the tin mug.

"I'm looking for the Chinese engineers," I said. "And possibly an Englishman who was looking for them yesterday."

He nodded a few times. "There are Chinese here," he said.

Kuan Yu elbowed Liu Zhi and grinned, the two of them apparently apprised of everything the shaman knew.

The shaman continued, "Yes, there are a few Chinese here, but fur traders, mostly. Did you say you wanted engineers?"

"Yes," I said. "Inventors, tinkers, anyone who works with mechanical things."

His face stretched in a sly, wide smile. "Oh. I think I know what you want. You want a factory."

Now, one thing I wasn't quite expecting here was a factory. It seemed too distant from everything, too remote—what could they possibly be making here? I supposed whatever materials were needed could be brought in by the freight trains, but still . . . I realized my face betrayed my doubt because the shaman laughed, leaning back, his elbows almost touching the floor behind him. "There are places between empires where they cannot reach, which are too distant or unimportant to pay attention to. And this is where hidden life thrives, concealed from the powerful eyes but known to those who are curious enough to notice such things."

"What is built at the factory?" I asked. My only familiarity with such establishments was limited to that distant day in Tosno, where we saw that awkward flying machine go up lopsidedly. Belatedly,

I felt a pang of guilt that I had never bothered to find out whether the freedmen we saw that day lived, after the contraption crashed somewhere in the peat fields.

It came like an echo from the past, an answer to some question I asked what felt like many years ago, in a different place, a different life, back when I was a proper girl. "Airships," Kuan Yu answered. "For Taiping Tianguo. Just don't tell anyone."

I looked over at Volzhenko, who clearly was a greater danger to secrecy than my modest person. He grinned back, and I remembered his attitude about accumulating experiences and decided that he was not very likely to tattle. "May we see the factory?" I asked politely.

The shaman nodded. "Just finish your tea," he said.

Somewhere between the disgusting tea and the piling back into the sleigh it occurred to me that none of us had asked the shaman about our supposed mission: the whereabouts of the horses or the Englishman who had disrupted the soldiers' lives at the fort. I wondered, though, if agents of Nightingale were still pursuing me . . . or Jack. If they were following Jack, they would find the factory . . . unless, of course, Jack had not gone there.

I sat in the sleigh, my heart in my mouth, finally understanding the reason and the nature of Jack's strange behavior: our separation and his notes, his promises to meet me and his reluctance to do so. I now doubted he would be at the factory he had sent me to.

It was the behavior of a steppe bird, the one that faked injury when a predator stalked her nest, and ran, dragging her wing behind her, refusing to fly and hopping ever so awkwardly, luring the enemy away from her nest and yet never wandering far enough away to lose the sight of it.

I bit my lip until tears beaded my eyelashes and froze, a string of pearls that refracted the light of the low sun just brushing the treetops of the forest. I smelled the fire pits of the village and the frozen spruce sap, and felt foolish and ungrateful as I thought of Jack who struggled and risked so much to keep Nightingale's attention on himself, not me. I only hoped the detour to the factory would yield its purpose soon, and that I would have enough smarts and the presence of mind to use this opportunity. After all, we were so close to China, I could almost taste it.

The shaman had explained the way to Kuan Yu. He now sat in the front, next to Volzhenko who refused to surrender the reins, and pointed the way. The road was slight but well packed, and the horses' hooves rang on it as if they were wearing glass shoes.

"There should be a turnoff soon," said Kuan Yu, and pointed. "Over there, by that log, I think."

"That is no log," Volzhenko answered and pulled on the reins, stopping the horses short of a dark heap marking the side path.

We got out of the sleigh. The horses, who already knew what lay there, snorted and neighed. The lively one in the center even got to his hind legs and danced, the whites of his eyes flashing wild.

The dark heap was a dead horse, already frozen solid, its mane all icicles and matted hair, its eye reflecting the treetops—filmed over, opaque as a cataract. Snow had been dug up by the thrashing of its front legs and the deep furrows crossed the beginning of the path, obscuring it while simultaneously marking it. A small spray of blood from the beast's mouth marked the snow in front of its muzzle, but we did not see any further injury—until we circled the body and saw that the horse was not merely swaybacked but that its back dipped and rose again at a sharp angle. Its spine was broken, I realized with a pang. The poor thing died a horrible slow and thrashing death as it flailed and struggled to regain its feet and failed.

"That was done intentionally," Volzhenko said. "What terrible bastards. Who'd do something like that to an animal?"

I had my ideas but remained quiet, and I hoped that the rest of my companions wouldn't notice a deep depression in the snow, near where the faint path turned between two closely growing spruces. It looked like an ordinary hole in the snow, brought about by a falling tree or a jumping deer, but I knew that if I looked closely I would find boot prints—the same boot that used the back of the poor horse as a springboard, the boot that pushed off with enough force to break its back.

As Volzhenko clucked his tongue and circled the dead animal, examining the uneven bumps of broken bones stretching its skin in small, gruesome tents, I looked for the traces of Jack's possible pursuers. There were a few hoof prints clustered about the stiff-legged corpse, which then continued down the road. At first I wondered at how they managed to miss the small side path, but then realized that there were more footprints running down the main road—gigantic strides that could only be Jack's. Like a bird leading away and then doubling up on his own footprints, to confuse the predators.

"Well, no saving this horse now," Volzhenko said. "We'll tell Kurashov to send some men to collect it—it ought to be good for dinner."

We helped him to push aside the dead horse and climbed back into the sleigh. We started down the narrow winding path, and I kept looking for other traces of Jack's passage. I prayed he would be waiting for us at the end of the trail.

The next depression created by Jack's leaps lay in the shadow between several spruces, and I would've missed it if I had not been looking for it. The path was a paltry sleigh track, two troughs winding between the silent, snow-covered spruces. It looked like a path that would lead to the kingdom of Morozko or some other imaginary place in a childish tale dealing with winter and frozen palaces and snow-covered woods. Nothing in those tales ever took place east of the Ural Mountains, and I thought of how even our fairy tales valiantly maintained the European gestalt of our national psyche.

Another hole in the snow, this time two-booted, with a spread-out hand print next to it, as if Jack had lost his footing; beside it—a few broken branches, some snow shaken loose in a small mound. I smiled to myself, already forgetting the dead horse at the beginning of the trail, and thinking instead of seeing Jack again. I did miss him, no matter how difficult I found it to return his feelings.

I missed my letter (confession) too. I missed the clarity granted to me by laying my thoughts and feelings down in a straight line—straight like the locomotive tracks, brilliant under the sunlight—instead of meandering as they tended to do when trapped inside my mind, going round and round, looping like this forest path, barely wide enough to allow the passage of the sleigh. Sometimes we moved so close to the trees that they dumped handfuls of snow on our heads, stuffing it down our collars.

If there were further traces of Jack's passage, they were too far from the road to see, or perhaps I was too lost in my recursive self-reflection—as my mother used to say, it is a bad habit of mine. In any case, when I looked up expecting to see nothing but trees, the forest opened up and the horses stopped and shied at the sight of a surprisingly large building built of logs and metal, squatting in the middle of a scorched, blackened clearing devoid of snow and life. The clearing smelled like fire and rust, and I tasted copper on the back of my throat.

The sleigh could go no farther and we dismounted and walked across the strange, dead crunch of sand scorched with such a hot fire that it felt bereft of life—maybe the surface of the sun would feel this way. Even though it had taken us no longer than half a minute to cross from the edge of this ghastly clearing to the door of the factory building, it felt much longer—a sense of desolation gripped my throat and made me take quick, shallow breaths. This place was not natural, and it seemed especially incongruous in such wild surroundings; it would've been more tolerable in a city. It was then that I fully grasped the destructive powers of mankind, its ability to alter its environment to a shocking, ruinous degree. The realization made me light-headed.

We knocked on the double doors, twice as tall as Volzhenko and wide enough to let our horses and sleigh through. There was no answer but a steady, low growling coming from inside and the rhythmic thumping and metallic clashing that served as a counterpoint to it. Volzhenko and I traded a look while Kuan Yu and Liu Zhi just shrugged at each other. Kuan Yu was the one who finally pushed open the gigantic door. It opened with a slow, weighty swing, and we peered cautiously inside.

I consider myself a person virtuous within reason, and as such do not expect to ever visit the depths of Hell and any of its rumored circles; but the moment I entered the factory, I felt I certainly had gained some notion of the experience.

The smell of sulfur was as thick as the hissing steam rising from gigantic vats filled with what looked like molten iron and water poured over it from buckets fetched by sweating coolies, dressed only in the lightest of linen pants and sleeveless shirts. I realized the vats each had a distinct shape, and recognized them as molds containing various parts of some large and alien mechanical contraption.

The feeling of desolation that had gripped me outside of the factory did not let go even though the factory teemed with people and shouts in both Chinese and Russian. There were men pulling ropes, and things hoisted in the air; there were complex membranous wings that reminded me of both dragons and dragonflies, and there were wooden hulls of junks. There was an abundance of life and inventive genius all around me, and yet all I could think of was the scorched ground and the dead horse outside.

Finally, one of the coolies noticed us—or rather, Kuan Yu, who seemed to have taken charge of our small expedition, shouted something loud. The coolie replied, and I studied his uncovered head, long hair, and beard. They exchanged animated sentences, and Liu Zhi joined in.

Volzhenko leaned closer, his mouth so close to my ear that I felt the moisture in his breath. "I keep wanting to learn Chinese, but there's never time or motivation. I wish I could understand what they are barking about."

"Talking," I said, and moved away. "They are talking."

Volzhenko laughed. "What's came over you?"

I just shrugged and watched two workers stretching animal skins, scrubbed and tanned, over the skeleton of hollow metallic tubes. It seemed to be too small for a proper airship wing, so I pegged it for a rudder.

There was no point in telling Volzhenko that I didn't like him calling Chinese speech barking because I disliked the emperor referring to my aunt's anger as hysterics, or my professors calling female students overwrought and irrational. I did not think that Volzhenko was a bad man, but I had no doubt that if I were to try and explain myself, he would tell me that he was just joking. It seemed better to say I didn't like something without any explanation, and let him come up with rationales he could trust for himself.

Finally, some sort of agreement was reached between Kuan Yu and his new acquaintance, and the coolie grinned at me, showing his teeth, some of which were conspicuously missing. "You," he said to me. "Are you the hussar we were told about, named Menshov?"

"Possibly," I answered, trying to keep my voice from trembling. "Who told you? The Englishman who was here earlier? Is he still here?"

The man shook his head, grinning. "No Englishman. My foreman. He told me to bring you right over to him. You'll come, won't you? Bring your friends."

Suitably intrigued, we followed him across the uneven wooden then concrete floor and along a long row of cooling iron parts, some of which were shaped like cups or bells, while others had more elaborate protuberances, like suns and stars drawn by small children or folk painters.

"Do you know who that foreman is?" Volzhenko whispered as soon as he caught up to me.

I shook my head. "I am curious though."

"Got many Chinese friends?"

"A few, only they are all in China, or so I think. He may know of me through my aunt. She has connections with officials and bureaucrats most everywhere."

"They all seem to be Chinese here. Or Buryat."

I smiled and hastened my step to catch up to the coolie who was walking quite fast. "I'm sure we won't have to wait long for the solution of the mystery."

The factory floor sloped down toward a trough that carried off the water and refuse dissolved in or floating on it. We had to jump over the revolting green and brown stream flecked with unclean foam. On the other side, the floor sloped upwards, and we had to circumvent a half-assembled ship, that looked half like a Chinese war junk, half like the ill-fated airship I had seen at Tosno. I wondered if the factory managed to build anything operational.

Volzhenko thought the same, apparently: he nudged me in the ribs and asked in a stage whisper, "Do you think maybe Prince

Nicholas had a point about the Chinese? They seem to be readying an invasion under our very noses."

I frowned, even though the same worry crossed my mind, but I chased it away quickly. "Nonsense," I whispered back, just as loudly as Volzhenko. "Prince Nicholas cannot possibly be right about anything."

Volzhenko snickered. "I see what you mean," he said. "Touché."

Behind the airships, there were stacks of both ingots and thin sheets of metal, and piles of bleached linen, animal hides, and anthracite—everything, it seemed, this factory could need, amassed in inspired disarray. Finally, we arrived at a warren of what I supposed were offices— small enclosures built of canvas and wood directly against the outside wall of the factory.

The coolie shouted something in which I recognized my name into the center of the labyrinth and then sauntered off, unconcerned about the outcome. Soon we heard quick, light steps, and a man in traditional Han robes emerged from the lackluster offices, very much like a beautiful butterfly exiting its drab cocoon, unashamed of its humble beginning.

The foreman, like everyone here, had long hair falling over his young face. I clasped my hands over my mouth as I recognized him. "Lee Bo!"

He peered at me, puzzled at first. His forehead furrowed but soon smoothed over as—between my short hair and my raggedy mustache—he deciphered my features. "Sasha," he breathed. "I'll be damned."

"You know each other?" Volzhenko said.

"We went to the university together," I said quickly in my most masculine voice and rounded my eyes at Lee Bo.

"Indeed." Lee Bo. "Before Mr. Menshov joined the hussars, it seems."

I smiled gratefully. "And what about you? I thought you went back to China!"

"I did," Lee Bo said. "Chiang Tse and I both did. But I was needed here. Taiping Tianguo is concerned about Russia allying with Britain, and with keeping the Qing as far from our factories as we can. So we came to Siberia—you could build an entire city here, and no one would ever know."

"Is Chiang Tse well?" I blurted out before I could bite my tongue. I felt myself blush and quickly added, "Have you seen the Englishman who helped us that night at the club?"

"Why, yes to both," Lee Bo said. He leaned against the makeshift office wall with reckless disregard as its integrity was threatened by even his slight frame. "Jack was just here—he left something for you."

"He's not here now?" I said, disappointed as well as relieved upon hearing good news about Chiang Tse.

"No. He had to go meet some people. He did leave you a package."

We proceeded to Lee Bo's office—a little kennel crowded with a drafting table and cylinder desk, filled almost to capacity with folded diagrams and broken models of wings and wooden propellers. There were feathers and crumbled pine needles crunching underfoot, and a small pile of plant parts on the cylinder desk. I saw sycamore and maple seeds, and smiled—I remembered Lee Bo talking once about taking inspiration from nature, and was glad to see that he looked to it in his airship design. At least, I assumed the maple seeds with their membranous, leathery wings were the inspiration for the hand-carved propeller sitting next to them.

Lee Bo went to work shifting papers and mumbling to himself in Chinese. I was curious to see him like that—until now, I knew him as one of the cohesive group of Chinese students, a soft spoken man who was rarely seen apart from Chiang Tse. Now, he was a confident engineer whose training in physics served him well. I was proud to know him, even though the sense of pride was somewhat muffled by a million questions and worries that weighed on my heart.

He found an envelope addressed in Jack's hand, and proffered it to me. "Take it," he said. "I was glad to meet Jack—glad to thank him for helping us that night back in St. Petersburg. And now, I have a chance to thank you—without your intervention, I would not be here today. I am glad to have this opportunity to return the favor. Jack said he could not transfer these papers to you before because you were being watched, and he hoped the pursuit has been diverted enough so you can continue your journey with everything you need."

I opened the envelope with trembling fingers, and glimpsed the pale blue ink with a sigh of relief, felt the crinkling of the tracing paper under my fingers. The diagrams of submarines and faded letters all neatly collated, all the proof that I would need to convince the Taiping leaders . . . if I were to go to the Taipings. I breathed deep, savoring the smell of dry papers and the trace of lilac perfume wafting off Nightingale's papers, a ghost of her fearsome presence.

"Lee Bo," I said. "I need to talk to you, in private if possible."

Volzhenko muttered something under his breath.

I touched his sleeve. "Think of it as an experience in being unimportant."

He couldn't help but laugh, and waved me on. "Go ahead, Menshov. I only hope that I'll find out what this cloak and dagger is all about."

Lee Bo grinned then. "Whatever it is, I do not think it is about starting another war."

I shook my head and waited for my friend to leave the office. It was strange, feeling my trust in someone who had shown me nothing but friendship, so suddenly lacking. But I couldn't risk it, couldn't risk questions and secrets. I told myself that it was for his own protection and felt a little better. I only had enough trust left for a single person.

It took me a few minutes to explain the reason for our travels to Lee Bo. He listened, straight-faced, never betraying any surprise. I showed him Wong Jun's letter, and only then did he frown. "Are you seeking an alliance with the Manchu?"

I shrugged. "I do not want to. But if Taiping Tianguo is just a short-lived government, if you think it will fall before long . . . "

"Taiping forces have taken Beijing recently," he answered. "Wong Jun is a good man and a friend, and his letter will help you if you ever encounter any Qing officials. But why make an alliance with a power that is on the verge of falling?"

"I just want to do the right thing," I answered, and felt very tired. I looked around for a place to sit, but there seemed to be no space for a human form in this kingdom of fragile models. "Do you think Taiping Tianguo will want an alliance with Russia?"

He opened his arms, as if embracing the factory from the inside. "Of course we would. We would like to be here legally, without having to rely on the willing blindness of that garrison. I hope Jack did not stir them up to too much action."

"They seem to want to stay as far away from the Buryats as possible."

Lee Bo nodded and folded his arms across his chest, thinking. "I will escort you to China myself," he said, "will take you to Hong himself if that's what it takes. I will make sure that the Manchu never bother you. You bring Russian support to the Taiping State. This way, we both avoid interference from the British, and the Qing will fall for the lack of support."

"I would like that," I said. "Will we go to Beijing?"

"Nanjing," Lee Bo said. "Beijing is still chaotic. Remember, Nanjing is the capital. It's much further south, in the province of Jiangsu."

"Is there a railroad?" I asked. "How much longer will it take? I would like to get back to St. Petersburg before the third quarter is over, you know."

Lee Bo laughed. "Who needs railroads when you can have wings?" he said and spread his arms, fluttering his wide sleeves, making me think for a moment he could fly like a bird.

Then I remembered the airships. "Do you mean . . . ?"

"Yes!" Lee Bo laughed. "I've been dying for a trial run, and this is an excellent opportunity."

"A trial run?"

"Don't be a coward, Sasha," Lee Bo said, still laughing. "Besides, you'll get to meet some of the new Governor-Generals Hong Xiuquan has been appointing. How exciting it is to see the formation of a new state!"

"Rather exciting," I conceded. "But really, I don't want to meet any officials, I want to make Hong Xiuquan promise to send a diplomatic mission to the Emperor Constantine, and then go home."

"Fair enough." Lee Bo still laughed. "Although I promise you that one of those governors would give his right arm to meet you."

I shook my head. "Very well. I will have to go back to the garrison to pack, but I'll come back tomorrow."

"I'll send a dog sled to pick you up in the morning."

Chapter 16

And just like that, everything was resolved and decided. Volzhenko and I would report to Kurashov about the dead horse in the snow, and apologize for not finding the others or any of the alleged English culprits. Volzhenko promised to say nothing of the factory, after I swore to him its existence would be no detriment to anyone.

The hussar confessed he felt a little guilty about not telling Kurashov there was an entire Chinese airship factory right under his nose.

"Don't be too concerned," I told him on our sleigh ride back to the garrison. "How would you hide something like this? It's like an awl in a sack. Lee Bo indicated Kurashov simply prefers not to know. He stays away and minds his own business."

"I always find it puzzling," Volzhenko said. "People who choose not to know."

I shrugged. "Only God knows what a man's limits are. This is why I pray for the souls of suicides."

Volzhenko smiled. "You do? You're a strange one, Menshov." He let the reins in his hands hang loose, and the horses slowed to an easy trot. "And you have friends everywhere—we go to the middle of Siberia, find a secret factory, and its foreman is a friend of yours?"

"I was led here," I said.

Volzhenko gave me a long sideways look. "Maybe so. Still, I do find it interesting. And you're telling me you're going to China on an airship?"

"Yes. A trial run."

He looked unsure whether he should laugh or not, and Kuan Yu interjected, "He is serious."

"They are coming too." I gestured toward Kuan Yu and Liu Zhi.

Volzhenko nodded a few times, thinking deeply. "I suppose the rotmistr will want to know where you went."

"You'll tell him we found other travel arrangements; that the Buryats offered us dogsleds and trailblazers and translators, and dogs are less conspicuous than trains."

"You won't tell him yourself?"

"I suspect he may already understand more than you think, my friend." The rotmistr had, from the beginning of our acquaintance, seemed most accepting of my continually extraordinary journey and done nothing to hinder me, only aid. Why he had so providentially taken me under his wing, I did not know, but was grateful he had.

"He knows you're on some secret assignment, but he would probably like to give you his best," Volzhenko said.

I sighed. "Tell him I'm sorry. And that I'm very grateful."

We continued in silence. The stars came out, showing in the jagged holes of black, torn from the fuzzy spatulate outlines of treetops, with gray wisps of clouds curling around them like my own breath curled around my face below. It was cold but still. It occurred to me that it was one of those moments when time stopped mattering: I could have ridden like this forever, or perhaps I had been or would be at some future date, but the trees and the silence and the pronounced absence of wind, the sense of being between—between Europe and Asia, train and airship, between different friends—compounded the feeling of being so very alone in the night, lost in the world in a place where one could be neither recovered nor missed. I thought of crying and imagined my dry frozen tears falling on the bottom of the sleigh like glass beads, and smiled instead. Melancholy could be sweet, if one only allowed oneself to enjoy it. We arrived at the garrison by the time the moon, globular and distended, tarnished like silver, struggled over the treetops and the clouds and looked over the fence, into the garrison, at its dirty snow and soft blue shadows of the stables. There was yellow light in the windows, but I knew that I would go inside quietly, pack my things and leave without saying goodbye.

WE DEPARTED EARLY THE NEXT MORNING. LEE BO'S DOGSLED, driven by a sleepy Buryat, waited for us before anyone in the garrison awoke. Kuan Yu, Liu Zhi, and I left quietly. Volzhenko was the only one to see us off. As we said goodbye, he embraced me, shyly but fiercely, and my heart panged at the thought of how many friends I left, with little hope of ever seeing them again. I was pensive and silent the entire ride back to the factory.

The airship waited for us, and the sight of its membranous wings, basking in long slanted rays of morning sun made my ennui disappear. The wings trembled a little with vibrations of the entire hull, and I heard the engine roar and hiss inside the giant beast.

Most of the ship's interior was taken up by the engine—as large as that of a locomotive, with a blazing furnace separated from the wood paneling with long strips of copper. Adjacent to the engine room, there was an enclosure filled with anthracite, and many barrels of water. There was a rudder in the back of the hull, and a few levers that rotated it lazily to the right or to the left.

With all the machinery and supplies necessary to run it, and people who were responsible for feeding the furnace—constantly shoveling the anthracite into the blazing furnace maw—there was barely any space for passengers. Our seating and quarters were just a small gondola furnished with two hard narrow benches, so we had to sit sideways, facing each other. There was barely enough space for four.

Lee Bo seemed not at all discouraged by the seating limitations of his craft. "It's cramped and it will get cold," he said. "So prepare all your furs and blankets."

"I thought these things were supposed to have balloons," I said.

He shook his head. "Not in this weather—too cold. Plus, they are unreliable, slow, awkward. This is an entirely new design; it will be improved with time, I am certain, but it is quite a bit more efficient than the balloon ones, if I may say so myself."

"It seems so . . . bulky," I said.

"It only looks heavy and lumbering," Lee Bo reassured me for the tenth time, after we were finally seated in the belly of the roaring creature. "But it is quite agile, I swear to you." With these words he disappeared to take one last look at the engine and all the other flying instruments.

"I hope it is not as agile as he claims," Liu Zhi whispered. "In fact, I hope it never gets off the ground at all—otherwise, we have a long fall before us."

Kuan Yu nodded in sympathy, and the three of us huddled close together, abandoning all ambitions of looking dignified.

Lee Bo soon joined us in the gondola that, in addition to being cramped, was beginning to feel downright fragile. "It's very safe," he said again. "We'll be in Beijing in no time."

I sat up straighter, and stopped clinging to Kuan Yu for a moment. "I thought we were going to Nanjing?"

"I received news that one of Hong's generals is in Beijing now; just the man you need to see. There's still fighting there, and there are airships of other types all over the place," Lee Bo said carelessly. "We won't stand out."

I was about to point out I was not interested in risking the dangers of warfare or the perils of capture or being mistaken for a spy and would overall prefer a much more modest means of arrival to a safer destination, but then something whined horribly, and there was rhythmic thudding and roaring of flames. I squeezed my eyes shut and felt the shuddering of the floor under my feet. At that point, I forgot I was supposed to maintain an appearance of masculine strength and grabbed Lee Bo's elbow.

"Do not worry." He touched my shoulder in careful encouragement.

The contraption started sliding on the snow, its propellers whining louder and angrier. Through the narrow windows, I could see only one membranous wing going up and down in a slow stiff flap, but then the movement grew faster and the noise became deafening. I was ready to forget all attempts at dignity and just fall to the floor and beg to be let off this horrible thing, when—with one final thundering roar and crash of a broken tree—the airship let go of the earth underneath it and took to the sky.

The wing flapped more now, and on the upward swing it lifted enough to allow me a view of the land underneath. I saw trees and the garrison all the way west, a lone pillar of cooking smoke reaching for the sky, and a Buryat village almost underneath us. Dogs barked and children ran, small and black on the ground, and the sound had grown muffled by the roar of my blood in my ears. The treetops of the tallest trees were now below us, and birds flew wing to wing with us.

I was starting to think that maybe we would survive unscathed and it was even possible we were not about to fall out of the sky and shatter into tiny pieces when Kuan Yu, who was clinging to the opposite embrasure, exclaimed in surprise.

I looked over, to see a long road below us—such a long, snow-covered road winding between the trees that it seemed to define the very meaning of "loneliness." There were three horses and several people on the road—most armed even though they were dressed in civilian tweed coats. Three rode on horseback while the rest walked. One of the riders seemed different from the rest, and I squinted, trying to see the details from a distance. I soon realized he sat with his hands tied behind his back, and his horse was being led by the bridle by one of the walking men with a ready musket.

As the airship passed over them, a few looked up; they were too far away to see their faces, but the bound man on horseback also had a hood or a sack over his face—when he tilted it up, the uniform blue over his face and shoulders was clearly visible against the dirty snow of the road.

"This is Jack," I whispered.

Lee Bo's fingers squeezed my shoulder. "Nothing we can do now."

"But . . . "

"I hope he knows you're on this airship," Lee Bo said to me. "I'm sure he does. Do you think they could have captured him unless he let them?"

His words were comforting, and yet I knew that Jack was not a god. Even the smartest and the strongest grew tired, even birds feigning injury grew too fatigued or too careless at times. Careless enough to be caught. And he had been running for so long . . .

The airship tilted and the people in the road disappeared from my view, yet I stared at the white wilderness below, at the trees and the snowdrifts, at the lakes encased in green ice and the black rivers, fissures in the very soul of the world. My fingers grew numb and my face chapped in the quick cutting wind that sliced like a knife, and still I clung to the window frame, as if I could see the people in the road, and Jack, so gangly and alien in his passive pose, his face blocked. I realized I was used to him always being in movement, often explosive and violent. It wasn't truly him, hands tied, head covered, bound to a horse led by someone. This was not how it was supposed to be. He was supposed to come to China with me . . . and yet, he left the documents for me, and he was captured empty-handed except for the Dick Turpin penny dreadfuls on his person. This thought made me smile despite the longing and fear I felt.

"I swear to you," I whispered into the whistling of the wind, the roaring of the engines and the creaking of the airship wings. "I swear I will return for you. I will follow and find you, if that's the last thing I do." I glanced at Lee Bo and Kuan Yu engaged in a quiet conversation next to me, and added aloud, "I swear that I will rescue you, Jack Bartram, even if I will have to miss the rest of the school year." That was as solemn a vow as could be expected out of anyone.

THE AIRSHIP TOOK SURPRISINGLY LITTLE TIME TO GET USED TO. Within an hour or so, I forgot to panic every time the engine whined or gave one of the choking gasps it seemed inordinately fond of. And after two hours, I whooped with joy when the giant green tear of Lake Baikal swam into view. Kuan Yu and Liu Zhi laughed and cheered, and Lee Bo did a little dance, restrained by our cramped accommodation as well as his own shy nature.

In three hours, I had grown bold enough to ask Lee Bo to show me the engine room. He led me through the narrow passage in the ceiling over the seating area, to the confining hot area where three shirtless men fed coal to the furnace.

"Who is steering?" I asked after I started to sweat under my furs but didn't feel ready to go back to the seating area.

Lee Bo smiled. "An engineer," he said. "The controls . . . are really more witchcraft than science, and it requires an artist and a man of great intuition to direct it. Would you like to see?"

"No." I swallowed hard, my apprehension returning to haunt me again. "I think we can go back now."

"It's not as terrible as you think," Lee Bo said. "Your friend Kuan

Yu had been learning to fly such ships . . . although he still has not mastered landing them."

Lee Bo was kind to me. Yet there seemed to be such a different quality to his kindness than Jack's possessed. Oh, how Jack haunted me! The sight of him, tied to the back of a horse like a common criminal, being transported like that . . . It wasn't the disgrace and the falsity of his crime—surely, he would have learned as much from his penny dreadfuls he was so fond of—it was the helplessness that tore at my heart. I did not like to think of Jack as helpless; doubly so (even though it was not flattering for me to admit) because his freedom and his protectiveness ensured my safety. Somehow, I trusted him more with it than even Volzhenko, or Lee Bo who had his own airship . . . maybe because Lee Bo had his own airship.

We had returned to the narrow benches, and I managed to sleep a little, wedged between soft, fur-lined side of Kuan Yu and the trembling wall of the airship's hull.

WE SAW BEIJING FROM THE AIR. IT WAS STRANGE TO CROSS BORDERS like that—before I even knew, we were crossing unfamiliar rivers and snow-bound vast steppes of Mongolia, and then I slept. I woke up in the darkness, an orange conflagration staining the sky sickly ochre; there was nothing but fire below and nothing but black sky above. For a few happy moments, I thought I was still asleep and snuggled deeper into my furs. Kuan Yu cruelly shook me awake, and I sat up, wide-eyed and sick to my stomach.

Arriving in foreign places is disorienting enough on its own; it is harder by the air since there are no check points and no officials ask you to show them your papers, and no landmarks you can recognize in the usual sense of traveling. There's only the whistling of the wind and the horrible crackling from below. For a moment I believed that we were dead, in hell, in some other punitive dimension of the afterlife.

"This is Beijing," Kuan Yu told me, as if hearing my panicked thoughts.

"It is Beijing," Lee Bo echoed, consternation and confusion making his voice thick in his mouth. "I had no idea it would be like this. We have to see what is happening here."

I had no firsthand experience with wars, but Eugenia's stories were enough to impart some expectations. "It is always like this," I answered, and recounted my Aunt's tales of Moscow burning and Napoleon, the stories passed down of the Tatars before them. How else could it be? There was no war without burning and fire, confused screaming and the thick flakes of ash suspended in the air, lodging themselves into throats and noses. I sneezed and mucus came out ash-black.

Lee Bo climbed into the airship, ostensibly to command landing; I hoped he would make sure we descended somewhere far away from the conflagration. But just a few moments later, the giant ship whined and tilted with its nose down, so that I slid on my bench until I was stopped by the comforting solidity of Kuan Yu.

"Easy there, young soldier," he told me and smiled. There was sadness in his eyes, in the creases of his eyelids, the smile could not chase away.

"I'm sorry," I whispered. "I . . . I forgot that those are your people."

He looked at me, curious. "Do you mean to say that you experience pain less if it is not inflicted on your countrymen but on someone else?"

"Everyone does," I said. "Otherwise, wars would not be possible—if we felt the pain of others like our own, no one would ever retaliate."

"I see your point," he said. "War then is just a failure of imagination."

"Exactly." I looked at the flames that grew larger as we descended and then fell away as the airship tilted.

It landed with a heavy thud, and my jaws clunked together with enough force to chip a tooth.

"Not enough snow for smooth landing," Kuan Yu guessed. "The fire melted it off."

The airship tilted and screeched, and then spun half a turn before almost rolling over and finally, finally stopping. I took huge panicked breaths, too terrified at first to realize my mouth tasted like ash, that ash and cinders ground between my teeth; my lips bled and their blood mixed with that seeping out of my nose. That would require a mustache change.

"You look a fright," Liu Zhi informed me as soon as the three of us disentangled ourselves from each other and stood on shaky legs.

I licked my lips, tasting ash and blood and metal. I then touched my nose: it was not broken, so I attributed the bleeding to the sudden change in altitude.

We tumbled out onto a flat patch of dirty snow and scraped sand. I grabbed a handful of snow, not caring how filthy, and pressed it to the bridge of my nose to stop the bleeding. Throughout, I kept a death hold on my satchel, not letting it go more of a second nature by now than trying to not get hurt. I wondered to myself if any dedication to any endeavor required simply letting go of the fear of death. I decided to finish that thought at a better time, or at least when finishing it would not make me shake and cry with fear.

Lee Bo and the men from the engine compartment, along with a tall, broad-shouldered Buryat (probably the engineer) joined us, and our small group had a brief but animated discussion what to do next.

"We need to find some officials," I said in English.

One of the coolies snorted. "And I would prefer to keep as far away as possible from any officials. Why do you think you're more important than us?"

Lee Bo raised a pacifying hand the moment he saw the look on my face—I supposed it was not pretty, with all the blood and the matted mustache. "You are free to go," he said to the men. "As long as you know what you're doing. We, however, need to think of the fates of countries, not just of our own hides."

"That was too harsh," Kuan Yu said, but Lee Bo paid him no mind.

Lee Bo waved his hand rather imperiously, and explained that everyone could do whatever he wanted, he really did not care one way or another, but he had to get me to a Taiping official and he would rather do that than stand around arguing.

After that, Kuan Yu and Liu Zhi followed us. The coolies and the engineer turned away from the burning city. I hoped they would be safe. We walked toward the orange light burning up half the sky.

We came to a large, sprawling aggregate of campfires and tents, overturned carts and oxen that lowed at our approach and then fell asleep again. I assumed that it was an encampment of the attacking Taipings, and puzzled at what we were doing here—I wanted officials, not generals. Then it occurred to me that if they were successful, generals would likely be in control of Beijing. This is why Lee Bo decided to stop there instead of going to any of the more distant and southern provinces. I sighed and followed, hoping that the Taiping generals would not be too vicious.

Despite the presence of Kuan Yu, Liu Zhi and Lee Bo, things got very confusing very quickly. Even though the Taipings wore their hair long—or at least they were supposed to—quite a few of them were new enough to still have it short, and some, who just joined, still had their queues. The men with these varied haircuts slept around the fires, while others sat, awake, talking or eating.

To my surprise, there were a few women among them, none of who looked like camp followers—they laughed and talked among themselves, and one of them, a girl of maybe sixteen, stood by one of the larger fires, leaning on a musket that seemed to be as tall as she. I stopped for a bit to smell the snow and the char, and the warm musk of human skin, and to look at the girl, at her dark face and the black crescents of eyebrows mirroring the eyes below them, and the reverse curve of her mouth. I envied that girl because she was not wearing man's clothing—as far as I could tell, she did not have to.

However, there didn't seem to be any generals in sight, and soon we ventured closer to the burning city, to the open area outside the city wall, where ash fell like snow. I tried to keep my eyes on the walls and the buildings beyond them, afraid to look at the ground lest I discove dead bodies. But there was only softness of ash under my feet, and the supportive hand of Lee Bo on my elbow.

We walked in circles from one campfire to the next, and I had to rely on Lee Bo to ask questions; Kuan Yu and Liu Zhi joined his conversations sometimes, but remained silent otherwise, and it occurred to me that they were tired.

"Let's stop," I told Lee Bo after a while. "I'm tired—it's like trekking through the purgatory."

"You want to rest?" he asked.

I nodded at Kuan Yu.

We settled at the nearest fire. A few men gave me sideways looks and Lee Bo explained they were not used to foreigners to begin with, and suspicious of them after the Opium War. I nodded that I understood, but doubted I was cutting an intimidating figure with my blood-smeared face and constant yawning.

Lee Bo engaged some of the soldiers in conversation, and since

I did not understand their words, I listened to the broken rhythm of their speech and studied their appearance in the uneven firelight. They all seemed not soldiers but peasants, with their long clothes made of unbleached rough fabric and shoes that were barely anything more elaborate than foot wrappings made of the same cloth as the rest of their attire. Their long unbraided hair and dark faces gave them a wild and untamed appearance, and for a while I thought of my dead papa who I hardly even remembered. I thought of his uprising and of how much more dignified it was—uniformed officers and well fed, well-cared for horses, their formations and their gracious riding into Senate Square, the cannons, the marching soldiers . . .

The men around the fire seemed a mob to me, as indistinct from one another as the freedmen in the factories of St. Petersburg, as the peasants who worked Eugenia's fields. I did not mention it to Lee Bo, of course, but they looked not like masters of destiny but its toys, tossed about in the waves of circumstance. And yet, I could not help but think about them in the same way I thought about my father and his co-conspirators, and I found my brain's insistence on finding this unlikely kinship quite irritating.

The droning of the voices soon made my eyelids fall closed, and I let the memory of the airship's whining drown out the rest of the sounds. I dreamed of falling and then I dreamed of being my dead Uncle Pavel, miraculously alive in 1825, when he (I) rode into Senate Square side by side with Lee Bo, both of us dressed as Chinese peasants and holding our sabers high, high enough to reflect the rising sun and the orange glow of the burning city that stood unknowable and phantasmagoric in my dream.

Chapter 17

The morning came, bleak and stiff with cold, tasting of ash and burning paint. I stretched and remembered where I was—sleeping in the snow, swaddled in my furs, which, although still comfortable, were beginning to smell of all the unsavory things we had encountered recently. I tried not to breathe in too deep as I sat up.

The true scale of devastation was mercifully hidden by the morning dusk and the curling of fog—or was it smoke?—that tendriled between the campfires, close to the trampled, black snow. I stretched and stood up, looking around. Our airship was not visible in the distance, but the stone walls of Beijing seemed just a few hundred yards away. Last night's fire seemed to have died down.

Lee Bo stood next to me, his hand with dirty and broken fingernails lightly resting on my shoulder. When I squinted my eyes just so, I could see every crease and every speck of dirt rubbed so deep into his olive skin. "What do we do now?

"The assistant general, one Feng Yunshan, and some of his army are inside the city," Lee Bo said. "The Qing have surrendered, or at least this is what everyone here thinks."

"So it is possible there's still fighting in the city."

"Everything is possible." Lee Bo shrugged. "However, if you want to speak to the Assistant General Feng, this might be a good opportunity to do so. If the Taipings solidify their position over the Qing, the alliance with your country may not seem as necessary as now, when everything is still teetering on the edge."

I sighed. The political maneuvering was starting to wear on me. The more I thought about it, the more I realized that if it were up to me, I would never leave the comfort of St. Petersburg or Trubetskoye again if I could help it, and if I did would make sure to remain within a hundred yards of a hot bath at all times. "I suppose. Isn't it dangerous, though, if there's still fighting?"

"We'll take Kuan Yu and Liu Zhi with us," Lee Bo said, as if that negated my point completely.

We came to the gates, that stood undamaged in the otherwise charred wall, but the gates were unlocked. Despite the destruction, I stared all around me, suddenly hungry for novel sights. The streets were wide and deserted, and I marveled at the beauty of the remaining houses—even though only a few still stood intact among the wreckage, I found their appearance as attractive as it was foreign: the houses, only one or two stories tall, boasted an abundance of wide windows and roofs with steeply arching eaves. They were painted green and gold and red, and plum trees, bare now, grew between the houses in small copses. Their bamboo and wood paneling, lacquered and brightly painted, gave the street a cheerful and peaceful air, belied by the burned out ruins all around us.

I let Lee Bo and the others lead the way, and trailed behind, keeping an eye out for troops. There were very few people in the streets, and I couldn't say I blamed them. However, there was no shortage of dead bodies—I tried to look away when yet another corpse, stiff and straight and white with frost captured my gaze. I stared instead at the roofs and the windows, trying to guess who was behind an occasional shadow that flitted behind the white screens guarding most of the windows.

After a few streets like that, we entered a part of the city where buildings were taller and streets were wider, giving way to several squares with large, imposing buildings. One of them, particularly sprawling, had a statue of a goddess in front of it.

"This is the examination hall," Lee Bo told me as we passed it. "Local students take their examinations here, and they get assigned to the official posts depending on how well they do."

"Did you do well?"

He grinned. "Not really. This is why I'm running a factory in Siberia. But Chiang Tse did very well."

The sound of his name pricked my heart like a small, sharp pin. "Oh? Was he the governor you wanted me to meet?"

Lee Bo only smiled.

"You have to tell me!" Suddenly, it seemed very important for me to know. "Where is he? Will I see him?"

Lee Bo laughed then. "I don't know. I haven't been home since October. We exchange an occasional letter, but last I heard, he was on duty in Gansu, his province."

We arrived at the bottom of the bridge that led to a set of very tall gates. The gates stood between us and the rest of the street, flanked by two white stone dragons; they were probably guarding something important.

I smiled, imagining humble and soft-spoken Chiang Tse as an imposing official figure. "I am sure he's governing well," I said out loud. And added, without thinking much, "Do you usually have several wives?"

Lee Bo waited with me at the foot of the bridge until Kuan Yu and Liu Zhi caught up to us. "Under the Qing, yes. Taipings? Just one. Chiang Tse, however, doesn't have any."

I blushed without meaning to. "I was just curious, in general."

"Of course," Lee Bo said, thankfully not laughing. "In general. Customs of foreign lands are so confusing." There was a hint of reproach in his voice.

"I thought it was the Chinese who wanted the foreigners to stay away. How do you expect us to know your customs?"

"I don't." Lee Bo's eyes met mine, and I was taken aback by anger I saw in them. "But look around you—this is what happens when you let foreign ideas into a country."

"I thought you supported the Taiping Tianguo."

"I do, but that is beside the point. Remember the Qing are foreigners, and the Hakka are among the most ancient people of China, with its original language and customs."

"I see," I said, very softly. "But I hoped that being at the foreign university had some benefits for you."

He looked at me as if he just saw me for the first time. "I didn't mean to take it out on you. But it hurts, to see it like this. And we keep arguing . . ."

"Yes," Kuan Yu said as he stood next to us on the steps. "Arguing, always arguing, and it's always the same words that run around like water in a circle, wearing down the bedrock."

"Yes," Lee Bo agreed, and looked pensive. "Shall we? This is the imperial residence, the English call it the Forbidden City."

I looked up to the place where the bridge ended at a flat square area just before the gates. Even though our view was largely blocked by the elevation of the bridge and the platform's edges, it was still clear there were people there—I heard voices and clanging of metal.

"Who's there?" I asked Lee Bo.

"Only one way to find out."

He headed up the bridge, Kuan Yu and Liu Zhi catching up to him and flanking him, so that the three walked almost shoulder to shoulder, with Lee Bo a quarter of a step ahead of the others. Something about their formation made me suck the air through my swollen lips and move the satchel into my left hand, while my right rested lightly on the hilt. There were only four of us and unknown multitudes up and ahead—what reason did I have to be nervous?

The men standing in front of the high red walls were Taipings, about twenty in number, and I drew a relieved breath. Dirty and long-haired or not, they were our allies, and I worked hard at trying to like them.

One of the filthy men stopped us by thrusting a spear he held against Lee Bo's chest sideways, like a gate.

Lee Bo stopped and said something in Chinese.

The man with the spear argued, and Kuan Yu joined in. The volume of their voices increased as the man with the spear only stood, feet planted wide of the chipped gray stone of the platform, and shook his head no.

A few others joined in, and Lee Bo shoved the spear away from his chest. This gesture was followed by further consternation and agitated hand waving. I looked from one group to another helplessly, hoping for some clue in addition to their outward hostility, something that would reassure me the argument would not end in bloodshed.

One of the other guards, a thin and sullen man with a beard long enough to brush against his rope belt, pointed at me. Even though I did not understand his words, I shook my head. "Not English," I said, rather contradictorily, in English.

The Taipings around us closed ranks and pushed closer, forcing Lee Bo, Kuan Yu and Liu Zhi to push back, almost leaning into our attackers. I kept my hand on my hilt.

The thin man who had spoken to me reached out—his long-fingered, yellowed hand splayed up in the air—and grabbed the front of my uniform jacket, visible between my open furs. I don't know whether he just wanted to see my insignia or whether it was a gesture of provocation; all I know is that I took an instinctive step back, to give myself room to draw my weapon and to end the unwelcome contact. The buttons and the gold braid, subjected to so much stress by travel and dirt, snapped and my jacket flew open, spitting forth the theatrical bill with Wong Jun's calligraphy.

I wrestled out of the attacker's hand, indignant, and quickly closed my uniform and buttoned my furs. Lee Bo tried to grab the bill out of the attacker's hand, but the other Taipings held him back.

"You don't understand," I started. "I am not here to see the Qing, I swear to you . . ."

But it was already too late, as the thin man pointed at me, shouting, and even though I did not know the word, its meaning resonated loudly. "Traitor!" he called. "An English traitor in our midst, a foreigner, carrying a letter offering alliance to the Qing!"

Lee Bo spun close to the ground, and in a fluid quick motion twisted the spear out of the hands of the large man; his foot swept in a wide semicircle, and the disarmed giant thundered to the ground, landing on his rear and elbows.

I already knew what Kuan Yu and Liu Zhi were capable of doing, but here, free of the confines of the train carriage, they took my breath away. I tried to fight, my saber parrying thrusts from the sword held by one of the Taiping guards, but my efforts were half-hearted, because even the threat to my very life could tear my attention from the acrobatic airborne miracles that were Kuan Yu and Liu Zhi. I do not think I had ever seen anything quite as graceful, quite as beautiful as their defensive display. Even the Imperial Ballet would appear a mere trundling of mincing cows in comparison.

Kuan Yu's feet, slippered like those of a dancer, left the ground as if elevated by some divine will. Unceremoniously, he planted his right foot on the knee of his opponent, who stood with his legs slightly bent, thus offering Kuan Yu an incidental foothold. Kuan

Yu pivoted, and his left foot arced through the air, striking several faces in quick succession.

Liu Zhi had disarmed one of the guards and used the spear as a staff to make a wide circle around him—he swung the spear to and fro, lashing viciously at everyone who dared to take a step toward him. Lee Bo, who had his back to Liu Zhi's, thrust his spear at the brutish man who was the first to attack him, and all three seemed quite unconcerned about the immediate threat—their faces were set in an expression of thorough concentration, but there were no traces of fear or panic, the emotions I felt certain my own face betrayed in abundance.

There was a swish of air, and I stepped to the side, deflecting a sword's point thrust at me. I am not a good swordsman: I had never had proper training, and all I knew I had picked up from the long summers spent playing with the children of engineers. Childhood play with sticks taught me to sidestep thrusts and to block direct hits; I had no form to speak of, but enough attention and strength to follow my opponent's attacks and to parry or avoid them. He increased his exertions, and I had to turn away from the sight of Liu Zhi rising into the air, using the spears of several of the guards as rungs of an invisible ladder.

I defended myself as well as I could, even though my attacker kept pressing, forcing me back to the bridge leading down, and I had to keep looking sideways to make sure I was not about to tumble down the stone slope. The man was stronger and would have overpowered me, but I remembered the satchel I still held in my left hand. I swung it at his face, and connected with a satisfying, solid slap. My attacker staggered back, and I used the opportunity to lunge at him and demand he surrender his sword.

Meanwhile, Kuan Yu and Liu Zhi did not waste any time. By the time I stumbled back to the knot of the Taiping guards, they had felled many of the enemy; still more of them ceased attacking and, instead, stepped back. I did not think anyone was killed—even though Kuan Yu and Liu Zhi punched and kicked and punched some more, their fists a gray blur of fast and precisely terrifying motion, their attackers appeared awed and stunned rather than seriously hurt. The only blood flowed from injured noses and lips, not from serious wounds.

One of the guards noticed my approach, and swung about, a spear in his hands gleaming with a sharp brilliant point. I had no time to react as the spear struck me in the shoulder, and with a twist its handle broke off, leaving the point embedded in the cork of my corset. I frowned, and ripped out the spearhead; I think I impressed my attacker—he stepped back, giving me an opportunity to run for the gates.

Lee Bo took another wide swing at the crowd, and his eyes met mine. "Go!" he shouted. "Go inside."

I ran across the stone paving, sheathing my sword as I ran. The Taipings intensified their efforts at not letting us through; Kuan Yu and Liu Zhi flew over them like two deadly birds. They seemed singularly undisturbed by gravity, and I left this question to be pondered at a more opportune time. I rushed to the carved double gates, red-colored wood covered in long, sinuous dragons and winding flower stems receding before me as if in a tunnel. They seemed so far away—until I slammed into them, full-tilt, and the doors slowly swung open, not making a slightest sound, as in a dream.

Lee Bo followed me right away, and I stopped.

"What are you doing?" he shouted, pulling the door closed behind us.

"Kuan Yu," I replied.

"They'll be fine, they can take care of themselves."

I did not doubt his words, of course, and yet worry gnawed at me—even flying men could be killed, especially if it was only two against twenty. Against an armed twenty.

"You fought well," Lee Bo said with some surprise, and sucked in his breath. "Come along now."

We found ourselves in a small courtyard, where only two Taipings guarded the passage to the rest of the Forbidden City—I gasped at its vast and serene appearance, at the bright pavilions and the gardens that stretched around us. Everything was lavishly decorated. There was gold leaf to rival the domes of the Moscow churches, and carvings that seemed to breathe, giving life to the taloned maned monsters that decorated them.

The guards paid us little mind. The outside gates, heavy as they were, did not let through much sound, and I did not suppose they would have a reason to suspect that two men would somehow get through the twenty outside without their consent.

"Where's Feng?" Lee Bo asked one of the guards—at least, this is what I thought he asked. I recognized the name *Feng*.

The guard waved his arm toward the large building off in some distance. Lee Bo translated. "Talking to the emperor, discussing terms of surrender."

"Just the two of them?"

"Some officials." The guard thought for a while, and then added, "And a Russian envoy."

"Who would that be?" Lee Bo asked me as soon as we passed the guards.

"No idea," I said. "I thought the Emperor Constantine did not want an alliance . . . but maybe my aunt has convinced him." I smiled then, hopeful my work would be easier.

The Forbidden City seemed the Abandoned City now. We walked along the path lined with strangely shaped rocks and pillars; what they were supposed to represent was obscured by the snow. The trees that craned their slender, snow-weighed branches over the path must've been magnificent in the spring, when the white flowers frothed and cascaded over the boughs, and I squinted and imagined that the snow mounding on the stones were white petals of plum and cherry flowers.

"This is the Palace of Earthly Peace," Lee Bo said and pointed at the large pavilion that dwarfed everything else around it. It also stood out from the surroundings because it had two roofs, one stacked on top of the other. The building itself was an arrangement of smaller pavilions, some lower and some taller. A wide staircase led toward it and several subordinate structures, topped with matching copper-colored rectangular roofs with steeply curved eaves.

"It is beautiful," I told Lee Bo, and really meant it. "I've never seen anything quite so . . . " I paused, searching for an appropriate epithet. It seemed so strange and otherworldly, especially considering that we just fought the people who were supposed to be on our side. "It's very beautiful," I concluded in a rather uninspired manner. "I am sorry for getting us into that fight—Wong Jun's letter . . . "

Lee Bo shrugged. "If we ran into Qing forces, that letter would've had an opposite effect. In any case, you're a barbarian, and it would be foolish to expect people to trust you."

"Kuan Yu does."

Lee Bo shook his head, smiling. "This is very naive of you. Do you think he is helping you because you're serving the purpose he finds agreeable, or because you're so precious that everyone who runs into you just has to help you?"

"The former." I tried not to sulk.

"Right. So don't take it personally, but do remember that people . . . people will do what suits themselves first. Don't expect them to stop everything because you happened to wander by and need help."

"I don't," I said. "Is it another one of those arguments you mentioned before?"

He nodded. We ascended the white staircase to the Palace itself, and I thought of how unlike the Winter Palace in St. Petersburg it was. Irrelevant and minor thoughts always plagued me at such important times, and I shook my head to clear it.

There were more guards here, but they wore Qing queues, and I wished I still had Wong Jun's letter.

My stomach growled and acted as if it was about to do a flip and exit my body through my mouth and disappear forever. I swallowed hard. "I am bringing important information about the British."

Lee Bo translated.

The guards did not seem especially spirited—they barely acknowledged our presence and let us through the double doors leading to the palace. I stepped through, simultaneously hopeful and apprehensive.

To my disappointment, we did not see the emperor. I supposed that he must have been rather discouraged by the woefully underdressed Taipings tracking muddy footprints across his beautifully paved floors and fine carpets. There were quite a few of them about; they gave us suspicious looks, but Lee Bo's banter seemed to put them at enough ease to let us through. The walls were decorated by friezes and hangings made of richly embroidered shimmering silk that moved in the breeze, and the people in the battle scenes, artfully depicted, waved their banners and raised sails of their war junks.

We found General Feng in one of the smaller halls of the palace—it was almost intimate, decorated with soft rugs and low, embroidered couches, almost European in their design. On one of these couches, Feng, a small man who looked to be in his early thirties, stretched luxuriously, oblivious to the fact that his leather slippers left a round wet stain on the upholstery. His long hair was pulled into a horsetail on top of his head, and his wide, curved sword rested across his lap. Otherwise, he looked like any of his men.

He sat up when he saw me, and spoke sharply in Chinese.

I smiled and shook my head, and opened my satchel. I always suspected there was a huge relief in stopping the struggle and simply giving up the thing that had motivated one for weeks and months and years on end. I suspected that Sisyphus himself heaved a sigh of relief when the boulder rolled down the hill and he stood on the slope, empty-handed and free for a moment, truly happy because in that brief instant he had lost everything again, and had not yet regained hope and motivation for the next impossible task.

This is how I felt when I extracted the blueprints and the letters detailing the English treachery, when I gave general Feng the signed copies of treaties between the British and Ottoman empires, as I piled proof after proof after proof that China and the Taiping Tianguo, if they were to survive, would have to form an alliance with someone, and Russia seemed a logical choice, a neighbor driven by the same necessity and less foreign than any other.

Lee Bo translated, pointed things out, answered the general's questions.

Feng's voice rose as he gestured at one of the papers. Lee Bo frowned and spoke faster and in a higher pitch. I looked from one foreign face to the other, suddenly aware of how much I did not belong here. My suspicions intensified when Lee Bo bowed his head, pressed his hands together before his chest, and spoke softer, but with the unmistakable strain of pleading that was always the same, no matter whether the language spoken was Russian, English, or Cantonese.

Feng listened and sat up straighter, his back growing rigid with resolution. When he spoke, he was not addressing either Lee Bo or myself, but rather talking over our heads to someone in the hallway just outside.

My heart sunk as Feng tossed the papers I had given him carelessly on the couch cushions, and waited for the two Taipings to enter and flank me, in a way much less reassuring than the manner in which Kuan Yu and Lee Bo had so shortly before. When their hands clasped my wrists, freed my saber from my sheath, and took my shoulders—gently, gently, like a mother cradling a helpless child—my spirit gave out. I did not sob but I did not struggle; I let my head droop and my thoughts swim, as I could almost see myself—like another person would; detached, floating—being led down a corridor, all golden lights and filigreed panels on the walls, flowers and fantastic beasts, my heels hitting the tiles too loudly.

Then we were outside. Deep snow in hidden courtyards littered with splintered bamboo shafts and shredded red paper muted my footsteps, and I thought of it as a relief. We arrived at a small pavilion, and I thought it was a jail. But instead it turned out to be a small shrine. There were several statues placed on a dais; one corner of the cold stone floor was covered by a threadbare straw mat. The stone rang hollow and frozen with my bootsteps, went silent as my legs gave way and I crumpled to the floor, just as the key on the other side of the door turned, leaving me more cold and alone than I ever thought possible.

I HAD TIME TO THINK NOW. THE RUSHING ABOUT OF THE PAST weeks came to such an abrupt and disreputable stop that the very cessation of motion felt more crushing than the imprisonment. And I was in prison, even though instead of a jailer I had jade statues of some unfamiliar gods and a goddess, and there were no bars, just a room with dais with rounded corners and a wooden door.

It was too cold to sleep, and I curled into a comma, pulling my worn pelisse over my shoulders, like a too-short blanket. The carved goddess looked at me from the corner of one eye, not to notice me, but looking nonetheless.

My only blessing was the realization of how lucky I had been until that day, and how an abrupt end of my good fortune cast the incredible run of luck that preceded it in stark relief. Of course my luck had to run out some day, and it seemed more than coincidence that it did so just a few days after Jack's capture.

I searched under the dais, not really hoping to find anything but to keep moving. To my surprise, in the dusty, cold darkness under the smooth wood my fingers felt a jagged piece of rock. I pulled it out and discovered it was a flint stone, and my heart squeezed tight in my already constricted chest, then let go again.

The empty sheath of my saber was not a very good weapon, but its steel-encased tip would serve as a perfect counterpart to the flint stone, if only I could find something to set fire to. Encouraged and newly energized by hope, I crawled on my hands and knees, looking into every crevice between the floor tiles, and under every side of the dais.

My reward was a thin splinter of bamboo lodged between the wall and a floor tile, and half of incense stick. It was better than nothing at all.

Then it struck me: I tore at my jacket, exposing the accursed reverse corset (which, I worried, was permanently altering the shape of my body) and tore off a chunk of cork off one shoulder, my fingers clawed and insensitive from cold. With my bamboo splinter,

I arranged the cork shavings into a small pile, and set to striking the stone against the sheath's steel tip.

Just moving about warmed me up, and the surge of blood to my face and hands chased away the ennui and sense of indifference which victims of cold are so susceptible to. When the cork began to smolder, it seemed an extravagant gift, and I spread my fingers toward the pale stunted flames.

I burned the incense almost as an afterthought, and the smoldering stick filled the shrine with thick smoke. I coughed and almost put it out, but a new idea occurred to me.

I shoved the burning incense tip through the keyhole in the door—I did not have enough fire to burn the door, or worse yet, risk suffocation, but I could send a smoke signal—much like in a James Fenimore Cooper novel. My only worry was that there was no one on the outside to care enough to receive it. And still I waited, until the smoldering red line crawled back through the keyhole and burned my fingers before going out.

THE NIGHT CAME AND WENT—I HAD NOT REALIZED IT, BUT WHEN my feeble incense stick ran out and I sucked my burned fingers numbly, a golden shaft of light forced itself through the keyhole. It seemed so tangible, so solid, that I imagined myself grasping it like a magical key and turning it, the door squeaking open and returning to freedom. It felt so vivid, the fresh air on my face . . . I shivered and curled back into a small depressed ball. Even if I could break through the door, there was an entire country beyond the shrine and the courtyard and the Forbidden City—a country whose language I did not speak and to whom I looked like an enemy. I only hoped that Lee Bo was working to exercise his influence over Feng—if he wasn't thought a traitor and locked away elsewhere, of course.

The door opened then, as if my thoughts and the power of conjured images compelled it to. I sat up and blinked at the flood of bright light, simultaneously pulling my jacket closed and hoping that the dents in my shoulders were not too obvious. Two dark shadows solidified against the blinding whiteness and resolved into my escorts from day before. I looked at them, trying to suppress any hope. It became easier the moment General Feng stepped inside.

It turned out he spoke passable English. He gestured to me and said, "We saw your smoke this morning. Thank you. It has been so busy here, I forgot about you. My apologies."

I did not have the standing to sulk, although I was tempted. I did not particularly relish being a forgotten casualty of a foreign and ultimately strange conflict where if I were to die no one would likely know my name or remember my face. "Thank you for remembering me," I said. I did feel some gratitude—not to Feng but to Fenimore Cooper. "Now are you willing to listen to my proposal?"

Feng took a step back, as if suddenly unbalanced. "We examined the papers you brought," he said. "There is some interesting information, but I doubt your ability to speak for your ruler."

"I never said I did," I answered. "I merely gave you tools so you may seek alliance with those who can help you and whose trust you would have to win."

Feng looked at me quizzically. "And you took it upon yourself to do so. What made you decide to interfere in the fates of empires?"

I could not tell him the truth—namely, that the decision was pure hotheaded foolishness on my part. Instead, I stared at the tips of my boots and said, "I was in possession of these documents as well as an opportunity to travel. I hope you are not suspecting any untoward motives."

"I was," Feng answered. "But today, we spoke to the Russian

envoy who confirms your offer, and even brings assurances of the Russian emperor. Would you accept my apologies and join us?"

I FOUND MYSELF BACK IN THE PALACE, WHERE LEE BO GREETED ME with exclamations of relief.

Feng spoke in Chinese again, relieved at the presence of Lee Bo.

Lee Bo translated. "He says, the Russian envoy will be here any second. Even though he is inclined to reconsider the meaning of your information because of new events, he will of course have to take it to Hong."

"Good." I was about to ask who the envoy was, when there was some commotion in the hallway, and a small bamboo litter was carried into the room. I doubted the necessity of traveling by litter indoors, and thus waited with interest to see who would emerge from it. The carriers set the litter down, the curtain at its side moved, and my Aunt Eugenia, her own black-clad and unmistakable self, stepped out, smiling, with tears in her eyes.

I cried as well, and I introduced Aunt Eugenia to Lee Bo, and Lee Bo introduced her to Feng, and Feng asked Eugenia and myself about our feelings on the Taiping philosophy, which he kindly offered to summarize right away for us, and did so. I stopped listening when he mentioned strict separation of the sexes, and hugged Eugenia, and she hugged me back, and even though we both felt like we should have no tears left by now, we cried some more, and it was all very exciting.

"Why are you traveling in this litter?" I asked Eugenia. There were so many questions vying for my attention and struggling for primacy, but it looked like the least important had won out.

Eugenia laughed and hugged me again. "They let me meet the Qing Emperor, only he was not happy that the envoy was a woman, and the Taipings—whom I had to deal with mostly—insisted on keeping me separate from everyone else, so I've been carried in this litter all over the Forbidden City and the palace—which is quite large; much larger than it looks from the outside. I guess it is easier for everyone to cope if I am hidden away in this little coffin with rails."

"They did have an empress," I said. "Dowager, I mean, but an empress nonetheless."

"The Russians have had more recent empresses," Eugenia pointed out sensibly. "The great world of good it did us."

"I gave Jack's documents to the Taipings," I said. "They seem like better allies."

"Yes, since they are winning," Eugenia agreed. "Come with me, Sasha, come for a walk in a garden. We need to talk."

The garden that lay just behind the palace and surrounded a small shrine with a round roof was quiet and white, graceful black branches outlined against the snowdrifts and walls. I wondered at my ability to even notice such things, even admire them, as so many other concerns should've been closer to my heart. "I worry about Kuan Yu," I said. "I hope Feng got it sorted out with his people at the gates."

"I'm sure your friends will be fine," Eugenia said. "You've done well. I received your message, and I was able to finally talk Constantine into listening to reason."

"How did you manage that?"

Eugenia smiled, sly. "I do have friends, and I followed your advice. Apparently, being old-fashioned and honorable doesn't get you anywhere, but being friends with the empress's former beau who still has some of her less discreet letters will assure you her help."

"Brilliant," I said with respect. "So she helped you get Constantine's ear."

"Apparently, men do listen to their wives." Eugenia stepped off the stone path and crouched down, black as a crow on the white snow. She picked up a handful of snow and rolled it in her hands absently. "The snow is so heavy and wet," she said. "Great for the crops, and I think a warm spell is coming."

I crouched down next to her. The stone of the path felt so heavy that I put my hand on it, to feel its aged-cold surface, worn smooth by so many generations of feet, and yet it managed to retain the tiny bumps and cracks on its surface. They made me think of the moon and the dark blemishes and long sinuous fissures one could see on it some nights in June. "Do you think we'll be back in Trubetskoye by the time they start sowing?" I asked.

"Depends on what else we have to do. I think the Taipings will accept the invitation from the emperor I've delivered, and you and your Englishman friend certainly helped to sweeten the deal . . . Where is he, by the way?"

I told her about Jack and his initial disappearance and his capture, of the way he kept close and yet managed to distract Nightingale and her contingent.

"I never liked that woman," Eugenia said. "I always keep thinking we women ought to stick together, and I keep telling it to the empress—because if we do, we can stand up to the men and to the way they run things. But the empress and that Nightingale, they value men's opinion over those of their own kind. And I don't know what to do about them."

"I don't know about the general principle," I said, "but I certainly would be quite comfortable with destroying her. Not killing, just making sure she would never interfere with my life again, and that she wouldn't hurt Jack."

"Where would they take him?"

I shrugged. "Maybe to London, and maybe to St. Petersburg. Is Mr. Herbert still there?"

"I believe so. I think I saw some mincing dandy the last time I was at the Winter Palace, who kept lisping into Nicholas's ear." Eugenia straightened and spat. "I swear it is a miracle that I managed to get myself sent here—Nicholas is in the pocket of the English and the Turks, and he has no inkling they are not his friends."

I stood too. "He does seem both dim and unpleasant. But I am really thinking that I should probably go do something about Jack before he is executed as a traitor and a criminal."

Eugenia gave me a long look and continued down the path, leaving tracks of snow clumps on the clean dry stones. "You keep some dubious company."

"I suppose. Will you come with me, at least some of the way?"

"Of course, dear. How far do you think they could've traveled?"

"If they took the train, they are at least three days ahead of us."

"Then I suppose we will have to convince Mr. Feng to lend us an airship. Otherwise, we will never catch up."

I sighed happily and caught up to Eugenia, throwing one arm around her shoulders. "Dear Aunt Genia, I'm so glad you're here. I feel like everything will be right now."

Genia's thin hand—traversed by blue, delicate veins—patted mine. I felt a surge of pity at her fragility and the sudden realization that she was getting old. "Well," she said. "I do not know if everything will ever be completely 'right,' but I can promise you this: if your prolonged absence gets you expelled from the university, the emperor himself promised to intervene on your behalf."

"Really?"

"Really." She smiled. "He said so himself before he stuffed me into a submarine."

"Is that how you got here so quickly?"

She nodded, pleased. "I felt rather like a sardine, but it took me from St. Petersburg to the Kara Sea and to Yenisey to Baikal quick enough. Then they found me an airship."

I shuddered at the thought. "The submarine sounds awful. I hope we get to travel by air rather than water. But I suppose we have to go and find out if we are required to take any messages with us."

Chapter 18

There were no messages, but General Feng informed us that Hong—the new ruler of China, if the treaty the Qing signed abdicating the throne could be believed—had decided to send an emissary to St. Petersburg, to bring the offer of an alliance and treaties to sign. We were invited to join the emissary, and Feng promised we would be sent by air, and reach St. Petersburg in no time.

Another surprise awaited me on the morning of our departure. The airship was positioned in the Sea of Flagstones, the open square before the building called the Hall of Supreme Harmony. The canal running in a semicircle around the square was frozen solid, and the footpath and the tiny bridges paved with multicolored blocks shone with frost. The roof of the Hall blazed in the sunlight. A small solemn army of Taipings had gathered to watch our departure; I was relieved to see Kuan Yu and Liu Zhi among them. I regretted I had too little time to explore this wonderful place—there were so many palaces and halls and pagodas, small hidden gardens, and the wells with poetic names Lee Bo told me and I immediately forgot. One, I thought, had something to do with concubines.

I also regretted not seeing Chiang Tse—I regretted it probably more than anything else, but I had difficulty admitting it to myself, not to mention talking to Aunt Genia or Lee Bo about it. And now it was too late. I tried to focus on getting home, on saving Jack, on seeing my mother, on going to the university again—anything but the sucking regret in the pit of my stomach. I stood by one of the tiny bridges, erect and straight-faced, my uniform clean and mended and my pelisse trimmed with new fur. All my belongings had been transferred into one of Eugenia's leather valises as my old satchel had been falling apart from all the abuse I subjected it to. I watched with dry eyes as an airship, of a design similar to the one that had brought me to Beijing, descended into the square and landed on its sturdy wheels with engines chugging.

The machine was much bigger than Lee Bo's, but I suspected it was born in the same Siberian factory. The seating was allocated to the belly of the ship instead of the flimsy freezing tiny gondola under it. The entire ship was more streamlined, with wider wings and narrower hull. Its front end was shaped as a snarling dragon snout, and the hull was painted with red and gold scales, as if reflecting the roofs of the palaces around us. I was by then thoroughly charmed by the architectural excesses of little towers and pagoda roofs all stacked on top of one another, and painted such bright red and gold and copper and green. Not even winter could dull these colors.

We waited for the emissary. When he appeared I could not, at first, see him as he was preceded by a sizeable entourage. Some of the Taipings waiting in the square joined it as well, including Kuan Yu. I was glad he was coming with us. "Is it one of the generals?" I whispered to Eugenia. "I hope they don't send a military man to negotiate such matters."

"No, Feng is pretty smart," Eugenia whispered back. "It is one of Hong's newly appointed governors."

"Which province, do you know?"

"Gansu," she whispered back, and this simple word made me see a black sun and white sky.

Chiang Tse had changed little—his queue was of course gone, but he had kept his gentle and dignified demeanor, and his dark eyes remained downcast even as he approached us. I agonized at first over whether he would recognize me; but surely Lee Bo must have told him.

He bowed to Aunt Eugenia. "It is a pleasure and an honor to travel with you," he said softly, and the sound of his voice tugged at my heart gently, like one of the large red-and-white carps that lived in the ponds in the imperial palace nibbling on my fingers. "It is my humble hope that as persons gifted with the trust of our rulers we can discuss the common interests of our countries, and come to a mutually beneficial set of agreements."

Eugenia seemed pleased. "We will indeed do so," she assured him. "Shall we?"

Chiang Tse smiled and nodded, and offered her his arm in a European fashion. His clothes, however, were that of an official, and his robes bore a patch with two embroidered cranes on them. Lee Bo explained its meaning, and even though I was hazy on the details, I gathered cranes were indicative of high rank.

Eugenia took his arm and they walked to the airship side-by-side with me following them and ten or so men of Chiang Tse's retinue bringing up the rear. I turned and saw Kuan Yu over my shoulder; I smiled and he grinned back. So much for a humble fur trader, and I was glad to have him travel with us again.

We settled on the benches that were refreshingly padded and rounded. They felt more like cradles than the hard wooden benches of the train or other airship. This trip was promising to be altogether more comfortable, and I sighed and stretched.

Chiang Tse and Eugenia spoke softly. I sat behind them, and could only make out the animated bobbing of Chiang Tse's head, agreeing with something Eugenia proposed.

Finally he turned around to face me. There was no recognition in his dark eyes, and I smiled.

He offered me his hand. "Chiang Tse," he said. "I am the Governor-General of Gansu."

I shook his hand. "Poruchik Menshov," I said.

He smiled then. "My friend Lee Bo told me you were the one who brought the evidence of the treacheries planned by the English."

I couldn't contain myself any longer. "But I see he failed to remind you of our previous acquaintance."

Chiang Tse smiled politely, and his eyes showed no recognition, which to me seemed the very height of hilarity. He squinted at me as I kept laughing, too overcome to say anything. Finally, I managed to pull my fake mustache off my lip, and his eyes lit with recognition—he forgot his dignified bearing and official position as he vaulted over the back of his bench to sit next to me and grasp my hands with a gesture so sincere that my reverse corset felt like a slab of rock, pressing on my chest and not letting me breathe.

"Sasha," he said.

I do not know what his retinue thought after that—but I am sure they had been selected in part for an ability to not talk about things they witnessed. Whatever the case, I did not care whether anyone was watching as I embraced Chiang Tse with an ardor that was perhaps a mite excessive for mere camaraderie. He gasped and held me too, and his quick breaths told me that he was as overcome as I. A moment later a hot wet drop on my neck told me he was crying.

If Eugenia noticed anything, she was of course too well brought up and too mindful of my happiness to turn around, and instead busied herself with her knitting. She rarely knitted, and I suspected the shapeless, dingy brown thing she worked on was the same one she had started when I was a child.

"I thought I would never see you again," Chiang Tse whispered and let go. His face was slightly reddened and more emotional than

I had ever seen. “I worked so hard on letting go of the very thought of you, and yet I begged Hong to send me to St. Petersburg.”

“I missed you too,” I mumbled, the words a pale shadow of my protracted longing and the upsurge of happiness I experienced when I saw him again.

We traded further inarticulate expressions of our delight for a while, and Chiang Tse would not let go of my hands.

“I guess you’re not taking this separation of genders tenet too seriously then,” I said.

He laughed. “I think it is acceptable as long as you’re dressed as a man.”

I wasn’t sure but I thought I saw Eugenia’s shoulders shaking with laughter.

WITH CHIANG TSE, IT WAS EASY TO TALK ABOUT JACK AND WHAT we should do about him. Chiang Tse remembered Jack as the one who—along with my own modest efforts—allowed for his and Lee Bo’s escape that night at the Crane Club. He was eager to return the favor.

I had favors to return as well. I felt overwhelming gratitude to Jack for all his help and self-sacrifice; yet, I felt burdened by my debt to him. I did not know if the same feeling motivated Chiang Tse, but for me helping Jack carried a two-fold purpose. I hoped that didn’t make me a bad person.

Chiang Tse mused. “They will have to change trains at St. Petersburg and Moscow. I think we can intercept them in either of those cities.”

“But what can we do to make them let Jack go? He is under English law, and I don’t think we have legal grounds to interfere.”

Chiang Tse pursed his lips. “Nothing the emperor could do?”

I shook my head. “I doubt he would intervene, especially now.

We might have to rescue him ourselves—by force if necessary."

"Or perhaps we could negotiate."

Aunt Eugenia turned then. "With what are you planning to negotiate, Chiang Tse?"

"With whatever I can," he said very earnestly. "The man saved my life, and he made sure that Sasha arrived in Beijing safely. There is nothing I wouldn't do to see him to freedom and safety."

I nodded that I agreed—and yet, every time I thought of Jack's devotion, of the consideration and fondness he showed me, I became more and more concerned. It did not make sense, but I was starting to fear him—after all, he was superhumanly strong and agile, and he was not the man one would want to upset. I hoped that Chiang Tse's diplomacy would be enough not only to save Jack, but to protect us from his displeasure if he ever were to be upset with us.

It was with no small amount of apprehension that I realized that some people made excellent allies but terrible enemies.

Travel by air was a lot less interesting than by train, once one got used to the idea of being up in the sky, as high as the birds flew. The windows revealed nothing but patches of sky and clouds. The usual rules of conduct felt irrelevant as well—at least, neither Aunt Eugenia nor Chiang Tse's retinue offered any criticism of his propensity to hold my hand, and no one even batted an eye when we whispered and laughed like conspiratorial children. On solid ground, Chiang Tse was reserved and often cold; in the sky he seemed younger, as if relieved from the weight of his responsibility.

The engineer guiding the airship had agreed to follow the railroad tracks below. Every now and then we wandered over to the engine room where the furnaces—red-hot, hissing, and spitting—blazed like the pits of hell. The thick round panes of glass in the belly of the engine room allowed a distorted and bleak view of what was below, and we tried to guess the landmarks we were passing over. We named rivers as they shimmered below our feet, and we pointed the dark tracks of the railroad. At night, we pressed our cheeks against the windows and tried to see the stars above.

We saw the train below in the morning. We were mere hours away from Moscow, and I quickly counted on my fingers to make sure that the time worked out. I did it several times, until I had no doubt left the train below was the one likely to contain Jack and the Englishmen who captured him.

"I think Jack is on that train," I told Chiang Tse.

He squinted through the thick, greenish glass on the floor of the engine room. "Very well," he said. "We'll intercept them in Moscow."

"Can you land the airship there?"

"I don't know. Let me talk to the engineer."

I followed him into the metal passageway, a narrow vaulted tube that connected the engine room to the engineer's cabin, where the brass levers that operated the airship's wings and rudder bristled from the walls like quills of some metallic porcupine turned inside out by some great misfortune. The engineer, a stocky Taiping with thick hair all the way down to shoulders nodded at us.

"Tang Wei," Chiang Tse addressed the engineer. "Do you see the train tracks below? Did you notice a train we passed a while back?"

Tang Wei nodded, and adjusted a knob to his left, making the airship tilt slightly right. "I saw it," he said. "You want me to follow?"

"You do not have to follow," Chiang Tse said. "But if we could meet the people on that train just as they disembark, and if we could do it discreetly . . . "

"We can do that," Tang Wei said. "I'll just need a station and a field. And maybe a town—we need more coal anyway. We are running quite low."

I wondered what the airship looked like from the ground; I wondered if people on the train noticed us, hovering so doggedly above them—or at the very least, saw our shadow on the ground and wondered at its shape. The airship had decreased its speed, and now matched that of the locomotive below us.

The train soon came to a halt at some deserted unnamed station, too inconsequential to stop at unless explicit orders were given or passengers present. Tang Wei made the airship circle above the station as we clung to the windows of the control room, which were both thinner and clearer than the ones in the engine room.

I looked through the windows as a chain of small black figures spilled out onto the snow, and Chiang Tse pointed them to Tang Wei. "Can you get to them?"

"Easy," Tang Wei said. "Nothing but fields here."

As the airship tilted toward the ground and descended, swooping lower and lower with every turn, the details of the procession below us resolved and grew clear. I saw Jack first: they had him in stocks, and I am ashamed to admit I felt a small prickling of relief. He was my friend, I reminded myself, there was no reason for me to fear him and certainly no reason to feel happy that his wrists were enclosed in a solid block of wood with his large, knobby fists protruding above it like two ugly growths on a tree trunk. It must have been hard to walk like this in the dead of the winter, when the wind howled and the ice dust in the air stung one's cheeks and eyes like powdered glass.

His ankles were held together by a similar contraption—he moved very slowly and awkwardly, as the wooden block and the heavy chain winding about his ankles allowed him only a slow shuffle with steps no longer than a couple of inches. I wondered if he could still leap, if he could push the earth away from him with both of his feet, if his strength would be enough to let him soar even with such an awkward start.

Or maybe his legs were strong enough to displace the entire planet from its orbit, and for a moment I imagined Jack getting angry and hurling Earth into the dark cold recesses of dead space, away from the life-giving sun . . . I shook my head at such a foolish fantasy, and went to the passenger area, to wake up Eugenia and to notify her that a small-scale conflict with Britain was upon us and likely unavoidable.

They headed down the snow-covered trail leading away from the station—it was almost like Trubetskoye, like so many small anonymous villages that curled up within a mile of the station, all their roads leading to the nearest depot like the spokes on the wheel. A few more years, and my entire country would be like this—circles of hamlets surrounding the beating hearts of the stations, the rectangular wooden platform by the shining rails signifying progress.

The airship touched the ground lightly, like a butterfly landing on a flower; its wings, still flapping, raised clouds of snow, obscuring for a short while the English. They did not try to run—I didn't suppose they would, with no other nearby cover than snow-covered platform. The locomotive had already departed, whistling its low forlorn note at a distance. And one's will to escape would surely be somewhat sapped by the sight of a giant metal airship, painted as a dragon, descending from the sky.

I walked next to Chiang Tse and Kuan Yu, their flanking shoulders giving me strength and courage, with the rest of Chiang Tse's retinue following closely behind, their swords drawn.

I was a little surprised to see Dame Nightingale—she was dressed in a long gray coat of the same cut and fabric as those of the men around her. Only her tall, laced boots with a small but noticeable heel bore any traces of femininity. I almost asked her where she had purchased them, before remembering myself.

"You," she said in my direction. She did not sneer, exactly, but her voice was icy with contempt. The snow under her feet crunched, betraying her otherwise imperceptible shifting. "You don't have to wear those boy's clothes anymore—they don't hide you that well."

"Neither do yours."

She smiled then. "It's for convenience."

"You're just copying me." I felt a small stirring of satisfaction warming my cheeks when I saw her flinch.

Dame Nightingale shook her head and smiled. "You can flatter yourself with whatever interesting ideas you have, but the truth is that Mr. Bartram here is a British citizen and is subject to the British crown, and your barbarian thugs can not help you." She clucked her tongue, her long eyelashes casting a blue shadow over her porcelain-white face, spared even by the frost. "Really, Sasha—you should know better than attempt anything so foolish."

"And yet you got off the train," I said.

"We decided to choose less predictable mode of transportation," she said. "Trains are nice, but the very fact that they run on schedule makes it difficult to work in an element of surprise—as you yourself must've noticed."

I nodded. Despite my better judgment, I couldn't help but feel a deep kinship with this tall woman, straight and strong as a pillar. I could even see her as a friend, should she have chosen a different occupation. "I've read your letters," I said. Half-confession, half-desire to hurt, I wasn't sure.

Her face turned scarlet—the color spread from her right cheek, as if I had slapped her. "And I've read yours," she said through her teeth. "That fool"—a toss of her head indicated Jack—"had it on him. At least, now he knows that he was leaping and dancing for your amusement to little effect." She turned away from me, to speak directly to Jack who was surrounded by a tight circle of men wearing gray coats and round hats. "How does it feel, hmm? You make a funny puppet, Jack—so long and gangly and silly looking. Surely, this girl had a good a laugh at your expense."

It was my turn to flush deep crimson. This was not going in the direction I had hoped, and yet I found strength to meet Jack's gaze.

He looked gaunter, longer, and his eyes had a haunted look about them, no doubt helped by the deep shadow of the stubble and the hollowed appearance of his temples. He looked back at me, his eyes dull and his face unmoving; then again, his chin was resting on top of a solid and likely frozen block of wood and his bare hands were blue from cold, so he would probably look miserable even if his heart wasn't broken.

He licked his lips a few times, as if getting ready to speak.

"Careful," I whispered. "If you wet your lips too much, they'll chap."

He smiled then, his lips cracking and blood seeping through the tiny fissures, slow as water under ice. "Too late for that," he said. "I didn't read your letter—I found it and I kept it to give back, and she was the one who read it and told me."

"That was an appalling thing to do," I told Nightingale. I'd have to explain the nonsense about letters to Chiang Tse at some point, but now was not the time for it.

She sneered in earnest then. "And what you did was right?"

"I read your letters for my country's good and for the sake of peace, not some petty revenge," I said. "Really, Dame Nightingale. I am disappointed in you."

She jerked her shoulder in an exaggerated shrug. "Well then. Do you want to scold me some more, or can we continue? We are on a diplomatic mission."

"Until Constantine expels you all as spies."

"Until then. In any case, Mr. Bartram is one of us, and he will have to travel abroad with his countrymen. I'm afraid there simply isn't much you can do about it, little girl."

This was too much, the last insult was the nudge I needed to suddenly feel all the fatigue and fear and anger I had been denying myself during this journey; the dam that had been holding my feelings at bay—constructed from pure stubbornness and desperation—finally burst in a starry flash of red. I felt my hands closing into fists and my legs propelling me toward Nightingale even as my shoulder drew back and my arm swung in a wide arc, like that of a drunk and a lowlife. The anger felt delicious.

A sensation of metallic cold on my forehead jolted me back to my senses and I held back my fist, which was only inches away from Nightingale's face. I saw the mother-of-pearl handle of Nightingale's tiny pistol in great detail, down to tiny cracks cobwebbing one of the larger panels, and felt acutely its barrel pressing against my brow, cutting a cruel red circle into my skin. My anger could not find release and pounded inside me, like a wave on some oceanic shore, my impotent rage that could not even find a simple relief accessible to any tavern brawler. How I wished then to break that beautiful, haughty face, and the impossibility of doing so boiled in my eyes and spilled as tears.

"Well," Nightingale said then. "Will you behave now?"

Out of the corner of my tearing eye I could see her left hand rise and motion to her entourage to stand by. "Yes," I whispered. I had to struggle to meet Jack's gaze, and shook my head ever so slightly. I saw his fists tensing too, and had no doubt that he could shatter his stocks if I gave a signal; surely he was strong enough. Only he would never endanger us—at least, that was what I was hoping for.

Jack gave a slightest nod that he understood, and I took a very slow step back, eager to end the contact between my flesh and

Nightingale's pistol. My forehead burned where the steel had touched it.

"There is nothing you can do," Dame Nightingale said simply, and let her pistol arm hang limply along her side. "You are outnumbered, and your friend Bartram here knows as well as I do that if he tries any of his tricks, I will not hesitate to shoot you and your barbarians."

"Unless we can bargain." My mind, still clouded with anger, was starting to clear and to cast about for possible solutions.

Chiang Tse, quiet until then, stepped closer to me and whispered, "What do you mean?"

"The ship," I whispered back. "Surely, you have more."

"But . . . " he started.

Nightingale looked at him, bored. "Dear boy," she said. "Don't worry. She doesn't know what she speaks of. You have nothing we want. Rather, nothing we do not have."

"That is not true," Chiang Tse said. "I heard about the robbery in the Crane Club. You want our inventions."

"We have some models," Nightingale said, smiling. "Remember—we don't really need anything from you; Britain won that war." And yet, I noticed her eyes stray toward the dragon airship resting behind us, twin streams of steam coming from the symmetrical holes in the side of its hull and making the wings undulate up and down.

Chiang Tse noticed too: he hooked his thumb over his shoulder, pointing at the ship. "Not even that?"

"We do not want blueprints; we already have them."

"Then it won't make any difference," I told Chiang Tse. "It's only the matter of time before the British can build their own."

Chiang Tse frowned. "But Sasha, we cannot give them such weapons. Our very survival—"

"—is a matter completely separate from the one at hand," I

interrupted. “Don’t you remember? You owe your life to this man, you owe him the very alliance between our countries.”

He shook his head, but then smiled, as if remembering something. “If you put it that way . . . What are matters of military security when you can save the man who risked so much for you?”

“Exactly!” I gave a quick sideways look to Nightingale. “If we have Jack on our side, the loss of one ship won’t matter.”

“I know there will be a war sooner or later,” Chiang Tse said, and looked at Jack with new appreciation. “I suppose he would be valuable.” He then turned to Nightingale. “Will you trade with us? That man for the airship. We’ll even provide an engineer to fly it.”

The English muttered among themselves.

“You won’t be in trouble?” I whispered to Chiang Tse.

He shrugged. “These things have a way of sorting themselves out.” He winked at me, amused at something I was missing.

Nightingale turned away from me for the first time since we got there, and consulted in lowered voice with her contingent. Her mind must have already been made up, for she didn’t pay attention to Jack, and he hobbled toward me.

“Jack,” I started.

He shook his head—rather wobbled it side to side, which was as much movement as his stocks allowed. “We’ll talk later,” he said. “I’m just glad to see that you are alive and well.”

“You too,” I said. “I wish they had not kept you in these wooden blocks.”

“Well, they bloody well had to, didn’t they?”

“You probably do not remember me,” Chiang Tse cut in.

“I do,” Jack said. “You are welcome.”

I could not believe that I had persuaded Chiang Tse to give up the airship—a beautiful, powerful machine—to his enemies. And yet, I couldn’t see another way; I only wished I would have the same clarity of vision every day of my life, the same ability to see through the conjecture and the imagined complications we tended to pile on top of everything, to see right to the heart of the matter: there was a man we both owed our lives to, and something we could trade for his salvation. It wasn't even a difficult choice once you looked at it that way—and I was glad that Chiang Tse was able to see it my way.

I brushed an unbidden tear from my eyelashes. "I guess I better go to the airship and get my aunt and her things. Does anyone know when the next train arrives?"

"You're close enough to Moscow," Dame Nightingale said. "There is a train every hour or so. And do send your people to fetch the rest of your belongings from the ship—we are not thieves, we just want the airship."

"You're accepting our offer then?" Chiang Tse said.

"Of course. You didn't think that he—" she gave another head toss in Jack's direction—"is important, did you?"

"Of course he is," I said. "He's important to you, enough to chase him all the way to Siberia."

Chiang Tse pulled on my sleeve. "Sasha," he said mildly. "Let's not prolong the pointless argument."

"I am sorry," I said to her. "We appreciate your willingness to negotiate."

"I hope your engineer doesn't mind taking us to St. Petersburg and then London," she said. "It seems like the emperor has had quite a change of heart, and I fear that soon we won't be welcome at his court."

"Of course," said Chiang Tse. "Wherever you have to go."

I bit my tongue, said nothing, only nodded. "Do you have the key for those stocks?"

Nightingale tossed the jangling knot of keys to me. I fumbled the catch, and they sunk into the snow by my feet. I dropped to my knees, my reddened, clawed hands digging in the snow. Who knew how deep the snow was, how far those keys had fallen? I had my arms up to my shoulder in snow, when I heard Nightingale's abrupt laugh. My fingers touched the steel and I drew a gigantic breath of relief.

"Don't let him out until we're gone," she said. "And forgive us for not waiting."

By the time I pulled the keys out of the snow, the steam of the airship had grown to two forceful streams. Aunt Eugenia and the rest of our companions had disembarked with speed that precluded dignity—I saw a man tumble in the snow, and recognized the engineer, Tang Wei.

I turned to Chiang Tse. "But he . . . "

"We sent a different engineer," Chiang Tse said as the English turned their backs on us in their hurry to get aboard.

I scanned the faces of the small crowd—my aunt, the diplomats, the crew . . . Kuan Yu was conspicuously missing, and I finally understood.

Jack waited patiently as I unlocked his chains and the locks. The wooden stocks split in half and tumbled to the ground, with a dull and splintering sound and the ship's wings were beating violently, like those of a panicked butterfly.

Aunt Eugenia joined us. "What did I miss?" she asked. "The Englishmen and that terrible Nightingale woman have the ship—did you mean to do that?"

"Yes," I said. "Don't worry. Aunt Genia, you remember Jack? Jack Bartram? We saw him at the opera house."

Jack stood in the snow, rubbing his wrists with an absent expression. I was starting to worry that he was damaged somehow, hurt beyond repair.

"Jack," I whispered.

His eyes snapped open, and he smiled at Eugenia. "It is a pleasure," he said, and shook the hand she offered.

"Pleased to meet you, Mr. Bartram," she replied. "I suppose we can get acquainted on the train since Sasha and Chiang Tse gave away the airship."

"Yes, they gave the airship . . . " Jack's voice drifted off and his eyes turned toward the ship, its wings unfurled, shuddering in anticipation of flight. It seemed alive now, breathing, almost the legendary creature itself come to life . . . I felt an acute pang of regret for letting Nightingale's unclean hands touch such magic.

"Well, we'd best all get to the platform so the next train will stop for us." Eugenia started striding across the desolate field, barely troughed by all the human movement to and fro. She seemed remarkably indifferent to the snow that was undoubtedly starting to melt in her shoes.

"Wait, Countess Menshova," Chiang Tse called. "There's still someone joining us."

"But—" Aunt Eugenia never got a chance to finish her thought as the roaring of the airship grew deafening, and its wings, shrouded in the sparkling veil of snow, flapped faster as it rose higher and higher into the air.

And then Jack leapt.

Eugenia and Chiang Tse, and even the Taipings who had all seen Kuan Yu in action, gasped—even though Kuan Yu's fighting was impressive, he could never leap so high. We watched Jack float up into the air, as high as the tallest tree in the forest, as high as the beating wings of the airship. He was vengeance personified, and already his gnarled blue fingers stretched, reaching, ready to tear the delicate wings of the ship and to pluck it out of the sky, like a cat leaping for an unsuspecting sparrow.

"Jack!" It was my own voice splitting the air, dry and strained like tearing of raw silk.

Impossibly, Jack stopped in the air—the momentum that carried him toward the airship ceased and he hovered there for a part of a second, a black gangly puppet against the light sky—just inches away from the ship—and then gravity took hold of him and he fell back to the trampled snow where the rest of our small group huddled close together, as the dragon airship glared golden in the sky, and the train whistled from far away.

"Wait," Chiang Tse repeated, this time looking directly at Jack. "No sense in killing yourself in a pointless task."

Jack, crouched down with the force of his landing, looked up, and straightened, slow and deliberate. "Pointless?"

"Jack, I think Chiang Tse means that Kuan Yu is flying the ship."

"He seems to be doing a fine job," Aunt Eugenia said.

"Kuan Yu? Our friend from the train?" Jack asked, confused. "I knew he was no ordinary fur trader, but surely he is not an engineer?"

"He isn't." I knew my satisfied expression befuddled Jack all the more, but I just could not contain my desire to tease him a little—after all, he did sent me on a chase after him.

The ship was now a mere gold coin against the sky, gaining distance. I strained my eyes until I saw a black speck, so small that I was not entirely sure I had seen it, detach from the ship and fall toward the Earth. "Look!" I called to Chaing Tse, pointing at the falling dot.

He smiled. "It is rare to find an ally who knows what you need him to do without ever asking. I would be a liar if I said I was not pleased with his admirable abilities."

Despite the distance, as the speck approached the ground, I could see it was shaped like a tulip—or a man with a substantial amount of fabric spread above and around him, bracing and slowing his fall.

"What of the ship?" I said.

Aunt Eugenia sighed. "Remember Tosno?"

I nodded, mute. The ship was so beautiful—it was beautiful still as it faltered and grew larger as it descended, as its wings hung limp. The steam no longer escaped from it, and I could only imagine the terror of the people trapped inside it—or rather, I tried not to. The golden ship wobbled one last time, and then plummeted somewhere into fields hidden from view by a narrow copse of bare aspens. Only a brief flash against the slowly darkening sky signaled its demise.

I turned to Jack. "I suppose you have your revenge."

He shrugged. "It's not proper revenge if you do not complete it yourself."

"At least this way you survived. I'm glad you have."

He nodded, looking unconvinced.

We shivered and waited for Kuan Yu to join us.

Epilogue

ALMOST A YEAR HAS PASSED SINCE WE GOT BACK TO ST. PETERSBURG. It is winter again, and I cannot wait until May when I can go back to Trubetskoye. I am a little upset that I have to repeat the first two quarters, but the work is easily accomplished the second time around.

I also find it comforting that Chiang Tse has been allowed to finish his education. He was granted leave from his gubernatorial post and now performs some diplomatic duties for the new Chinese ambassador to the imperial court—but not enough to interfere with his studies. The Crane Club is still gone, but now that the English have left the Northern Star, we've made it a favorite spot to get together and listen to the mechanical pianist.

Wong Jun was released from the Ravelin, but decided to stay in St. Petersburg—being a Manchu is now a precarious proposition in Beijing. He seems content to come to classes every now and again between bouts of complaining and dark moods. He claims to find some comfort in writing poetry, but he never allows the other Chinese students to read it.

And then there is Jack. He also attends the university and takes classes; he still walks me home every now and again. As for our adventure, we speak little of it. He has expressed regret over the poor horse, and the fright he gave the garrison. I have imparted some of Volzhenko's theology and told him of the Aardvarks. The subject of my ill-fated letter is never mentioned between us, but the knowledge of it hangs over us. We both know I do not return his feelings, just as we both know he has not yet abandoned hope that someday I will. He seldom speaks to Chiang Tse, but both are polite and do not seem to wish ill to one another.

Jack seems concerned about the English expulsion, and makes occasionally vague predictions about the Secret Service traveling to Mongolia to make connections with the Qing Dynasty, but I think he worries a little prematurely. As Eugenia says, no point in planning for winter when you don't know if you'll live through the summer.

Eugenia remains at Trubetskoye to keep my mother company and to make sure the family estate runs as smoothly as could be desired. All summer, the two were the same as always, and I expect to find them so when I visit Trubetskoye at winter recess; I do not expect people their age to change. I would not want them to, for the world grows less familiar with every day, and one needs to have a steady constant flame of familiarity one can return to when the dragon airships are gone and the reverse corsets are packed away in oak chests. Any adventure must give away to familiarity of routine, and I look to what lies ahead of me, clear eyed and level headed, knowing that both changes and constancy have their place in the world, and that I can survive either.